A BONE FOR THE DOG

BY

Phyllis Maclay

visit PhyllisMaclay.com

For my husband, Alan
And our children
Matthew, Courtney, Katherine, Philip, Emily, and Ali
You are the best part of me

To honor my mother and remember my father
For the best childhood a kid could have

And to Dutch
For helping Mom find happiness after grief

ISBN 1-59113-497-8

Edited by Kathleen Cook

This book is a novel.
The characters and small towns are imaginary and fictitious.
To construe as anything else would be in error.

You have collected all my tears and preserved them in your bottle.

(Psalm 56:8b TLB)

Part One
SHAWN

ONE

Her car wasn't in the driveway. The tall man with sun-streaked hair thought nothing of his wife's absence. His tanned face betrayed his love of the outdoors, and his blue eyes were trained to be aware of his surroundings. But nothing seemed amiss as he tried to remember if Jolene had told him where she would be. *Must be at her mother's.* Shawn hummed, *on the road again,* as he hurried across the dusty yard to feed the animals before the last rays of sunlight were snuffed out by the hovering darkness. The small wooden door to the feed room squeaked open as he ran his hand along the wall for the light switch. "Yeeow!" he yelped. Pain seared his finger as his foot stomped the scampering scorpion that had fallen to the floor.

Shawn examined his index finger. Red and swelling more each second, it was already stiff and painful to wiggle. He stooped over the spigot by the rabbit pens and ran cool water over it, scooping up mud from his feet, spreading it over his throbbing finger. The light in the west was shrinking.

Got to get a move on. He went inside the feed room and dug the metal scoop into the bucket of rabbit pellets. An image of Rachel squealing with delight, patting the blinking bunny's head while Shawn held her over the hutch made him smile. Rachel. *Daddy's girl.* He quickly filled the rabbits' dishes and gave them fresh water. "Hey, Bucky. How's it going, Fluffy and Muffy?" His large hand rubbed their ears as they hopped over to him. He closed the hutch doors and returned to the feed room to fill another bucket.

The chickens interrupted their roosting to swoop at him when Shawn scattered corn over the dry, cracked ground. The yellow kernels were scratched and pecked by their searching, hungry beaks. He checked the nest boxes for eggs, putting them in the cartons he kept near their nests.

The small farmhouse was an embarrassment to his wife. So Shawn had bought a retail nursery business in addition to his full time job managing at OK Wholesale Plants. With the extra income he bought land to build them a home and raise cattle. Now Jolene complained about his long hours, but Shawn was sure once they moved in (hopefully before Rachel's second birthday) his wife would be happy. *Our house, is a very, very, very fine house…*

Happy. Something Jolene was not these days. There had been lots of upsets in the Stevens household the past few months. For instance, after they had brought their baby home from the hospital, Jolene had insisted on living with her mother- just the baby and her. "Mom will help me learn to be a good mother," was her reason.

Shawn had been patient. Gave her time to gain confidence with a new baby. Jolene was always the nervous type, so he would understand. But as the days stretched into weeks he longed to hold Rachel and wanted his wife with him. Amid the fury of Jolene and her mother, he had packed up his family and brought them home. That was almost eighteen months ago and she still had not forgiven him.

Then there was the sleeping arrangement feud. Jolene insisted on keeping Rachel in bed with them, even after the baby crawled over her and tumbled to the floor. "She sleeps here or with me at mother's." She didn't have to finish the rest of the message. And even though she had won again, Shawn was sentenced to sleeping on his side of the bed while Jolene cuddled with Rachel on hers.

Shawn put the bucket away and the eggs in the refrigerator in the feed room. Darkness pressed the last bits of light into the flat horizon while he searched the sky for familiar stars. *Where is she?* He picked off the dried mud from his finger. It stung, but the swelling had gone down. He would need to put meat tenderizer on it.

As he scanned the sky for familiar constellations, a paw pressed on his boot, startling him out of his thoughts. "Hey, Bell, whacha doin', old girl?" The big dog thumped her tail on the ground as she trembled to keep herself from jumping on him. He scratched her ears. "Where're my girls tonight? Where'd they go, Bell?" Shawn held her chin and softly sang, "Where, oh, where are you tonight? Why did you leave me here all alone?" The dog tilted her head to listen, but approaching headlights sent her bounding for the driveway. *Good. They're home.*

His smile faded when he failed to recognize the car under the streetlight. A man got out and tipped back his cowboy hat. His huge belt buckle reflected the light onto the papers he was holding. "Evenin'. You Shawn Stevens?"

"Yes, sir."

"Here." Shawn reached for the official-looking papers the man had in his outstretched hand. He turned them around and held them up to the light. *Suit* was all he could make out of the legal papers. Something was terribly wrong. He wondered if Mr. Belt Buckle noticed the shaking papers. His tightened throat was making it difficult to breathe.

"What is this?" Shawn forced his eyes back to the papers, straining to focus on the print. The man said something but Shawn couldn't hear it through the pounding in his ears. "What?"

"I said I can't read it to you, fella."

The papers rattled in his hands. "You gotta help me," Shawn croaked.

Mr. Belt Buckle took the toothpick out of his mouth and rolled it between his fingers. He leaned close, the rim of his hat brushing Shawn's baseball cap. "Your wife's suing you for a de-vorce, Son." He patted Shawn's shoulder and quickly returned to his car.

It had to be a mistake. Belt Buckle had the wrong guy. Sure, things weren't the greatest between Jolene and him but this…

Shawn yanked open the back door to the house and fumbled for the light in the kitchen. He saw dirty dishes in the sink and counter, and an ashtray spilling over onto the table. *Nothing different here.*

He kicked a beer can out of the way as he raced to their bedroom. With a click of the light switch, he discovered opened drawers gaping with the announcement Jolene had, in fact, packed her bags. He sank into the unmade bed and dropped his head. His mind was tangled with a million thoughts. Shawn tried to absorb what Jolene had done. It took him three tries to dial the right number for Jolene's mother.

"Edna? Is Jolene there?"

"Yes, Shawn. Just a minute."

"Hello?"

"Jolene, what are you doing?"

"Oh… I guess you got the papers."

"What's going on? Come home. You and Rachel come back home."

"Not this time, Shawn. It's over. Didn't you read the papers?"

"It's not over. You and Rachel are my family, the most important thing in the world to me. What did I do? Come home and we'll talk about this."

"There's nothing to talk about, Shawn. I don't love you any more. I just want this to go smoothly and be over with as soon as possible."

Shawn swallowed away the urge to cry. "Jolene, I love you. Please, I'll do anything. We'll get counseling, whatever you want. This is our family, Jolene, we need to work this out."

"Nope. We're getting a divorce, Shawn. We'll be doing our talking through lawyers after tonight. Don't call me."

"But what about Rachel? She's my daughter, too."

"We'll work that out. Bye."

And just like that, Shawn's family was gone.

TWO

During the divorce, Shawn repeatedly begged Jolene to return home with Rachel. But Jolene had grown tired of him and was ready to move on. Shawn discovered she was back with her first husband, and that worried him. Flint was a man who was into drugs, big time, especially heroin. If Jolene was going to go through with this divorce, then he would spend his time trying to rescue Rachel.

He received another shock the month after Jolene left. Between what little the letter carrier was allowed to tell him and the information on his bills, Jolene had been intercepting the mail to keep him from finding out she was running up the credit cards. He knew now. Boy, howdy! He was told it was his legal obligation to pay them since they were in his name.

The day they went to court to finalize things, Shawn pulled Jolene aside. "This is our last chance. We can still salvage this marriage." She pulled her arm away. "If you go through those doors, that's it, Jolene. Don't be asking me to get back with you." She turned her nose upward and marched though the door.

"Let's do it!" she proclaimed. The doors closed on Shawn and his dreams for his family.

*****

Two weeks later, Jolene called Shawn at work. He sat back in his chair at his desk and listened to her sobs. "Shawn, I screwed up. I'm so sorry. I want us to get back together."

Sorry? You mean you and Flint split the sheets. He had to be careful what he said or she would use Rachel to punish him. "Didn't I tell you, Jolene, we won't be getting back together?" he said gently.

"Fine. Don't pick Rachel up early today as planned. Come at your scheduled time." She hung up on him. So much for being careful.

Shawn finished his stack of work orders and signed out of the greenhouse. He drove around Wagontown, trying to find Jolene's

11

new apartment. She had already moved twice since she left her mother's.

He pulled into the parking area in front of Jolene's apartment. The peeling yellow paint and torn screens depressed him when he thought about his baby living here. He followed the sound of a revving motor behind the building.

Shawn found Rachel sitting between the legs of a skinny, greasy man, riding in circles on a motorcycle. Each lurch forward snapped Rachel's head back while Jolene, holding a beer in one hand and a cigarette in the other, squealed with laughter. Fear grabbed his chest and squeezed out his breath.

"What are you doing?" gasped Shawn. He ran over and stood in front of the motorcycle. "Are you crazy, Jolene?" He grabbed Rachel and held the trembling little girl close.

"You sure are late," slurred Jolene. "You were supposed to be here an hour ago." Her green eyes seemed to swim in their sockets.

"You told me I couldn't get her early. Remember?" Rachel clung to him as Shawn leaned toward the greaser. "If I ever catch you putting my daughter on your bike again, you'll be riding a wheelchair." The squirrelly man squinted up into Shawn's eyes, taking in the height and build of the tall, angry man before him.

"Cool. Don't want no trouble."

"You have her home by six, Mister," yelled Jolene as Shawn carried Rachel away. "Six oh-oh!"

Shawn wasn't late returning Rachel. He carried her up to the front door and knocked, but there was no way Jolene could hear through all the loud, heavy metal music. He pushed open the door and strained to see through the smoke. Only candles lighted the front room. He stumbled over a pair of legs stretched across the floor. They belonged to a teenager giggling behind a beer can.

"Where's Jolene?" yelled Shawn as Rachel buried her head in his shoulder. The girl nodded toward the next room. Shawn turned off the music, blew out the candles, and flipped on the ceiling light. Pushing open the door to the kitchen, he saw a pot of spaghetti on the stove, the sauce dried and cracked. Somewhere under the pile of dirty plates and coffee mugs was a sink. The trashcan beside the stove looked like a volcanic eruption of garbage, the refrigerator was streaked with dried food and red punch. His shoes stuck to the floor. Jolene was propped against the counter.

"I can see why you had me pick up Rachel at your mother's the last two weeks. Gave you time to remodel the place. Love what you've done to it, Jolene. Early American pig sty."

"Shut up, Shawn." Jolene's face was puffy; her skin was the color of the gray pot on the stove.

Death warmed over comes to mind. She swayed as she poked Shawn's shoulder with her finger. "Don't talk to me like I'm your wife."

"You do happen to be the mother of my child. How do you think it makes me feel leaving Rachel here in this filth? And you're going to get in trouble giving beer to minors like that girl in there."

"Are you worried about me getting into trouble, Shawn? Don't tell me you care!" He turned his head to avoid the kiss meant for him. Jolene slid off the stool as Shawn caught her. When she stood up he noticed how her clothing hung on her tall, bony frame. *She looks like those pictures of Holocaust victims.*

"I care about Rachel and how she has to live, Jolene. How can you do this to her?"

"Come here, Baby," Jolene clapped her hands and took the little girl from Shawn. "She's fine where she is. Don't you start anything."

Shawn kissed Rachel goodbye and wound his way around beer cans and litter to the front door. He sat in his truck until the teenager left and the lights blinked out in the apartment. He vowed he would keep track of everything Jolene did until he finally had enough to go to court to get custody of his child. *Before it's too late.* Until then, his baby had to live like this.

Shawn leaned his head against the steering wheel and cried.

13

THREE

"Shawn, I want to talk to you. Can we meet somewhere?"

Her words grated on his ears as he clenched the phone. Over the past two years Jolene had said these words a dozen times. She was getting a job. She was going to move to Santa Fe. She was going to get her GED. That she managed to do. There was a nurse's aid program she was going to take. She didn't get the part about actually having to attend classes. Jolene had even told him she was going to place herself in rehab for her drug problem. Shawn hurried to his lawyer with this information in hopes of getting Rachel, but was told it was too late. No judge in Oklahoma would take a child from its mother while she was getting her act together. It didn't matter Jolene only stayed a week.

"Shawn, are you there?"

"Yeah. "

"How 'bout the "Longhorn"? It's kind of like *our* place - to meet and talk."

Shawn showed up at the restaurant at "six-oh-oh," just as Jolene requested. She sat at a booth, wearing another new outfit. In fact he didn't remember her wearing the same thing twice in the past few weeks. *Wonder who she found to tap this time.* He had heard rumors on several candidates.

Shawn slid into the booth across from her. "Where's Rachel?"

"At Mother's." Jolene's eyes dropped to the table for a second.

"I thought Edna was on vacation." A hint of pink surfaced on her pale cheeks.

"She came back early."

"What's this all about, Jolene?"

She reached across the table with her manicured hand and patted his arm. "Don't be in such a hurry. Let's order first, okay?" He noticed the ring - maybe a ruby - and the gold tennis bracelet. *She found money this time. Poor sucker.* He started humming, "Can't Buy Me Love," as he scanned the menu. "They didn't know about her," he murmured.

14

"What?" Jolene closed her menu.

"I'll have chowder." He smiled and motioned the waitress over to their booth.

Shawn wanted to ask for extra time with Rachel this week so he thought it best to humor Jolene. He listened to her chatter, nodding and smiling at all the right times during the meal.

Jolene leaned back and lit a cigarette. As always, she tried to redirect the smoke as if doing him a big favor. "Want dessert? I'm treating."

"No, thanks. I have to get to the nursery."

"I was hoping maybe we could see a movie or something."

Shawn shook his head. "What is it you wanted to tell me?"

Jolene pouted her lips. "All business and no fun. Well, here goes." She leaned toward him. "You remember Paul Frank?"

Ah, one of the rumors was true. "You mean the car salesman that lived beside your uncle when you were a kid?"

Jolene nodded. "He wants me to move into the little house he owns next to his."

"I thought he lived in that mansion on Tumbleweed Drive."

Jolene laughed and swept back her black hair. "Well, he hasn't been doing too well betting on the race horses or at Vegas lately. He sold that and moved into one of his houses on Sunset View. He still has his ranch up country."

"You want to practically move in with a man you never cared for as a kid."

"It wasn't true about him hitting his kids." Jolene was rocking in her seat.

She's getting nervous. "A man old enough to be your father, with a gambling problem. Good choice, Jolene. Great father role for Rachel."

"You're her father, Shawn. No one will ever take your place."

"Why am I just now finding out about Paul? Why all the secrecy, Jolene?"

"I didn't want to hurt your feelings."

Laughter escaped him. *She doesn't even get the absurdity of her words.*

15

"Rachel really likes him." Jolene grabbed his hand. "He's very patient with her, you know how she can be so-"

"Okay."

"What?"

"You know there's nothing I can do about any of this. The mother gets all the rights. At least this home should be in better condition than any other place else you've had Rachel."

"So, you're okay about Paul and I?" She sounded disappointed.

"Just as long as Rachel is being well taken care of, Jolene. I have to go."

She grabbed his arm. "I still love you, Shawn."

Shawn's head dropped. "You love me but you're going to hook up with Paul."

"Someone has to take care of me. I'd rather it was you. I screwed up when I left you."

Shawn slowly pulled his arm back. "Can I have Rachel Monday and Tuesday? I'd like to make it a long week end and go camping."

He waited for her answer. As always, it depended on how she felt at the moment.

"Sure. She'd be bored helping me move anyway."

"I'll pick her up as usual."

"At Mother's." Jolene toyed with her lighter. "Have fun."

"Yeah." Shawn saw his chance to escape. He flopped on his cap and nodded to her.

"Shawn?" He turned back to her. *Almost made it.* "Shawn, I still love you."

"Gotta go." He hurried out to his truck and glanced at Jolene's Nova SS. Beer cans were scattered on the floor in the front and back. Dirty diapers and fast food trash surrounded the child seat. Shawn snorted. *Nova Super Slob.* Maybe Paul Frank could clean her up. Maybe things would be better for Rachel.

FOUR

Shawn went through the suitcase Jolene had packed for Rachel, who was chattering excitedly about their trip. Four pairs of long thermal underwear, a half dozen sweatshirts, blue jeans, and heavy socks - all still with the price tags on. *Overkill as usual. Did I tell her we were camping in the Yukon?* He placed all the extra clothing on Rachel's bed. "What's this?" Shawn held up a plastic baby bottle in front of the grinning girl.

"My puppy bottle," giggled Rachel. She pretended to drink from it.

"Rachel, come here." Shawn sat on the bed and swept her onto his knee "How old are you?" Rachel wrestled with her hand and proudly displayed three fingers. "Do you remember how I told you last year that you were too big to drink from a bottle?" Rachel nodded solemnly. "I got you a big kid's seat for you to ride in my truck instead of the baby one, didn't I?" Another nod. "Well, big girls who ride in big kid's seats don't use this."

"What are you going to do, Daddy?"

"*You* are going to throw this baby thing out and drink from a cup, like the big girl you are."

Rachel burst into tears. "I don't want to throw out the puppy bottle, Daddy." *Thanks, Jolene.*

Shawn brushed away her tears. "Don't cry, Rachel. I'll tell you what. We'll find a nice little baby who could use this bottle, and I'll try to find you a puppy *cup.* Good deal?"

Rachel's eyes, blue like his own, rolled to the side as she considered this. "Okay." Shawn scooped her up and hugged her.

"Now let's get going. We're camping in the mountains where they have pretty trees."

"I love you, Daddy! Let's go!" Rachel danced out the door as Shawn picked up the baby bottle and disgustedly tossed it in the trashcan. Remembering his promise to Rachel, he took it out. "Well, little puppy, you've been saved this time."

"Daddy! I'm still ready!"

Shawn laughed as he took the suitcases out the door.

*****

Their camping trip over too quickly, Shawn found himself knocking on Jolene's front door. It was a modest little house, but it was clean and kept up - at least for now. "Where can she be, Daddy?" Rachel squinted, trying to figure out her mother's absence. "I want to tell her how much fun we had camping."

"Don't worry, we'll find her soon." He took Rachel's hand and walked to the back of the bungalow. Rusty bedsprings and old mattresses were piled against the house. The back yard was small and ended with a sharp drop-off to a rocky drain ditch. "Never, ever come out here yourself, Rachel. You could fall way down there."

"Maybe Mommy's next door at Paul's." They walked across the drive to the larger house. It was constructed with the same dark clapboard as the bungalow, and also seemed to be neat and well kept.

Knocking on that front door was fruitless. "We'll drive over to Granny's and see if she's there." He noticed the frown crinkling above Rachel's eyes. "Don't worry, we'll find Mommy." They spent the next hour driving all over Wagontown, trying to find her.

"Maybe she went to Nuevo Lago, Daddy." Rachel's small voice quivered.

"Why would she go there?"

"They like to go to see the race horses. Her and Paul. Sometimes they take me. But I think it's kind of boring."

"What do you do while you're there?"

"Mostly hold Mommy's beer while she watches the races."

"Does Mommy drink a lot of beer, Rachel?"

"She likes it. She says, 'I have to have my beer!'"

"We'll try one more time at your new house. Maybe she forgot she lives there now." They both laughed. Shawn was relieved to see some of the worry leave the child's face. *Why does Jolene do this to her?*

Jolene's Nova was in the drive. "She's here!" squealed Rachel Shawn carried her and her suitcase to the door, which flew open before he could knock.

"You're late, Mister. You were to be back at six-oh-oh, and in case you haven't noticed, it's after seven!"

Shawn sat the suitcase down. Jolene was clad in a red robe with her long, wavy hair wrapped in a thick towel. She held onto the door jam to steady herself.

"We were here on time. You weren't." Rachel squeezed his neck. *What's it going to be, Jolene? Another war?*

"I was taking a shower. You could have come in."

"Your car wasn't here."

"I give you permission for extra time with my child and you do this to me."

"What did I do to you?" Rachel squeezed him harder.

Jolene flicked her cigarette past him. She tilted her head back and blew out a stream of smoke, her lips dry and cracked. "You're always messing with me. You can forget about seeing her tomorrow night."

"Now, wait a minute, Jolene. I have a right to see her Wednesdays."

"No, you don't". She poked his shoulder with each word. "I let you see her out of the goodness of my heart." Rachel buried her head in Shawn's shoulder.

"Check your papers, Darlin'. I'll be here to get her tomorrow."

"We'll see about that! I'm sick and tired of this!" Jolene reached behind her and picked up a black coffee mug. She drank from it, licking her lips as she set it back.

"What are you talking about, Jolene?"

She leaned closer. The smell of beer on her breath made him back up. "I hear things, like you're dating that girl from Hampton. If I catch the two of you together, I'll kick her butt." Jolene was screaming and shaking her fist in Shawn's face. He felt Rachel tremble, her tears dampening his neck.

"Now look what you've done, Shawn. You made her cry. Come here, Baby."

Shawn pulled back. "You're a real piece of work, Jolene. Rachel couldn't wait to tell you about our trip, but you're drunk. You ruined it for her."

"Are you done preaching? Give her to me, *now*."

Shawn knelt down with Rachel and dried her tears. Her sad eyes looked up at him. "Bye, Daddy," she choked.

Shawn held Rachel's face in his large hands. "Bye, Sugar. I love you."

"I love you, too, Daddy." Jolene tapped her slipper on the wooden planks.

"See you tomorrow." Rachel threw her arms around his neck. *How can I leave her?*

"That's enough." Jolene picked up Rachel. "Come on inside and see what I bought for you, Baby."

After the door slammed in his face Shawn hurried home to call Jolene's cousin, Jane. She had always shown a special interest in Rachel, and Shawn was counting on that as he told her, "I just dropped off Rachel and Jolene's drunk." Jane told him she would hurry over there.

He wondered when the time came, if Jane would help him get custody of Rachel. He wondered how much longer he'd have to wait. He wondered if when he called his lawyer in the morning he'd say again it wasn't enough, but Shawn already knew the answer to that.

*****

Jolene didn't have to worry about the "girl" from Hampton. As their relationship grew more serious, they had talked about having children, which Shawn wanted more of, and Annie did not. That discovery put a damper on their dating, so they decided to part as friends.

He hoped Jolene didn't think her threat had anything to do with it. The image of lanky Jolene trying to whoop anyone made him laugh as he unloaded the heavy poinsettias from his truck. He closed the cap and took inventory of the white and red ocean of petals on the tables before him. The greenhouse was ready for Christmas. Shawn hoped it would be a good season. He was happiest here at his nursery, especially when Rachel was helping him with potting plants or watering the roses. Shawn wanted to have an enterprising business to pass on to his daughter - and hopefully his other children.

Shawn looked up as a black car drove under the "Stevens's Nursery" sign and parked next to the Christmas tree area. Rachel jumped out of it and raced toward him with outstretched arms. "Daddy! Look, I'm here, Daddy."

Shawn scooped her up in his arms. "What a nice surprise!"

"I'm going to stay with you, Daddy. For five days!"

Shawn looked past her and watched Jolene approach them. Her pale lips were barley visible against her chalky skin. She carried her coffee mug.

"Rachel, I told you I wanted to talk to Daddy first." Jolene pouted her lips at the child. "I hope you don't mind. Can you take her for a few days?" Shawn had made plans to perform at a pub in Buckshot over the weekend. He and his friend Karen had been singing and playing guitar the weekends he didn't have Rachel, earning him extra money for Christmas. He could never tell Jolene, or she'd threaten to kick Karen's posterior, too. He'd figure something out.

"Sure, any time. When will you bring her by?"

Jolene swirled the liquid in her cup. A new watch sparkled at the edge of her sleeve. *Looks expensive.*

"I was going to leave her with you now."

"Where are you going?"

"Paul and I are going to the Yucatan. Mother will give you our phone number. And I have a baby-sitter lined up for when you work."

"You don't have that information for me now?"

Jolene shook her head. "You know me, Shawn, I'm so stupid. Just bring her home Wednesday night at the usual time."

"Who is she?" asked Shawn.

"Who?" Jolene asked after sipping her mug.

"The baby-sitter. Will I take Rachel there or is she coming to my house, or what?" Shawn tried to hide the irritation in his voice.

"She'll come by here tonight. I told her to be sure to come before six. Y'all can work out the details." Jolene looked back at the car. "I didn't pick up supper for Rachel. Paul is so fussy about eating in his precious car." Jolene's green eyes rolled under her raised eyebrows. "He just doesn't want to get his fat butt out and have to clean it."

"I *am* hungry, Daddy." Rachel tugged on his arm. "I have an idea. Let's get tortilla burgers at the cancino."

"Let me go inside and ask Maria if she'll close tonight. I hope so since you haven't had anything to eat."

"I'm sorry, Shawn. I screw up so much. I'm so, so stupid. I better go before Paul gets impatient. Next he won't buy me anything in Mexico." She squatted down to Rachel. "Bye, Baby. Be good for Daddy, and I'll buy you lots of stuff."

"Goody!" squealed Rachel, her auburn curls bouncing as she jumped up and down. She squeezed her mother's neck. "I love you, Mommy."

Jolene turned to Shawn. "You be good and I'll bring something back for you, too, Shawn." Suddenly, there was no daylight between them. "I'll miss you as much as Rachel," she whispered in his ear. He smelled it. *Beer.*

"Just make sure the sitter shows up so I can get to work."

Jolene giggled. "I will, I promise. Oh, save me seven of those gorgeous poinsettias you have inside, the huge hanging ones. Paul put me in charge of Christmas gifts for his employees."

The man's a fool. "They're not cheap, Jolene."

"Doesn't matter. He's good for the money." Already her back was turned to him as she hurried to the car.

FIVE

Maria agreed to stay, so Shawn and Rachel drove to Sala's Grocery Store. They climbed up the cement steps and pushed open the heavy wooden door. The smell of grilled onions triggered his hunger, and Shawn remembered he had not eaten all day. Rachel galloped to the back of the store.

"Hurry, Daddy, or my stomach might eat itself!" Rachel rested her chin on the "Order Here" counter. The place was noisy with waitresses barking orders, customers chatting at their tables, and the sound of sizzling burgers on the grill.

"Hello, Mr. Stevens." The round, smiling woman pulled an order pad and pencil from her spattered apron.

"Hey, Rosa. *Como esta?*"

"Busy. Y'all want the usual?"

"My kind of woman. Tell Tomas he better watch out."

Rosa giggled wickedly. "Y'all still have to pay, no matter how much you flatter me."

Rachel led him to the table by the window. Shawn looked out across the flat land and saw thunderheads piling their white ominous clouds on the horizon. The field before them that had been bursting with cotton bolls in August was now desolate and barren. Gusts of wind whipped up swirls of the dark dry dirt. *I'm like that field,* thought Shawn. *Lonely, waiting for something to grow.*

"Daddy, she's coming. Stop daytime dreaming!" Shawn laughed. He watched Rosa waddle over to their table, balancing a round tray of food in one hand and carrying soda cans in the other.

"Here you are. Y'all enjoy." She tossed two wrapped straws onto the table and hurried away.

"Grace, Daddy, close your eyes and say grace." He opened his eyes a slit and watched Rachel fold her little hands in earnest prayer. She frowned furiously, trying to shut out all distractions.

I love her so much.

The child's eyes burst open. She lifted her tortilla burger to her mouth. Shawn reached over and tickled her chin. "Now, eat so we can get back and meet this sitter."

"Then we'll go home and feed the bunnies!" Rachel stood up and clapped her hands.

"Sit down, Rachel."

"Let's take our food home so we can see the bunnies now."

"No, sit down." He pulled her to her seat.

"But it's getting dark."

"I'll turn on the floodlight. Rachel, don't argue. Sit down and let's have a nice supper." She reluctantly sat on her chair.

"Mommy wouldn't make me wait."

Shawn stopped chewing. "Do I look like Mommy?"

Rachel took a bite of food. "She lets me do what I want."

"Mommies and Daddies aren't supposed to let their kids do everything they want."

"Why not?" At least she was eating.

"Because kids don't always know what's best for them. You're hungry, so you need to sit and eat. You better hurry so we can go home and feed the bunnies. Okay?"

They finished and stopped by the nursery to help Maria close up. Shawn was angry the baby-sitter hadn't arrived. He'd have to make his own arrangements for next week.

They had just entered the front door of his house when the wind blew in a storm. Rachel shrieked as the night sky ripped open with a searing bolt of lightening. She clung to Shawn's leg while he hung up his cowboy hat.

"Hey, hey, Darlin, we're safe in here." He carried her to the sofa and held her until they only heard the sound of the rain pounding on the roof.

"Daddy, what about the bunnies?"

"They're dry in their hutches."

Her round eyes stared into his as she grabbed his face. "But they'll be so hungry. Can we go now and feed them?"

"Maybe. Let's go look." Shawn turned on the floodlight and opened the back door. The yard from the side of the house to the fields was flooded with dark water racing toward the drainage ditch. "It's pretty deep by the hutches. We better wait until morning."

"But Daddy, they'll starve!"

"They'll be okay. Rabbits in the wild don't always get to eat their supper."

"But these are our bunnies and they need to eat." Rachel yanked free of his grip and ran down the first two steps. Shawn grabbed her and pulled her inside.

"Listen to me, young lady. The water is too deep for someone who's only three. And there's a good chance the flooding may have washed out some snakes. Don't you dare go out there without me."

"Then let's go now!"

"No! It's not safe." Rachel burst into tears. "The bunnies will be fine until morning. Now let's get you to bed. You look tired."

"Okay." Shawn was surprised at her sudden obedience. She was used to getting her own way with Jolene, and it usually took a day or two for Rachel to adjust to his discipline.

After he had tucked her in bed, Shawn turned on the TV, kicked off his boots and stretched out on the sofa. He yawned, surprised at his sudden fatigue. The old blue sofa knew the shape of his long body, lulling him to sleep.

He sat up. *What was that?* Screaming. *Out back.* Water. *Deep water. The rabbits.* Shoving his feet into his boots, images of Rachel being bitten by a rattler or swept away to the ditch flooded his body with panic.

"Rachel!" he roared and bounded down the steps into the pelting rain. He ran toward the shrieks and found her outside the feed room, clutching a bucket of pellets, standing in water over her knees.

"Daddy, help me, help me!" The bucket splashed into the water as Rachel clawed and slapped her legs. Shawn raced to her. *What is it?* Then he saw. Baseball size masses of quivering fire ants were floating by. Some had washed up against Rachel's legs. She desperately tried to brush them off. Shawn grabbed her and rubbed her legs.

"Ah, Baby, poor Baby." He carried her to the house and stripped off her clothes and shoes on the porch. Rachel wailed in pain.

25

Shawn scanned her body for more ants, knowing just one would bite and sting her over and over. He brushed them off her stomach and back.

"It hurts! It burns. Daddy, make it stop!" Rachel shook in is arms as he carried her to the bathroom and wrapped her shivering, wet body in a towel. He held her, reaching for the phone in his room to call his neighbor.

"Mama Mae. It's Shawn. Sorry to wake you but Rachel just got swarmed by fire ants. What should I do? ... All right. The back door's open."

Rachel shrieked in agony. Her hands continuously scratched her legs and feet. "I'll be right back, Rachel." Shawn tried to lay her on his bed but she tightened her grip around his neck.

"Daddy, don't leave me!"

"I'm just going into the bathroom. I'll be right back I promise." He forced her hands from his neck and went to the next room. Her wails filled the house while Shawn got a bottle of ammonia from under the sink and cotton balls from the drawer.

"Daddy! Hurry!" He ran back to his bedroom.

"Mama Mae told me this will make you feel better in a few minutes. It will sting at first, so you'll have to be a big girl for me and let me put it on you."

"No, don't, it already hurts."

"Let me look," said Shawn as he tried to open her towel.

"No!" yelled Rachel.

"I'm just looking." Rachel sobbed but released her grip on the towel. Shawn unwrapped it as anger surged his veins. *Look what they did to her.* Her stomach, legs, and feet were dotted with red welts. He knew what just one of those felt like. Fire ants were one of the curses they had to live with and learned to hate.

"Looks like you're gonna need help with that." Mama Mae's raspy voice was sweet music to his ears. She handed him a book and motioned him to read to Rachel as she picked up the cotton and ammonia.

"I'm glad you're here, Mama Mae." Shawn leaned closer. "Look what they did to her."

Mama Mae tilted her head so she could examine the bites through her bifocals. "Now, Rachel, I didn't get up this time of night to listen to no screamin'. Your Daddy's right, this will hurt. But you just listen to the story Daddy's gonna read to you, and y'all forget about me and what I'm doin'. If you don't fuss too much, Puddin, you get to keep the book. Understand?"

Rachel bit her lower lip and nodded. "Now we got to get goin' or this won't do any good." Shawn pointed to the pictures, blocking Rachel's view of her body with the big book. Mama Mae's wrinkled, weathered hands quickly rubbed the cotton ball soaked in ammonia over the child's tummy, legs and feet. Rachel kicked and screamed in protest.

"I'll blow on it, Honey. Now, we need to turn you over."

Shawn coaxed Rachel's attention back to the book, then helped Mama Mae turn Rachel over. "Almost done, Puddin, keep readin', Shawn." He placed the book under Rachel's chin while she propped herself up to follow the story.

"I'm trying not to scream, Daddy, but it hurts!" she cried.

"You're doing great, Rachel. She's almost done."

"Blow on it, Mama Mae, please blow away the burn." The frowning woman brushed back a strand of salt-and pepper hair and blew puffs of air on the disappearing welts. She gently turned Rachel onto her back and examined her work. The swelling was gone, tiny red dots the only sign of the vicious attack.

"What a brave little Sooner you are, Rachel."

Rachel smiled as Shawn covered her up. "Do I get to keep the book?"

Mama Mae bent over. "You bet, you earned it. Now, try to sleep. Have a feelin' you and I need to have a talk about listening to your Daddy tomorrow. But that's another day, let's finish this one first. Now, give me some sugar." Rachel leaned forward and kissed Mama Mae's tanned cheek.

"I love you, Mama Mae."

"I love you, too." She turned to Shawn. "I'll wait in the kitchen."

Shawn watched the slim woman disappear through the door. He stroked Rachel's hair until she was quiet. "Try to sleep, Darlin'. I'll carry you over to your bed later."

"Can I sleep with you, Daddy, please?" Rachel clutched the blanket under her chin. Red blotches surrounded her eyes, her nostrils still quivered.

"Nah, you're too big." He would have liked to keep her there, to comfort her. But he feared of what Jolene might accuse him if he did. She was capable of anything. "I'll be back after Mama Mae leaves and sit with you." He kissed her and turned out the light. "Night, Rachel. I love you."

"I love you, too, Daddy."

Shawn went into the kitchen. Mama Mae had two shot glasses filled with brandy on the table. She was putting the bottle back in the cupboard above the sink. "Being the good Baptist I am, I'm doing this only for medicinal purposes."

Shawn chuckled. "And for what ailment would this be, Mama Mae?"

"Nerves. You look like a bar of soap at the end of a long wash day."

"And you?"

"Lord knows it shakes me up when I see what those fire ants do." With that, they tipped back their heads and swallowed their medication. "You know, during flooding those durn ants travel in balls that rotate, so they take turns getting air. Why God made them with such smarts to survive is beyond me."

Shawn leaned back in his chair. "She sneaked out."

"Of course she did. Jolene never makes the child listen. She's afraid to say 'no' to her about anything. She thinks Rachel won't like her. I wonder who's the parent in that relationship sometimes. You know what you got to do, don't you." Before he could answer, she continued, wagging her finger at him. "Put hooks on these doors. High and out of reach. And you got to start locking up. Robert Hill's place got broke into last week. They think it was kids on drugs. Gangs are driving out from Nuevo Lago, breakin' in and stealin'." She pushed her chair back and tied a bandanna over her hair. "Now, I got to get home before Luke knows I left his bed. Daybreak will be creepin' under my door before you know it. And you get some sleep."

"Can I ask you one more favor?"

"Sure, Shawn." He walked over to the doorway with her and saw the rain was stopping.

"Can you watch Rachel tomorrow night?"

"Pub engagement?" Mama Mae's green eyes twinkled. "Or do you have a date?"

"No, no date. I haven't been having much luck there lately. I'm too busy anyway." He held the door open for her.

"I can't tomorrow night, but don't worry. I'll have a sitter here for you." A smile threatened to break out on her face. "How long are you keeping Rachel?"

"Until Wednesday night. I need someone next week, too."

"I'll arrange it. What time should she come?"

"Seven is good." Shawn cocked his head. "What's her name, Mama Mae?"

She turned and went down the steps. "Laynie Whiteman. She's single. Has some kids of her own. They'd be good for Rachel to play with. I'll tell her to bring them along."

"But-"

"Don't you trust my judgment, Shawn Stevens?" Her hand was on the car door, pulling it open. "Go back inside and get some sleep." Mama Mae ended the conversation with a slam of her old Lincoln and drove east to her home down the muddy road. Shawn closed the door and started for his bedroom to carry Rachel to her bed, then stopped. Hearing Mama Mae's voice scolding him, he smiled and locked the front and back doors.

SIX

Rachel was unhappy Shawn was leaving for Buckshot. She blocked his exit from his bedroom as he carried his guitar. "I want to come with you, Daddy." She was jumping side to side.

Shawn put his guitar by the door and his hand on her shoulder to quiet her. "You can't, Rachel. It gets too smoky and you would be up too late."

The child stamped her foot. "I'm used to Mommy's smoke and she lets me stay up late as I want."

Shawn picked her up and went to the kitchen window, watching for the new sitter. "You shouldn't be around anyone's smoke, Rachel. It's bad for you and I don't know why Mommy does that. And little girls who are three need to get to bed at a good time. Mama Mae said Laynie has some kids of her own to play with you."

"Will it be fun?"

"Do you think Mama Mae would have it any other way?" Rachel smiled and pointed out the window.

"Is that them coming down the back road?"

"Could be." Suddenly, Shawn was nervous. *Dumb.* "Yup, she's pulling in the drive." The dome light of Laynie's car showed her releasing three bouncing children from their seat belts. He opened the door for them before they could knock.

"Come on in, come on in," proclaimed Shawn. Tallest to smallest -boy-girl-boy - came in the door, followed by Laynie, her brunette curls framing wide, brown eyes that stared into his. There was a small dimple under her lower lip, just one the left side, when she smiled. And her smile captured his eyes...

"Hi, Shawn, I'm Laynie." When his hand enclosed around hers, something surged through him as music filled his mind. *Thunder and lightning. So very frightening...* He was speechless. Laynie studied his face, then dropped her eyes as a hint of red surfaced on her cheeks.

She felt it, too... I think. I wonder if she heard the music.

Laynie slid her hand out of his grip and turned to Rachel, who was frowning at them. "You must be Rachel. Mama Mae was right. You are a pretty little girl."

"A big girl." Rachel scanned Laynie head to toe. "Are you going to tell me your kids' names or are you and Daddy going to stand there and look at each other all night." Laynie raised her eyebrows and the two adults laughed nervously.

"Okay, Rachel. The oldest is Zack. He's twelve. This is Madison, we call her Maddie, and she's seven. This little guy is Joey. He's just a little younger than you."

"Hey, guys, I'm Shawn and this is Rachel. She'll show you around. I have to go or I'll be late."

"What's in the sack?" Rachel pointed to the large brown bag Laynie had put on the table.

"You'll find out, after your daddy leaves. I promise you'll like it."

Rachel reached for him. "Well, I guess you better get going."

Shawn picked her up and laughed. "Laynie, all the numbers you'll need are on that table by the phone."

She smiled. Why was his heart thumping? "I've nothing to worry about with Mama Mae down the road."

"Oh, she's home?" he asked.

"She wants to be in case I need her. I told her we'd be okay, but you know Mama Mae."

He certainly did. "What else did she say?"

"Just that it might be a little difficult for Rachel when you leave because you don't go out much."

Laynie laughed. He liked her laugh. He liked how she looked when she laughed. And how she looked when she wasn't laughing. He knew he was staring. Shawn winked at her and this time he saw a full-faced blush. "I'm not going to tell you what she told me about you," he teased. "And with that, I'm outta here."

"What time will you be back?"

"Have the boyfriend out before one," he chuckled.

Laynie rolled her eyes. "Not me. I've been in a dry spell."

This made Shawn happy... hopeful. He kissed Rachel goodbye, was showered with more goodbyes from all the children as he hurried out the door to his truck.

"Shawn, don't you need this?" Laynie stood on the porch holding his guitar.

"Well, now, Laynie, I've heard of a girl being pretty enough to make a man forget to eat, but never to forget his guitar." She leaned close to him and pressed the instrument into him.

"But I'm not," she whispered.

"Pretty?"

"I'm not a girl. I'm a woman, in case you haven't noticed." This time she winked at him. Her face was close to his. He wanted to kiss her, he almost did. *Too soon. Boy howdy.*

All night, he could not get her out of his mind. *Laynie. Nice name. Nice girl - I mean woman.*

At the end of their gig, Karen followed him off the small stage and tapped him on the shoulder. "You sounded really good tonight, Shawn," she said as they put their guitars in their cases. "You in love or what?"

Shawn laughed. "You know my track record. Well, I got to get home. I have Rachel and I don't want to keep the sitter too late."

"Ah, she's pretty, right?"

"She's very nice and has three kids that are either already asleep or need to be."

Shawn gathered up his things and hurried out to his truck. He hoped he didn't smell too smoky. He hoped Laynie wasn't in a hurry to get home. He hoped she liked him. Seemed to, but maybe she was just being nice. On the drive home Shawn thought how nice it would be to be in a good relationship, to (touch her hair) have someone to talk to, someone to (hold close) confide in. He parked beside her car and carried his gear inside. Laynie walked in from the living room as he set his guitar in the corner of the kitchen.

"Hey, Shawn. How'd it go?" She yawned and tousled her curls. He wanted to do that. He wanted to hold her and kiss her sleepy eyes. *Slow down, cowboy.*

"Great. How did Rachel do?"

"She was good. I did have trouble getting her to stay in her bed, so Maddie offered to sleep with her and the boys are on the floor. Rachel showed me where you keep your sleeping bags."

"How 'bout a cup of coffee?"

"No, thanks, Shawn. I need to get my kids home and in their own beds. If you could carry Maddie, I'll wake Zack and carry Joey."

"Why don't you leave them here? You could sleep on the couch or come back for them in the morning."

Laynie blinked away the rest of her sleepiness. "I don't think that's such a good idea."

"I was hoping you and I could talk a little."

"I'm really tired. Would you help me?" When he followed her into Rachel's room, she had already wakened Zack and was picking up Joey. He bent over and looked at the blond haired girl snuggled next to Rachel. The boys looked like Laynie, but Shawn guessed Maddie looked like her father. She did have curls, although they were tighter ringlets and blonde. Laynie was whispering to Zack, who took the brown bag and held open doors as the procession made its way to the car. She buckled her sleeping children in and thanked Shawn for helping her.

"What do I owe you?" Shawn leaned against her car.

"It's okay. Maybe you can return the favor for me sometime when I go out."

Ouch! "Maybe I could take you out to dinner or something. You like to dance?"

Laynie frowned. "I have to go. Bye, Shawn." He watched exhaust curl around her taillights as she drove away.

What went wrong? Was Rachel too wild? Is it me?

Shawn took his disappointment to bed, and it would not let him sleep. He tried to sort out the night's events. When he left for Buckshot, Laynie seemed happy, even flirting with him. When he returned, she couldn't get out of the house fast enough. Perhaps some things just were not meant to be.

SEVEN

"Mornin', Daddy. I had fun last night with the kids." Rachel climbed up on the chair across from him at the kitchen table. She rubbed her eyes. "They play silly games and Zack is funny."

"Did you and Laynie get along?" Rachel's cereal pinged in the bowl and he dowsed it with milk.

"Oh, yes, Daddy. She had lots of cool stuff in her bag. Play-dough, Popsicle sticks and glue. Look what I made!" Rachel jumped off her chair and picked up her project from the counter. "Look, Daddy, a star. It has glitter and everything. Laynie says I should hang it on our Christmas tree."

"Wow, that's really pretty, Rachel. Now, sit down and eat." Shawn poured juice into her new puppy cup. "What else did you do?"

"Played." Rachel stuffed her mouth full of cereal and crunched. Milk leaked out over her lips.

"Too much. You'll choke." He dabbed her mouth with a napkin. "Were you nice to Laynie? Did you listen to her?"

"Yeah. She only made me do time-out once."

"Uh, oh, what did you do, Rachel?"

She shoved another spoonful into her mouth. "Said a bad word. I said 'chickensh-"

"Okay."

"Mommy says it. But Laynie said I should use a better word. She said that word gets you in trouble. I said it again to see if she meant it. She did."

Shawn laughed. "Did she say anything about me?"

"She asked a few questions, but mostly played with us."

Shawn sipped his coffee. *Should I call her?*

"I did get into trouble one other time." Rachel picked up her bowl and slurped the remaining milk.

"What did you do?"

"I got into her purse while she was on the phone." She wiped her mouth on her sleeve.

"Rachel!"

"Laynie wasn't too mad. She just told me to put the stuff back and go play with the kids while she talked to Mommy."

"Mommy talked to Laynie? For very long?"

"Well, I got to look at almost everything in her purse and I looked at all her pictures. She's got some toys in there, too, mostly for Joey, some gum."

"Okay, Rachel, That's really none of our business. Don't do that again, understand?"

"Yeah. Can the kids come over and play today?" The phone was ringing.

"I don't know, Rachel. They might have other plans." He hoped it was Laynie. He needed to know what Jolene told her.

"*Hola*, from sunny Cancun, Shawn!"

"Jolene."

"Don't sound so disappointed. Did Rachel tell you I called last night?"

Now what? "We were just talking about that."

"I don't appreciate you going out when you're with Rachel, Shawn. You're supposed to be spending time with her."

"Look, Jolene, I was working to make a little extra money. Besides support, I'm still paying you off for the land, remember? And your baby-sitter, if there ever was one, never showed up."

"Okay, okay. Your baby-sitter seemed nice. Who is she?"

"Someone Mama Mae found. But I guess you already know that since you talked to her."

"It's all right if she's a friend of Mama Mae's."

"What did you say to her, Jolene?"

"I just let her know a few things about Rachel. She mostly talked to me about her kids."

"That's it?"

"Did she say I said something wrong? I was nice, Shawn."

"No, she didn't even mention you."

"Anyway, we'll be home Wednesday. I got you something."

Shawn noticed her slurred speech. *It's another tequila sunrise…*

"I'll have Rachel back at your house by six, right, Jolene?"

"Yes, Shawn. I miss you."

"Have fun with Paul." *Please.* He hung up before she could say any more.

A crash in the kitchen brought Shawn running to Rachel. She was standing on the floor surrounded by orange juice racing towards the stove. Broken glass fanned out at her feet.

"Daddy, I'm sorry."

"It's okay, Rachel, just don't move."

Rachel bent down. "I'll clean it up."

"Don't touch it!"

"I'll be careful, I'm big."

"No!" But Shawn knew he wouldn't be able to out-race her determined hand as it grasped a large piece of glass. She shrieked when blood streamed out of the gash in her palm.

"Rachel, I'll help you. Try to calm down." Rachel gulped air and screamed, gulped and screamed. Shawn grabbed a dishtowel out of the drawer and held her over the sink as he ran cold water over the wound. The flow of her bright crimson blood caused her to squeal in fright.

"Why is it doing that, Daddy? Make it stop leaking!"

Shawn wrapped the towel around her hand and applied pressure. Every time he opened it to look at the cut, blood raced out.

"Rachel, we're going to go get this fixed."

"Where, Daddy?" Her wide eyes radiated fear.

"To the emergency room where a doctor will help us."

"No! No! No!" she screamed. Shawn held her across from him and looked into her eyes.

"Rachel, listen to me. You have to calm down. You'll have to be a big girl. I need your help. We must go get you fixed up, I can't do this by myself. Are you going to help me?" Shawn wiped away her tears as she nodded.

"Good. I knew I could count on you. I need you to hold the towel really tight against your hand, like this, while I drive. You can do that, can't you?" She nodded again, trembling a little less. Shawn scooped her up and carried her out to the truck. All the way to the hospital he talked, trying to quiet her panic.

"Here we are, Sugar." He cradled her in his arms and hurried toward the glass double doors. They swished open as they went inside. Rachel sobbed while Shawn filled out all the forms. He shoved the clipboard back under the reception window. "How long will it be?" he asked the woman who took his papers.

"I'd guess about forty-five minutes. Unless more serious injuries come in." Turning away she dismissed him. Shawn sat down and put Rachel on his lap. She closed her eyes and leaned against his chest as he stroked her hair. He elevated her hand against his shoulder and felt her quivering body.

"Shh, shh," he soothed, stroking her long hair. A teenage girl with stringy brown hair hopped over and flopped into the chair beside him, followed by, he guessed, her boyfriend. While their cowboy boots matched, she was only wearing one. On her bare foot, around her big toe, was a high school ring.

"Don't ask," she giggled and held it up for Shawn to see. "It was sure easy to get on, but I can't take the darn sucker off." Her boyfriend grinned and tipped back his hat.

"Try soap? Butter?" Shawn asked.

"Yup. Now my toe's swollen from trying to get it off." Shawn bit his lip and suppressed the urge to laugh. "Go ahead, mister. Everyone else has laughed at me. It is kind of stupid."

He winked at her and said, "Maybe they'll have to amputate."

"Hey! Now that's not funny." She laughed anyway and leaned toward Rachel. "What happened to your little girl?"

"Cut her hand on broken glass."

"Poor baby," the girl cooed. A nurse walked up to her chair and handed her a metal tool. "What's this?"

"A jeweler's cutting tool. Just put it on the ring like this and turn the screw. Maybe it will work."

"Maybe?"

"You got a better idea?" The nurse pushed her glasses up her nose and left them.

"Okay, Rob, get over here and do what she said." The boy looked at Shawn and shrugged, got on his knees and tried the tool. Shawn looked at the people across from him. A young boy sat between two men who were trying to soothe his sobbing. A large fishhook pierced his thumb; the barb was completely under his bloodied skin.

Hooked on a feeling... The music played in his head. "I'm a sick man," he murmured to himself. "Poor kid." Rachel shifted positions and closed her eyes again. A woman sat on the other side of him with a boy about Rachel's age. His cheeks were flushed, and he leaned against his mother. "Sore throat?" Shawn ventured.

The woman turned to him. "Earache. It just rags me the doctor doesn't see kids Saturdays. You call and all you get is that dang recording telling you to go to the ER."

The woman ran her hand through her tangled hair. There was grayness under each eye, like the dark half of the moon. She yawned. "You stay up all night with your sick kid, then have to camp out in this place. They seem oblivious to the fact we have a life, too. You wait in their offices, you wait in that little exam room, and you wait in here. Imagine how it feels to be the sick kid."

Shawn was nodding. "I called the doctor one Friday afternoon when Rachel had a sore throat. The receptionist told me they were booked for the day. I reminded her they were open two more hours. She said sorry, no way. I asked her what I was supposed to do all weekend."

"Go to the ER."

"Right."

The woman yawned again. "What did you do?"

"I drove Rachel to the clinic told them I wasn't leaving until the doctor saw her."

"Bravo! Lions 0, Parents, 1."

"Rachel Stevens!" barked the receptionist.

Rachel jumped. "That's us, Darlin'," said Shawn. He looked at the woman. "It was nice swapping complaints. Good luck."

Once they had gotten in the examination room, it didn't take long to have Rachel's hand tended to by the medical student. Shawn gathered up the insurance papers and carried Rachel out to the truck. "I'd say a brave girl like you deserves lunch. What do you say, Sugar?" He placed Rachel on the seat and buckled her.

"But we just had breakfast, Daddy."

"It seems so, but that was hours ago. Let's get a bite to eat, then we'll go by the drug store and get the things we need to take care of your hand. I'll have to show Mommy what to do."

"Oooo, Mommy, might not be able to do that. She gets freaked out when I'm hurt."

When they arrived home Shawn gave Rachel medication for the pain and put her to bed. He tried to call Mama Mae but she wasn't home. He wanted to tell her about Rachel's latest encounter with disaster, and to ask her for Laynie's number. Instead, he cleaned up the mess in the kitchen and changed the oil in his truck. When he came in to check on Rachel, the phone was ringing. *Laynie?*

"Hi, partner. *Como esta?*" Shawn instantly recognized his friend's voice.

"Carlos? I thought you died. Where are you?"

"Still in Florida. But not for long. I got a problem I was hoping you could help me with, amigo."

"Name it."

"I got to get out of here fast. You know that shopping mall I was putting in? My investors pulled out and stuck me with all the bills. Isabelle and I need a place to hang out until things cool off and I can figure this out."

Shawn chuckled. "When will you be here?"

"Ah, man, you're the best. We'll be there in a few days."

Shawn was looking forward to it. Isabelle was a great cook, and he and Carlos had quite a history together. Remembering their "wild oats" days, he smiled as he went into look at Rachel.

EIGHT

His time with Rachel, as always, went too quickly. Shawn drove to Wagontown and pulled into Jolene's driveway. The streetlight showed no signs of her car. *Here we go again.*

Remembering the last time this happened, he carried Rachel to the front door and knocked. "I don't think she's home, Daddy. Do you think she forgot me?"

"Now how could anyone forget you? No way. Maybe she's asleep or something."

"But where's her car?"

"Does Paul ever drive it?"

Rachel nodded. "He says he wants to fix it up for her. Go inside, Daddy. Mommy always forgets to lock the door. I want to show her my stitches."

At least the fire ant bites have disappeared. Only one storm to weather.

"I'll do it, Daddy." Rachel wriggled down to the porch and opened the door. The instant it swung open a vile, rancid odor assaulted Shawn's nose.

"What's that smell, Rachel?"

"Eeew, Daddy, I don't know. I'll turn on the light."

What the light revealed made Shawn sick. Wet diapers were strewn all over the living room. He walked toward the kitchen, stepping over several piles of animal waste.

"I guess Mommy forgot to clean up after Wags. Yuk!"

"Wags?"

"My puppy Paul got me. I wonder where she is. Wags!"

"Just sit on the sofa while I look for Mommy."

Shawn went into the kitchen and looked in the refrigerator. Empty, except for a six-pack of wine coolers and some pudding. He slammed the door and headed toward the sound of running water.

The bathroom door was open, so he reached in and turned on the light. Water was leaking out of the running toilet. Piles of sopping towels surrounded it. The smell made him gag.

"Come on, Rachel." He plucked her from the sofa and hurried out to the porch. "How do you and Mommy live there?"

"We don't very much, Daddy. We mostly stay with Paul."

"Is his place cleaner?" He put Rachel back into his truck.

"He has Raul take care of the house."

"Raul?"

"Paul calls him his 'boy'."

"Oh. He works for Paul."

"Yup."

"But he isn't a boy, is he?"

"No, Daddy. He's old. Even older than you."

Shawn laughed, then frowned. "It's not right to call Raul a boy. It makes Raul, well, sad when he hears it, even if he doesn't show it. Understand?"

"Yeah. I wonder where Mommy is."

Me, too. As they stepped off the porch, Shawn scanned the yard and driveway, trying to figure out what to do.

"When can I play with Zack and Maddie and Joey again?"

"I don't know. I got their phone number from Mama Mae and left a message, but Laynie hasn't called me back."

"I don't think Mommy's coming Daddy."

Shawn got eye level with Rachel. "You know what? I'll put a note on her door to call us when she gets home. Maybe they got stuck in traffic or something." Rachel's brows crinkled. "Don't worry, Sugar. Paul will watch out for her."

They never heard from Jolene that night. Shawn called Mama Mae and made arrangements to have her watch Rachel while he worked Thursday. Rachel cried when he told her she would stay with him, convinced something bad had happened to her mother.

See what you do to her, Jolene. When he tucked her in bed, they talked, as every night, about how she would try to wake up when she had to go to the bathroom. He didn't know if it was all the stress Rachel lived with, or Jolene's lack of working with Rachel, but she still had to wear diapers at night. *If only I had her. I'd give her the life a little girl deserves.*

He watched TV and thought about calling Laynie again. *No, she's probably getting the kids to bed.* He lay in his bed that night, his thoughts swimming in his head. Usually he enjoyed his solitude, but tonight it crushed him. Shawn was lonely. He had liked being married. He wanted more children. Images of Jolene's place and Rachel living there haunted him. If he took Jolene to court now, she would say she's not living there, but at Paul's. Paul would lie about her drinking. Rachel was stuck in the middle of all that mess. His stomach twisted. Shawn turned his head and tried to bury his worries in his pillow.

*****

Fifteen minutes before quitting time, Shawn was paged for a telephone call. "The un-wife," he muttered to a giggling secretary as he picked up the phone. Jolene called him three or four times a week, always the same time.

"Shawn, we're back. Where's Rachel?"

"Where were you?"

"Paul wanted to stop by his horse ranch and check on things. He might give me a job there."

"As what?" Many suggestions went through his mind, none of them kind.

"A cook." Shawn laughed. "I know, I know, I don't do much of that, but Paul would teach me." A memory of Jolene in their kitchen filled his mind. She had wanted to try to make chicken soup. He could barely eat it, but he did. He discovered later she had merely poured canned chicken broth over the overcooked, mushy noodles.

"You should have called me, Jolene."

"Were you worried about me?"

"Rachel was." No response. "I'll bring her over after supper."

"No, you've done enough. Besides, I want to give you something. I really don't want Paul to be along. He always puts the damper on things. What time should I come?"

"How about seven?"

"Fine. And Shawn?"

Here it comes. "What?"

"I really missed you. I kept thinking about the time we went to Cozumel."

"I have to get back to work."

He hung up quickly and shook his head as he swished past the rows of potted palms. Back at his desk he made notes to fertilize the hanging ivy and trim the palms to be ready for shipping.

Shawn picked up Rachel at Mama Mae's and brought her home for supper together. She was excited about showing her mother her bandaged hand and wondered what she had bought her in Mexico. He and Rachel were rinsing off dishes to put in the dishwasher when Jolene arrived, an hour early.

"Where's my baby?" she squealed as she threw open the kitchen door.

"Mommy! I missed you! Look at my hand!"

"What happened? Shawn, why didn't you call me? I need to know if she so much as stubs her little toe." She clutched Rachel.

"It would have helped if you had given me a number to call."

Jolene blinked. "Mother was supposed to do that."

Lie. You do it so easily.

"I know you take good care of her, Shawn. I couldn't ask for a better Daddy for our daughter." Jolene picked up the two bags she had dropped to the floor.

"Did you get me something, Mommy?" Rachel pulled on her arm.

"You know I did, Baby. Daddy, too." She handed a bag to Rachel. "Go in the living room and look what I got you." Rachel ran and dumped the contents of the bag on the sofa, laughing in delight.

"This one's for my other baby. Here, Shawn." She held out the other bag.

"You didn't have to, Jolene."

"Look inside. I know you'll like it." He pulled out a tee shirt. "Go try it on. I'll help you, if you want." She looked at him coyly.

"That's all right."

"Can we have a cup of coffee together?"

He glanced at the clock. "I have to get to the nursery."

"Work, work, work," she pouted. "You never change."

"Do you know how many poinsettias you'll need for Paul's employees?"

Jolene frowned. "I think nine should do it."

"Nine? Jolene, they're forty dollars a piece."

"He's good for it. I'll write you a check when you deliver them. You *will* deliver them for me, won't you? I could never carry those big things and knowing me, I'd drop one or break it."

"How about tomorrow when I come to get Rachel?"

"Sounds good."

Shawn said goodbye to Rachel and promised to pick her up the next afternoon for his regular weekend with her. "Good luck with your new job, Jolene." Jolene beamed as she waved goodbye.

He missed his little girl already. At least Carlos and Isabelle would be there soon. He'd have to set up a cot in his room for Rachel and get her room ready for them.

Shawn loaded up his truck with things he'd need and drove to the nursery to see if he had to run down to Dallas again to get more poinsettias. Maybe he'd try to call Laynie from the nursery one more time. Maybe this time she'd be home.

*****

Shawn closed the cap of his truck and blew out a sigh. Not one stem broken on the poinsettias. He drove the fragile cargo carefully to Jolene's house to deliver them and to pick up Rachel. He wondered if he'd be driving all over Wagontown looking for her.

Good. She's here. Rachel raced out to him. He was shocked to see Jolene had cut off her long hair. It now hung just below her ears in a blunt cut that accented her long nose and her thin lower lip.

"You don't like it, do you?" Jolene carried a coffee mug and a cigarette in one hand, fluffing her hair with the other.

"What?" Shawn was in no mood for being drawn into her game of "tell me I look nice."

"My hair. You hate it."

Boy howdy! "Do you like it, Jolene?"

"Yes."

"Then that's all that counts." He buckled Rachel in the truck. "Do you have the money for Paul's poinsettias? They're in the back. I'll unload them if you'll ask him where he wants them."

"What poinsettias?" asked a gravelly voice. Shawn turned toward it and saw a huge man with red sideburns and half glasses on the end of his nose ready to slide off any minute. His belt threatened to give way to the bulging belly it encircled. He had about three strands of hair that made their way across the top of his head.

I don't remember Paul being so follically challenged. Shawn smiled inwardly.

Jolene's eyes widened. "Oh, nothing, Paul. Go back inside and watch your movie." Paul snorted and disappeared.

"All he does is sit on his fat-"

"Jolene, does he really want these?"

She bit her lip. "No."

"No. That's just great. I hauled them up here for nothing."

"Don't get mad at me. He's the one who changed his mind."

"If that's true, couldn't you have called me?"

"I was busy, Shawn."

"What, learning to cook? Studying your books for nursing school? Watching your soaps?" Shawn knew he had to bottle his anger in front of Rachel. "Never mind, Jolene. What time should I have Rachel back Sunday night?"

Jolene sipped her mug and squinted at him. "Six oh-oh. On the dot. Don't be late."

"Fine. And Jolene - your hair - it's a new you."

He meant it as a subtle jab, but she smiled as if this pleased her. Shawn drove away quickly before she rolled it over in her mind and turned it into an outright compliment.

NINE

"Shawn, telephone." 3:45. The unwife. He walked over to the office and picked up the phone.

"Hello, Jolene."

"How did you know it was me?"

"Lucky guess."

"I have something very important I need to talk to you about."

What's left? "I need to close up a few things here at work. Can I call you when I get home?"

"I don't want to discuss this on the phone."

Of course not. "I have to go out to the nursery after work. Things are pretty busy out there."

"I'll drive out and bring you something to eat. You have to eat, you know."

"You don't have to do that."

"It'll be fun. I won't get in the way, I promise. I'll see you later."

What was she planning this time? Maybe she and Paul were getting married.

Laynie.

He hadn't thought about her in several days, didn't see much sense in it. It was obvious she wasn't interested. Shawn signed out of the greenhouse and hurried to his nursery.

He hurried over to Maria. *"Hola, senora,* been busy?"

She flashed him a smile as she counted change into a customer's waiting hand. The man had bought a white poinsettia Maria had wrapped in red foil paper, tied with a bursting red bow.

"I'm so glad you came, Boss. I need to wrap more of these and make a silk arrangement. You can handle the customers."

"Yes, ma'am," he chuckled and waited on the people drifting up and down the rows of plants inside the greenhouse. Shawn loved working with his plants, and now his hard work was paying off. The ivies and hoyas he had grown from cuttings were now rich green plants that tumbled out of their hanging baskets and pots. Looking at them made him feel at peace.

The last pinks and purples were fading from the sky when Jolene arrived. She walked up to him with two bags of take-out food.

"Look, Shawn, Chinese, your favorite."

"Thanks, what do I owe you?"

"Nothing, silly. My treat."

With Paul's money. "Let's go inside and eat at my desk. You can tell me what's so important you drove all the way out here. I have to get back to work before Maria gets swamped."

"Okay. But who's that talking to her?"

Shawn looked in the window of the silk shop and saw a younger Hispanic woman standing next to Maria, getting out ribbons and silk flowers.

"Oh, that's Patricia, our new designer. I didn't know she was here."

"It's good she is. Now we won't get interrupted."

"Go in my office while I ask her to tend the cash register." Jolene nodded eagerly and walked to the other small building next to the silk shop. Shawn opened the door to the silk shop and leaned in. "Patricia, I need you to tend the greenhouse. I won't be long."

"Ah, boss, what's she up to this time?" asked Maria. She rolled her eyes while she tightened the bow around the plant in front of her.

"Who knows? If I'm not out in fifteen minutes, come rescue me." Maria giggled. "If you don't, you're fired."

"You couldn't run this place without me and you know it." She wagged her finger at him.

Shawn laughed and walked toward the office. A heavy feeling settled in his stomach. He pushed open the door and walked around the railing to his desk in the back. Jolene had put the food on Christmas paper plates and placed the plastic forks and knives on green napkins. Soda was in red plastic cups and a white candle burned in the middle of it all. He felt like the fly looking at the web.

"Sit down, Shawn." She pointed to his chair and pulled another up for herself. "Do you like it?"

He tossed his jacket over a chair and sat down. "It's nice, Jolene, but I really have to get back to work in a few minutes. What did you want to talk about?"

"Wait. I have one more thing for our meal."

What? Tinsel? Santa hats for us to wear?

"Close your eyes."

"There's no time for this, Jolene."

"Please. It's from Rachel."

"Where is she?"

"With my cousin, Jane. Now close your eyes. Don't peek." Shawn obeyed and squeezed them shut. "Now, open your eyes and look up." She was leaning toward him, holding something over his head. He raised his head and it registered too late what it was.

Mistletoe.

Jolene leaned further towards him and kissed his lips. He sat back in his chair while she laughed at him. *Drinking again. Ho, ho, ho, and a bottle of beer.* She reached over and wiped her lipstick off his lips with a napkin, then laid her hand on his cheek. He jumped up and walked toward the door.

"What is it, Shawn?"

"I thought I heard someone come in."

"You're acting like a nervous school boy. Now sit down and eat."

Shawn sat down and shoved food into his mouth before she could pull any more tricks. He watched Jolene push her food around her plate with her fork. "Aren't you eating yours, Jolene?"

"Guess I'm excited about what I want to tell you."

"So tell me."

Jolene put down her fork. "Okay. We have a beautiful daughter, don't we?"

"That we do."

"Don't you just love everything about her? She's funny, she's smart, and she's so pretty. We make beautiful children, Shawn."

"Child, Jolene. We only made, I mean, had one."

Jolene took his hand. He saw the diamond on her finger. *So that's it. When's the big day?*

"And isn't that a shame? We have only one."

Shawn pulled his hand away and looked in her eyes. "What are you saying?"

"I want us to have another baby."

"What?"

"I wouldn't ask for child support or anything. Just for you to be as good a daddy as you are with Rachel."

"You want you and me…"

"I have all the details worked out."

"I don't even want to hear about those. No. No, no, no." Shawn knew he was blushing. Just as the walls began to shrink around him, the door opened and Maria stuck her head in.

"Boss, we need you. Now."

"I've got to go, Jolene. Just eat this stuff, or leave it, but I gotta get out of here."

"Shawn!"

"It's busy out there. And I have to make deliveries. Flowers, that is. And well, thanks for the food." Shawn grabbed his jacket and tripped over the mat as he fled the office. He opened the door to the silk shop. "Thanks, Maria. Please tell me you have some deliveries for me. I have to get out of here, fast."

"That bad, huh? Okay, but you have to tell me the juicy details later."

"You won't believe this one."

"Yes, I will. We're talkin' about Jolene."

Shawn grabbed the keys to the old Suburban Maria had loaded with flowers and the list of deliveries. Maria was telling him something when he spied Jolene coming out of the office. "Tell me later, Maria, I'm outta here."

Shawn hopped in and drove off as quickly as he dared with the fragile flowers. *Of all the crazy, hair-brained ideas she's come up with, this one takes the cake. Boy howdy.*

Fortunately he had several runs out in the country, and the Suburban had been packed with plants and arrangements for delivery. When he finally returned to the nursery the "Closed" sign hung at the front gate, and Maria and Patricia were restocking tables in the greenhouse with plants.

Maria handed him a stack of receipts. "Don't worry, Boss, she's gone. She didn't look too happy."

Patricia laughed. "Jolene told Maria to never interrupt you two again when you're together. Said she could have her fired for that."

"I was really scared, Boss." Maria flashed a grin.

Patricia opened her purse and looked for her keys. "I have to go. My baby needs me."

"Why don't you do the same?" Shawn asked Maria as he took money out of the register. He locked it and put the cash in a bank bag.

"Not before you tell me what happened in there. You sure looked like you had the devil at your heels when you came out."

"I did, Maria, I did. Ready for this? She wants us to have another baby."

"What!" Maria's hands flew to the sides of her face.

"Said she had all the details worked out."

"I thought she was getting married to that bigot car salesman."

"You heard about that?" Shawn shook his head. "Every time I think I've heard it all with her, she manages to come up with something wackier than ever. I don't want to talk about this any more. Go home."

Maria called her husband to come and pick her up. She hung up the phone and picked up her jacket. "I almost forgot. Someone was here looking for you."

"Who?" Maybe Isabelle and Carlos had arrived. He hoped so.

"She didn't say. She came up to me and asked me where you were."

"What did she look like?"

"Big brown eyes, brown hair. Short. She seemed really nice."

"She was short?"

"No, her hair. Dark complexion, but she was Anglo."

Shawn snapped his head toward Maria. "Was her hair kind of curly?"

"*Si*. You know her?"

"When was she here?" *Please let it be while I was delivering.*

"When you were in with Jolene. I told her you were busy in there but she said she wanted to surprise you."

The noise. He *had* heard the door open. *Ah, Laynie. What did you see?*

"She was only in a minute or two and came out. She asked who was in there with you."

"Maria, why didn't you tell me this before I left?"

She crossed her arms. "Don't yell at me! I tried to tell you when you were racing out of here."

"Did she say anything else?"

"No. She just went back to her car and drove off. Who is she, Boss?"

"Laynie." It was almost a whisper. "I met her a couple of weeks ago. Mama Mae got her to watch Rachel for me. She never returned my calls."

"But she came out here to see you. That says something."

"You're right, Maria. I'll see you tomorrow."

Shawn gathered up the receipts and money and went inside his office. He flopped everything on his desk and grabbed the phone. He knew Laynie's number from trying to call so many times before.

No answer. Not even the answering machine.

What are you thinking, Laynie? How can I reach you?

Shawn drove home and fed the animals, deep in thought about Laynie. *Why had she come out to the nursery? Should I keep trying to call her? I wonder where she lives.* In the darkness, he stumbled over something. He shone the flashlight on the motionless object in front of his boot. *Oh, no, Fluffy. How did you get out?*

He picked up the limp body and examined it. In the darkness he couldn't tell if dogs or a coyote had gotten her. Rachel would be heartbroken.

Shawn put the dead rabbit in an empty feed sack and put it in the shed until the burial in the morning. He checked the cage and saw a hole near the door when he heard the phone ringing from the house.

Mama Mae would shoot him for leaving a window open. He quickly slid the water dish over the hole and hurried into the house.

"Daddy! It's me!"

"Rachel! What's going on?"

"Mommy said she saw you tonight. I wish she had told me she was coming to see you. I would have come along."

"I sure wish you would have. I miss you."

"I miss you, too, Daddy. Can you come get me now? Let's go for ice cream."

Shawn looked at the clock on the wall. "It's too late now, Rachel. Everything's closed. You should be in bed anyway. It's after ten o'clock".

"Mommy's not in bed, yet. I have to wait for her."

"Where are you?"

"Paul's house. We stay here most of the time now. I have my own bed but I like to sleep with Mommy. Oh - she wants to talk to you. I love you, Daddy."

"I love you, too."

"And I love you, too, Shawn." Jolene's voice was thick with inebriation. She giggled.

"I was talking to Rachel. Why is she up so late?"

"You know me. I need you to make me a better Mommy. I need *you*. I still love you, Shawn. I really screwed up when I left you. I was so, so stupid. Please, let's get back together."

"That's not possible, Jolene."

"Don't you love me just a little itty bit?" She started to cry. "You're Rachel's daddy. We should be together. We're a family. I love you, Shawn."

"Jolene, where's Rachel?"

"Right here."

"She's hearing all this?"

"Our daughter wants us to be together, too."

"Let me talk to her." He heard Jolene tell Rachel to come to the phone.

"Daddy, why did you make Mommy cry?"

"Rachel, I didn't. Mommy's drinking beer, and the beer makes her cry." He heard Jolene coaching her to say something.

"Why don't you want to live with Mommy and me?"

Shawn gripped the phone. "Rachel, you should be in bed. Where's Paul?"

"He's in the living room watching TV."

"Go ask Paul to read you a story and put you to bed. Be a big girl and sleep in your own bed tonight. Will you do that for me?"

"What about Mommy? She's crying."

"We'll talk about all this when you and I are together. Mommy will be fine. I love you, Rachel. I'll see you tomorrow, okay?"

He hung up quickly. He was about to go out and repair the hole in the rabbit hutch when the phone rang again.

"Shawn? Paul Frank here. What's going on?"

"What do you mean?"

"I come into the kitchen and Rachel and Jolene are in tears. Jolene said you upset Rachel and that upset her. I don't know what's going on, Buddy. Do you have an explanation?"

"Yeah, I'll tell you..." but Shawn stopped himself. If he told Paul about the conversation, it might break them up, and Jolene could end up in some shack with a greasy biker or pill-popping junkie. At least with Paul, Rachel had a decent place to live.

"Rachel's upset because I wouldn't take her out for ice cream tonight. It's too late."

"Is that what this is all about? Jolene gets so dramatic. Everything's a big deal with her. Glad to know one of you believes in a kid having a bedtime. You want to talk to them some more?"

"No. Just get Rachel to bed. Tell her I'll see her tomorrow."

"Will do, Buddy."

The phone rang a third time. He almost ignored it, wanting instead to fix the rabbit pen, but he gave in to the ringing. "Shawn, why did you hang up on me?"

Jolene. Should have kept going out the door. "When?" He was almost out of patience.

53

"You had Rachel on the phone and hung up." He heard a pop, then the hiss from the can she was opening. "You and I weren't done with our conversation."

"Where's Rachel?"

"Paul's putting her to bed."

"Okay, Jolene, we're not getting back together. Not now or ever."

"Are you seeing someone? I'll kick her butt."

"I'm not, and it doesn't matter. I told you if you went through with the divorce that was it. Remember?"

"I really ruined you, didn't I? You're all alone. I'm so sorry I screwed up, Shawn. I still love you. You're Rachel's daddy."

"What about Paul?"

"He wants me to marry him. Everyone wants me to. You can't believe the pressure I'm under."

"What do you want?"

"I don't want to marry him."

"Then don't. "

"Maybe I will. Marry him. Maybe I'll just do that. I'll let you know."

His head spinning, Shawn hung up and hurried out into the crisp darkness. He needed something normal to do to get the craziness of Jolene out of his mind.

TEN

Rachel was chatting with customers at the nursery who were buying the last of the poinsettias this bustling Saturday morning. Shawn was up the ladder, stapling down plastic that the blasting wind had whipped off the night before. Maria was yelling that she and Patricia needed his help, that he could fix that later. He smiled as his foot hit the ground and turned her.

Maria waved her finger at him. "*Mira*, all these people. You might have to go get some more plants." He really didn't feel like driving down to Dallas this afternoon, but Maria was right. He was grateful business was good.

"*Hola, amigo*. You look like you could use some help."

Shawn grinned and turned toward the man who had spoken. He recognized the trademark ponytail of his friend. "Carlos, man, it's good to see you! Did you just get in?"

"We went by the house and unloaded some stuff. I remembered where you hide the key."

"Where's Isabelle?"

"Here I am."

Shawn turned to a petite woman with long, black hair and hugged her. "Pretty as ever. Did you shrink? You seem shorter."

She gently punched his arm. "It's those high heeled tennies you have on today."

"Did Maria see you?"

Carlos scratched his beard. "Yeah, she still threatens to shave this off me. And cut off my ponytail. She told Isabelle-"

A shriek pierced their conversation. Maria was screaming for Shawn. "*Mira, mira*, Shawn! Rachel is up on the ladder!"

Shawn followed Maria's pointing finger. His heart froze when he saw Rachel near the top of the ladder. He pushed through people who were staring at the child with their mouths open, some gasping and clutching at their chests. Shawn, Carlos, and Isabelle moved toward the ladder, Shawn silently climbed the up ladder. Rachel stopped her ascent.

"Daddy, look what I can do!"

The taste of metal flooded Shawn's mouth. Rachel was leaning away from the ladder, holding on with only one hand.

"Rachel, put two hands on the ladder! If you don't listen, I'll make you come down from there right now."

Rachel's free hand grabbed a rung. "I listened, Daddy."

"Wait there until I come up to you, Rachel. Don't go up any higher." Shawn slowly climbed as he talked.

"I want to go to the top." Shawn heard gasping from below.

"There's spiders on the top rung. Stay where you are."

"I don't want to see the spiders, Daddy."

"Just stay there, Sugar." *Almost there.* When Rachel turned to wave at him, her foot missed the rung and she slid down toward him. Her hands skidded down the sides of the ladder but her kicking feet couldn't find the rungs. As he watched her plummet toward him, Shawn wondered if they'd share hospital rooms.

At that instant Carlos yelled behind him. "Catch her." Shawn had been unaware he was right behind him. Carlos wrapped his arms around Shawn's legs and the ladder. Shawn reached toward a shrieking Rachel.

She slammed into him, kicking his chin but he held firm. He almost welcomed the pain. Almost.

The spectators clapped and cheered. "Hey, man, I think my shoulder's dislocated," said Carlos as he loosened his hold. After Shawn placed Rachel on the ground, he turned to lay the ladder down but his knees turned rubber. He almost buckled to the ground but Isabelle and Carlos grabbed his arms.

"How many more kids do you want someday?" laughed Carlos.

Shawn was trembling. He sat on a bench and grabbed Rachel. "How many times have I told you not to do anything here without asking me? Do you know you could have been hurt?"

Rachel crossed her arms. "But I didn't fall, Daddy."

He turned her toward him. "Yes, you did. And you were scared. I heard you screaming."

"But I'm okay."

"Thanks to Carlos. Don't you ever do anything like that again, understand?" Rachel nodded and hugged him. "You scared me, you really scared me, Sugar. I should have put the ladder down."

The crowd had gone back to browsing and Shawn felt his knees had solidified enough to put the ladder away. He held Rachel close and motioned Carlos and Isabelle to follow him to his office.

"Rachel and I have to run to Dallas. Can you help Maria?"

"Sure, Shawn. We know the ropes." Carlos grinned. "I need a job anyway."

"Close up and I'll meet you at home after I unload here."

Isabelle patted his shoulder. "I'll cook you a nice supper. Hurry back."

*****

Traffic was surprisingly light on the trip to get the poinsettias. Back at the nursery Rachel helped to unload the small pots and Shawn quickly lined up the bigger ones on the tables. "Let's hurry home to Isabelle's fajitas!" said Shawn as they locked the nursery gate.

"Bet it's enchiladas," guessed Rachel. They pulled out onto the dark road.

"Has Mommy learned to cook yet, Rachel?"

"We mostly eat pizza or burgers."

"Oh, take out?"

"Yeah. Sometimes she cooks me spaghetti."

"Is it good?"

"Yes. She buys my favorite kind."

"It's from a can?"

"Yeah, the one with the guy on it with the funny hat."

At least she's mastered the microwave. "How do you and Paul get along?"

"He's okay. He keeps telling Mommy she needs to spank me."

"Like when?"

"Like when I tell her to shut up."

Shawn whistled. "You tell Mommy that?"

"She doesn't care."

"What else doesn't Paul like?"

"He says she buys me too much. That she and I leave stuff all over the house."

"Are you sleeping in your own bed?"

"Not much, Daddy. I like to sleep with Mommy. She likes it, too. I just crawl between them." Shawn gripped the steering wheel. If he talked to Jolene about this, she'd just deny it and punish him by taking his extra time with Rachel. *What should I do?*

"We're here!" sang Rachel. "Let's go, Daddy, I'm starved!" He scooped her into his arms and hurried toward the back door. Maybe Carlos had a few ideas about how to handle this.

*****

"Why don't you just take off with her? I could help you settle in Mexico."

"Life on the run?" Shawn pushed back his plate and watched Rachel playing in the living room with her dolls.

"Desperate times take desperate measures." Carlos chewed on a plain tortilla. "Just run away."

"I couldn't do that to her. She'd miss Jolene too much at this point in her life."

"Wouldn't be much of a life for her, anyway," added Isabelle. "Always looking over your shoulder."

"You could always go back to Jolene." Carlos grinned.

"Now there's a scary thought. Living with Jolene again. Even if I could bring myself to do that, it wouldn't be long until she'd be looking for greener pastures."

Isabelle filled another tortilla and handed it to Shawn. "She's nuts for having left you. She's always looking for something better and losing what good things she has right under her nose. You deserve someone who would appreciate the good man you are."

"Don't worry, Isabelle. I'm not going back to her."

"So what are you going to do, man?" asked Carlos.

"My options are lousy, aren't they? Leave Rachel with Jolene and hope she straightens out her life, or watch and wait until things are bad enough for me to get custody of Rachel."

"Be realistic, Shawn. You're going to have to wait until she does something bad enough for the court to give you Rachel." Isabelle rose and gathered up their plates. "And hope and pray nothing happens to that little girl in there in the mean-time."

"Jolene did shape up while she was pregnant," said Shawn. "I couldn't get her to stop smoking, but at least she didn't drink."

Isabelle laid her hand on Shawn's shoulder, frowning. "I hate to tell you this, but she didn't give up her beer. Jolene only got good at hiding it. I was here once visiting her, when she was in her sixth or seventh month. She got out a beer and asked me if I wanted one. I didn't and stared at her as she drank. Then she heard your truck and she jumped up from the table and hid her beer behind some stuff on the counter. 'Don't you tell!' she said. She took a long drag on her cigarette as you came in the door. She was so calm and cool."

"Why didn't you tell me, Isabelle?"

The slim woman shrugged. "I didn't know the two of you very well then. I wasn't sure what to do, so I kept quiet. Wish I had said something."

"Don't beat yourself up, Is." Shawn pushed back his chair. "There are a lot of things I wish I'd done differently. But you can't change that. You move on and do the best you can. So, how long will the two of you be staying in *mi casa*?"

Carlos finished his tortilla. "I'm working on an import business. I just need a little time to get it going, find investors, you know how it works."

"Take all the time you need. Can you work at the nursery tomorrow, Isabelle, while I take Rachel back?"

"Sure, what time?"

"Come by about five. Then when I come back we'll close and the three of us can go out for a bite to eat."

"Sounds like a plan." Carlos leaned back and stretched. "That will give me time to do some running I need to do. Isabelle would rather work for you anyway."

59

"And now I need to get one little rug rat to bed."

As Shawn tucked Rachel in her cot in his room, he entertained the thought about fleeing to Mexico.

"When do I see Mommy?" Rachel yawned and hugged her stuffed puppy.

"Tomorrow. Do you miss her?"

"I'm afraid she's sad."

Shawn brushed back an auburn lock. "Why would she be sad?"

"She tells me when I'm over here she misses me so much she cries for me. She says I'm her only friend."

Shawn looked into his daughter's troubled eyes. "Paul is her friend, isn't he?" Rachel frowned a she thought about that, then nodded. "And doesn't Tina come around?" Another nod. "See, Mommy's all right. She has friends. You're our daughter, Rachel. You're supposed to have fun when you're with her and when you're with me. That's your job, having fun." He leaned over and tilted her chin in his hand. "And I haven't counted your ribs today!" Rachel squealed as he walked his fingers over her sides. "One, two, three, hey I have to start over, you're too wiggly!"

"Don't Daddy, don't. They're all there. Stop!"

"Only if you promise to stop worrying. That's a grownup's job, not yours."

"I promise Daddy, I promise."

And I promise I'll never stop trying to give you the normal life you deserve, Rachel.

ELEVEN

"Where's Carlos?" asked Shawn as he parked his truck beside his office. Isabelle locked the office door.

"He called and said to go without him. He got tied up with his investors." She looked around to see if everything was in order. "We had a good day today. How did it go returning Rachel?"

"Uneventful, for a change. Jolene was pleasant with no earth shattering plans. She wants me to tell her if she should marry Paul or not. I won't do it."

"She wants you to decide everything for her. She should leave you alone."

"Let's not talk about her any more. Still game for supper?"

"Sure. Let me get my coat and I'm ready."

They drove a short distance to a small restaurant. He pulled into a parking lot while the aroma from the kitchen reminded him of his hunger.

"Here we are. I'm starving. Carlos missed his chance for me to treat, Isabelle."

They walked under the "Chat and Chew" sign and across the tile floor to a booth. Isabelle was good company and easy to talk to. They were eating and laughing over old times when a woman across the room rose to leave with a man about her age. In the dim lighting of the restaurant Shawn saw something familiar about her. She ran her hand through her curls and headed toward them. He grabbed her arm as she walked past.

"Laynie!" Her dark eyes widened as she stopped, the man behind her bumping into her.

"Hey, Laynie, I didn't see your brake lights." He laughed and turned to Shawn. "You a friend of my sister's?"

Relief flooded Shawn. The last thing he wanted to find out was he had competition. He stood. "I'm Shawn. This is Isabelle Mendoza."

"I'm Hunter, and late for my date tonight. I'll make a call, Laynie, and wait for you outside."

"I won't be long, Hunter." The young man nodded as he got his cell phone out of his jacket pocket and pushed through the door.

"It was nice to meet you, Isabelle. Shawn, tell Rachel I said 'hello'."

"How do you know Shawn?" asked Isabelle.

"I baby-sat for him."

"I see." Isabelle was studying Laynie like she was the enemy.

"Why don't you come by and tell Rachel yourself?" asked Shawn. He hadn't realized how long her lashes were. He was remembering again the effect her presence had on his pulse. He wanted to touch her lovely chin…

"Sure, Shawn. Let me know when you're ready to go out again."

"But I meant-"

"Goodbye. Enjoy your meal."

She was gone.

Shawn started to slide out of the booth, but Isabelle reached across to stop him. "Where are you going?"

"I have to talk to Laynie."

"She doesn't want to talk to you."

"I'll be right back." He hurried out the door and saw Laynie getting into her car. "Laynie! Laynie, wait." He ran over to her door.

"I have to go, Shawn."

"Why, do you have a heavy date?"

"You better hurry back to yours."

Shawn laughed. He put his hand on the roof of her car and leaned closer to her. "She's married. To my friend."

"Does he know you're with her?" Her eyes sparked with anger.

"Of course. Look, Laynie, she means nothing like that to me."

"Don't tell her that. That woman is in love with you, Shawn."

"That's crazy, Laynie."

"Look. I don't know what weird idea you have of relationships, but I don't want to get mixed up with you."

"What?"

"Don't even call me to baby-sit. Goodbye." She pulled on the door and he jumped back before it slammed shut. Hunter looked at him and shrugged as she drove out of the parking lot.

I don't want to get mixed up with you? What did I do?

"Did you catch her?" Isabelle asked him as he slid into the booth. "What's going on with you two?"

"Nothing. Absolutely nothing. That's the problem."

"Guess you'll never see her again. She was pretty mad."

Shawn cocked his head. "She was angry, wasn't she? That means she cares."

"What are you talking about?" Isabelle grabbed his hand. "You're making no sense."

"If she didn't feel anything for me, she wouldn't be so angry. Come on, I'll tell you all about it on the way home." He laid money for the check on the small plastic plate left by the waitress and went to his truck. Isabelle had little to say as he related all that had happened between Laynie and him.

"She thought you and I were a couple." He better not tell her the crazy part about Laynie thinking Isabelle was in love with him. That one was way out in left field. Out of the ballpark. "I need to know what Jolene told her that night she baby-sat Rachel."

"I could guess, Shawn. Jolene still the stranger to truth she used to be?"

"She'd tell you that the sun was shining if she was standing in the pouring rain. And she'd expect you to believe her."

"She still tells you she loves you?"

"Yeah. And then the next minute she's considering marrying Paul Frank."

"Some women will go to extreme measures to keep their man. I have."

Shawn looked over at Isabelle. He hadn't noticed before, but she seemed even thinner than the last time he saw her. Under the flash of the streetlights he watched her pick at her fingers as she talked.

"What do you mean? You and Carlos having troubles?"

"You know Carlos, Shawn. His eye isn't the only thing that wanders." Shawn stared straight ahead. He dared not meet her eyes right now, because what she said was true. Carlos never had any qualms about extra activity beyond his marriage. In fact, when Shawn had been married, Carlos was amazed at his fidelity, even when things were going badly.

"I found out he was seeing Donna, his old girlfriend. And it was on a regular basis before we came here. I hadn't been feeling well, so I went to the doctor and when I came home, I told Carlos of my cancer."

"Isabelle! I didn't know! Why didn't either one of you let me know?"

"I made Carlos promise not to tell. I told him about my chemo treatments, and I insisted I went alone. I was hoping he would wait at home for me and feel guilty about cheating on me."

"Oh, Isabelle. How awful for you!"

"He seemed sorry. He started going places with me; was even telling me he loved me again. I was so happy."

"Has, I mean is the cancer, um, are you going to be all right? Should you be still getting treatments?"

"I'll be fine."

"How do you know?"

"Because it's all a lie."

"What!" Shawn yelled. Isabelle dropped her head.

"I made it all up. I didn't have cancer. I just drove around when I told Carlos I was getting treatments."

"Isabelle!"

"Shawn, I was desperate. I was losing Carlos."

"Does he know this?"

Isabelle's laughter was flat. "Carlos found out the truth. He was suspicious and followed me one night when I said I had a treatment. He was furious and said he was leaving me. He almost did."

"What changed his mind?"

"This mess with his business. Suddenly, he needed me."

"How are things now?"

"How do you think? We both lied to each other. Ironic, isn't it? I've never followed him to check up on him like he did me. Do you really think it's always business that takes him away, like tonight?"

"You don't think he's…"

"I don't know what all he does. We might not see him until after Christmas. You know how he is about the holidays."

"He hates them. But that's because of his family, not you, Isabelle."

"He can't seem to keep them separate. He believes I'm the cause of most of his problems."

They pulled into his driveway and he pulled the keys out of the ignition. "Isabelle, I'm so sorry. I didn't know." He leaned over and held out his arms. She hugged him back. "But no more lies, please. I've had enough of those for a lifetime." She leaned back and wiped tears off her face. "Let's go inside and eat popcorn and see if we can find an old movie on TV." He opened his door.

"You're a good man, Shawn Stevens. Jolene was a fool." The telephone was ringing when they went inside. He left Isabelle in the kitchen and hurried to answer it.

"Carlos! You missed a good meal! Where are you?" Shawn heard music in the background and women laughing.

"Still in Mexico."

"Are you through with… business?"

"No, man. I got more wheeling and dealing to do. I'll tell you all about it when I come back."

"When will that be?"

"A couple more days. Tell Isabelle for me, will you?"

"She's in the kitchen. Why don't you tell her yourself?"

"Ah, she gets all bent out of shape when I have to travel."

Shawn turned his back to the doorway and lowered his voice. "Come on, Carlos. Can't you wrap it up soon? She needs you."

"She's used to it. Besides, I know you'll take good care of her."

"Business huh? Sounds like a bar to me."

"I got to go. Later, man." He hung up.

The aroma of buttered popcorn drifted into the living room. Some of the kernels were still exploding inside the bag as Isabelle held the corners and pushed the microwave door shut with her elbow. She glanced at him as the steaming popcorn tumbled into the bowl on the table. "He's not coming home tonight, is he?" Shawn shook his head. "Bet he said he'll be a couple of more days, right?"

"He had some business."

"Don't." Isabelle held the bowl and pulled on his arm. "I've heard it all before. I don't have to hear it again." Shawn was glad she said that. He felt like he was lying when he relayed Carlos' excuses. And Shawn was sick of lies.

TWELVE

The holidays were over. Jolene had promised to let Rachel spend part of Christmas with Shawn, but ended up calling him from Paul's ranch near Dry Gully, saying they were running late and wouldn't be back until the next day. Carlos still hadn't returned from Mexico. So he and Isabelle feasted on the turkey dinner she spent hours preparing, as if a great crowd were showing up to eat. Shawn felt a little silly sitting down to such a spread of food, with Isabelle fussing over all of it. But he remained quiet, as if all the fussing would hide her husband's absence. Carlos hadn't even called her to wish her Merry Christmas.

It was Saturday and he was almost glad the nursery was slow. Maria could handle things herself, and he needed time to figure out how to talk to Laynie. Isabelle was at the mall, taking advantage of the sales.

Shawn inhaled the aroma of his coffee, savoring that first moment when it filled his lungs. He sat down at the table with his steaming mug, sipping as he read the newspaper. Outside the sound of a familiar engine approached, then stopped.

"Oh, no," he moaned, slapping the paper on the table. "Now what?" He rose and looked out the kitchen window. At least Rachel was with her.

The back door exploded open as the little girl burst inside. "Daddy! We're here! Mommy and I came to see you!"

"Well, come here and give me a hug." *Maybe Jolene is taking off again. Maybe she's getting married.*

"Hi, Shawn. We were driving by and I saw you were home. I need to talk to you."

Yeah, right. Just happened to be on the back road by my house. With no particular place to go. Hail, hail, rock and roll...

"Rachel, give me another one of those hugs, then go in the living room and play with your toys Santa left here for you." He never knew what Jolene would say in front of Rachel.

"Paul wants to set up a college fund for Rachel." She crossed her arms. "I want your name on the account. If it's in mine, I'll spend it all. You know how I am with money. Got any more of that coffee?"

"Sure." Shawn poured a mug and slid it toward her as she sat at the table. He leaned against the counter and sipped his coffee. "What brought on this money for Rachel?"

"Don't be so suspicious, Shawn. He just wants me to marry him."

"Do you want to?"

"You can't believe the pressure I'm under from everyone." She opened her purse.

"Not in here, Jolene. Smoke outside."

"Right. Don't know what I was thinking. Am I stupid or what! I'm just so nervous all the time."

Shawn noticed her trembling hand. Her hair, now long again, was pulled back in a ponytail. She apparently had been up early enough to put on make up so she didn't have her early morning washed-out look. It was the best he'd seen her look in a long time. He had forgotten how pretty she was. "What do you have to be nervous about?"

"Oh, so much, Shawn, so much. If you only knew."

"Does Paul treat Rachel okay?"

Her head jerked toward him. "Yes," she snapped. "She's fine where she is."

Pretty defensive today. "Do they get along all right?"

"Sure." Her lipstick was making red waves across the top of her white mug. "He thinks I need to discipline her more. But you know me. I can't say 'no' to her."

"You're going to regret that real soon. And you're not doing Rachel any favors, Jolene. Kids need to know their boundaries."

"That's why I need you, Shawn. To help me with Rachel."

"No, Jolene, Rachel needs me."

"So do I."

We're dancing the dance.

"Are you going to marry Paul?"

Jolene's teeth gnawed at her bottom lip. "I might. If I do, would you give me away?"

Give you away? Shawn's jaw dropped. "That's your Dad's job, isn't it?"

Jolene drummed her nails on the side of her mug. "I can't count on him to show up, let alone be sober enough to walk down the aisle. You know how drunk he is all the time. He's worse than ever. He dried out last month, but that only ever lasts a couple of weeks. He doesn't care how his drinking affects his family."

Shawn stared at her. *Do you hear yourself?* "Just be sure this time, Jolene. For Rachel's sake."

"I screwed up when I left you. I screwed up a lot. I should have stayed with you."

"But you didn't and that's history."

"But I still love you."

Shawn set his mug down and looked toward Rachel. She was coloring in her new book. "When does Paul want to set up this account for Rachel?"

"What? Oh, I don't know."

"Have him call me and we can get together and do this. Sounds like a good idea. Rachel, come here," he called into the next room. She ran to him. "Want to go outside and find Belle?" She nodded and pulled on his hand. They all walked out the door and Rachel cupped her hands around her mouth.

"Here, Belle! Here, girl!" Rachel squealed with delight as the old dog trotted from behind a bush, her tail swinging in a circle. "Come get me, Belle, catch me!" Rachel raced around the yard, the dog following in a slow gallop. They disappeared behind the feed shed.

"Stay in the yard, Rachel," yelled Jolene. The wind was whipping strands of hair blowing loose from her rubber band. She tried to keep them off her face as she turned to Shawn. "She loves to come here."

"Do you need me to keep her this weekend?"

She playfully punched his arm. "No, silly. We're going down to Dallas for the weekend. Want to come along?"

Shawn laughed. "No." He wanted to say much more, but it was safest to just say that. "Guess you'll be leaving soon. Let me say goodbye to Rachel and send you off to pack."

Rachel hugged Belle once more and ran over to Shawn after he called her. She was halfway across the yard when the movement of something under the rabbit hutch caught Shawn's eye. He ran toward Rachel.

"Run, Rachel, run to me really fast!"

Jolene saw it and screamed, pointing to the animal stalking the small girl. Rachel stopped and turned to where her mother was pointing. "Run, Rachel! Run to me!" Shawn hollered. But she froze, staring at her attacker. The rooster aimed his razor-sharp feet toward her.

"Fall down and cover your face!" Shawn was almost there. Rachel collapsed to the ground and buried her head in her arms. The rooster landed beside her, flapping up to strike. He squawked in surprise at Shawn's swift kick. In his rage Shawn didn't feel the cut on his arm as he grabbed the rooster's feet. He held it at arm's length and threw him into an old hutch. Rachel ran over to him, sobbing.

"Are you all right?" Shawn held her out as his eyes raced over her. "Did he hurt you?" She shook her head. "I don't know how he got out, Sugar. I'm so sorry. He won't ever do that again, I promise you. He's soup."

"What do you mean, Daddy?" Rachel tilted her head, her blue eyes blinking out the last of her tears. Jolene grabbed Rachel from Shawn and held her against her.

"Baby, are you all right? I was so scared! Oh, my heart's just a-racin'! Did that bad, bad rooster hurt you? He scared Mommy so bad. That awful, bad, bad thing."

"She's okay, Jolene. I'm sorry this happened."

"Look what he did to your arm!" Jolene held his arm. "Should we take you to the hospital? Is that deep? Just look at that awful gash!" Rachel started to cry again. Shawn threw Jolene a look to keep quiet.

"I'm okay, it's not bad. I'll go in and wash it up and put a bandage on it. One of yours that looks like a big crayon. Then I'll be just fine."

"Do you want help?" asked Jolene, tenderly. She pulled his arm toward her but he turned away.

"I'll be *fine*. Now, Rachel, I hear you're going to Dallas. Give me a kiss and tell me all about it when you come back."

"I will, Daddy."

Shawn picked her up and hugged her. "We'll make that rooster into soup next time you come over for a weekend."

"And eat him?" Shawn nodded. "That'll teach him to chase me!" She giggled and hugged him again.

Jolene drove off, Rachel's hand waving wildly out the window at him. "Be safe, Rachel," he muttered. "Watch over her, God. I can't." He watched the dust billow around the back of the car until it disappeared into the flat brown landscape.

THIRTEEN

Shawn still hadn't heard from Laynie, and Carlos hadn't been back since before the holidays. Isabelle and Shawn kept themselves busy at the nursery and spent many evenings alone or with Rachel at the supper table. Shawn felt a little uncomfortable at all the cooking Isabelle did for him, but it seemed to keep her mind off Carlo's absence.

"I'm going down the road to visit Mama Mae. Want to come along?" Shawn held the back door open for Isabelle to follow.

"No, thanks. I'll take care of these dishes then curl up with a good book. Maybe Carlos will call." There was a sadness about Isabelle that surrounded her and deepened each day of her husband's absence. There seemed to be something else that tormented her, but Shawn could not figure out what it was.

"Not a very exciting way for you to spend a Friday night."

"You should talk. Tell Mama I said 'hey'. Will you be late?"

"No, Mother," teased Shawn. Isabelle threw a tea towel at him as he ducked out the door, relieved to see her smiling. In a few minutes he was rapping on the old wooden screen door at Mama Mae's.

"Well, look at what the cat dragged in. You haven't been by here in a month of Sundays. Come on in, Son, but you can't stay long. I'm on my way out." The feisty woman wrapped a strand of gray hair behind her ear as she shooed him into the kitchen. "Got time for one cup of coffee."

"I'd rather have your lemonade, if you made some."

Mama Mae smiled as she filled a glass. "No one makes it like me, right?"

"Now, let me see." Shawn drank half the glass. "Nope. No one."

"Slow down, boy, you'll get cramps drinking like that. You drink faster than a parched cow on a hot day."

Shawn held the glass as she refilled it. He loved her kitchen. The cookie jar always had cookies, a cake was always in her big

72

round container, and a pie was always in the refrigerator. With all the work of a farmwoman, she managed to have her kitchen sparkling clean.

"Where are you off to, Mama Mae? You and Pop goin' dancin'?"

Mama rummaged through her purse, taking inventory of keys, tissues, and mints. "He's at the lodge planning a project. You're the one who should be going dancin'."

"I hate to go alone."

She closed her purse and leaned toward him. "Well, maybe you could *go* alone. But you still might find a nice partner. I happen to know a pretty one will be at the Boot Scooter tonight."

Shawn laughed. "The last one you steered my way got scared off for some reason."

"What do you mean?"

Shawn set his empty glass on the counter and stared at it. "Laynie. I thought we hit it off, but now she acts like I got the plague."

"What did you do?" Mama Mae's frown expected the truth.

"Nothing. I never even had the chance to blow it. One minute she's giving me signals she'd like to go out with me, and the next it's like she can't get far enough away from me. She ever say anything to you?"

Mama Mae shook her head and put Shawn's glass in the sink. "I haven't seen much of her. But maybe you can straighten this all out tonight. I'm baby-sitting for her so she can go out. She and some friends from work are going to the Boot Scooter."

"But what if she's with a date?"

"I doubt that, but you can always ask her to dance. You can be very persuasive, Shawn. Just sweet-talk her with that deep voice of yours," she laughed.

Shawn entertained the scene in his mind. What the heck, the worse thing that could happen was she'd say "no." "Guess I'm going home to get ready to go dancin'. Thanks, Mama Mae." He kissed her cheek as she waved for him to hurry out the door.

"Have fun and don't worry about the time. If you stay out late, I'll just fall asleep on her couch."

Shawn hurried back to his house and found Isabelle working on her needlework. She looked up in surprise to see him. "Where's the fire?" she asked as he hurried past her.

He went into his room and pulled off his shirt. "I've decided to go out. I'll tell you about it after I shower."

Isabelle whistled when he returned to the living room, ready to go. "You look nice. I've never seen that shirt before. What's the occasion?"

"I'm going out. I'm hoping to run into Laynie."

"Oh, the one with all the kids." It almost sounded like an accusation.

"Three, Isabelle. She's not the woman in the shoe." He rubbed his socks over his newest boots and slipped them on.

"I thought she wasn't interested in you."

"I'm hoping to change that. Or at least find out why." Shawn went into the bathroom for one more look. His brown hair was almost dry and only curled a little. His blue eyes stared at him through his glasses. Great. He was starting to sweat.

"I don't know why you waste your time trying." Isabelle stood up as Shawn grabbed his keys. "She's a fool for not jumping at the chance to go out with you the first time."

Shawn laughed. "Thanks. Guess I'll just have to show her the error of her ways. Wish me luck."

"Are you bringing her here?" Isabelle sounded... alarmed.

Of course, she feels awkward. "I doubt it." The phone rang. He watched her smile as she talked.

"It's Carlos! He's coming back this week."

"It's about time," yelled Shawn so Carlos could hear him. "I'll see you, Isabelle. Don't wait up for me." He hurried out into the darkness.

*****

Shawn pushed open the door and the man wearing a black cowboy hat and boots to match held out his hand for the cover fee. He waited a moment for his eyes to adjust to the dim, smoky light and scanned the room. Someone bumped his own hat as he crossed the floor. He adjusted it and chose a seat at an empty table near the dance floor.

He ordered a drink from the waiter and sat back in his chair, searching for Laynie indiscreetly, he hoped. Shawn hated coming to these things alone and didn't care much for sitting by himself at a table. The smoke burned his eyes. It was hard to believe he used to smoke two packs a day. Then one day he was driving along in his truck and rolled down the window to smell the fresh cut grass along the road. But he couldn't. Couldn't smell a thing. It was the cigarettes, slowly robbing him of his sense of smell. Too big a sacrifice, Shawn drove to a dumpster and tossed in his last pack of cigarettes.

Now he couldn't get over how quickly smoke irritated him. He hoped he found her before the headache that threatened to break out from the back of his head exploded with pain.

There was laughter in the corner behind him. Shawn looked back and saw her, laughing with three other women. Laynie shook her head as two of them got up and went to the restroom. A man from the bar approached their table, and Shawn sighed with relief as the other woman followed him to the dance floor.

"It's now or never," he sang to himself. Laynie was watching her friend dance as he sat down beside her. She drew in her breath when she saw him next to her. "Hey, Laynie. Can I talk to you?" He folded his hands nervously on the table.

"Are you here alone?"

"Yeah."

"Where's Jolene?"

Shawn laughed. "I don't know. Why do you ask?"

Laynie frowned. "Does she know you're here?"

"I hope not. She tends to ruin my chances with women."

Laynie stood up. "That's a terrible thing to say about the woman you're about to marry. Re-marry, I should say."

"What are you talking about? Please, sit down and tell me."

"And then that married woman you're sneaking around with. Your friend's wife, no less."

"Isabelle?"

"I want you to leave me alone. You're already a busy boy."

"Laynie, sit down and give me a chance to talk to you. I don't know where you've gotten your information, but it's all wrong." She remained standing.

"I don't know why I should. I guess if you're a friend of Mama Mae's, there must be something good about you. Unless you've got her snowed like you did me." She slid back into her chair. "Hurry before my friends come back. You don't want to be embarrassed in front of them by what I might say." Laynie's cheeks flushed.

"I don't know how to begin."

"Try the truth."

"I will tell you the truth, Laynie. Just listen. First, Jolene and I are not getting remarried. We never had plans to, and never will."

"That's not what she told me when she called the night I baby-sat for you."

"What did she say?"

"She went on and on about the plans y'all were making about getting back together and how happy Rachel was about it. Said you had had a roving eye but she relented when you begged her to forgive you, and you told her she is the love of your life."

Shawn shook his head. "Reverse that, Laynie, and you'll be a lot closer to the truth. I know you don't know me from Adam, but check it out with Mama Mae."

Laynie crossed her arms and sat back in her chair. "What about your cozy little dinner at the nursery? After all your messages on my machine, I thought maybe, just maybe, Jolene wasn't telling it straight. She sounded drunk to me that night on the phone. So I thought I'd surprise you and pop in on you and we'd talk. Only I'm the one who got the surprise."

"Ah, Laynie, I know how it must have looked."

"It looked like kissing to me."

"Jolene blind-sided me. She's always calling me, needing to talk to me about something or other. It's always life and death with her."

"Can't you say 'no'?"

"Then she'll punish me by using Rachel." Laynie's face softened. "I told her to go in and wait for me. She said she brought a bite to eat. I walk in and there's this spread of food and she's waiting for me."

"Like the spider in her den." She was smiling. Ah, maybe she'd believe him.

"Boy, howdy! Jolene even had mistletoe. She told me to close my eyes because she had a surprise from Rachel. Before I knew it, she was kissing me."

"Never close your eyes in front of a spider." Laynie seemed more relaxed, resting her chin in her hand.

"When I found out you had been there, I tried to get in touch with you."

"What about Isabelle?"

Shawn pushed back his hat and rubbed his forehead. "She and her husband, Carlos, are staying with me until they get back on their feet. Carlos is traveling all over Mexico putting some kind of business deal together. He asked me to take care of Isabelle. He'd do the same for me - if I had a wife, that is."

"I hate to tell you this, partner, but that woman has feelings for you."

"Isabelle? Nah. Why, you jealous?"

"Don't push it, mister. I'm still trying to absorb all this."

"That's easier to do while you're dancing. You know how to two-step?"

"Only if I've got a good partner." Shawn guided Laynie and to the dance floor. "Careful, it's been a while since I've done this." She laughed as he led her around the floor. The song ended and was followed by a slow one. Shawn held onto Laynie and tilted his head. She nodded. They moved in silence for a while. He breathed in the smell of her, wanting to pull her closer but not daring to.

"Laynie, there's so much I could tell you. Believe me when I tell you if Jolene says it, it probably isn't true."

Laynie laughed. "I guess there's a lot we don't know about each other, Shawn." She leaned back at looked up at him. "Just don't you lie to me. Okay?"

"I won't. And if you'll agree to see me again, I have to warn you, Jolene will do everything she can to break us up. And I'm trying to get custody of Rachel. It won't be easy."

"If you hold me a little closer, you'll be able to tell I've got a backbone back there."

Shawn didn't have to be told twice.

FOURTEEN

Carlos promised to be home by Valentine's Day. Things were going well for him, and they would be able to move out by April. Isabelle was excited about finding a house for them to rent and made big preparations for his homecoming.

Things were going well for Shawn, too. Life was good when you could share it with someone. He and Laynie did things with the children, and Rachel loved being with "the kids." He was dreading the phone call that was inevitable. Rachel must have told Jolene about Laynie by now. Shawn wondered what was delaying her interrogation of him.

He was driving Rachel back to Jolene's after what was supposed to be another one of her trips to Mexico. Her car was in the drive, but Paul's wasn't next door at his house. "Rachel, I don't think they're back yet." The child burst into tears.

"I made Mommy a Valentine and everything," she wept. Her small hands clutched a pink piece of paper with a heart covered with glitter Shawn had helped her make.

"Don't cry, Sugar. We'll go home and try again tomorrow. Valentine's Day is a few days away, so it won't be late."

"But where is Mommy? She always does this!"

Shawn dried her tears, holding her chin in his hand. "I know, Rachel, I know. Let's go back and have some of those good cookies Isabelle made."

"And I helped."

"That's why they're so good." He tickled her and headed back home.

The snack and bedtime rituals over, he had just tucked her in when Jolene called. "I'm back. I'm coming for Rachel." *Uh, oh. Snippy voice. Trouble.*

"That's not a good idea, Jolene. I just put her in bed. You can come get her tomorrow. Where were you tonight?"

"I'll come for her in the morning. At nine-oh-oh."

"What's wrong?"

"Nothing. I just want to see my baby."

Shawn didn't like the way she sounded. *Gonna be a big storm. Wonder what it's about this time. "When the storms of life are raging, stand by me..."*

He walked to Isabelle's bedroom and knocked on her door. "Come in." She was sitting on the bed paying her bills.

"I'm going to be in my room the rest of the night. The war department is coming in the morning to get Rachel."

"You heard from Jolene?"

"Yeah, she called, you know... the usual. Are things still on schedule for Carlos' coming home?"

"Just a few more days." She looked tired.

"Then he's here for good?"

Isabelle's lips pressed together. "He might have to make one more trip."

Shawn saw the anxiety in her face. He didn't know how to comfort her. "If there's something I can do, tell me." She sighed and shook her head. "Well, then, goodnight."

"Goodnight, Shawn. I wish you didn't have to deal with Jolene."

"Me, too." He closed the door, and quietly entered his room. Rachel was sleeping on the cot, her arm around her stuffed puppy. "You're my little puppy," he whispered as he pulled the blanket up to her chin. He pressed the power button on the TV, turning up the volume gradually so Rachel would not awaken. She never even stirred.

Shawn lay down and pressed the remote as he scanned the channels. *I forgot to lock up. Oh, well, I'll get it before I fall asleep. I did promise Mama Mae.* He looked at the clock. A little after ten. Laynie would still be up. He leaned over and dialed her on the old blue rotary phone he didn't have the heart to get rid of.

"Did you decide what you want to do tomorrow?" he asked her.

"We've got the whole day, right?" He grinned as he heard the excitement in her voice.

"The whole day. Maria's got everything under control at the nursery. I can hear you smiling, Laynie."

"One of my friends from church will take care of my kids. She wants them to sleep over. Wow, a whole Saturday for us to be together and no deadline."

"What do you want to do?"

"Let's go to the lake."

"Great. We'll eat at our favorite restaurant."

"I've been looking forward to this all week, Shawn."

"Me, too - whoa! Hold on." The door opened. Jolene was inside his bedroom. "What are you doing?" demanded Shawn. *This takes the cake.*

"I've come for my daughter." She leaned over and picked up Rachel.

"We agreed tomorrow would be better for her."

Jolene kicked open the door. "My lawyer advised me to do this."

Shawn was incredulous. "He told you to drag a sleeping child out of her bed at night?"

Jolene hurried out. He heard the back door slam shut.

"Shawn! Shawn, what's going on?"

He picked up the phone. "Jolene just barged in here and took Rachel while she was sound asleep."

"Can't you stop her?"

"She's already gone. And no, there's nothing I can do. This was extra time for me with her."

"Is there anything I can do?"

"No, Laynie. There's nothing anyone can do. That's the problem."

FIFTEEN

Shawn glanced at the kitchen clock as he carried the cooler away from the sink. Almost nine o'clock. Laynie would soon be back from taking the children to her friend's. He loaded the last of the things they'd need for the lake and pushed the tailgate shut. He was almost inside when Jolene honked at him as she pulled in the drive. *Now what?* She got out of her car and hurried over to him. "Good. I wanted to catch you before you went to the nursery. Can we talk?"

Shawn leaned against the gate. "Not for long."

"I want to explain about last night. My lawyer advised me to get Rachel."

Yeah, right. "Jolene, if he told you to quit feeding her, would you still listen to him?"

"Now look, Shawn-"

"No, you look, Jolene. What kind of a mother are you to drag her out of her bed when she's fast asleep like that? Tell me, what kind? I have a problem with the way you take care of Rachel. Her living conditions are at times worse than that of a dog's."

"I don't have to listen to this crap. I'll just move away where you can't bother me any more."

"And I'll fight you tooth and nail for custody if you do."

"You'll lose." Jolene squinted in the morning sun. She quickly put sunglasses over her red eyes.

"I'll slow you down. Just where do you think you'd move to?"

"Dallas. Or Stillwater."

"What about Paul? How would you live? Do you have a job?"

"Stop it, Shawn! I just came out here to explain last night to you."

"And what was I supposed to say, Jolene? 'Oh, well, if your *lawyer* told you to do that, then it's okay.' Is that what you expected?"

She crossed her arms. "I expected you to be civil about this. All you want to do is fight with me."

Shawn put his face in front of her. "No, Jolene. All I want is what's best for Rachel."

Jolene lowered her head. "I know. I love her, too. I try my best. I just screw up a lot. You know me, I mess up all the time, I'm so stupid. It's the way I am. I'm not going to move, at least not far away. Well, you better get to the nursery. I'll see you Wednesday when you get Rachel." She hopped in her car and drove off. Shawn watched her, shaking his head as he tried to figure out what this episode was all about. He pushed it all out of his mind and went inside to lock up. He had a very important lady waiting for him, and he didn't intend to be late.

*****

"I never get tired of the lake. It brings out the little kid in me." Laynie's eyes danced as she scanned the water.

He watched her and caught a glimpse of the little girl she spoke of as she watched in fascination. Laynie looked at him. "Shawn, don't look at me, look at this panorama," she scolded. "It's such a beautiful sight."

"Yes, it is," he said as he pulled her close. "And I'm not talking about the scenery."

"I think I have the better view," she said as she touched his face. He kissed her.

"Let's go make some memories," Shawn said as they walked hand in hand to the water's edge.

*****

It was one of the best days of Shawn's life. Laynie and he walked and talked like they had known each other for years. At lunch, Shawn opened the tailgate, where they sat and ate out of the picnic basket Laynie brought. Afterward they spread a blanket on the ground and watched the waves ripple in. They talked about everything from kids to parents, from their past to their future dreams, oblivious to the chilly air.

"Tell me something about yourself no one knows," Laynie challenged.

"You first. I'm no fool," answered Shawn.

"Okay, chicken. Let me see. You know how I love chocolate. Well, before I eat it, I discretely hold it under my nose and breathe in that wonderful aroma. I close my eyes when I'm alone."

Shawn laughed. "I hate to tell you, Laynie, but that's no secret."

"It isn't?"

"It's all over town. Everyone in Wesley is talking. I heard about it last week."

Laynie pushed him back onto the blanket. "Ha, ha. Now it's your turn." She leaned on her elbow to listen.

"Don't laugh. This is crazy, but I'll tell you."

"Go on."

Shawn looked out across the water. "Sometimes, when somebody says something, or does something, it, like, well it triggers a song… in my head."

"You're scaring me, Shawn Stevens."

"You think sniffing chocolate is normal?"

"Touché. Give me an example. Are you hearing music now?"

"Yeah." He sat up and hugged his knees. "I hear 'So Happy Together'."

Laynie sat up and brushed sand off her tee shirt. "By the Turtles? I like that song."

He slid his arm around her shoulders. "You make me happy, Laynie. Happier than I've ever felt before. We're good together, you and I. We share a lot of the same dreams, the same values. I like being with you, I think about you all the time we're apart." She was looking deep into his eyes, capturing every word. "I don't know about you, but I don't want to see anyone else," he added.

"Neither do I," she whispered. "Wanna go steady?"

Shawn laughed and kissed her. "Yeah, I sure do." He stood and pulled her to her feet. "Let's go for another walk and then look in a few shops before supper."

The rest of the day raced by. They watched the sun set as they ate along the water. They drove to Laynie's house outside Wesley, where they watched "Lonesome Dove," falling asleep on the sofa before the movie was over. Shawn awoke to Laynie gently shaking him out of his peaceful sleep.

"Hey, cowboy. It's almost two."

Shawn stretched and put his arm around her. "Guess I better get out of here. We don't want the neighbors talking." He held her close. "This was one special day, Laynie."

"For me, too." She cuddled close to him. "Thanks, Shawn. My only complaint is you make the day go too fast."

"Boy, howdy. I better watch out hanging with you. Before I know it, I'll be an old man." They walked to the door where Shawn slipped on his coat. "I'll call you tomorrow. Dream about me."

"Exclusively." She smiled and put her arms around Shawn's neck. "Good night." He held her close and kissed her. Shawn didn't want to leave her soft lips. But it was time to go.

"Hey, now I hear it," Laynie whispered.

"What?"

"The music. 'Happy Together'."

Funny. So did he.

SIXTEEN

Shawn made a quick check of things at the nursery Sunday afternoon. Maria had everything in order after what had apparently been a slow day. Business hadn't been good since Christmas. Customers should have been stopping by for Valentine gifts, but unlike most places in Oklahoma, the people of Wesley were a fickle clientele. He'd seen many businesses go under in this town.

He was closing the gate when Jolene drove up in her Nova. It had a new paint job, and the chrome gleamed. Shawn walked over to her as she rolled down the window. The inside looked like a trash can on wheels. She quickly kicked a beer can back under her seat.

"Hey, what's going on?" Shawn asked her.

Jolene leaned against the steering wheel. "You want to tell me? I tried calling you all day yesterday and came out here to find you. All I got was a bunch of 'I don't knows' from Maria. I drove out to your house three times."

"Is something wrong with Rachel?"

"She's all right." Jolene grabbed her purse and took out a cigarette and lit it with shaking hands. "You didn't tell me you weren't working."

"What did you want?" Shawn wanted to end this and get back home. He'd hoped to see Laynie today.

"I wanted to know if you'd keep Rachel."

Shawn drummed the car roof. "You never said anything yesterday morning."

"Where were you?"

Shawn walked away. "I have to go, Jolene."

"But I need to talk to you."

Shawn stopped and slowly turned. *You talk too much...* Laynie would laugh at the music in his head. "So talk, but make it quick."

"You don't have to be rude. I'm thinking of moving out."

"Moving *out*? As in leaving Paul Frank?"

"Maybe. I might. But don't say anything yet. I'm not sure."

"What happened?"

Jolene bit her lip. "Nothing. It's just not like it used to be. You know, it's not special any more."

"Okay. I have to go, Jolene. Give me the details later, when you know them. Just let me know where Rachel is. And, yeah, I want Rachel. Anytime." Jolene slowly drove away and Shawn hurried home to call Laynie.

*****

It was good to see Carlos. Despite all his many faults, Shawn valued his friendship. Isabelle was smiling again, and Shawn hoped this time it would last. But with those two, he had his nagging doubts.

They were at the Boot Scooter, celebrating Carlos' homecoming and success at starting up his import trade. He would be driving down to southern Mexico to bring up blankets and ponchos from Guatemala. They were all excited about the potential business. Shawn was going to introduce Laynie to them, but she had called him as he was about to leave to pick her up telling him Joey had an earache and fever. She urged him to go without her, and they'd make new plans after Joey's recovery.

Shawn watched Carlos and Isabelle on the dance floor, two-stepping as most as the other couple did. To look at them right now, you'd think they were newlyweds. Carlos was talking and Isabelle laughed at everything he said. He wondered what ghosts from Carlos' past tormented him, pulling him down at times into an abyss of depression. He treated the holidays like they were a parasite, sucking all the joy and happiness out of his life. But to look at him now, you'd never know he suffered from such turmoil. They whirled over to the table, Carlos panting like he'd just run the mile.

"You're gasping for air like you're an old man, old man," teased Shawn. Carlos flopped down in his seat.

"I don't see you up there moving your bones around the floor. Here, you dance with her. She never has enough."

"Want to, Shawn?" asked Isabelle, holding out her hand.

"Sure." He slid back his chair and they glided easily around the dance floor. "You sure look happy tonight, Isabelle."

"I am. The only thing that could ruin it is if Carlos tells me he has to go away again. I know he has to make regular trips to Mexico, but that shouldn't start until next month. Our apartment will be ready by then and I'll be busy moving and I won't miss him so much."

Shawn glanced at Carlos, who was intently watching the blonde at the next table. He turned Isabelle's back so she wouldn't see. *Not tonight. She's so happy. Come on, Carlos. Give her tonight.*

The band took a break and they returned to their table. Shawn rubbed his eyes. "I'm going to get out of here soon. I'm getting a headache."

"Can't take the night life, huh? And you said I'm getting old." Carlos leaned toward him. "So, is there really a lady in your life, or is it a figment of your imagination, *amigo*?" Carlos' dark eyes danced with mischief. "You don't get out of here until you give us a few details."

"Carlos!" scolded Isabelle. "Don't be so nosy."

"At least you met her."

"Not really. It was only in passing when Shawn had taken me out to eat. If you would have been with us as planned, you would have met her, too."

Carlos leaned back and grinned. "What can I say? I had business to take care of. Which reminds me, I'm going to have to leave tomorrow."

"Carlos," cried Isabelle, "tomorrow's Valentine's Day. You promised you'd be here."

He patted her hand. "I will be, Isabelle. Just not all day. I won't have to leave until noon."

Isabelle's perfect night had just been ruined. Shawn could see it all over her face. Her sad eyes looked at him, and he had to look away. *Your cheatin, heart...* No. Stop the music. He would give Carlos the benefit of a doubt.

"When will you be back?" Shawn asked. "I could use your help to fix some fences at the ranch."

"I'll be gone three days tops. I know I owe you, Shawn, and I'll be back to help."

"I'll hold you to it. I don't want to be chasing cows all over the county." He held Isabelle's chin in his hand. "We'll go get him if we have to." A faint smile broke out but Isabelle's eyes were full of aching from broken promises. He looked at Carlos as he put on his jacket and hat. "We really will come and get you. Three days."

"You got it, man," assured Carlos. "We're going to stay here a little longer. See you in the morning."

Shawn waved and headed for the exit. He glanced back and saw Isabelle pushing open the door to the women's room. Carlos was leaning over, talking to the blond.

*****

Carlos got up early enough to talk to Shawn before he headed out to OK Wholesale Plants. Shawn admonished him to be home in three days, and Carlos reassured him he would. The phone rang and Shawn almost ignored it, thinking it was probably Jolene. It was unusually early for her, but if it were she, it might concern Rachel.

"Hi, Babe." Shawn let out a sigh. *Laynie.* "I don't want to make you late for work."

"How's Joey?"

"That's why I called. I'm taking him to the doctor's this morning. He cried all last night with earache. I'm going to have to cancel our plans for tonight. I'm sorry, I know it's Valentine's Day and all."

"Don't be silly. Joey needs his mama. I do, too, but I'll wait my turn. Want me to come over?"

"Yes, but I don't think that's a good idea. You know how kids are at times. They want all of Mommy's attention."

"I hear you. I'll miss you."

"I'll miss you, too. Don't sit home. Do something. After all, it *is* Friday night. Maybe by tomorrow Joey will feel well enough for company."

"I'll call later and see how he's doing. Poor little guy."

Shawn was disappointed, but he knew this was the way it was when you have children. Maybe Jolene would let him have Rachel tonight, although he dreaded calling her on Valentine's Day.

Shawn tried calling Jolene all day, but guessed they were out of town, probably at Paul Frank's ranch. He returned home from work and found Isabelle sitting on the sofa amid the long shadows crossing the room as the last rays of daylight streamed in the west window. "Hey," greeted Shawn as he turned on the light on the end table. He sat next to her and saw her red eyes. "You and I can form the lonely hearts club tonight."

Her eyes lowered, Isabelle turned her head. "What do you mean?"

"Laynie has to stay home tonight. Joey's still sick."

"I'm sorry to hear that."

"Carlos get off okay?"

She nodded. "Oh, yeah. It's what he's good at. He's had lots of practice."

"Look, it's going to be a long night if we sit around here and feel sorry for ourselves. I have reservations for two at Reflections. How 'bout you and I get ready and go eat? Then we can come back and crash. I'm still tired from last night."

Isabelle's eyes met his. "Gosh, Shawn, you are getting old. I remember when you and Carlos stayed out late night after night."

"That seems like a million years ago. Want to go?"

She straightened up. "You mean that place that has the polished copper tables and a candle on each one?"

Shawn nodded. "And one wall is a big mirror so all that candlelight is reflected."

"Sounds nice. I've heard about it but never been there. I'd love to go."

"You can use the bathroom first while I'll call Laynie. I want to see how Joey is."

"I won't be long. I know exactly what to wear." Shawn was glad to see her smiling. He dialed Laynie's number.

"Pediatric Center," said Laynie.

"Uh, oh. Don't tell me. Who else is sick?"

"I had to get Maddie and Zack from school, so we all went to the doctor's together. Too bad they don't give group rates. They've been on their antibiotics all day, so tomorrow will be better. What's going on with you?"

Shawn explained the situation with Isabelle. "So you're taking her to Reflections?"

Shawn was surprised at Laynie's voice. "Yes. Remember, you told me to go out."

"I didn't mean with a date."

"Laynie, she's not a date. She's just a friend."

"Maybe to you. But it's different for her."

"I wasn't expecting you to react like this."

"It doesn't feel right to me, Shawn. Reflections is so romantic. And it's Valentine's."

"Look, Laynie. Isabelle loves her husband."

"But she's lonely and disappointed. You're warm and caring. It's a bad combination, cowboy."

"I only care about you, Laynie. You're my Valentine, Darlin', whether I'm with you or not. We'll make up for this. But if it really upsets you, we won't go."

"That'd really win Isabelle over to my side. No, go. I guess I'm being silly. There's no sense in all of us staying home, lonely and forgotten on Valentine's Day."

"Laynie-"

"I'm *kidding,* Shawn. Really, go on and call me tomorrow. But not too early. It's going to be a long night again. I'm tired. I guess that's why I'm so grouchy."

"Okay, Isabelle and I will cancel our plans to go dancing and watch the sun come up."

"Don't push it, mister."

"I'll miss you."

"You better."

Shawn chuckled as he hung up the phone. Isabelle came out and whirled in a circle before him. "Is that what they call one of those little black dresses?" he asked her.

"Do you like it?"

"You look nice."

"Here, put this necklace on me." She turned her back to him and held up her long hair. "I bought this to go out with Carlos tonight. I wasn't going to let it go to waste."

"If he'd see you now, he'd have wished he'd be here. Give me about twenty minutes, and we'll be off."

They had a nice dinner and excellent food. The restaurant was crowded with couples celebrating the day of romance. Shawn was enjoying Isabelle's company, but it was Laynie he thought of most of the evening. *She'd love it here. I'd watch the candlelight sparkle in her eyes, as she'd chatter away about the kids, her work, and try to get me to talk some more about myself.* He smiled.

"Shawn, *Shawn!* The waitress wants to know if you want dessert."

He blinked himself back to reality. "I don't know about you, Isabelle, but I'm stuffed."

"Me, too. I'm going to have to take mine home in a doggie bag."

The waitress placed the bill beside Shawn and promised to return with the doggie bag. "Was the stuffed flounder good, Isabelle? That's one of Laynie's favorites."

"Your mind's been on her all night, hasn't it?"

Shawn leaned back and patted his stomach. "Good food, and a good woman. What more could a man want?"

"How about Jolene giving you Rachel and then leaving you alone."

"Amen to that, Sister."

"How do you think Jolene's going to react when she finds out about *her*? She'll never let you have custody of Rachel. She's her link to you. It's going to get worse, you know."

Shawn leaned forward. "I can't let that stop me from going on with my life, can I Isabelle? Not only is Laynie good for me, she's good for Rachel, who needs to see what normal mothering is like. She needs to know what it's like to have siblings, to play with other kids."

"You sound pretty serious about *her*."

Her. Wonder why she never says Laynie's name. "Isabelle, did you ever meet someone you felt was the love of your life? You know, like you read about, that once-in-a-lifetime thing?"

"Yes, I have."

"That's Laynie. I've never felt this way before, and I've been around the trail a few times." Isabelle smiled. "I can talk to her, tell her anything. I trust her. I never thought I would trust a woman again."

"You can trust me, Shawn."

"I know, Isabelle, but I mean this differently."

"Have you told her you love her?"

"No. I don't want to rush things."

"Are you afraid she doesn't feel the same?"

"I sure hope she does. I can't imagine my life without her. You know, I should tell her. Sometimes you wait too long and then it's too late. Maybe she's waiting for me to say it first."

"Any woman would be thrilled to hear you say those three words, Shawn."

"I don't know about that, but I am going to tell her. I'm glad we had this talk. Thanks." Shawn followed Isabelle to the truck. Silent sadness shrouded her as Shawn tried to get her to talk on the way home.

"I'm really sorry Carlos isn't here, Isabelle. I'm sure he'll be back on time this time."

"I don't want to talk about Carlos."

"Okay, what do you want to talk about?"

He heard her sigh as she faced him. "Don't you want to know about the love of my life?"

"Carlos?"

"No. I mean, I love him, heaven knows I do or I wouldn't put up with all his antics. But he's not my love-of-your-life person."

"Then tell me."

"You have no idea, do you? It's you, Shawn. I'm in love with you."

Shawn's heart leaped into his throat. "Me! Isabelle, it can't be me!"

"You don't decide with your head who it will be, Shawn. It's a decision of your heart. You touch my heart like no other man has. You're strong, but kind. You're funny and smart."

"Isabelle, Isabelle, this can't be. You're married, and to my best friend."

"I know. Ironic, isn't it? Don't worry. I won't cheat on my husband. It's just not something I'd do. And you're so wrapped up with Laynie, you never saw this coming."

Shawn wished they were back at the house. The truck suddenly seemed too small for the two of them.

Isabelle looked at him. "Relax, Shawn, I'm not going to do anything dumb. No one else has to know. Tonight the two of us were alone in a romantic restaurant on a romantic holiday. I just couldn't keep it inside any longer."

Laynie knew. Boy, howdy.

"I don't know what to say, Isabelle."

"Don't say anything. We'll say goodnight and tomorrow act like this conversation never happened. I've hidden it all this time pretty well, haven't I?"

Except from Laynie. She knew.

"I don't want this revelation to ruin our friendship. You've been so generous to Carlos and me. I don't want to make you feel awkward in your own house."

"Okay. But you have to forget about this." At last they were home. They walked into the house in an uncomfortable silence.

"I'm going in my room. Thank you, Shawn, for a wonderful evening. I'm sorry I said anything, but tonight was so beautiful, I couldn't keep it inside me any longer."

Laynie was really right about Isabelle. The romantic place, the special day... I've got to learn to trust her judgment more often.

Isabelle turned her head. "I'll get the phone." He hadn't even heard it ringing. Isabelle was beaming when he walked into the living room as she hung up. "It was Carlos! He called to wish me Happy Valentine's Day!"

"Good!" Shawn was still at a loss for words. Isabelle hugged him. "This really was a wonderful evening." The next instant she was closing the door to her room.

Shawn looked at the clock. Nine thirty. He wondered if Laynie was coping all right. Of course she was. He just wanted a reason to talk to her. He dialed her number and waited to hear her voice.

"Hey, Doctor Whiteman. How are the patients?"

"Hey, yourself! You really didn't stay out all night. The kids are all asleep. I can't believe it."

"Want some company? Or are you too tired?"

"I'd love you to come over. But I'll probably fall asleep if we watch TV."

"I won't stay long. I have something I want to tell you. And it's Valentine's. I want to be with you."

"Me too. I miss you."

"Not for long. I'll be there soon." Shawn grabbed his keys and a small wrapped box from the shelf on the hutch and hurried out the door.

*****

"Shawn, it's beautiful!" Laynie exclaimed as she held up the necklace. "Help me put it on." He wasn't about to tell her it was the second time he'd done that tonight. He decided on the way over he'd wait to tell Laynie about the Isabelle thing. Wouldn't be too smart to say, "Laynie, I love you, and by the way, Isabelle told me tonight she loves me."

"Did you pick it out yourself? I love the crystal heart." She turned around. "How does it look?"

"Beautiful. Just like you."

"Right answer," she said as she slid her arms around his waist. "Thank you, Shawn." Laynie kissed him. His pulse was thumping in his ears. "Are you hearing music?" she teased.

"Yes."

"What?"

"Wise men say," he sang softly, "only fools rush in. But I can't help falling in love with you." Her eyes studied his face. "I love you, Laynie. I know it's kind of soon to say that, but I know what love is and I-"

"I love you, too," she whispered.

"What?"

"You don't have to explain, silly. I know. I feel it, too."

"You do?"

"Are you really that surprised? Shawn, you have a lot to learn about women."

You got that right, Darlin'. "I love you, Laynie. I feel like I can't say it enough. It feels good to say it."

"It feels even better to hear it. Now, sit down here and tell me some more." They sat on the sofa, both forgetting their fatigue and remembering how good it was to be in love.

SEVENTEEN

Carlos returned by his deadline, and he and Isabelle moved into their apartment. After few weeks, they were finally able to get together with Shawn and Laynie to eat dinner. Laynie had to be blind to miss the look Isabelle gave her when they walked in the door to meet them at Elaine's Eatery. How could Shawn have missed all the signals from Isabelle? At least Carlos was oblivious to it all.

Carlos' reception of Laynie made up for the chilliness of Isabelle's. He had Laynie smiling and laughing before they were finally called from the café area to their table. Laynie went out of her way to win Isabelle over, even doing that "girl thing" of asking her to go to the rest room with her.

"I really, *really* like Laynie," said Carlos while they were gone.

"That doesn't surprise me. She's a woman."

"No," protested Carlos." I mean it. She's pretty, she's smart. She's funny. What's Jolene think of all this?"

"I don't know. I'm surprised there hasn't been some kind of big dramatic scene."

"Is she still with Paul Frank?"

"Yeah, for now. Look, can we not talk about her tonight? I'm having a good time."

"You're right. Sorry."

The four of them had many more good times together, and Shawn was glad Isabelle and Laynie became friends. He hoped Isabelle had laid her feeling for him to rest. Six feet under.

Isabelle was often over at his house while Carlos was away, but so was Laynie, and the two of them ended up chattering away about whatever it is women talk about.

Laynie's kids and Rachel were meshing well. They felt comfortable enough to fight and confide, to laugh and to cry together. *Like brothers and sisters.*

Zack was good with the younger ones and Rachel adored him. He'd tote her on his back and take her for walks with the others.

Rachel learned how to pretend. Shawn would watch them building imaginary forts and chasing imaginary bandits. Maddie had gotten over her shyness with him, and clung to his hand whenever there was an open one free.

Joey worshipped Rachel, and Shawn could see a special bond between them. Their two little heads would often be together, scheming a trick to "scare" Zack or inventing a new game to play with Maddie. At times, Shawn even heard Rachel sharing her thoughts on things troubling her. Joey grew fiercely defensive of her.

Shawn knew Laynie was the woman he wanted to spend the rest of his life with. His love for her was so complete, so genuine, like none ever before.

Laynie never spoke much about her divorced husband. He'd moved to Wyoming and forgot his promises to be in touch with the children. Laynie seemed happiest to forget him. Shawn wished he had that luxury with Jolene.

They had taken the children to the zoo. The kids were in awe of the animals. Laynie and Shawn watched the kids as they all rode the train around park for the third, and under much protesting, last time. He looked at Laynie as the wind tossed around her dark curls, wondering when the time would be right to ask her the big question. She turned to him and smiled.

"Shawn," she said, leaning close to him. "When are you going to ask me to marry you?"

"Right now." He took her hand and enclosed his around it. "I love you, Laynie. I want to spend the rest of my life with you, and only you. And also the kids," he laughed. "I want you to be the woman I always come home to, to share my life with. I want to grow old with you. Will you marry me?"

Her smile radiated from her soul. She placed her hand on his cheek, a gesture that always tugged at his heart. "Yes, Shawn. I feel the same way."

"It won't be easy," he warned. "We have a lot of battles ahead."

"I know. But we'll face them together. Always together." He leaned over and kissed her. A group heckling arose from the children about the kiss.

"I love you," laughed Laynie.

"I don't think we should tell the kids until I tell Jolene."

"I know." Laynie placed a finger on his lips. "I'll wait. But let's not think of her or anything else that dampens this day."

Shawn decided on the drive home he would get it over with and meet Jolene the next day. Then he pushed all thoughts of her out of his mind and listened to the discussion of his family-to-be trying to decide on burgers or chicken for the stop on the way home. It was a new song, and sweet, sweet music to his ears.

*****

"I couldn't believe you wanted to meet with me." Jolene tossed her purse on the seat of the booth and slid in. "This really has become 'our place,' hasn't it?" Looking pale and tired, her hair hung straight to her shoulders. Jolene squinted at Shawn, as an array of tiny lines fanned out from her eyes.

"Are you still with Paul Frank?"

"That could change if you want it to." She leaned toward him, tilting her head. "Just tell me you want me to leave him."

"That's not for me to decide, Jolene." The waitress appeared with their coffee. "I went ahead and ordered."

"Just coffee, Shawn? We're not eating?" she pouted.

"You never do. You just push the food around on your plate. Have you lost more weight?"

"Are you worried about me?" She brushed his chin with her finger. He sat back, out of target range. Jolene laughed and reached for his hand. Shawn slid it off the table.

"Don't you want to stay well for Rachel's sake?"

"I'm fine. I'm in great health. Except for my heart," she whined. "It breaks every time I hear Rachel talk about Laynie. Laynie, Laynie, Laynie. I could scream every time I hear that name."

Great. Hold your ears, folks. He took a deep breath and began. "Rachel likes Laynie." Jolene scowled and sipped her coffee. *Hey, no screaming.*

"And just when were you going to tell me about *her*?"

"How about now."

"I don't think I'm going to like this." She got out her cigarettes. "And don't tell me not to smoke. This isn't your house and it's my life. You're making me nervous. You're screwing with my feelings again." Her fingers trembled as she struggled to light up.

Shawn was afraid she was about to unravel. He hurried on. "Laynie is a good person, Jolene, and she's good with Rachel. I've been seeing her for quite a while now. She makes me happy, and I love her. We're going to get married."

Smoke fumed out of Jolene's nose while she pounded out her cigarette in the ashtray. "I guess there's nothing more to say. I don't see how you can throw away your family like this."

"What!" He leaned toward her. "*You* were the one who left."

"I give you a wonderful daughter, I tell you I still love you, I let you know I'd leave Paul the second you tell me, and you have the nerve to do this to me!"

I wanna get out of this place. If it's the last thing I ever do... Shawn shook away the music. Jolene was leaning toward him, her nose almost touching his. "Just when I was thinking of allowing you to have custody of Rachel. You can stuff that idea where the sun don't shine." She grabbed her purse and stomped put the door.

Well, that went well. He chuckled, despite Jolene's display of indignation. It could have been much worse. *Yeah, right you were going to give me custody. Is this the part where I'm supposed to run after you? Not in this story, Jolene. That's not how I'd get Rachel. But I'll never stop trying.*

And now he had a partner.

EIGHTEEN

May finally arrived. Everything was set for the wedding. The simple ceremony was held at Laynie's church (and now his) and the reception at Mama Mae's. Carlos and Isabelle stood for them with Zack paired off with Maddie, and Joey as ring bearer and Rachel as the flower girl. A weekend in Oklahoma City was all they could afford for their honeymoon, but Laynie was excited about spending those few days in that beautiful city.

Since it was part of his salary they decided to move into Shawn's small house until they sold Laynie's. Shawn was amazed how the children adapted to the cramped living space. The three little ones were in one room; Joey and Maddie on bunk beds and Rachel in her own. Zack rearranged the furniture in the front room, blocking off an area for his bed, desk and bureau. They were all pleased with their temporary conditions. He looked forward to the bedtime rituals of stories, prayers, and listening to Laynie sit on their beds and sing their favorite songs.

Shawn was hearing from Laynie about the endless phone calls she was receiving from Jolene: she asked her directions to the new mall; she told Laynie about the troubles she was having with her family; she complained about her sister Tanya's snooping; Jolene even wanted advice on raising Rachel. Laynie was baffled how Jolene could be so warm and friendly one day, and sulky and cold the next. He hoped it wasn't wearing Laynie down.

Shawn told Laynie to record her phone conversations with Jolene. He was doing all he could think of to help him get Rachel.

One evening after putting the children to bed, Laynie placed a tape in Shawn's palm. "You won't believe this conversation. I felt like I was dancing with the devil. I'm going to the store for a few things. Listen to it while I'm gone and the kids are asleep."

"Okay. I love you."

"I love you, too, Shawn. We'll get her out of there, Babe. No judge in his right mind would let a little girl stay in these conditions when she could have a good home with you."

"With *us*," he corrected. He closed the door behind her.

Shawn looked at the tiny cassette and frowned. *Might as well get this over with.* He placed the tape in his answering machine and pressed "messages." Evidently Laynie didn't have the tape ready when Jolene called. It began in mid conversation.

JOLENE: I never get angry. That's part of my problem. Paul found me a psychiatrist and that's what he told me. I have to let out my anger. But I don't, Laynie. It's just not me.

LAYNIE: I see.

JOLENE: But when I do get angry, it's usually at the person that deserves it least …um, it's, it's usually Shawn. (*She's drunk,* thought Shawn.) I get so angry, I take out all my fuh-shtrations on him. Are your kids all in bed?"

LAYNIE: Yes.

JOLENE: I don't know how you do it. Three of 'em. Paul says till Rachel is thirteen, she'll be telling me to go to hell. That's because she told me to shut up. "What do you want me to do?" I asked him. I have no control over Rachel. He wants me to spank her. I told him you, me, and Shawn are the only ones to, to…

LAYNIE: Discipline Rachel?

JOLENE: Yes. Shawn would *never* abuse Rachel. Or any kid.

LAYNIE: He's a very good father, Jolene.

JOLENE: (sighs) Does Rachel wander to y'all's bed?"

LAYNIE: She used to, but not any more. She stays all night in her own bed now. Does she come to your bed?

JOLENE: In the worst way. If she's at our house, she gets in bed with me. If we're over here, God forgive me, I know I'm not doing the right thing sleeping with Paul Frank. God will punish me-but I don't want to get married. Paul lets Rachel get in bed on his side. She climbs right over him and sleeps between us. I tried to put Rachel in her own bed because you and Shawn do. (Sound of a can hissing open and Jolene swallowing.) The doctor said this is my problem, not Rachel's.

LAYNIE: What?

JOLENE: I switched doctors because that first one wanted to put Rachel on medication.

LAYNIE: Oh, no, Jolene, don't do that.

JOLENE: I guess you think I'm crazy… maybe I am. Dr. Ronald- that's the one I'm at now and I like him- told me "it's not your child, it's you. She needs you to say 'no' and mean it."

LAYNIE: Sounds like good advice for a parent.

JOLENE: My dad, and my older sister, Tanya, specially righteous Tanya, and my mom get on my case about how much I let Rachel be with y'all.

LAYNIE: We love having her here, and the kids think of her as their sister. Shawn and Rachel have a special relationship.

JOLENE: And you're good to her. I love y'all and y'all's kids.

LAYNIE: I have to go, Jolene.

JOLENE: Okay. Me, too. Have to go. To the bathroom (she giggled). Bye.

Shawn's stomach twisted. Images of his little girl sleeping between Jolene and her lovers sickened and angered him. He slammed his fist on the phone table. "What else must she endure?" He reminded himself the children were asleep, and went outside to sit on the back step. He looked at the dark sky sprinkled with stars and a scooped out moon. "How much longer?' he whispered. "Help me, God. Help me save my little girl."

*****

It was Friday and his weekend to have Rachel. Laynie called Shawn and said she would be able to pick her up before he came home, because Jolene was going away.

The children raced over to him when he pulled into the drive, arms outstretched for the hugs-to-come. Except for Zack. He was much too mature and too cool to do that. He sauntered over and waited for the mass of hands and happy faces to greet Shawn and run off to play, then gave him a smile and said the usual, "Hey, Dad. How's it going?"

After Zack disappeared into the house, Shawn called Rachel back. "What, Daddy?"

"What happened to your lip?" She ran her tongue over the round sore.

"It was my fault. But Laynie said it wasn't my fault."

"Who said it was your fault?"

"I think you better talk to Laynie."

"Okay. Love you, Sugar."

"I love you, too, Daddy."

Shawn watched her return to Joey and Maddie, who were climbing all over the swing set he brought over from Laynie's house. The smell of supper drifted through the screen door to greet him, and he saw Laynie stirring something on the stove while Zack was placing plates around the table. "Smells, good Laynie," he said as he slid his arms around her waist.

"Chicken noodle soup, Mama Mae's style." She leaned her head back on his shoulder.

"Mmmm. Soup smells good, too."

"I'll leave," said Zack as he rolled his eyes.

"Supper's almost ready," said Laynie as he disappeared out the door. Shawn pulled out a chair and sat down. He patted his legs for Laynie to sit on his lap.

"What's with Rachel's lip?"

She sat down and brushed back his hair. "Jolene called Rachel over to her and she jumped up to be held by her mother."

"It's a cigarette burn! The stupidity of that woman..."

"I told Jolene she needs to stop smoking around Rachel. I reminded her of Rachel's chronic cough. I was surprised how she took that coming from me. She agreed and said she'll stop."

"Yeah, right... she didn't get mad?" This was way too easy.

Laynie laughed as she stood and dipped out steamy bowls of soup. "She's going away for the entire month of June. She wants us to keep Rachel, and not to tell her family she's away."

"Great. Good. Where's she going?"

Laynie placed the bowls around the table as Shawn slid his boots off and tossed them out to the mudroom. "She's being very mysterious about that. Said she would call us later with all the necessary information."

"I've heard that worn out tune. Hey, we'll have Rachel for a month! Maybe we can work on her bed-wetting and nail picking."

"One more thing."

"Uh, oh. I don't want to hear this, do I?"

"You have to. The kids took a dip in the pool this afternoon. When I was helping Rachel put on her bathing suit, I noticed a bruise on her bottom, the size of a half dollar. Look at it when you dry her off after her bath tonight."

"What do you think it's from?"

"I don't know, Shawn. She acted really funny when I asked, and said, 'Paul didn't mean to spank me.'"

"It's time, Laynie. Time to go to court. I'm going to file and Jolene can be served after she comes home. It will be the end of extra time with Rachel. That will be the tough part."

"It's a real mess, isn't it? But we surely have more than enough to prove to a judge Rachel needs to be with us."

"Yeah, we have our diaries, the tapes, she's had several live-ins, has one sugar-daddy now, no job, horrible living conditions, gets drunk." Shawn washed his hands at the sink. "And maybe I can get her family to help."

Laynie placed a plate of peanut butter apples on the table. "You think they will?"

"If they care anything about Rachel they will. How could anyone who loves that little girl allow this to go on?"

"Blood's thicker than water, Babe."

"That's what I'm counting on. Her Aunt Tanya and Jane, Jolene's cousin, claim to care for Rachel a lot." Shawn made a mental note to call them after he talked to his lawyer.

Laynie poured milk into the waiting glasses. "Good. Then we'll get started. It would be nice to have her here before school starts. Can they schedule things that fast?"

"We'll find out. Now, let's have that soup. I'll call the kids."

Shawn watched them run in after he hollered for them to "come and eat!" The thoughts of the bruise on Rachel disturbed and angered him. It was time to end all this craziness.

*****

June passed too quickly like Shawn knew it would. Laynie and he had worked with Rachel and she was "dry all night" almost the first two weeks and no slips the last two. Rachel was proud of herself. She stopped picking her nails about mid-June, and her chronic cough cleared up. She did worry about her mother. Jolene called only once, and that was toward the end of the month to say she would be home in a week. The message was left on the answering machine when she knew they would be at church.

Shawn noticed Rachel started calling Laynie "Mom." When she'd talk about Jolene, she would say "my mom" or sometimes "Jolene." He guessed it was because the other children called her that.

Jane and Tanya said they couldn't answer Shawn about helping him in court. He was irritated with them and reminded them they would be helping *Rachel,* not him. His lawyer said the hearing would be in November. Now all he had to do was wait for the bomb to drop.

And explode it did. After Jolene returned and was served the notice, she stripped Shawn's visitations down to the bare minimum. Even though he expected that, it was difficult for him and the whole family.

With her coming less often, they saw a change in Rachel. She was distant with Laynie when she'd first arrive, and separated herself from the other children. She was particularly cool with Joey, who tried valiantly to win her back. Shawn understood Joey's frustrations with her, because he felt them himself. Rachel was defiant with him. She asked Shawn why he and her mother weren't together. And she was wetting the bed every night. Laynie and he were deeply saddened and concerned at Rachel's regression, and could only guess what was causing it.

One day Laynie told Shawn she ran out at Joey's crying and there he was at the foot of the back steps. Rachel had pushed him down. The next day Rachel came crying to Shawn with two red miniature C's on her nose where Joey had bitten her. He hated seeing the children struggling with all this new anxiety.

Shawn was glad when his folks called and said they would be coming by for a short visit. They left their home in Indiana and had been traveling in their motor home.

Jolene had softened a bit and allowed Rachel to come the morning after their arrival to stay with them during their visit. His parents wanted to talk to Jolene when Rachel was to be picked up. Shawn warned them it would do no good, but they felt they had to give it a try. They were going to get Rachel while he was at work. Shawn was anxious to get home at lunch to hear how things turned out.

After they had eaten, the children ran outside to play. "Tell me about your meeting with Jolene," Shawn said.

Laynie started first. "We knocked on her door, but she wasn't there. We walked over to Paul Frank's and knocked. Rachel came out and your dad told her to get her mother. Rachel returned and said her mom would be out in a minute, and I told her to play with her puppy under the tree while we talked with her mom."

"You should have seen her, Shawn," said his mother. "She was in her nightgown! I said, 'Jolene, we want to talk to you for a few minutes. Why don't you go put some clothes on and come out here?' She was nervous. And she had her coffee mug. I wonder what was in that coffee mug." His mom shook her head. "You were right, Shawn. It was fruitless trying to talk some sense into her. Dad asked her if she could see her future, where would she be in one year."

"She couldn't answer," said Laynie.

His father cleared his throat and finally spoke. "The woman has no idea about her future. Or Rachel's. Mom asked her to think about letting Rachel be with you so she could get herself together. She said to her, 'Would you have given up one of your kids?' Mom told her that wasn't fair, that the two circumstances were entirely different."

107

"Then the lies began," said Laynie disgustedly. "She said she wasn't drinking any more, she's going to nursing school, and she and Paul would be married next week."

His dad folded his hands on the table. "I could see it wasn't going anywhere, and I was afraid she'd change her mind about letting Rachel come with us. So I thanked her for listening to us, and asked her to think about the future, and especially Rachel's."

"Thanks for trying," said Shawn. "Now, I have to run up to the nursery and check on a few things. I won't be long."

His mother began stacking plates. "Why don't you go along, Laynie? You two probably never get to be alone. Dad and I will do the dishes and watch the children."

"We'll even put them to bed if you decide not to come back," laughed his dad.

They thanked them, and after the endless goodbyes to the children escaped in Shawn's truck. On the way, he told Laynie how his boss was giving him a hard time at work, always undermining things he did. He felt his responsibilities were being taken away from him. "I asked him if I had poor job performance and he said, 'No, I just want to be more involved in the operation.' You know what, Laynie? I think *he* has a drinking problem. I saw in the paper he was arrested for a DWI."

"I wonder what it will take for Jolene to get help. You should have seen what she looked like when she first came to the door, Shawn."

"Can we not talk about Jolene any more tonight?" Shawn glanced at Laynie. Her hurt eyes silently questioned him.

"Okay."

"I get tired of it. I live with it, then I hear about it all over again when we're alone."

"I live with it, too, Shawn."

"Then let's not dwell on it."

"I wasn't aware I was dwelling on it. It just happened today, for Pete's sake. It helps me to talk about it. I need to tell you how she gets to me."

"I think it's better to push it out of your mind. We can't do anything about it right now. And I don't want my parents to worry. You didn't tell them about the bruises, did you?"

"No." He caught the anger in her voice.

"Don't be mad, Laynie."

"Of course not. We'll just push it out of our minds and pretend everything's wonderful." She kept her gaze out her window the rest of the ride. Shawn gave up trying to get her to talk to him. At the nursery she avoided him, and they drove most of the way home in silence.

"What's your problem, Laynie?" he asked as they went the last mile home.

"Look, Shawn, we deal with this Jolene thing differently. What you call 'pushing out of your mind' I call 'bottling up.' And if I do that, I go crazy. It's the way I am. I'll just have to find someone else who will listen to me. And don't worry, it won't be your folks. But really, Shawn, don't you think they have most of this whole thing figured out?"

He parked the truck in their drive. The lights were on in the house and they could hear the children talking and laughing. "I don't think they need to know all the details."

"Your mom *wants* to know." Laynie's hand was on the door handle.

"Just tell her some things, okay? Now, look. There's a full moon out. Want to star gaze a little with me before we go in?"

"No, thanks," Laynie opened her door. "I need to talk, so I have to go call a *friend*." She slammed the door and went in the house without him.

NINETEEN

Shawn's folks left and Rachel went back to Jolene's. Zack, Maddie, and Joey were spending a three-week stretch with their father in Wyoming. Laynie drove them up and spent a few days with her family. Shawn missed his family.

Of course, Jolene found out they were all away, and suddenly became "forgiving" of him and allowed Rachel to be with Shawn more often. It started on a Tuesday, when she called him at work, promptly at 4:45.

"Are you picking Rachel up tonight or tomorrow night?" she asked him.

Huh? Tonight? Okay, I'll play along. Shawn blinked away his confusion. "Tonight, if that's okay."

"I'll be waiting, Shawn. See you soon."

Shawn put his charts in order, and drove over to Jolene's. He was sure Isabelle or Mamma Mae could watch Rachel tomorrow while he worked. Rachel and Jolene were waiting on the porch when he pulled into the drive.

"Daddy, you're here!" Rachel raced out to meet him. Jolene strolled behind. Her face was slack and she stumbled when she was almost beside him. He grabbed her arm to keep her from falling. She was so thin, he was afraid he would break it as he pulled her up.

"Jolene, have you been drinking?" he whispered in her ear. She turned and waved him away, laughing. "No, silly, it's my medication."

He released his grip. "Medicine for what?"

"I'm so nervous all the time. When you had Rachel so much, I felt like an abandoned mother. Now I have to take care of three homes. Mine, Paul's, and the ranch in Dry Gully."

"Sounds like you need to get your priorities straight."

She sighed. "I know, I know. Hey, Rachel, tell your Daddy you got to feed a calf a ba-ba."

"A what?" Shawn asked.

"She means a bottle, Daddy." Rachel tugged his jeans leg. "I fed a calf with a bottle. Let's go."

"You got it." Shawn opened his truck door as Rachel crawled inside. He felt Jolene's hand on his shoulder. He turned to her.

"I hear you're a bachelor again." Her huge pupils almost hid the color of her eyes.

What's she on now? "Laynie will be home this weekend. She misses her family and old friends. The trip gives her a chance to catch up on everything."

"Let me know if you need anything. *Anything.*" Jolene caressed his arm.

"Come on, Daddy. I want to feed the bunnies!"

Thank goodness Rachel was impatient. "I'll bring her back tomorrow night." He quickly closed the door and headed home.

"How you doin', Sugar?" He looked at Rachel and noticed bags under her eyes. "Are you feeling all right?"

"I'm mad at Mommy. She gave away my dog again. And my cat. She did it when I was at cousin Jane's. I came home, and Sneakers and Tiger were gone. I cried."

"Why did she do that?"

"I don't know. She got rid of Pepper the same way. And Tabby." She yawned and leaned back against the seat. "She said she was going to take me to get another puppy last night. But she didn't. Mommy's a liar." Rachel crossed her arms.

Her words cut through him. "That's not the way Mommies should be, Rachel. Mommies and their daughters should tell the truth."

Shawn looked over at his little girl. Her arms had slid down each side of her as her head rested on the door. She was asleep.

*****

The phone was ringing when he came out from tucking Rachel in bed. He hoped it was Laynie. "Shawn. This is Jolene."

Again. "What's up?"

111

"I need the child support check early. Can you put it in your mailbox and I'll be by tomorrow morning to get it?"

This was becoming the norm. "Can't I just give it to you tomorrow night when I bring Rachel back?"

"I really need it earlier, to pay my gas bill. I could come and get it now."

"No. I'll put it in the mailbox tomorrow."

"Is it raining hard there?" Jolene asked.

Shawn held the curtain aside and peered out. Rays from the floodlight cut through the driving rain. He could see water racing down the drainage ditch.

"It's not too bad."

"I hear it's to keep up. Oh- that reminds me. Bring Rachel to Paul's tomorrow. I'm staying here because there's water in my place up to my ankles."

Shawn shook his head as he hung up. *You live on a rise in a house on piers and there's water up to your ankles. Better build an ark, Jolene.*

He looked out at the rain splashing on the hard ground. He wished Laynie were here. This reminded him too much of his lonely days before their marriage. Even though it had taken him time to adjust to the new noise and activity level of the new family, he knew the others had had a lot of adjusting, too. They had been used to a bigger house, but surprisingly complained little about the cramped space. He and Laynie were still looking for a home, and were waiting for the person who put an offer on hers to get mortgage approval.

Shawn decided to sit down at his desk and do the unpleasant task of getting some things ready for the hearing. He made a list of things he wanted to go over with his lawyer.

Moved
  1. Her mother's
  2. Iris Avenue (evicted)
  3. Johnson Road (evicted)
  4. Little Spring Apartments
   5. Paul's bungalow

6.*Tina's (when she had been angry with Paul)*
7. *Paul Frank's house*

    -<u>Admitted</u>- *Said I'm the better parent. I give Rachel food,*
clothing, shelter, religion, structure, and discipline. But Jolene won't
turn her over to me.
    -<u>Sleeps with Rachel</u>
    -<u>Bedwetting</u>- *we had Rachel trained in June. Has regressed.*
    -<u>Horrible living conditions</u>
    Can't count on Jane or Tanya. They think Jolene is doing
better.

    Shawn tossed the pen in the tin cup Maddie had decorated for him in Sunday School. She had given it to him Father's Day, when she announced she was going to call him "Dad." She didn't know it, but that was the better gift.

    Dredging up the past chewed at his insides. Shawn needed Laynie here to push him to do this. He just didn't have the stomach to write more.

    Enough. Rachel was here with him tonight. He got up and opened her door to peek in at her. Her hair covered her face and spilled over her pillow. Shawn gently pulled it away and smoothed it against her head.

    "I love you, Rachel. You're safe with me tonight. Sleep. Sleep peacefully. You deserve that." He kissed her cheek and quietly closed the door.

TWENTY

Maddie was excited about starting second grade in her new school, but Zack was anxious about junior high. Things seemed to get better for him after he found a good friend in Preston Matthews. They were always happy to have the friendly teenager over, and Laynie felt comfortable in taking Zack over to Preston's house.

Jolene had called Laynie one day and said it was "sad, so sad Rachel has no one to play with. Since the call, Rachel was over almost every weekend and often half the week.

It was a Friday in the middle of an unusually warm October. Shawn was going to pick up Rachel for the weekend, then stop and get pumpkins. He would drive them out to the lake tomorrow and have the kids carve them, right there on the picnic tables.

Jolene was on a lounge chair under the big live oak tree in front of Paul Frank's. Several bags were on the porch, and she had something on her lap. She smiled and got up as he pulled into the drive.

"Here. It's apple. Your favorite." She handed him a pie wrapped in foil. "Rachel made it."

Shawn took it and placed it on the floor of his truck. "Where is she?"

"Come to the porch, I have some things for the kids. For Halloween."

Great. Laynie's going to blow a fuse. It *was* hard to understand the sudden flow of presents for the children coming from Jolene. Notebooks and pencils for school: water guns and coloring books; sodas and candy. Laynie made it very clear she didn't like it. Shawn was supposed to have talked to Jolene about stopping it, but never had the nerve. He didn't want her to take his extra time away with Rachel.

"Rachel! Your Daddy's here! You better hurry, young lady." Jolene turned to Shawn. "First, here's her medicine."

"She was sick?"

"I thought I called and told you. I guess I didn't. I'm sorry, Shawn." The wind whipped at her white blouse flapping over her jeans. Losing more weight made her seem even taller. *If the wind was any stronger*, he thought, *she might blow away.* Jolene handed him a small bottle. He held it up, squinting at the label.

"It says 'Patches'! The name on this medicine says 'Patches'!"

"Oh, Tanya got it filled at work. She told Dr. Mason her cat was sick. She can get it much cheaper than I could from a people doctor. It's the same thing, Shawn. Tanya asked Rachel what name she'd like to have if she was a puppy or kitty."

"But she's not an animal, Jolene. You had a veterinarian make a prescription for medicine for our daughter! How do you know the amount is right?"

"Calm down. She's been on it all week and she's fine. You only have to give it to her tomorrow. Rachel! Your Daddy's *waiting*!"

"Jolene, I don't like this at all." At that moment Rachel landed on the porch, the screen door banging behind her.

"Daddy! Look what Mommy got for the kids!" She picked up one of the bags and held it open for him to see. "Look! Halloween candy! And stickers and a little stuffed spider for all of them. And make-up to dress up and-"

"I'll look at it later. We have to go. You take a bag and I'll bring the rest." While Rachel was buckling herself in, Shawn turned to Jolene. "Look, Jolene, I know you mean well with all these gifts for the kids, but it's well, it's awkward."

"But Rachel wanted me to."

"She just said you bought this stuff."

"But she wanted me to." Jolene squinted at him through the window. "Does *Laynie* have a problem with it?"

"We both think it's… confusing."

"They're Rachel's brothers and sisters."

"Yes. But that's *my* family. We'll take care of buying them things."

"My, my. All Laynie has to do is pop her whip." Jolene laughed and walked around to Rachel's window. "Bye, Baby. Hope the kids like the stuff we got them. Be sure to give it to them. Maybe give Laynie a spider." She looked at Shawn and laughed again.

He spied a trashcan at the roadside stand where he and Rachel stopped to get pumpkins. Shawn was tempted to throw the bags from Jolene in it. It would save a lot of trouble at home. But he didn't know how he'd explain it to Rachel. And besides, it would be a waste to throw it all away. He did toss the medicine into the barrel. Shawn would not give his daughter a prescription from a vet.

They loaded four pumpkins in the back of the truck and headed home. The children raced up to the truck where Rachel proudly displayed the pumpkins. She then ran off with the kids, laughing and yelling with them. Shawn's smile faded when he gathered the bags and pie to "face the music." *"War, huh? What is it good for? Absolutely nothing!"* Funny, he was hearing less music in his head these days. He guessed it was either because his thoughts were too filled with his family, or because he had Laynie to talk to every night. But he was hearing music now.

Laynie wasn't in the kitchen, but the table was set with foil over the plates and bowls. He backed up and quickly placed the bags and pie out of sight on the chest freezer.

Shawn found her in their bedroom, putting clothes away from the wash basket.

"Hey, Baby, sorry I'm late. I forgot to call you. I decided to get the kids' pumpkins on the way home. Hope supper's not ruined."

She slid his socks drawer shut and stood next to him. "Pumpkins! I guess it is almost Halloween." Laynie slid her arms around his neck and kissed him. "No wonder you were so late. I bet they were busy selling pumpkins." He held her close, thinking how good it felt to hold her.

"I missed you today," he murmured.

"Don't worry," she teased. "Supper's not ruined. Mr. Reynolds and I took care of that."

"Foiled again," said Shawn. Laynie moaned. "I really did miss you today."

"I missed you, too. Now, let's feed our starving family." He followed her into the kitchen. "I'll call them in while you wash up," she said over her shoulder. Shawn watched her walk toward the back door. She was looking at the things on the freezer.

"What's all this?"

"Jolene sent that stuff over for the kids."

Laynie put her hands on her hips. "I thought we talked about this, Shawn. We agreed this isn't right. You said you talked to her."

"I did."

"When?"

"This evening. That's another reason I was a little late."

"You talked to her for the first time today?"

"She'll use Rachel to punish me, you know that."

"You let her use Rachel to dictate our lives. You never make her accountable for anything. You just let her go on like we're blind and stupid to her schemes."

"Schemes?"

"First she calls the kids on the phone when we're not here. Remember what Zack told me when Mama Mae was here? She talked to all of them. Then she asked to take them to the circus. Then the lake. The movies. She never takes 'no' for an answer. Now she buys them stuff all the time. And *you.* She buys you Father's Day, birthday, and Christmas gifts. And don't tell me just because her name's on the cards they're from Rachel. She would never pick out shirts and cologne."

Here we go again, Shawn sighed. "What do you think her scheme is?"

Laynie's mouth dropped. "Isn't it obvious? She wants to be part of this family. I want you to stand up to her."

"She'll take away our time with Rachel."

"She'll get over it. Jolene needs us to take care of Rachel because she doesn't want her family to know how often she goes away, or does whatever it is she does."

"Well, I tried today. But the conversation went right over her head."

"Maybe it was because at that same moment you were taking all her gifts home."

"What was I to do? Rachel was right there."

117

"I don't know, Shawn. I only know this is crazy and I don't like it." She pushed open the screen door and called the kids. He shrugged and washed his hands at the sink. The children paraded into the bathroom to wash up as Laynie took the foil off the bowls and plates.

After they said grace and devoured lasagna and salad, Laynie rose to cut the pie. She placed a piece in front of each of them. "Oooo, apple," cooed Maddie. "I didn't know you made pies today, Mom!"

"I didn't." Laynie placed a huge piece on front of Shawn and sat down. "Rachel made this one."

"Wow, Rachel," said Zack. "I didn't know you knew how to make pie."

"It's easy. All you have to do is dump in the apple stuff from the can into the frozen crust from the store. My mom did the rest."

Joey was staring at his piece, frowning. His brown eyes studied the pie. "Where's the lid?"

"What?" asked Maddie.

"The lid. There's nothing on top." All four pair of children's eyes riveted to their dessert. Shawn bit his lip to keep from laughing as he met Laynie's eyes.

Laynie glanced at Rachel and stood up. "That's so you can put ice cream on top."

Zack rolled his eyes. "Yeah. It's an open face pie."

Shawn saw the look Laynie shot Zack and he pressed his lips together. Laynie got ice cream out of the freezer and placed a scoop on each piece. He loved her for saving the day, even though he noticed she wasn't having any.

After supper, Shawn saw Laynie go out, unnoticed by all but him, and feed the rest of the pie to the chickens.

TWENTY-ONE

The lake was almost deserted as they parked the mini van next to a picnic table. Laynie placed a pumpkin and special pumpkin-cutting knife in front of each child with strict instructions for carving. Joey and Rachel waited for help, but Maddie and Zack immediately started surgery on their pumpkins. They sawed off the lids and used the big spoons to scoop out the meat and seeds. The wind coming off the water tugged their hair as they concentrated on their masterpieces. The sound of the choppy waves washing up behind them was peaceful to Shawn. He looked at his family and smiled. This is how a Saturday should be: Zack was giving advice to Joey and Rachel on how to carve the perfect Jack-o-lantern; Maddie was in her own world, concentrating on the mouth she was creating; Rachel and Joey struggled to make their knives saw through the pumpkin skin, and Laynie was revolving around the table like a satellite.

No worries, no anxieties… no Jolene.

No, not today. Won't think of her today. Don't want it ruined.

"Look, sea gulls!" said Zack. "They must have come up from the Gulf. Let's see if they want the leftovers." He scooped up a handful of seeds and stringy pumpkin and tossed it toward the water. Almost immediately, the gulls circled and swooped down, devouring Zack's offering. The other children did the same, and then Maddie took a bucket and filled it with water from the lake to wash off their table. Laynie and Shawn loaded the pumpkins in the back of the van, and unpacked their picnic lunch on the next table. After they ate and cleaned up, they walked around the lake, skipping stones and talking.

The shadows of the trees stretched longer as the sun dipped toward the horizon. Laynie reminded Shawn the kids would be grumpy if they stayed too long past suppertime. Amid moans of protests, they loaded up and went home.

"It was a good day," said Laynie as she took his hand and kissed it. "What a good idea to carve pumpkins by the lake!"

"I hope it's something they'll remember."

"They will. Thank you, Shawn. For being such a good father, for giving them memories like this. I just wish we didn't have to take Rachel back," she said quietly.

"Me, too." But it was always there, always menacing in the back of his mind always lurking like a thief in the night, even after a day like this.

Rachel has to go back to Jolene.

Laynie turned to him. "I don't understand Jolene. She's got to know she needs help. Why doesn't she get it- for Rachel's sake?"

Here we go again. "I don't know."

"Can't she see how she's affecting Rachel? The least she could do."

"Laynie. Not now." Shawn saw the hurt in her eyes again. "I don't want to think of her now."

"Okay. What *may* I talk to you about?" He didn't miss the sarcasm in her voice. But he was able to draw her into conversation about planning a vacation next summer. Laynie loved to talk about going to Colorado.

"Did I tell you I got some brochures this week on Pike's Peak and Echo Lake? They look so beautiful! The Rocky Mountains!" Her voice was wistful whenever she spoke of them. "Do you really think we'll get there, Shawn?"

"If we get your house sold, I don't see why not. Remember, we've got that ongoing invitation from Carol and Missy to come up and stay with them."

"Maybe we'll fall in love with it and move there some day." In the dimming light he saw her eyes wide with her dreams of living in the Rockies. It never left her.

"Who knows?" mused Shawn. "The job market has to be better than here."

"Amen to that. I *am* glad you have the job you do."

The children tumbled out of the minivan and placed their pumpkins on the back porch, facing the dirt road. "That way Mama Mae and Pa Luke will see them!" said Maddie.

"Now, inside for supper," said Laynie as she shooed them through the door. "What's this?" Her foot struck something under the steps. Shawn pulled out a shopping bag and looked inside.

"Four little pumpkins!" he said as he opened up the paper taped to it. "I bet Mama Mae dropped these off." But when he saw the handwriting under the porch light, he knew Jolene had struck again.

"They're from Jolene, aren't they? " Laynie took the note from him and read it aloud. "Dear Shawn, I saw these and just had to get them for the kids. Aren't they cute? See you later, Jolene."

"Guess it's not going to stop," said Shawn, daring a look at Laynie.

Her eyes met his. "Not if it's up to you and Jolene. You tell me not to make you think of her. Don't you think it's about time you tell her the same thing?" She crumbled the note in her fist. "I hear Rachel calling you. Why don't you go in and start their showers. I need a minute to cool off." She turned her back to him so he went inside. He didn't dare touch the pumpkins. Their fate wasn't as important as peace in his family.

Later that night Laynie showed Shawn more brochures on Colorado. She seemed to have forgotten the pumpkins as her eyes sparkled when she talked about how the kids would love climbing the boulders at the Garden of the Gods.

They'd be getting up for church in the morning, so they decided to go to bed early. While Laynie checked on the kids one last time, Shawn sneaked outside to the garbage can. He peered in and saw four small pumpkins in it, and he sighed. Tomorrow he would toss them to the chickens. It would be a shame to waste them completely.

TWENTY-TWO

Shawn was grateful it was Sunday. He was tired from working two jobs and fixing fences at the ranch. After church, he planned to stretch out on the sofa and vegetate, if that was possible with a house full of kids.

But it was Laynie who found him first. He had just gotten comfortable when she sat on the floor beside him, and stroked his hair. "Don't get too comfy. I found a great house. It has four bedrooms and a two-car garage. Lots of trees, Shawn, pecans, live oaks, even walnut." Her eyes danced. "It used to be for sale by an agent. Now the owners are selling it at a lesser price. It's on seven acres, five fenced in, and it has a barn. *And* two wells!"

"You've seen it?" he yawned.

"I called the number on the sign and the lady was awfully nice and told me all about it. I drove by it several times this week. She said we could come by today and see it."

Shawn moaned. "Maybe tomorrow." He felt like he was cemented to the sofa.

"But till we eat supper after work and get there it'll be getting dark. Come on, let's go. She said to bring the kids. They can play outside while we look and ask questions."

"I'm really tired, Laynie. How about next Saturday?" *Please, let me sleep.*

"By then it might be too late. Someone else might buy it. And remember, the closing on my house is tomorrow. It would be a perfect time to make an offer. How many four bedroom houses do you think we're going to find in the country near Wesley?" Laynie was standing now, pulling on his arm. He closed his eyes. His body felt like lead.

"I'll get the kids ready. I'm leaving in fifteen minutes. I'd rather you come with me, Shawn. Please? You'll be glad you did. Really."

He peaked through a crack in his eyelids. She was gone. He heard Maddie and Rachel run into the bathroom. Well, he'd go. But he was going to be grumpy and not care who knew it.

Laynie smiled when she saw him lumber out to the kitchen. "I'll drive. Load up kids."

"Yee haw!" yelled Rachel as she and Joey raced to the mini van.

"Move 'em out," said Zack as he and Maddie followed.

"Come on, cowboy." Laynie tugged his arm and nodded toward the door. "It's only sleep. I'll tuck you in real early tonight." She wasn't doing a very good job of trying to contain her excitement as she practically skipped down the steps. He didn't know how she did it. She was just like his dad, getting by on only about six hours of sleep. And so dang happy in the morning. But she *had* learned not to talk much to him before his first cup of coffee.

Laynie kissed his cheek before putting the van in reverse. "Why don't you take your nap on the way there?"

"It's somehow not the same as the sofa." Shawn knew he was being difficult, but doggone it, he was tired.

"Okay, Grumpy."

He did close his eyes and actually dozed off until he felt the van jerk as it made a sharp turn into a crushed stone drive. "Here we are!" announced Laynie.

"Cool!" said Zack. "You were right, Mom. It does have lots of trees."

"Hey, it's green," said Joey. "The house is my favorite color, Mommy. Let's buy it."

"Joey, don't you know anything?" said Maddie "You don't buy a house because it's a certain color. You have to make sure it has more than one bathroom."

Shawn laughed. "Amen to that, Maddie." He looked out at the ranch-style home. Okay, he was curious.

"If we buy this house, Daddy, will Mommy move in with us?" Everyone froze at Rachel's question.

"Mommy has her own house. And she takes care of Paul Frank's and the one at his ranch. I think that's enough for one person, don't you?" asked Shawn.

"I guess so."

"Besides, Rachel," said Laynie as she parked the mini van. "You, Paul, and your mommy are one family. Zack, Maddie, you and Joey, Daddy and I are another, separate family. We live in two different places and do different things. We want a bigger house because *this* family, *our* family, needs one. Okay, Sweetie?"

"Okay. Can we get out now?"

"Yes. But," cautioned Laynie, "I want all of you on your best behavior. You may look a little inside, but mostly play in the back yard. It looks pretty big to me."

Laynie was right about the house. It was great. The living room was small but had a fireplace. The bedrooms were big, as was the barn out back- and it had a workshop. But what impressed Shawn the most was the water. It tasted good without any sulfur odor.

"We're over an Artesian well," proclaimed Alfred, the owner. He led them to them kitchen window and pointed toward the barn. "How do you like that pump jack, Shawn? If the electric goes out in a twister, you can pump water yourself."

His wife, Aggie, insisted Laynie look in all the closets and cupboards. Laynie's eyes shone when she cornered Shawn outside by the corral. "What do you think, Grumpy?" she whispered.

"I think I love you."

"Good. But I mean about the house."

Shawn took her hand and walked toward Alfred and Aggie. "I think we better sit down at their table and write up an offer they can't refuse."

"You mean it?" Laynie threw her arms around his neck. "Oh, Shawn, I knew you'd love it."

"And I'm sorry for being such a bear."

"Forgiven. And forgotten." Shawn was about to own his first house.

TWENTY-THREE

Laynie told Shawn to read her latest diary entries while she picked up the kids at school. The hearing was only a week away, so Shawn forced himself to deal with getting everything ready. It dredged up so many nightmarish memories. He lay down on the bed and read Laynie's words:

Jolene dropped off Rachel. Was happy when first arrived. I was on the phone when the kids said someone was at the door. I hung up and heard Rachel fussing, picking her nails, near tears. Jolene had come back, so I said "hi." She ignored me. I heard Jolene saying to Rachel, "I can't." I asked what was the matter, and Jolene whined, "Rachel wants me to stay." I said, "If you go now, in a minute she'll be fine." Jolene looked indignant, closed the door, left.

Later that evening I talked to Rachel alone. I asked her, "What does your mom say when you come here?"

Rachel- "That she cries for me when I'm here."

Me- "How does that make you feel?"

Rachel- "Makes my tummy hurt."

Me- "What else does she say, Rachel?"

Rachel- "She says she doesn't want me to come here. She tells me in the car, when we're just about here."

Shawn snapped the diary shut. *Dear God, this is too much for a four-year-old.* He opened and read Laynie's last entry:

Tanya called after Shawn left to return Rachel this weekend. (Jolene had asked us to keep her, even though it was not our weekend.) Tanya wanted to know if she could come and get Rachel and take her out for a hot dog. I told she was on her way back to Jolene's. Tanya wanted to know if we had Rachel all weekend, I said "yes." She said, "I knew Jolene lied to me when I got on her about dumping Rachel on you all the time. I told Tanya when Rachel is here, we do not consider it being "dumped on."

The phone was ringing. He looked at the clock. Almost five. Laynie was a little late. He hoped she didn't have a flat.

"Shawn, y'all can forget about getting Rachel this week. I'm keeping her home."

The War Department. "What's wrong, Jolene?"

"You and that Dr. Spock of a mother you're married to, let her get all bit up. She's covered with mosquito bites."

"Look, Jolene, calm down. It was my fault. I was at the nursery with the kids and they ran out back in the woods to play. I didn't realize the mosquitoes were in there this time of year. When I found out they were being bitten, I kept them out front. I didn't even have repellent along. It caught me by surprise."

"You can't think of *everything*, Shawn. You have Rachel and *Laynie's* kids to look after."

He let that ride for now. "Just put alcohol on the bites (*or you could just breathe on them*) and try to keep her from scratching them. I didn't realize she had so many."

"Well, there's about ten on her legs and four or five on her arms. You know me. I panic. I try to be the best mother I can."

Yeah, with the hearing coming up.

"I'm not going to marry Paul. I think after the hearing Rachel and I are going to move."

Why didn't I record this? Too late now. "What happened?"

"Nothing. Nothing happened. I just want to be on my own. Rachel and me."

But first you need Paul to foot the lawyer bills.

"I must go and make supper for Rachel. Then I'm taking her to dance lessons."

Cook and dance lessons? Making it look good for the hearing. The judge will see through your transformation.

"Bye, Shawn. Call me if you ever need to talk."

The dogs were barking outside. He heard Laynie's and the kids' voices as they opened the screen door. He hoped by next week, Rachel's would be heard, too.

*****

It was Wednesday and they had just finished supper when Laynie answered the phone. "It's Jolene," she whispered. "She's crying."

He grabbed the phone and sat on the sofa.

"Jolene?"

"Oh, Shawn. My mother is in the hospital. I have to go in. She's having respiratory trouble."

"Is she in intensive care?"

"Yes. It's so awful. If only she would quit smoking. She just never can quit. I'll be by to pick up Rachel in an hour. Have her cleaned up, I'll bring nice clothes."

"Do you really think this is wise? I mean, don't you think it would upset Rachel?"

"But I need her there."

"I know you're upset, Jolene, but Rachel wouldn't understand what's going on. She'd have to wait and wait, and it would upset her to see you cry. Go with Tanya and leave Rachel here overnight. It will be one less thing for you to worry about."

"All right. But I'm not going with that righteous Tanya."

"You go and don't worry about Rachel. We won't tell her anything until we know more."

"Okay. I wish you could go with me."

"Is Paul with you?"

"Yes."

"You better get going, Jolene. Call us and let us know how Edna is doing."

Jolene did call close to midnight and related to Shawn her mother's progress. She was stabilized and would be moved to a regular room if she had a restful night. She should be home in a couple of days. Shawn was to bring Rachel home Thursday night, to *her* house, not Paul's. Jolene also said she was absolutely, definitely moving out. She had found an apartment in Wagontown that was subsidized by the government. "It's the Windy Way Apartments," she said. Shawn knew where they were. "It's better this way. Paul and I will still see each other. My lawyer advised me to do this."

When Shawn took Rachel back, Jolene's porch was full of high school kids drinking beer. He told Rachel to stay in his truck while he talked to Jolene, who was sitting in a lawn chair near the front door. He took her arm and pulled her down the steps. "Don't you know you can be arrested for giving them beer?"

"Their parents don't care. And it's private property."

"That doesn't matter. What's wrong with you?"

"It's just a little celebration with some friends. Mother's doing better and will be home tomorrow. And I'm moving out this weekend."

Just in time for the trial. "I can't leave Rachel here."

"You have to, Shawn."

"Tell them to go home. Now."

Jolene turned to the teenagers and announced, "Okay! Party's over. My husband wants to spend some time with me alone." The surprised kids scattered and shuffled down the street.

"See? No one's driving. No one's hurt."

"I'm not your husband, Jolene."

"You should be. You threw your family away."

"You're drunk. Is Paul home?"

"Do you want me to go over there?"

"Yes." Shawn went and got Rachel out of the truck. This whole incident made him sick. Just a few more days…

TWENTY-FOUR

Shawn clutched Laynie's hand as they sat on the bench outside the courtroom. Last night he had tossed and turned, trying to remember everything important that had to be brought out during the hearing. Every time he looked at Laynie, she was lying in the moonlight, staring at the ceiling. They admitted defeat in trying to sleep and just held each other until dawn sneaked in through the cracks around their curtains.

His sleepless night drained him of all his energy. Laynie, though, was charged. On the way to the courthouse she reviewed what they would tell the judge. As they waited on the bench in the hall, she was finding it hard to sit still as they waited. Her foot tapped the drab tiled floor.

"They should brighten up this place. Yuk! Shades of brown. Everything. The walls, floor, even the ceiling. How depressing."

She was nervous. Shawn smiled at her and was grateful she was there beside him. He glanced down the hall at Jolene and her crew sitting on a bench. No family. One young woman and one soon-to-be-ex-lover, Paul Frank. Shawn would bet the farm on that.

Laynie and he had arrived with charts, diaries, and phone recordings. But their lawyer had told them "judges don't like things like tapes because it drags out a hearing." Laynie had argued with him that they were vital to their testimony. She wasn't comfortable with the time Grady Martin had spent with them in preparation for the hearing. He had dwindled down their lists of witnesses to one friend (to testify about their family life) and their pastor. This troubled Laynie. But people in Wesley had told Shawn not to let his small stature fool them; Grady was good.

They were called inside and seated after the bailiff announced Judge Robert Jenkins's entrance. Laynie was allowed to sit next to Shawn, which surprised him.

Jolene took the stand and folded her hands in her lap as she quietly answered her lawyer's questions. When Grady asked her about putting Rachel in bed with her and Paul, she denied it. Laynie

129

tapped Shawn's leg. "Now we have to play the tapes," she whispered. "It'll prove she lies under oath."

Shawn nodded and patted her hand. It was stone cold. He rubbed it between his hands, knowing she was as desperate to get Rachel as he. How he loved her for that.

Grady was not as hard on Jolene as Shawn wanted him to be. But the lawyer explained that Jolene was coming across as the victim, and harshness from him would draw sympathy from the judge. "She's doing the 'I'm doing the best I can for a struggling mother all alone in this great big world and all I have is my daughter' thing," Grady said.

"Isn't this supposed to be what's best for Rachel, not about what Jolene needs?" asked Shawn.

"You would think so, but in reality, it's not."

Jessica Bender was called. The plump, yellow-haired woman that had sat next to Jolene in the hall now took the stand, her eyes darting about the room. She ran her tongue across her lips, clenching her hands on her lap.

Jessica's testimony was an assurance that as Jolene's newfound best friend, she had now stopped drinking. According to her, Jolene was a dedicated mother and always put Rachel's concerns first. Jessica said she had seen Jolene almost everyday for the past year and now lived right below her.

Grady rose to question Jessica.

"How long have you known Mrs. Jolene Stevens?"

Jessica looked down at her hands. "Over a year."

"How do you know she's stopped drinking?"

Jessica tilted her head. "I see her almost every day. She don't drink. She would tell me if she started again." Jessica stared at Jolene with questioning eyes. Jolene smiled at her.

"She's a good mother," she added.

"I didn't ask you a question."

Judge Jenkins put down the paper he was reading and looked at Jessica over his glasses. "Wait until you are asked a question."

"I'm sorry, your Honor. I never done this before."

"Now," said Grady, "You can't be with Jolene *all* the time, can you?"

"No, sir."

"So, you can't say for certain that she never drinks any more, can you?"

"Well, we talk every night."

"Yes or no, Miss Bender."

"No, no, not for sure."

"You have a son?"

"Yes, he's Rachel's age."

"Are you married?"

Jessica's eyes widened. "No. I don't know where my son's father is at."

"Does Jolene do favors for you?"

"Well, I don't have a good car. She drives me places. If I'm short of cash, she gives me money for gas or to pay my electric bill. She's very generous." Jolene was glaring at Jessica.

"What else does she do for you?"

Jessica looked steadily at Grady. "She done my laundry for me a couple of times. She takes me out to eat. Jolene even bought me some clothes." Jessica's grin disintegrated when she saw Jolene. Her mouth snapped shut in her confusion. "Um, she's watched my son for me a few times. She's a very good person."

"I didn't ask for your opinion, Miss Bender. That will be all."

Jolene's lawyer popped up like a piece of toast. "One more question, Miss Bender. You testified Jolene has taken care of your son."

"Yes." Jessica's brows knitted together as she looked again at Jolene, whose lips pressed together so tightly they where white.

"You wouldn't let just anybody watch him, would you?"

Jessica's jaw dropped. She got it. "No, sir. I don't let hardly *nobody* be with him. Just me and Jolene. I don't trust nobody else."

"That's all, Jessica. I'm finished with this witness, your Honor."

Shawn was furious at His Honor. He had looked at Jessica only once during her testimony. If Judge Jenkins had watched her, he would have seen so much more than her words conveyed.

It was their turn. Shawn took the stand. It was difficult to think. There were so many things he wanted to tell the judge. It was very warm; his heart was hammering in his chest. Shawn followed Grady's lead and told the court about Rachel's living conditions since Jolene had left him. Jolene's lawyer tried to get him to say Jolene was a good mother. For a moment he panicked. If he said "no" and they lost, Jolene would punish him with Rachel for years. Rachel would suffer so much. What should he say?

He saw Laynie. Her eyes were wide with disbelief. Ever so slightly, she shook her head. Shawn leaned forward. "No. She is not a good mother."

Shawn hoped the truth would prevail.

He returned to his seat. Grady patted his arm and whispered, "We're doing well. You were great up there, describing Jolene's horrendous living conditions. We'll save Laynie for last."

When Laynie was finally called to the stand, she took her notes and diaries with her. Grady asked her about the phone conversations with Jolene, and questioned her about various incidents. Laynie looked panic-stricken as Grady announced, "That's all, your Honor." Her eyes screamed silently at him, and Shawn knew, like him, she wanted desperately to play the tapes for the judge.

"Why didn't you ask her about the tapes?" he whispered to Grady.

"This has gone on long enough. Look at the judge. He's yawning. He's been reading papers that I'm sure have nothing to do with this case. He's losing interest. It's time to close."

Jolene's lawyer approached Laynie. "You testified Jolene Stevens was drunk, Mrs. Stevens. How do you know she was drunk?"

"Her words were slurred. I heard her opening a can while we were talking on the phone."

"Perhaps it was her medication affecting her speech."

"Medication in a six pack," retorted Laynie. She fielded more of his questions, and was excused. It was announced the judge would need a short recess to think about his decision.

Grady leaned over to them. "I think it went very well. There was lots evidence today that showed the judge Jolene is an unfit mother. He can't argue the fact she has a drinking problem and smokes around the child. She depends on a man for her income, and even a place to live. She has no job, so it's clear Frank is keeping her, even in her new apartment. You, on the other hand, offer a healthier, more nurturing environment. And Jolene evidently doesn't object to Rachel being with you by all the extra time you've had her. The calendar showing that was very effective, Shawn. We're in good shape. Don't go far, we'll be back in session soon." Shawn watched their lawyer stroll out the door. Grady joked with Jolene's lawyer in the hall. Adversaries one minute, colleagues the next. It was all business to them. It was Rachel's life to him.

They returned to the courtroom, all eyes on the judge. As they were seated, Laynie grabbed his hand. Shawn's heart sounded like a mad drummer in his ear. He tried to focus on all the legalese the judge proclaimed, and then there it was. *The decision.*

"The court's going to deny the motion to modify conservatorship, but I'm going to be very blunt with you." The stocky, white-haired man tugged on his glistening mustache as he leaned toward Jolene. "If I hear of any drinking, I will have to take this little girl from you. You got that?"

Jolene nodded her head like one of those bouncing Chihuahuas on the back seat of a car. "Yes, your Honor."

"Because," continued Judge Jenkins, "if anything happens to that child because of your drinking, then we're going to be in a very bad place. If there are complaints about your drinking, I'd be glad to hear another motion to modify and you will lose her. You understand I'm giving you a chance to prove yourself, that you're going to quit this drinking."

"Yes, your Honor." Jolene's hands were in a fist at her chest.

"And no smoking near her. You need to change the way you are parenting this child. Now. Today. You understand this?"

"Yes, your Honor." Jolene widened her eyes as she made this hollow vow that sickened Shawn.

"We've struck a deal?"

"Yes, sir."

"Okay. It's on the record, Ms. Stevens. What else we got?"

Shawn only heard bits and pieces as the lawyers discussed child support. He turned to Laynie. Her face was buried in her hands as she sobbed. Grady motioned for Shawn to take her out of the courtroom.

"You have to leave or be quiet, Babe. I'm sorry."

"I can't move and I can't stop crying. How did this happen? " Shawn watched Laynie's body tremble as she struggled to end the crying. Suddenly, he felt as though it was all a dream. Emotions bombarded him so intensely he could only sit and stare at the table in front of him. Coldness spread through his body, leaving him numb with grief. He watched the judge hurry out. *Yeah, your Honor. Play the mother card and run. Don't stop and think about what you've done. Stay with tradition like a good ol' boy and give the child to the mother, no matter if she's a lousy parent.*

Suddenly, the room was empty of all but Laynie, Grady, and Shawn. The lawyer quickly gathered papers and files and leaned over to him. "I don't know what went wrong. It's hard to get a child from the mother. Guess you found out the hard way. I'm really sorry. I'll be sending you the new custody papers to look over and sign."

"Let's get out of here. This place makes me sick," Shawn told Laynie. He helped her stand and they walked out to their car. Facing the courthouse, he yelled, "Halls of justice? My word, Laynie, what do we have to prove to save our little girl?"

"I don't know, Shawn. But we won't give up trying to find out. We'll never give up on her." She slipped her arms around him, but he felt nothing. Shawn was dead inside.

TWENTY-FIVE

Shawn moved his family into their new house just in time for Christmas. After the New Year, Laynie announced to him she was pregnant. Shawn was ecstatic. Their baby wasn't due until fall, but already Laynie was trying to pin him down on a decision on names.

Then one Friday in April, Shawn's boss called him in, and after seventeen years of managing the wholesale nursery, told him not to return Monday. Just like that. House payments, baby on the way, increased child support. No job.

Laynie nodded grimly as he told her the news on their front porch. "Well, at least you won't have to put up with any more of your boss' antics. You'll find another job before your unemployment runs out."

"But it's tough to find a decent paying job in these parts, Laynie."

"Then we better start looking."

They struggled and managed to pay the bills. Laynie was doing well as her pregnancy progressed, but Shawn was sick with worry about Rachel. She was losing weight and had a chronic cough. When he had her at the house, she was either in constant, frenzied motion or she fell asleep only minutes after getting in the truck.

Jolene took all extra time away from them, then after a few weeks was calling and asking Shawn to keep Rachel more than their scheduled time. She told him she wasn't seeing Paul Frank any more. Of course not, the lawyer bills had been paid.

Once Shawn had pulled into the parking lot of the Windy Way Apartments and seen a slim, dark haired man walking out of Jolene's apartment toward his car. "Who's that?" Shawn asked Rachel as she got in the truck.

"That's Stanley. He's Mommy's friend."

"Do you like him?"

"He's nice."

"Does he visit much?"

135

"Sometimes he stays overnight to keep Mommy from being scared."

Shawn stifled a laugh. "Scared of what?"

"The dark. Mommy's afraid of it. So am I."

Jolene came down the steps of her apartment carrying Rachel's stuffed puppy. "You almost forgot this, Baby," she said and handed it to Shawn through the window. A black haired boy about Rachel's age ran up and tapped on Rachel's window. She giggled and rolled it down.

"Bret!" she squealed. "I'm going with my daddy. I won't see you tonight."

"Who's this?" asked Shawn as he waved at Bret.

"Jessica's boy. She's becoming such a pain," whined Jolene. "She asks me to drive her everywhere."

Ah, my heart bleeds for you, Jolene.

"Bye, Bret!" Shawn heard Rachel sing. She was leaning out with her lips puckered.

Jolene's face scrunched in horror. "No!" she yelled as she ran around to Rachel's side of the truck. She stood between Rachel and Bret and put her face in front of Rachel. "We don't kiss *them*."

"Them?" Shawn demanded.

Jolene leaned inside. "You know. Mesicans. Well, he's half," she whispered.

"Stop it, Jolene. Don't teach Rachel your prejudices."

"You know what they're like, Shawn. They just use you." She turned and marched up the steps to her door. It was always incredible to Shawn how Jolene described her own traits in others. *They just use you...*

*****

Through all this, Shawn saw Rachel cling to Joey as her grounding wire. They sought each other out during her time with them, and he was steadfastly protective of her.

The two of them had been riding their bikes with training wheels, when Joey ran to Shawn. "Dad," he gasped, "come look at my bike. The one wheel's like this." Shawn chuckled as Joey leaned to one side and raised his leg. "It's cocksided."

"Let me look at that." He pushed the wheel back down and tightened the nut. "There you go. You and Rachel going to ride some more?"

"Rachel's tire went flat as a pancake, Dad. I'll air it up for her."

"I don't think you can, Joey."

"I can use the hand pump. I'm big enough."

"I'll get it later. Why don't you show Rachel the new kittens in the barn?"

Joey's brown eyes lit up. "She can help name them. 'Cept for Midnight, I already named her." He ran off calling for Rachel while Shawn went back to fixing a fence between the pasture and the driveway.

He was almost finished when he heard Laynie call for supper. Rachel raced into the house, but the bikes sidelined Joey. The dark haired boy sauntered over to Rachel's, eyeing the flat tire, then the pump, then the tire. He glanced around, and then looked at the end of the rubber hose coming out of the pump. Shawn hunched down and watched the little boy study the pump.

Joey inserted the pin into Rachel's tire and quickly placed his feet on the metal feet of the pump, and pushed and pulled furiously. Suddenly, when Joey pushed down on the pump, it toppled over as one of the feet broke off. Joey's hand ran through his dark curls as he gasped, "Oh, no!" He fell to his knees, folded his hands and dropped his head. "Now I lay me down to sleep," he proclaimed. "Our Father which art in Heaven, hallowed be thy name, with liberty and justice for all, please fix Dad's pump!"

"Joey!" called Laynie from the kitchen window. "Come and wash up."

Joey rose and stared at his surprise-gone-wrong, then ran inside the house. Shawn walked over and snapped the foot back onto the pump. "He might not have the right words, but he sure had the right idea." Shawn chuckled. "I know you're a busy God, so here's a little help in answering prayers from me." He finished pumping up Rachel's tire and went inside.

They were all waiting for him after Shawn washed up, with an extra face at the table.

"Hey, Preston. Glad you could see me. Always room for one more."

"Thanks, Mr. Stevens. I just love it, how y'all sit down together and eat. And Mrs. Stevens's killer meat loaf is the bomb."

"Is that good?" laughed Laynie.

"That's good, Mom," said Zack. "And it is the most superb meat loaf in all Oklahoma."

"What do you want, son?" Laynie's brows raised in anticipation of his asking permission to do something.

"Dearest Mother and Father, Preston has asked me to go to the lake with him and his family tomorrow morning." Zack wore his sugar sweet smile.

"And since we'll be leaving before dawn, Zack could come to my house this evening and stay over."

"That way, we wouldn't disturb anyone in the morning," added Zack.

"My, how considerate. You've thought of everything. How could we refuse?" Laynie looked at Shawn and smiled.

"Do you need to do anything for your mom before you go?" asked Shawn.

"Yeah, the dishes," giggled Rachel. "Make him do the dishes, Mom."

"Thanks, Rach. I *was* going to help you guys fly your kites this evening before I go."

"Can we eat?" demanded Maddie. "I'm famished and starved. And I'm hungry."

"Good idea," agreed Shawn. All their voices blended together as they prayed, "God is great..."

There was little spoken as plates were heaped with slices of meat loaf and mountains of mashed potatoes that held ponds of brown gravy. Amid the usual protests, vegetables were passed and put on each plate. "I don't like peas on a stick," reminded Joey.

"They're green beans, Joey," corrected Maddie. "They're supposed to be good for you. But why things that are good for you have to taste so bad, I'll never know. I would have made them taste like chocolate. Or marshmallows. I don't think we were really supposed to eat anything green. If I were God-"

"How fast does God answer prayers, Dad?" asked Joey.

"Wow, Joseph. How profound!" teased Zack.

"He is not, he's just asking," defended Rachel. Preston and Zack laughed.

"Why do you ask?" said Shawn. "By the way, I saw Rachel's tire was aired up. Thank you, Joey, but next time let me do it, like I told you. You could have broken the pump or something."

"Did you see the pump, Dad? I mean, did you put it away?" Joey had forgotten how badly the green beans were and chewed a mouthful profusely.

"Yep."

"That's all you want to say to me?"

"Yes, Son. Why?"

Joey's angelic smile tugged at Shawn's heart. "God is really cool, Rachel. God listens to little kids." Shawn winked at Laynie's questioning face.

"Yeah, and God forgives us, too," Rachel added.

"I knew that," said Maddie. "We learned that when we studied the projecul son in Sunday School."

Zack laughed. "Prodigal son, Maddie."

Joey swallowed his vegetables. "Mom, I have another question. What's a homey turtle?"

"A what?"

"A homey turtle. Its name is Lee."

Zack laughed. "Where did you get this?"

"I was asking Mom."

"Where did you hear about this... homey turtle, Sweetie?" asked Laynie after she gave Zack *the look.* Shawn chuckled.

Joey stabbed his last green bean with his fork. "We sang about him in church."

"Sing it for me." Laynie gave a warning glance to Zack and Maddie.

Joey sang in his small voice, "Our homey turtle, Lee." Laynie's napkin covered her mouth and stifled her laugh.

"I believe the words are, 'our home eternally,' Joey," said Shawn.

Zack, Preston, and Maddie snickered. "At least he was trying," defended Rachel.

After their meal, Zack and Preston did the dishes and left. Laynie was singing to the children before tucking them into bed. Shawn knew she needed a night out soon, and thought about suggesting they go out with their friends Henry and Delilah. Laynie tiptoed out of Rachel and Joey's room, smiling. "They switched places tonight. Rachel wanted to be on the top bunk and Joey said, 'sure.'"

"They're a pair, aren't they?"

Someone was knocking on the front door. Shawn opened it and saw Henry and Delilah standing there, waving away bugs beating around the porch light. The last shower a few days ago and warm weather brought out insects in swarms already.

"Hey, I was just thinking about you two." Shawn said.

Henry pointed toward the driveway. "Do you want your wagon of hay to be on fire?" he asked. Shawn and Laynie ran to the porch and looked. In the pasture across the driveway flames slowly consumed the square bales Shawn had stored on the wagon under a tarp.

"I should have taken off that tarp after the rain," said Shawn. "Guess we better get busy before we lose the wagon."

Shawn and Henry battled the hay fire into the night with the help of a passing neighbor. They pulled down bale after bale as smoke billowed over their heads. When they were finally finished, they assessed the damaged amid mounds of smoldering black hay and tangled hoses. The weary neighbor went home.

"The wagon's a loss," mused Shawn. "But I can rebuild it." The four friends sat on lawn chairs and talked until they were sure the threat of the fire starting up again was gone.

"How's the job hunting going?" asked Henry. He wiped sweat off his face with the back of his blackened hands. Soot streaked his forehead.

"I was hoping we could make a go of it with our own nursery. But Wesley is a funny town," said Shawn. "Lots of people couldn't keep their businesses operating, like ours. I'm going to have to find something else."

"It is tough here," said Henry. "And with your growing family," he grinned at Laynie," you'll need something with benefits."

"It's hard to run the nursery with a family," said Laynie. "Both are so demanding. And if it doesn't bring in that much income, Shawn and I decided it would be foolish to keep it open."

"How are things with Rachel?" asked Delilah. She was pulling off Henry's boots and dumping out hay and soot.

"Things are going downhill." Shawn leaned back in his chair and gazed at the stars. "Jolene has men coming and going. All in front of Rachel. She had an Easter party for Rachel, and when I picked her up afterward, I saw beer cans on the kitchen table and a few of Jolene's teenie bop crowd still hanging around. Some party for a kid."

"We need something that would make that judge sit up and listen," said Laynie. "And we need it soon."

Shawn and Laynie said goodnight to their friends and showered off the dirt and smell from the fire and smoke. He snuggled up behind her in bed, and held her until her heard her steady breathing as she drifted off to sleep.

Like most nights, Shawn lay there in the darkness, praying for some way to save his daughter.

TWENTY-SIX

Shawn was picking up groceries for their Fourth of July barbecue when he walked past the bakery section of the store. He decided to surprise the kids with some donuts. As he tried to decide between getting a variety or playing it safe and making them all the same, he heard someone call his name. He lifted his head and was looking into the gray eyes of the young, chubby woman wearing a white apron and plastic gloves standing behind the counter. He frowned as he tried to remember where he had seen her before.

"I'm Jessica, Shawn. I was at the hearing for Rachel."

"Oh, yeah, Jolene's friend. The one who lives below her and swears to Jolene's sobriety."

"Her what?"

Shawn shook his head. "You said Jolene wasn't drinking."

Jessica scanned the area, then leaned toward him. "I feel so bad about that. It wasn't the truth. Jolene's never stopped drinking. She told me to say that. She told me she really would stop after the pressure of the trial. She promised."

"A promise from Jolene? That's about as good as a three dollar bill."

"What?"

"Never mind. Go on, Jessica."

She bit her lip. "Jolene's worse than ever. She drinks all the time. Sometimes she comes down to my place at night, after midnight, cryin' and crazy because she can't git Rachel to go to bed. 'What should I do, Jessica? What should I do? How do you git Bret to sleep?' Crazy like that, over and over."

"This still going on?"

"Yup, almost every night. And her lawyer, he knew she was still drinkin'. He came by once to give her some papers and she had a beer in her hand. He laughed and said to me about her 'being loaded'. They even had a beer together."

"So much for his ethics."

"His what?"

"Forget it. What else?"

"She's drunk every night. When Paul Frank comes over, he tries to git her to read these books on being an alcoholic, and Jolene gits mad and cusses at him. Oh, her language! She's a terrible mother. There's hardly no food in their apartment. But there's beer in the refrigerator. And cigarettes. She always had money for that. Poor little Rachel, living in all that smoke, and that filthy apartment! She's always coughing. And she's so wild for Jolene, like a wild animal..."

"Anything else I need to know?"

"I feel so bad about what I did in court. Shawn, I want to make it right. Things are bad, so bad. Jolene passed out in the shower last night. Stanley was there this week and he poured her beer down the drain after she fell on her face. I saw her drive away drunk with Rachel in the car. And when she's drunk, oh, Shawn, she rants and raves and is so crazy mad! She yells and throws tantrums. She gits so mad at you and she *hates* your wife."

"Would you be willing to testify to this in court, Jessica? I need to know."

She nodded vigorously. "I sure would. I feel so guilty about before. It's awful the way Rachel has to live. It keeps gittin' worse. That poor little girl. I want to help her."

Shawn's skepticism gave way to excitement. "Let me have your phone number."

"I don't have no phone."

"Okay. I'll give you my number. I'm going to contact my lawyer today. You call me and tell me anything else I need to know. This might get us a new hearing, Jessica, hopefully soon. You're not going to change your mind, are you?"

"No, Shawn. I want to help Rachel."

"Good. Just keep thinking of that."

In his newfound hope, Shawn almost forgot the donuts. He hurried home to tell Laynie his news and to call his lawyer. Grady wanted Jessica to come in and sign papers of her testimony.

"What did Grady say?" asked Laynie as he hung up the phone. She rubbed her back, which ached from her increasing size.

"He's going to file for a hearing tomorrow. After what the judge said to Jolene, not to drink or smoke again, this is it, Laynie. He has to get Rachel out of there."

Shawn and Laynie took the children to Nuevo Lago to see the Fourth of July fireworks set off from a boat on the lake. Shawn gazed at the sky as it burst with colors, and felt noisy explosions of the display slam into his chest. *Just like a concert in the old days.* He looked at the children's faces as flashes of light revealed their fascination. *But these days are better. Children make the best memories. I love my family, God, so much. Let Rachel be with us soon. Please.*

The next day Grady called him to tell him the hearing was set for September. Shawn prayed there would be no delays so Rachel would soon be safe.

Shawn visited with the manager of the Windy Way apartments. He didn't want to go to court, but gave a written statement about Jolene: Jolene's apartment was filthy, full of trash, unfit for a child; Jolene was "loaded" on a constant basis; she had been given an infraction of the lease notice for having her boyfriend live there.

Shawn was hopeful. The evidence was building.

*****

Jolene tightened visitation time after she was served the papers for a new hearing. When he dropped off Rachel, Shawn noticed Paul Frank's car was more often than not there. Jessica would call Shawn late at night with reports of Jolene's drunkenness and neglect of Rachel. He urged her to go in and sign her papers of testimony. She assured him she would, and she would be at the courthouse the morning of the trial. When he hadn't heard from her for several weeks, he stopped by the bakery and talked with her.

"I'll be there, Shawn," she promised. "But Jolene's driving me crazy. She's always in my face about something."

"Just one more week, Jessica. I'll never be able to thank you enough for your help. Let me drive you to my lawyer to sign those papers."

144

"Jolene would find out. I'll get a ride, I promise. Don't worry."

The day before the trial, Laynie went into labor. All the kids but Joey were in school, so Shawn took him along.

Joey sat on the widow seat and watched TV during the delivery. After his new sister was born, the baby was whisked away to a small table where the nurses hurriedly cleaned and wrapped her.

"Why isn't she crying?" demanded Laynie.

"Just a minute," called one of the nurses over her shoulder. "The cord is around the baby's neck. I'm unwrapping it. It's good you had a quick delivery."

Shawn panicked as he watched the practitioner suction out the baby's nose and mouth.

"Why isn't she crying?" repeated Laynie. "What's wrong?" As a nurse wrapped the baby, one loud wail filled the room.

"She's fine, but she's a little blue, so I'm going to put her under the light until she warms up."

"Are you sure she's all right?" asked Shawn.

"Yes. You can hold her in a few minutes."

"Be sure to shield her eyes from the light," said Laynie. Shawn bent over and kissed her. "I wish I could see her better, Shawn." Her eyes never left the baby.

"She's beautiful. Thank you, Laynie." He felt like his heart would burst.

"I want to hold her. Why are they taking so long, Shawn? How's Joey?"

Shawn stroked her hair and laughed. "He's fine. It's good he found cartoons. You did shake him up a few times when you were yelling."

"Me? What reason would I have to yell?" she laughed. Shawn moved back as nurses quickly tended to Laynie and handed her the baby. She held her close and kissed the small face under the knit pink and blue hat. "Hello, Hayley Kathleen. This is your mommy and daddy. Joey, come see your baby sister." He crawled off the seat and came over to the bed, grinning. "Sit down, Sweetie, so you can hold her."

Joey sat in the black vinyl chair and cradled the baby in his little arms. Shawn got out the camera and took pictures of all of them. He held his new daughter, taking in this new creation lying so innocently in his arms. He was filled with overwhelming love and instinct to protect her. These feelings filled him like the Oklahoma floodwaters, as he whispered their baby's name, "Hayley Kathleen." He handed her to Laynie to nurse her.

"Oh, you meant for me to come right away," said a short, stocky woman in a lab coat at the door.

"Yeah, Dr. Spane. You're a little late," said Laynie.

"Looks to me like everything's under control," she said.

Henry came and took Joey home and stayed with the other children until Shawn returned. When they were finally alone, he took the baby from Laynie and held her.

"Guess you'll have to go solo tomorrow to the hearing, Shawn. I wish I could be there."

"Don't worry, Babe. We'll be fine as long as Jessica shows up. You just stay here and hopefully afterward, I'll pick you up with good news. What a great week this will be. A new beautiful baby daughter, and Rachel home with us soon. Finally, things are turning out the way they should, Laynie."

He kissed Hayley and blinked back his tears. The love for his children was something that surprised Shawn. It came from deep inside him, intense and unconditional. Whether it was for the older children or this new baby, he knew his love for them was something they could always count on.

*****

Shawn went to the top floor of the courthouse to look at the list posted outside Judge Jenkins's door.

Stevens vs. Stevens. Courtroom #1.

Wish she'd change her last name. Shawn turned and descended the dim stairway to the ground floor, waiting for Grady. He scanned the hallway for Jessica.

146

I should have made sure she had transportation. Grady strolled down the hall to him, grinning. "I just saw Paul Frank's car pull into the parking lot. Guess she didn't dump him completely."

"Wait until after today."

"Where's our star witness? " The lawyer put on a wrinkled suit coat and adjusted his tie.

"I don't know. If she doesn't show, we might as well forget this whole thing."

"Where's Laynie?"

Shawn told Grady about the birth of their new baby as he followed him into the courtroom. He sat next to Grady and frantically looked out the door. Jolene came in the side door with her lawyer and sat at their table beside his. Her hair was severely pulled back, her lips pinched; she looked like ice ran through her veins. *It's hard to believe we were ever married. How she's changed! Or maybe I was blind. Maybe she was a good actor. Look at her now; ready for another performance for the judge...* Shawn shifted his weight in his seat. It was hard to sit still with his heart thumping and his mind racing. *I wish Laynie were here... Jessica better get here soon!*

Shawn could see Paul sitting on the bench outside the courtroom. Just as the door was closing, he caught a glimpse of Jessica hurrying down the hall. He leaned back in his chair and sighed. "She's here, Grady. Jessica came through."

"Good. This shouldn't take long. Jolene has only Paul on her witness list. Judge Jenkins likes short proceedings."

"It's his job to listen to all of it."

"Yeah, but it's good to keep him happy."

Jolene took the stand and declared her sobriety was intact, her motherhood was all sacrificing, and her life was in order.

Paul Frank testified he never saw Jolene drink alcohol since the last hearing. He should know, they were together almost every day, even though she moved away.

Shawn testified his latest updates about Jolene and her negligence with Rachel.

"We notice your wife isn't here today, Mr. Stevens," said Mr. Hagley, Jolene's lawyer. "Is there a problem?"

Shawn smiled. "No problem. She's in the hospital." Jolene's head dropped as she stared at the table. "We had a little girl yesterday afternoon. Rachel has a new little sister."

Hagley's mouth snapped shut as he regained his composure. He smiled. "Nothing further."

Jessica was called in from the hall. She was sworn in and quickly took the stand. Shawn kept waiting for her to look at him, but she kept her eyes on Grady. *She's really nervous. Wonder if she's worried how the war department will react to her testimony. Get ready for the storm, Jessica.*

Shawn glanced at Jolene. She was whispering to her lawyer.

Grady asked Jessica the usual mundane questions about her identity, then asked her about Jolene's care of Rachel.

"What do you mean?" she asked.

Come on, Jessica. Don't be so nervous.

"Okay," said Grady as he tossed his jacket on the back of his chair. "Have you, since the last hearing, seen Jolene intoxicated?"

"You mean drunk?"

"Yes, Jessica."

"No. She don't do that. She's a good mother."

Shawn jerked front in his chair. His eyes bored into Jessica, but she would not look at him.

"Miss Bender, didn't you stop Shawn at the bakery where you work and tell him you were worried about all the drinking and smoking Jolene was doing, especially around Rachel?"

"No. I'm always too busy with my job to talk to nobody."

Shawn gripped the table as the room spun around him. *What is she doing?*

"Did you not call Shawn and tell him Jolene stumbles into your apartment drunk, crying when she can't put Rachel to bed?"

"No, sir, I did not. Not me. Jolene don't drink no more."

Grady's eyes bulged with exasperation as he approached Shawn. "She's killing us. I've got to stop."

"Jolene got to her somehow," Shawn croaked.

Grady faced Jessica. "Has anyone suggested you change your testimony today from what you had told Shawn you would say?"

Jessica's hands flew to her chest. "Oh, no! That would be against the law to lie! I never said nothing bad about Jolene to Shawn."

"Yes, Jessica, it is against the law to lie under oath. Let me ask you one more time as you remember that. Didn't you tell Shawn there's only beer in Jolene's refrigerator, and Rachel needs to be with Shawn?"

"No, sir. It's not like that. Jolene is a wonderful mother. She buys things for Rachel all the time. The child has everything she needs. She loves Rachel very much. She's a good person and mom."

"I want nothing further from this... witness," hissed Grady.

Shawn glared at Jessica, who hurried out of the room with her head down. Jolene sat wide-eyed and calm as a smile tugged at her lips. As if it were all a dream, Shawn heard the judge say that not enough of evidence was introduced and Rachel was to remain with Jolene.

TWENTY-SEVEN

It was autumn, but the trees seemed reluctant to give up their leaves, letting only some of them float to the ground when the wind tugged them off their branches. The sky was filled with the honking sounds and dark V lines of geese flying south. Hawks migrated in huge spirals, like lazy tornados in slow motion.

The grass was brown from the drought like it was August instead of October. Shawn was glad they had two wells for his family and the cattle. Now the trick was finding hay to supplement the cattle since the pastures were brittle, and hope the rain would soon come. He drove to Wagontown, scanning the desolate fields, seas of brown dirt occasionally kicked up by a mischievous eddy. He passed tractors driven by desperate ranchers cutting and baling the grass along the highway and on the median, hoping it would be enough to feed their cattle until the rain came. Shawn slowed to turn into the parking lot of the Windy Way apartments.

Rachel ran out to him with her mother following her. Jolene's hair now fell past her shoulders when she didn't pull it back. The wind whipped it around her face as she spoke. "Hi, Shawn. I just wanted to know if y'all needed any food."

"What?"

"I have plenty of cereal and things. I got on welfare, to help me out." She leaned toward him and whispered, "You know, food stamps. Until I find a job. I don't need all the things we get, so I thought you should have it."

"No, thanks. We're fine. Let's go, Rachel."

"Why are you so mad at me, Shawn? I'm not the one who keeps dragging us back to court. Rachel's fine where she is."

"Not now, Jolene." He was glaring at her. She disgusted him.

On the way home, Rachel talked about her kindergarten teacher and how pretty she was. "How is school going for you, Sugar?" asked Shawn.

"Good. I get mad when Mommy wants me to stay home."

"What do you mean?"

"She calls and tells them I'm sick when I'm not. She says it's okay to say that, because she's the one who's sick."

"What's the matter with Mommy?"

"She feels bad sometimes in the morning. She has awful headaches." Rachel squinted her eyes, recalling her mother's mornings. "She can hardly get out of bed to call the school. I get mad, but then I see she looks awful. I have to be real quiet because the loud makes her head hurt. I can get my own breakfast, Daddy. Donuts and a soda. I'm big enough."

"Donuts and a soda." Shawn snuffed.

"I watch TV until she's feeling better. She and Paul had a big fight. He was mad she let Will stay overnight."

"Will?"

"Mommy's new friend. She really likes him. He has a little girl named Dara. I play with her sometimes."

"What is Will like?"

"He's nice. Mommy's not sick so much since she got Will."

Got Will. Poor sucker. "Has Mommy seen a lot of Will?"

"Yup. She says she wishes they would get married."

"Married?"

"Are the kids all at home?" Rachel frowned. "I hope so. Can we carve pumpkins again at the lake like last year? Please, Daddy?"

Shawn pulled into the driveway. "Sure can. And the kids are all here."

"Can I hold Hayley?"

"You bet. Let's go inside and see what everyone's up to." He watched her race inside as he slammed the truck door shut. *Will... could it be? You'd think the guy would have learned the first time. Boy howdy!* Will Starks. Jolene's former boyfriend was in her sights as husband number three.

*****

Jolene was like a tornado, sucking the life out of things and leaving chaos in her trail. Shawn never knew where he was supposed to return Rachel until Jolene would call him and tell him. Sometimes

151

it was at the apartment, sometimes Tanya's, or Jane's house, sometimes Tina's.

Rachel was eating poorly and talked of sleeping on floors and falling asleep in school. She still wet the bed. Shawn was frustrated at his helplessness. He decided to visit Rachel's teacher. He wanted her to know what was going on, and told her to call him if she noticed anything he needed to know.

Jolene called him a few days later, screaming on the phone. "I don't appreciate these rumors you spread about me with Rachel's teacher. I know Judge Jenkins personally and I called him about this. Yes, I did. This is slander," she hissed. "My lawyer says so."

Her retaliation was deception. She told Shawn she would bring Rachel to church for a special service that Sunday. He stood outside and waited for her, searching the streets for Jolene's car. It was only after Zack came out and told him the program had started he gave up and went inside with the rest of the family. He called Jolene that evening and asked why she hadn't brought Rachel to church. She hung up on him.

The next night Jolene called him, chatty, asking him about his recent back injury, imploring him to take care of himself, especially with "all those kids to take care of." Shawn shook his head in disbelief, as Jolene yelled for Rachel to come to the phone and "talk to the only father you'll ever have." *Welcome to the circus,* he mused.

"I hope we can always be friends, Shawn. All of us. If I can help you, I want to." Shawn didn't know how to answer or how to handle her new onslaught of phone calls. Jolene called almost every day. She made Rachel perform her spelling words on the phone. She wanted his help with a Halloween party she was having for Rachel.

She called to ask Shawn if he could eat lunch with Rachel "every Tuesday and Thursday." (Her speech was slurred.) "I'll go Monday, Wednesday, and Fridays. That way we can be sure she eats her lunch every day. Otherwise she throws it out and then she wouldn't be eating right."

She was moving again, still staying in Wagontown, but in a different elementary school district. So the first weekend in November, after being told where to return with Rachel, Shawn found

their new home on Lantana Avenue. He parked in front of a small
brick ranch house, where a tall slim man with short red hair
approached him from the porch. Shawn recognized him. Rachel was
pulling on his hand. "Come inside and see my new room, Daddy."

"Not now," the man said to her. "I want to talk to your dad,
your mom's inside. She got you a present."

"Bye, Daddy." Rachel kissed him and disappeared through
the front door.

"I'm Will Starks." The way he said it, Shawn felt like he
should salute him.

"I know." Shawn reluctantly shook his outstretched hand.

"Jolene and I are living together now," he informed Shawn.
"I'll take good care of Rachel. I have a girl of my own. They play
nice together."

"Isn't this all kind of soon? Couldn't you just date?"

"We already know each other, Shawn. We've both grown up
since our first relationship, which I'm sure you know about. We were
just kids. We've both matured since then." Will seem quite impressed
with himself as he presented this revelation to Shawn.

"So you think y'all are all grown up now." It really wasn't a
question Shawn was asking.

"Of course," Will snorted. "Most definitely."

"I'm tired of Rachel being jerked around."

"I agree, one hundred percent. Okay. We're good. Well, you
have a good week, Shawn. I'm glad I met you. Jolene says you're a
great father. I'll be good to Rachel."

"I'll hold you to it."

Shawn tried to shake off the uneasiness that gnawed at him.
Will was certainly smooth, seemed to be in control. Maybe too much.

*****

Shawn and Laynie took the children to see the Christmas
parade in Nuevo Lago that December. They squealed with delight as
they watched the decorated boats glide by on the lake, their colorful
lights reflecting on the smooth water. Afterward, they drove the mini

van around to admire Christmas lights. When Shawn returned Rachel Sunday evening, Jolene tapped on his window and motioned for him to step outside the truck.

"I want to talk you," she said, pulling on his arm. "Come inside."

"Can't we talk out here?"

"It's cold and Will's waiting inside. Please, Shawn. It won't take long. Then you can run on home to Laynie."

Shawn shrugged. "All right." He followed her through the front door, and waited for his eyes to adjust to the dark room. An olive green blanket hung over the front windows in the living room, giving the room a dismal, oppressive atmosphere. Will entered and motioned for Shawn to sit on a chair across from the sofa where he and Jolene sat. "It's good to see you, Shawn. We've something to tell you."

Shawn sank into the stuffed chair. The air was stifling in the room, stale and choking from cigarette smoke. Rachel sat on his knee.

"Should she be here for this?" Shawn asked them. Somehow, he knew Will would be the one to answer.

"Sure. She already knows. Jolene and I are going to be married this month. Right before Christmas." Will put his arm around Jolene's shoulders.

"My lawyer said it would be best if we got married," Jolene added.

"Your lawyer..." Shawn stopped. He couldn't even begin to say what he wanted to. It was all so useless. "I just hope this gives some stability to Rachel," said Shawn. "She's been through so many changes."

"I agree," said Will, standing. "She needs more order in her life. One hundred percent correct. Thank you for understanding that."

Shawn rose to go. "Look, I want this to be a good thing for Rachel. Her life's been crazy." Jolene stared at the floor.

"I know that. But things are going to change for them. I got them out of those apartments and off welfare, didn't I? I have a good job, so Jolene can stay at home." Jolene was silent.

Shawn scooped up Rachel and kissed her goodbye. She jumped down and ran to Jolene. "Where's my present, Mommy? You always buy me something."

Shawn walked out and filled his lungs with the crisp evening air. He wondered how all this would be for his daughter. Once again he was watching her being forced through all these changes.

TWENTY-EIGHT

After the holidays, Laynie sank into a depression so unlike her. Shawn knew her anxiety about Rachel was getting to her, and she missed her family and friends in Wyoming. Their financial situation was a continuous burden. He had started a new job at a convenience store, where the pay wasn't great but the benefits were affordable.

Laynie had just put Hayley to sleep and was out hanging wash on the line. He watched her through the window as she neatly hung the socks in pairs. The shirts she hung out earlier were already dry and flapping in the wind like they were waving at invisible passersby.

Laynie lugged in the wash basket full of shirts on her hip. She smiled at him as she folded the laundry on the dining room table. "What's on your mind, cowboy? You're in deep thought."

Shawn smiled at her. "You need to go home again."

"We can't afford that now."

"You could drive."

She turned to him and laughed. "Twelve hour drive with a baby? What'd I do to you?"

Shawn chuckled. "Go over spring break next month. You wouldn't have much traffic because everyone will be heading down to the Gulf. Take the kids, they'll help you, and stay overnight midway."

"Without you?"

"I can't take time off already. Besides, Rachel is with Jolene this year for spring break, so I'll be here for our regular visitations."

Laynie smoothed out the last shirt and laid it in the basket. "But Rachel would be disappointed if we went without her."

Shawn placed his hands on her shoulders. "You need this. Think of it as making you a more relaxed mother." She smiled.

"I've been that bad, huh?"

He pulled her to him and put his arms around her. "No, you've been great. But it's been tough on you, ever since we got married. Never an easy moment."

156

"Same for you." Laynie leaned back and looked at his face. "I wish you could come."

"I know, but I can't. Maybe if Isabelle's around, she'll go along, especially if Carlos is away again."

"All right. I've got a month to make plans and get everything ready. Are you sure we can afford this? I mean, the motel and all."

"We'll be okay. I'll sell a cow if I have to, but you need to go home."

She kissed him and whispered in his ear, "Thanks for understanding."

And so it was, when the second week in March arrived, Shawn found himself waving goodbye to his family - except for Rachel- as they drove out the driveway. He was glad Isabelle was along to help with the navigation and the children. A menagerie of hands frantically waved out the windows accompanied by a chorus of "goodbyes."

When they were out of sight, he turned to face the silence of the house. He walked into the living room, swallowed by the oppressive quiet. No footsteps, no voices, no laughter. No one yelling for Mom, no one studying the inside of the refrigerator, no click of the baby swing, no radio blaring. Just a deafening hush that reminded him of his loneliness before knowing Laynie. A nagging fear invaded his thoughts, of losing them. *Drive, safe, Laynie. Be careful.* Shawn looked at the clock on the wall and realized it was time to get Rachel for the weekend.

Good. He could only take so much quiet.

*****

At first Rachel was ecstatic about having her dad all to herself, but by Saturday afternoon she was whining for the kids. Shawn took her out for tacos that evening, which cheered her just a little. She stayed with Delilah while he worked, where she rode horseback and played with their dogs. Shawn spent the rest of their time together at the house or in Nuevo Lago visiting the museum.

Their last day together they visited Mama Mae and Pa Luke, who fussed over Rachel. Shawn thought Pa looked tired, and his color was not good. He took Mama Mae to the side and asked her about his health.

"He goes to the doctor's tomorrow to have some blood work done. He's been real tired lately. I don't think he'll be able to finish helping to plant cotton, he's so tuckered out. I'm worried, Shawn."

"Call me and let me know what you find out," Shawn ordered. Mama Mae promised she would, and it was time to take Rachel back.

"Give me some sugar," said Mama Mae to Rachel as she puckered for a kiss. Rachel threw her arms around her neck and kissed her, then Pa Luke. "You be a good girl, Shug. Mama Mae says so."

"Yes, Ma'am," agreed Rachel, her blue eyes solemn. They got in the truck and headed to Lantana Drive.

"How are things going with your mom and Will?" Shawn waited for Rachel to answer, but she dropped her head and sighed.

"Darlin', what's wrong?"

"Mommy and Will got in a big fight, Daddy. Will pushed Mommy to the sidewalk."

"You saw it?"

"I was on the porch. I don't know why they were yelling at each other. Then Will pushed her down. She hit her head. She called the cops."

"Why didn't you tell me?"

"Mommy said not to. She said it was all fixed up now. She told the cops to go back. She said Will didn't really push her. Mommy was wobbly."

"Did you see Will put his hands on her?"

Rachel nodded. "She was wobbly, but not so she would fall. He pushed her. I saw."

"I need to talk to your mom, Rachel. This is wrong."

Rachel's eyes widened. "Oh, no, Daddy, don't," she gasped. "She'll be mad at me for telling."

"No, she won't, Rachel. She won't be mad at you."

They pulled into the drive a little early. Shawn and Rachel got out and went to the door and knocked. Rachel turned the knob, but it was locked. "They're not here. Where can they be?" she asked. Her face was full of worry.

Shawn saw the blanket hanging in the window move. He leaned over and saw a pair of brown eyes staring at him.

"Dara!" squealed Rachel. "Dara, let us in!" Rachel's fist knocked on the window.

The chubby girl stood and pulled back the blanket. "I can't," she yelled through the glass. "The door's locked and I can't open it."

"Get my mom," said Rachel.

"She's not here."

"Then get your dad," Rachel answered.

"He's not here either." The glass in front of her mouth steamed up.

"You're alone?" yelled Shawn. The girl nodded, and then dropped the blanket. Shawn took Rachel back to the truck and they sat inside. "Do they do this often, Rachel? Leave Dara alone like this?"

"Just sometimes. She doesn't behave very good, so they have to."

"They have to? Do they ever leave you alone?"

Rachel frowned. "Not much. Just sometimes with Dara. They lock the doors so we're safe."

"Rachel, what if there was a fire? How could you get out?" Her eyes widened as she considered this. "The two of you are way too young to be left alone."

"But I'm big."

"Rachel, listen to me." Shawn leaned over and looked directly into her face. "I'm going to tell Mommy to never let you home alone or with another kid again. If she does, you fuss and yell. Promise me."

Rachel sat up straight. "I promise, Daddy. Look, here's Mommy now."

159

Will parked his truck in the drive and Jolene jumped out. "Sorry we're a little late." She smiled and stumbled over to them as Shawn and Rachel got out of his truck.

"Dara's in there alone!" said Shawn, pointing to the house. "She's just a kid!" Will fumbled for his keys to unlock the front door, and disappeared behind it.

"I know. We just went to an open house." Jolene was frantically twitching her fingers. She grabbed Rachel's hand and pulled her to her side. "I missed you, Baby. I have a surprise in the house."

"What did you buy me this time, Mommy?" Jolene walked toward the house. "I didn't kiss Daddy goodbye!" Rachel ran back to him and kissed him.

"Jolene, we have to talk about a few things here."

"I can't now. Will's waiting for me."

"I don't want Rachel being locked in a house alone like that. She's too young to be by herself."

"Oh, Shawn, I would never…"

"And what's this about Will pushing you?"

"Don't you start anything, Shawn. Rachel exaggerates everything. It was just a little misunderstanding." She turned and stomped inside the house.

When he got home he looked up the number for Bev Starks, Dara's mother. She seemed indifferent to the report Shawn gave her about Dara being locked inside the house alone. Her voice was thick and slow, and Shawn hung up, disgusted. He turned and stared out the window as darkness crept over the flat land.

"What are you getting Rachel involved in this time, Jolene?"

The phone was ringing. It was Jolene, wondering if she could have her check early.

*****

The day after Laynie and the children returned home Shawn got a call from Mama Mae that Pa Luke had cancer of the liver. He took his family over to visit and talk to them about what help they would need in the future. Both seemed hopeful about Luke's prognosis, but Shawn noticed the yellow cast of his skin.

"Did you notice his eyes?" asked Laynie as they lay in bed that night.

"You mean the yellow? That's not good, is it?"

"No... I wonder how much they really know." Laynie sighed and mover closer to him.

He put his arm around her and kissed her. "They know. It just takes time to let it sink in. You'd think they'd have a cure for this by now." Shawn held Laynie close to him until she fell asleep. He wondered what it was like to learn your life partner was going to die. Mama Mae and Pa Luke were married sixty-two years. How could you wake up in the morning and suddenly remember you had to face the day without that person? Never again to shuffle out of bed together or share your first cup of coffee; anticipating talking about something funny that happened, only to remember there was no one to tell; hearing your spouse's voice inside your head but never again at the supper table. Night after night, falling into bed alone...

Shawn pulled Laynie snugly against him. "I go first," he whispered into her hair. He kissed her forehead and silently pledged his love to her for all his life.

TWENTY-NINE

"Dad, can you come here?" asked Zack as he motioned for him to come into the living room. "I just got off the phone with Rachel. She wanted to talk a minute. You know, big brother," he grinned.

"What's going on?" Shawn asked as he sank into the sofa. Zack sat beside him, his brown eyes serious with concern.

"Rachel said she skipped kindergarten today, just because she didn't feel like going. I heard Jolene yelling at her to tell me she was sick. So Rachel goes, 'Um, I was sick, Zack. Oh, and I dumped Brandon. Now my boyfriend is Tad. We went away last night with Tad, like a date.' I said aren't you kind of young for that and then Jolene kept telling her what to say to me. Rachel yelled for her mom to shut up! Jolene told her she better behave or the judge will take her away." Shawn shook his head. "Can't we get her away from Jolene, Dad? Isn't there something we can do?" Zack's face revealed his deep concern for his sister.

"I've tried, Zack, but nothing convinces the judge."

"Why does he care more about Jolene than Rachel?"

"That, my son, is the fifty million dollar question. If only we could ask him. Write your phone conversation down in our diary, and then give it to me. You know where we keep it. Thanks for telling me about this." He patted Zack's knee and filed this new worry away in his mind.

Later Shawn picked up the diary and scanned what Zack had written. He noticed Laynie had written an entry before Zack's:

Jolene calling more and more. When I picked up Rachel last time at Nan's, Jolene's friend, I saw Jolene had a beer in her hand. She tried to hide it under the table where she was sitting. Rachel told me she sleeps with her mother and Will. She still loses weight while with her mother, and then gains when with us.

Shawn picked up a pen and added that Jolene and Will had gotten married sometime that month. Jolene was being secretive about it, which baffled him. She hadn't changed her last name either. She was writing bad checks all over Wagontown, and he was embarrassed about the reputation she was attaching to his name.

Laynie came into the room with tears in her eyes. "What's wrong?" he asked, closing the diary.

"I just came back from Mama Mae's. They don't think Pa Luke will last the night. The whole family is there now."

"Should we go?"

The phone was ringing. "It may be too late."

Laynie was right. It was Pa and Mama's son, Jake, sobbing with the terrible news that Pa Luke had just died.

*****

Shawn had expected to see Jolene at the services for Pa Luke. She had known him even before he had, and Pa and Mama Mae were always kind to her, no matter how much her behavior provoked them. But she never came, and he knew Mama Mae was hurt.

Mama Mae's health deteriorated after Pa's death. She seemed to shrink each time he visited her in the rambling farmhouse. Shawn could see a bottomless loneliness in her eyes. When he talked to her it seemed as though she was not really hearing him, but listening for a voice she would never hear again.

That's why he was not at all surprised when Jake called him to say Mama Mae had died in her sleep. This time Jolene came to the viewing before the funeral with Tina helping her walk to the casket like she was an invalid. Jolene gripped the side of the casket, threw her head back and wailed dramatically before the entire church. Shawn dropped his head, embarrassed by the dramatic display.

He took Laynie and the children to Mama Mae's home where the family gathered to console each other and to eat the increasing casseroles and cakes brought by neighbors and friends. Shawn remembered the look of desolation in Mama Mae's eyes his last visit and smiled sadly. Shawn knew Pa Luke and she were together again. This bittersweet thought would help him deal with her sudden death.

Laynie came over and took his hand. She searched his face for a clue to his thoughts, then, as if she knew, put her arms around him and held him close. Life was hard. Life was unfair. But he thanked God he had Laynie. He could travel this unpredictable journey called life as long as he had her to take his hand and walk beside him.

Part Two
RACHEL

ONE

She just could not hold them up any longer. Her kindergarten teacher's image drifted away into a fog as her eyelids fluttered shut. Rachel buried her head in her arms atop her desk and was immediately asleep. Their fighting lasted a long time last night, keeping her awake. She could never close her eyes until she was sure her mother was safe beside her, sleeping.

Last night Will stormed into the living room where she and her mom had stretched out on the mattress her mother hauled in there so they could watch TV until they fell asleep. Just like a pajama party every night, her mom said. Like two girlfriends. But Will didn't like the idea one little bit and he let them know that.

"You're my wife and you'll sleep with me!" he'd bellowed. Her mother had jumped off the mattress and put her face very close to Will's, screaming that she'd sleep where she pleased. Will's face turned the color of her mom's lipstick when he shoved her to the floor. Her mother yelled back at him and Rachel couldn't remember all the bad words they called each other. Back and forth they screamed, like Rachel on her swing at recess. Back and forth, Will, then her mother, taking turns at shouting ugly things.

Rachel whimpered as she wrestled with those images in her restless sleep. Someone was gently shaking her arm. She opened her eyes and was looking into her teacher's face. The classroom was empty.

"My, my," soothed Mrs. Antone as she stroked Rachel's hair. "This is the third time this week you've fallen asleep. Thank goodness it's Friday. You need to catch up over the weekend."

Rachel raised her head and smiled. Mrs. Antone was so nice. And pretty. Rachel loved her teacher's long brown hair. She always wore colorful ribbons or bows in it.

"Where'd everybody go?" she yawned.

"They're out playing, but they'll be in soon. I wanted to wake you before we get back to work. Rachel, is everything okay at home?" Mrs. Antone's eyebrows looked like two little brown rainbows over her hazel eyes.

167

"Everything's fine."

"Are you sure, Baby? You've been so tired lately. I really should call your mother and let her know."

"Don't do that, Miz Antone. You know my mom. She'd freak." Her teacher nodded. "It's just that, well, we're going to be moving soon, into this really awesome house. So we've been busy packing and stuff."

She hadn't really lied to her teacher. They were moving soon. But they hadn't started packing yet. It was okay to lie sometimes. Her mother said so, if it was necessary. Rachel figured this to be one of those necessary times.

"All right, Rachel. We'll give it a little more time. But if you continue to fall asleep in class, I'll have to talk to your mother. I'm worried about you."

Rachel watched her walk away as the other children rushed in the door from the playground. *I have to try harder to stay awake. I have to keep my eyes open.* She pinched her arm to make sure she was wide-awake. Hard enough to last through the rest of the day. But the thing that really helped was when her mother came to eat lunch with her, she brought her the usual fast food with a cola. Thank goodness for the cola. Already Rachel knew the power of caffeine and how it would help her stay awake the rest of the afternoon. In fact, now it was very hard to sit and listen to Mrs. Antone. She just couldn't keep her feet still. And she had so much to tell everyone. Mrs. Antone frowned at her many times that afternoon, and before the day was over, Rachel's name was on the board three times for bad behavior.

When she got home her mother said they were going out for pizza for supper. Again. *I'm going to turn into a pizza. Mom will look in bed some morning, and there I'll be, all red and round with pepperoni all over.* She didn't know why, but Rachel felt like being mean to her mom. Maybe it's because she never cooked supper for her the way she heard other little girls say their mothers did. Like Mandy saying her mom made her barbecued ribs, her favorite, for dinner last night. Kaylee said her mom made fried chicken with real mashed potatoes and gravy. That made Rachel's mouth water. But she would have another night of eating pizza while kids yelled and threw plastic balls as they waded through them and begged their moms for more tokens to play games at Playtime Pizza.

At least afterward they picked up Dara. When her mother told them to behave as they ran into the house, Rachel retorted, "Shut up!" Dara giggled. When Rachel stuck her tongue out at her mom, Dara roared. Rachel laughed wickedly as she pulled Dara into her bedroom and yanked her up onto her bed.

"Jump, Dara. Let's jump!"

"On the bed? Can we?"

"Sure. I never sleep on it anyway." Rachel's laughter was loud and harsh as she plunged her feet, shoes and all, into the mattress. Dara copied, and they were soon jumping in glorious rhythm. Rachel was just getting the knack of turning while she jumped, when she saw Dara freeze on the bed, her mouth opened and closed in silence.

Will stood in the doorway, a belt wrapped once around his right hand.

"You know y'all aren't to jump on the bed. Don't you!"

"Yes, Daddy." Dara sounded like a baby.

"Looks like you two need a lesson in listening."

"No, Daddy. We won't do it ever again. We promise. Don't we, Rachel?" A tear slid down Dara's frightened face.

"It's my bed, Will. And you're not my dad." That felt really good to say. But it frightened Rachel to see how dark Will's face got.

"You little…" he grabbed Rachel's arm. "You stay right there, Dara. Don't you dare move!"

"I won't, Daddy!" Dara backed into a corner and hugged herself as she stared at her father. Will jerked Rachel toward him, then pushed her across the bed. She heard the snap about the same time she felt the pain burn across her upper back legs.

"Run!" yelled Dara as she threw her arms around Will's legs. "Run, Rachel!"

She rolled off the bed and clawed at the floor to get out of her room. She had to find her mother. Rachel dared to look back and saw Dara sprawled across the bed as Will's belt smacked against her bare skin. Dara howled in pain after each slap of the belt. Rachel almost threw up her pizza, but forced herself to yell for her mother.

"Mommy, make Will stop! He's hitting Dara with the belt."

"Where?" Her mother dropped her cigarette into the beer can on the coffee table. She jumped up and followed Rachel.

"In my room," Rachel screamed. "We were jumping on the bed and, oh, just come with me and make him stop!" Rachel pulled hard on her mother's arm and guided into her room. Dara lay curled up, sobbing into the pillow she clutched against her face.

"Stop it, Will!" Jolene stood between Dara and Will.

He turned and stared at them with cold gray eyes. He laughed, one short time, and nodded. "I think she's learned her lesson." Will strolled out of the room, jingling his car keys. "I have to go out for a while." They heard the front door slam.

"Dara was so brave, Mommy. She stopped Will from hitting me more."

Jolene grabbed her shoulders. "He hit *you* with the belt?" Rachel nodded. "Let me see." Her mother slid her jeans down to her ankles, said a bunch of bad words as she examined her red marks across her legs. "Welts, too," she fumed. "Let me see you, Dara."

The sobbing child slowly straightened out her legs while she lay on her stomach. Rachel held her breath. Unfortunately, she was wearing a dress. Dara's legs were already black and blue. Jolene left the room and returned with ice cubes in a baggie. She gently laid them on Dara's bruises.

"It's cold, Miss Jolene."

"I know, Dara, but we have to do it. It won't look so bad if we do this. You just stay here and leave this on you while I take care of Rachel." Dara hugged the pillow as they left the room. Her mother led her to the kitchen, where she put ice on her legs.

"This will never happen again, Rachel, I promise."

"Are we going to leave Will, Mommy?"

"Maybe. But don't tell anyone about this. The judge will take you from me if you tell. Far, far away from me. I would never ever, ever see you again. Ever. Do you understand?"

Rachel's heart pounded in her chest. "I won't tell, Mommy."

"And where would I be without my best friend?" She smiled and stroked Rachel's hair. "Mommy would be so, so lost without her baby girl. That would make me cry buckets of tears. That would break my heart. I need you so much, Baby." The thought of her mother suffering because Rachel had done something to cause their separation was more than she could bear. She threw her arms around her mother and sobbed into her shoulder.

"Now, let's put Dara to bed, and you and I will watch videos till the sun comes up. Okay?" Her mother smiled at her, bobbing her head side to side while she talked.

"Can Dara watch, too?"

Her mother frowned. "Nah, it'll just be us." She tickled Rachel, then went back the hall and helped Dara go to bed.

"Aren't you going to read to me 'n Dara, Mommy?" Rachel watched her mother slide a video into the VCR and flop down onto the mattress.

"No, Baby, not tonight. I'm too tired. Go into the kitchen and get me my cigarettes and a beer, purty please with two scoops of ice cream and whipped cream and a big fat cherry on top." Rachel giggled and skipped out to the kitchen. The beer was easy to find in the refrigerator, because it was the only thing in it, except for the left over pizza and soda. She grabbed a cola for herself. She wanted to stay awake with her mom.

As Rachel picked up the cigarettes, she felt guilty about poor Dara back in the bedroom, all by herself. Especially after she helped her escape Will's belt. That was pretty brave. She sat next to her mom and popped open her soda, licking the erupting bubbles off the top. They tickled her tongue.

"Shouldn't we let Dara watch, too, Mommy? After all, she did keep Will from hitting me with the belt again."

Her mother's hands were squeezing Rachel's shoulders as she turned her. Her face was only inches from Rachel's, and it was red as a stoplight. "I told you to never talk about that again, young lady." Rachel was dismayed at her mother's burst of anger. "The judge will take you away and I'll never see you again. I told you that, didn't I?"

171

Rachel squeezed her soda can. "I'm sorry. I won't say it any more. It's just that Dara-"

"Dara's fine where she is. She's probably already asleep. Now, do you want to ruin our little party, or have a good time?" Her mother popped opened her beer can, and drank from it. Rachel watched her tilt back her head and swallow, swallow, swallow. She put the can on the floor and smiled at her.

"Sorry I'm jumpy, Baby. It's just that Lieutenant Dan there gets on my nerves." She pointed to a picture of Will and Dara on the end table. When she saluted him, Rachel giggled. Her mother could be so funny, especially when she had her beer.

"What will we do when Will, I mean Lieutenant Dan, comes home?"

Her mother looked surprised at the question as she lit her cigarette. Rachel guessed she hadn't thought that far ahead. She knew her mom never thought much about what might happen next.

"He'll probably come back stoned," her mother laughed. "Don't worry about it, Baby. Let's watch the movie."

Rachel tried to concentrate, but she kept seeing Will's face when he saw them jumping on the bed. She kept hearing that awful crack of the belt as it smacked her legs and poor Dara's bare skin. She wanted to talk to her mother about it, how scared she was feeling, but that was forbidden. She was supposed to pretend it didn't happen.

Rachel made many trips to the kitchen that night to get her mom beer. She was getting sleepy and remembered Mrs. Antone said she was supposed to catch up on her sleep this weekend. "Mom, is this the weekend?" Her mother looked at her with funny eyes. They looked lazy and the middles were dark.

"Last time I checked, it was." Her mom laughed wildly. Rachel wasn't sure what was so funny, but she laughed, too.

"What time is it?"

Her mother squinted at her watch. "Two o'clock. Why all the questions? You think you're Lieutenant Dan or what?"

Rachel wasn't sure if her mother was angry or not. She sounded like she was talking with some slushy in her mouth. "No, Mom. I'm kind of sleepy." She laid her head on her pillow and slid under the blanket her mom had draped over them. As she drifted to sleep, Rachel thought about her bed at her dad's house and how nice it was to know it was there, the same bed - *her* good ol' bed - waiting for her every time she went over. This past week she and her mother had slept at her Aunt Tanya's, and twice at Tina's house. Her mom had been mad at Will (again) and so she took Rachel and left the house several times. It was good to fall asleep without a fight raging in the background, but they never got to bed early when they stayed somewhere else, either.

Rachel wished she was at her dad's, but immediately felt guilty about her wish. Her mom needed her. She had to make sure Will didn't hurt her mother. She got things for her mom when she was too tired, like her beer. And she was her mother's best friend. That role lay heavy on her small shoulders.

She closed her eyes and hoped her mom would remember she said they might leave Will. Rachel hoped she meant it. She was so tired of the fighting...

TWO

Rachel was feeling all mixed up about so many things. She loved school but was afraid to go because she might fall asleep. Or that something would happen to her mom while she was there. She wanted to go out for soccer but was bored with it after a few practices, so she quit. Her mom was going to be a Camp Out leader, bought all the books and everything. That made Rachel happy. But the meetings never happened, not even one. That made Rachel mad. And now her mom was telling her Will and she were going to buy a big beautiful house on Pueblo Avenue.

"But you said we would leave Will!" she yelled at her mother.

"Well, things will be better after we move into this house. It's so big and *expensive*. It's even nicer than Aunt Tanya's."

"How will a new house make things better?" Rachel hated it when her mother acted like she was stupid.

"It will, you'll see. Now come with me to the convenience store so we can buy Grandad a birthday present."

"What am I giving him?"

"Cigarettes."

"I'd rather give him something else."

Jolene opened the car door for Rachel and motioned for her to get in. "Like what?"

"I don't know."

"See? He's hard to buy for. He'll like cigarettes."

So that evening they were at Grandad's house, all three of them, acting like everything was fine. Grandad brought out the beer and whiskey. It was getting too smoky for Rachel in the living room, with Will, Grandad, and her mom all blowing their smoke into the air like the whales she saw on public television. Only that wasn't smoke. It didn't burn anybody's eyes or make you cough.

Rachel was glad her mother's much younger sister Penny arrived. They went in the dining room and talked. She wanted so badly to tell Penny about the BELT, but remembered her mother's

174

admonishments. So they talked about school and dance lessons and videos. Rachel did tell Penny her mom and Will had given away her cat, Puffball.

"Why?" asked Penny. "Didn't they know you loved her?"

"We're moving into a big house and they don't want a cat there."

"Oh," said her aunt, frowning. "Do you know where Puffball is?"

"My mom said she gave her to a nice family."

"Well, that's good." Penny stopped talking and cocked her head toward the living room. Voices were getting louder and louder. Rachel put her hands over her ears.

"There they go again. Even here."

"What do you mean, Sweetie?"

"Fighting. Mom and Will."

"Sounds like Grandad, too."

Rachel put her hands down and listened. "Grandad's yelling at my mom. Mommy says he's mean when he drinks." Penny just looked at her and shook her head slowly. "Let's go see if we can stop it, Penny."

"I don't think we should, Rachel. Let's just stay here."

"I have to see if my mom's all right."

Rachel walked into the living room and saw her Grandad slam his fist on the coffee table. Her mother was yelling, stabbing her finger at Grandad. Will would shout, then fold his arms across his chest, and then shout some more. All of their faces looked like red beets. Rachel saw Grandad pour more whiskey into his glass, even while he was yelling.

"You both need to go to AA," hollered Will.

"And you need to go to CA, Mister," retorted Rachel's mother.

Suddenly, Grandad laughed. "What the blazes is CA?"

"Cocaine!" screamed Jolene.

Rachel ran into the kitchen. Her ears hurt and her heart threatened to pound right out of her chest. Things would get worse, you could count on that. She had to do something. She spied

Grandad's broom in the corner, grabbed it and swept the floor viciously. Rachel neared an opened cupboard door by the oven where she saw Grandad's whiskey bottles.

Her small hands picked one up and opened it. She tilted it sideways and dumped it into the sink. It smelled like Grandad's kisses on her cheek. The empty bottle was tossed into the wastebasket as she reached in for another bottle. The amber liquid gurgled out into the sink and down the drain. She heard the clink of glass when the bottle landed in the trashcan. Five bottles had been emptied when the door opened. Rachel sighed with relief as she saw Penny come over to her.

"What are you doing, Sweetie?" Not nearly as tall as her mother, the petite young woman stroked her hair, just like Mrs. Antone.

"I, I... I don't know." Rachel threw her arms around her aunt and sobbed. Her head was spinning with all her troubles. She just wanted to be like Mandy or Kaylee and only have to worry about what to wear to school or what color to paint the princess' dress in her coloring book. Being her mother's best friend was so *hard*.

"It's okay, Sweetie. How 'bout I take you home and put you to bed tonight?"

Rachel squeezed her neck. Penny would read to her and tuck her in. Plain and simple, just like that. "Yes, Penny. Please. Tell Mommy."

So amid the screaming, bad words, and red faces, Penny and Rachel escaped to her house. It was a refuge for now, but only until her mother and Will returned. *How will they ever get home together in the same car?*

It was nice being with Penny. Rachel wished she didn't live so far away, so she could see her more often.

"Are you still sleeping on the floor?" asked her aunt as they walked into the living room.

"Yeah."

"Maybe after you move, you'll have your own room. That would be better for you, Rachel."

"I like to sleep with my mom." Now the next thing she was ashamed to tell Penny. It was what kept her from sleeping overnight at her friend's house. After she had her pajamas on, she looked into Penny's eyes and whispered, "I have to wear special pants."

"What?"

"I, well, you know, I still wet the bed."

"Oh. Okay. Do you know where they are?" Rachel was glad she didn't make fun of her while she quickly slid on a pair and hopped onto the mattress. "Are you sure you don't want to try your bed, Rachel?"

"No. This is where me and my mom sleep." So Penny read to Rachel and pulled the blanket up to her chin and kissed her. "Turn on the TV, Penny."

"No, Sweetie. You look tired. I'll sit here and read while you fall asleep."

"Can I have a soda?"

"No, I don't think you should drink anything else tonight. Now, close your eyes and go to sleep."

Rachel thought about telling Penny that her mom lets her drink soda any time she wants and watch TV until she falls asleep. She was a lucky girl, sometimes. Her mom let her do most anything she wanted. She thought about telling Penny these things, but much needed sleep dimmed her thoughts and snuffed them out until another day.

THREE

Bedtime at her dad's was so different than at home. For one thing, Rachel slept in a bunk bed, with Joey on the top. Laynie said it wouldn't be long until Hayley's crib would be in there, too. That would be so cool.

They went to bed at the same time every night- no TV, no sodas. Rachel usually complained about going to bed so early, but it never changed her dad's or Laynie's minds. The good part was there was always a bedtime story or two, and Laynie sang to them. Joey and Rachel took turns asking her to sing three or four songs each, unless they were running a little late. If there was only time for one song, Joey would pick "Yellow Bird," and Rachel would choose "It's Mice That Make the World Go 'Round." She loved that song. Mice made the world go 'round, cats made mice go 'round, dogs made cats, boys the dogs, girls the boys, love the girls, and finally God made the love go 'round. Nice things to think about before bedtime. Cats, dogs, God. No blowout fights, no ugly words. Then they would say prayers with Daddy. She and Joey almost knew the whole Lord's Prayer.

They talked and thought about different things at her dad's. Like God. Rachel liked Sunday School. Church was a little boring, especially when the preacher guy talked and talked, but they sang cool songs in kids' choir.

Once Laynie asked her what she wanted to be when she grew up. Rachel couldn't answer, because she never thought about that before. "I'll just find a man to take care of me," she answered. That made Laynie frown.

"Rachel, women can take care of themselves, if they choose. Look at our neighbor, Sara. She has her own house, a car, and a good job." Rachel nodded as she considered this new idea.

"Jane and your Aunt Tanya have jobs. Aunt Penny, too."

"But my mom says she needs a man to take care of her."

"Not everyone feels that way."

"I'll probably be like my mom." Laynie sat on the sofa next to her.

178

"Try to imagine *something*. If you could be anything in the world, what would it be?"

"I don't know." But it occupied her thoughts all that day. Could she possibly grow up to *be* something cool?

Rachel was often mixed up about her feelings for Laynie. When she would first come over, she pretended Laynie wasn't there. Rachel was mad she had married her dad, because her mom wished *she* were still married to him. Her mom said she still loved him, and if Laynie wasn't there, they could all be a family again.

But as the weekends wore on, Rachel found herself confiding to Laynie about things that bothered her. She even told her about the BELT. Laynie was so upset; Rachel thought she was going to cry. Especially when she told the part about Dara's black and blue legs and how she went to sleep by herself that night.

She would never forget the talk they had about love. Rachel had been calling Laynie "Mom." It felt okay, and besides, all the other kids did, too. And she didn't want to mix up Hayley. But then her mother said she should call her "Laynie," that *she* was her mother, that Rachel was *her* daughter.

Rachel told Laynie what her mom said. "That's too bad, Rachel," she said. "Your mother doesn't understand love. She thinks it's like a pie."

"A pie!" Rachel giggled. "What do you mean?"

"You cut a pie into pieces and give them away, one by one, to different people. When the last piece is taken, there is no more pie. Some people think love is like that."

"Isn't it?"

"Oh, no, Rachel. Love is like a flame on a candle. If I light a candle with that flame, what happens to the flame?"

"It's still there."

"Right! It stays the same. It doesn't get any smaller. And I can light another and another candle from the first, why I could light a whole room full of candles, and the first flame would still be there. That's love, Rachel. You can give it to this person and that person, and another one, and it never burns out. It doesn't change the flame of the other candles. It doesn't change the love you have for someone else. Understand?"

Rachel saw in her mind a whole circle of candles burning brightly all because of one candle in the center. "I see it, Laynie. I mean, Mom. I have enough of love in me for my mom, you, dad, and everybody."

"And if you love me, that doesn't mean you love your mom any less."

"And I won't run out of love for her."

"That's absolutely right. But that's what I think she's afraid of. So, if you want, you can call me 'Mom' here, and 'Laynie' over there, if it is easier for you. Okay?"

Sometimes Rachel was so glad she talked to this mom. But sometimes it backfired.

She came home from school, happy that she had stayed awake the entire day. Will wasn't home yet, so maybe her mom and she could go away before he came home. Her mom was on the phone again. Rachel watched her punch out her cigarette on a saucer as she yelled into the phone.

"That did NOT happen, Shawn." She turned to her and put her face so close to Rachel's their noses almost touched. "You were NOT hit with the belt, young lady. You quit your lying!" Her mom's breath was gross. But her pinched up face was worse. Rachel pulled away and ran to her room.

She *had* been hit by the belt. Her stomach hurt. It felt like she had eaten pins or a cactus or something. *Mom said I was lying. And with Dad listening.* Her door swooshed open and her mother flopped down on the bed beside her.

"Rachel, when you tell them things like that, it makes big trouble for me. They just want to take you from me. Besides, it's none of their business. Laynie's not your mother, and your daddy left me the day you were born."

Rachel's heart froze. Would he do that? Why wouldn't he stay to be with her? Daddies are supposed to stay with their little girls, aren't they? Rachel never knew these things for sure.

"And now, if it weren't for that perfect, *darling* Laynie, your daddy would be with me."

"But you're with Will, Mommy."

"Heavens to Betsy, girl, I'd leave him in a second to go back to your dad."

"Is that why you call him all the time?"

"Yes, Baby. I miss him. I love him so much." She was crying. Rachel didn't know what to do. She patted her mother's arm and watched her tears roll down her face.

"And Laynie's trying to take you from me, to turn you against me. She's jealous of how much you love me, and only me."

Rachel thought about explaining love, and pies, and candles, but she was afraid she might get it mixed up and make things worse. It was so simple when Laynie said it, but now, here with her mother, Rachel's mind was muddled. Besides, she didn't think her mom would get it. "Would you like me to get you a beer, Mommy?"

Her mom wiped her face on the back of her hand. "Sure, Baby. Mommy needs her beer. You get it while I make a phone call."

When Rachel handed the beer can to her, her mom was saying to someone on the phone, "We'll leave now. See you in a few minutes."

"Where are we going, Mommy?"

"To the Corn Crib to eat. Stanley is going to buy us supper. Let's go before Lieutenant Dan gets home. I'll write him a note and tell him we went to Tina's or shopping, or something."

"Is Stanley your boyfriend again, Mommy?"

"Kind of. Not really. Now, hurry."

Rachel wasn't sure she could eat. Her tummy still ached and her legs felt like clay. But her mom was counting on her. And best friends do what their moms need them to do.

FOUR

Sometimes she hated Joey. She didn't know why, she just did. It gave her great pleasure to watch his face turn from all silly smiles to frowns when she ignored him. Rachel could change him just like that. Other times she was so relieved to be with him. She could tell him anything. Even though he was a little younger, he listened like a big brother, and she usually liked the undivided attention he gave her.

But today he kept asking her if she wanted to ride a bike or go to their fort in the brush in the back pasture. Rachel didn't want to do either. She pretended she couldn't hear or see him, and it was driving Joey crazy. It was so funny. His voice was getting louder and louder as he tried to get her to answer him. She put her nose in the air and lifted her eyebrows, indifferent to his pleas to talk to him. She didn't know why, but it felt good she had power over Joey like this.

He stomped off in frustration, his voice quivering as he asked, "Why are you like this?" and she saw the tear that escaped out of the corner of his eye. He quickly wiped it away before he thought anyone saw. But she had, and it made her smile.

Rachel watched Joey run into the barn. *Cry baby.* When she turned, she bumped right into Laynie.

"What are you doing, young lady?" *Busted.*

"Nothing." She turned her back to shut her out, too, but Laynie wasn't going to let her get away with it.

"Turn around and look at me when I talk to you. Why did you treat Joey like that?"

Rachel met Laynie's dark eyes. She looked right into them "What?"

"You know what. You're being mean to him. He was so happy to see you, and all you could do was ignore him. We talked about this before, Rachel. I told you I'm not going to let you do this to him."

Boy, she sure had talked about it! A gigantic lecture about how family members treat each other with respect and get along and blah, blah, blah. Now she was calling Joey. Great. Just great.

He reluctantly approached them, his eyes carefully avoiding Rachel's. "Come here, Joey. Your sister wants to apologize to you for being so rude."

"I don't want to talk to her."

"Joey." He looked at his mother as she whispered his name and smiled at him. He hung his head and waited. Rachel stared off to the side, pretending she didn't know what she was supposed to do next.

"Rachel, apologize to Joey." Rachel could tell by Laynie's voice she had pushed things as far as she could without getting into major trouble.

"Sorry."

"You have to look at whom you're apologizing, Rachel. And you have to say why you're sorry."

This mom was so picky about everything. Rachel looked at Joey, who raised his brown eyes to meet hers. "I'm sorry, Joey, for ignoring you."

"Okay." Joey always forgave her. Rachel had a battle within her. She didn't want to let go of the control she had over him moments ago. But the sadness in his eyes made her feel badly.

"Now give him a hug, Rachel. Without rolling your eyes."

Laynie and her big ideas. She was always pushing this stuff. But as her arms went around Joey's waist and his around her shoulders, she had to admit it was hard to be mean or mad when you were getting and giving a hug.

"Now, say 'I love you' to each other."

"Mom!" they both protested.

"I mean it," she said sternly. "You have to look at each other's eyes, and say it. Without smiling."

"I love you," they giggled as they looked at each other.

"Hey, I said no smiling!" scolded Laynie as she grabbed and tickled them. "Now, doesn't that feel much better in here?" she asked

Rachel as she pointed to her chest. "Go play and come in when I call you for supper."

"Come on, Rach, let's go to our secret fort. I got some boards Dad said we could use. You can sit on the green chair."

Wow, Joey sure could be nice. The green chair was his and usually no one sat in it but him. He found it, he painted it, and he owned it. Rachel found a wooden crate and painted it blue for her seat.

Yeah, she was glad she had apologized. Rachel looked at Joey's happy face as he motioned her to sit down. She didn't know why she had been mean to him. Sometimes she got stuck in those awful feelings. This was better. Lighter inside. Her tummy didn't hurt and it felt as though her heart was smiling.

She would be nice to Joey the rest of the weekend. Joey was her best friend. And her brother. Rachel remembered what this mom had said over and over about family. Respect and love each other. You are to each other what no one else can be. Brothers and sisters, sons and daughters, mom and dad. Such a special thing.

Family. It was all so clear over here. If only her mom could understand.

FIVE

What her mother said and what her mother did were usually entirely different things. Last night they had another fight. Will left the house to go for a walk, to cool off, he had said. While he was gone, her mother grabbed Rachel and out the door they went to Tina's house where they had stayed all night. Her mother promised they would leave Will.

The next day Rachel stayed with her mom, even though it was Friday and she was supposed to be in school. Her mom was going to go back and get some things out of the house while Will was at work. Too afraid to go alone, she made Rachel accompany her.

Rachel was so terrified on the ride back to the house she almost threw up. Her mother told her to watch the drive for Will's car while she threw some clothes into a bag. Rachel whimpered like a puppy as her eyes scanned the street. "Please don't let him come home, please don't him come home," she whispered over and over. Her thumb rubbed furiously over her finger. She felt like she would burst out of her skin. "Hurry, Mom, *please hurry!*"

They made it back to Tina's safely. Friday evening Tina and her mom were drinking lots of beer and laughing. Rachel was sitting at their feet watching *The Lion King* when the phone rang.

"It's Will," said Tina. "He's sorry and wants to talk to you." *Say 'no', Mom.*

"No." Her mom finished the beer she had in her hand.

"He said he has a 'please forgive me present' for you." *Don't talk to him, Mom. Please. I'll get you a present.*

"This better be good." Rachel watched her mom talk on the phone. She looked so tall and thin, standing there in a baggy blouse and jeans that slid past her hips. She waited for her to tell Will they would not be back.

"All right," she was saying. "We'll be there in an hour. Yes, I can drive." She hung up and sat next to Rachel. "We need to get our things together, Baby. We're going back."

"But, Mom, you said we wouldn't!"

"He's really sorry, Rachel. Besides, some of it was my fault. I shouldn't call your dad so much, I know it makes Will mad."

"What did he get you, Mom?" Rachel was standing now. She felt like her chest would explode. What present could Will have possibly bought that would make her mother go back?

"A motorcycle jacket. Just like I always wanted. I've said all my life, I wanted to own one before I was forty, and Will made my dream come true."

"The jacket today, the bike tomorrow," giggled Tina.

"Can you picture Will on one, Tina?" They laughed and laughed wildly. "That will have to be another man," predicted Jolene.

So the next morning Rachel and her mother were sleeping on the floor in their own living room until noon. Later, Rachel chewed on a doughnut as she watched her mom walk around the kitchen, wearing her new black leather jacket. Will came out and she handed him a cup of coffee and kissed his cheek. Rachel stared at them. Her tummy was quiet but her heart felt cold.

She had just finished dressing when her mother came into her room. "Guess what, Baby. Today is Will's birthday. Let's have a party for him tonight."

A birthday party? Rachel looked at her teeth in the dresser mirror. She didn't want to talk about Will and pretend nothing happened. "Mom, when can I go to the dentist? You missed my last three appointments. My teeth need cleaned with that special stuff. It feels so good afterward. Your teeth feel slippery when you run your tongue over them afterward. I like that."

"Rachel, pay attention, this is important. And I need my girlfriend's help." Jolene stroked her hair. "Will you help Mommy?" Rachel looked into her mom's green eyes. They looked funny already. Her poor mother.

"Okay."

"Good. We have lots of running around to do. First, I have to call and invite people. Then we have to get a cake, munchies, soda, beer, and decorations."

But her mother's mood had soured by the time they were leaving the house. "Hardly anyone's coming. Jane, Tanya, Nan, even Will's friends, all have plans. So they say."

"Why would they lie, Mommy?" Rachel sat in the front seat as they went to pick up a cake. She was never allowed to sit up front at her dad's. But with her mom, she didn't even have to buckle up if she didn't want. "Maybe they really did have plans. We didn't let them know about the party soon enough."

"Well, phooey with them. Tina and a couple of others are coming. Penny's still in town. We'll have fun. We'll surprise Will."

Rachel and her mom returned to quickly clean up the house. They threw lots of things in closets and drawers and under beds. They sprayed with Lysol and air freshener. They hung streamers and balloons and put out candles and flowers.

Tina arrived first that evening with a friend named Cassie. Rachel was excited to see Penny come with her boyfriend, Camden.

The food and beer were passed around and consumed. Rachel noticed her mother never ate, only drank beer. Penny handed Rachel a soda. "Where's Will?" she asked her mom. "Shouldn't he be here soon?"

"He better be," said Jolene. Her words sounded weird again. Mushy. She sighed. "I need to make a call." Rachel thought she would be trying to get a hold of Will, to tell him to hurry home, but when she sat at her mother's feet, she realized it was her dad on the phone. "Yeah, we're having a birthday party for him, and he's supposed to be here by now," she said. "Remember when I had a surprise party for you, Shawn? I loved you so much, then. I still do. You know that. I sure screwed up, didn't I?"

"Can I talk to Daddy?"

"Okay, but only a minute. I'll go wait for Will." She almost gave the phone to her, but put it back to her ear. "Here's our little girl, Shawn. She wants to talk to her daddy. The only one she'll ever have. I love you, Shawn." She finally handed the phone to her.

"Hey, Sugar, how are you?" Hearing her dad's voice made Rachel smile.

"Fine, Daddy. We're having a party for Will."

"Are you doing all right, Rachel?" He sounded worried.

"Yeah. What's Joey doing?"

"He and Maddie just went to bed."

"Already? What time is it?"

"It's after eight. We have Sunday School tomorrow. Next week's Easter Sunday and you'll be with us. Mom's almost finished with your dress. She finished Maddie's yesterday."

"Cool. Where's Zack?"

"He's at Preston's house. He'll be home in about an hour."

"Oh." She would have liked to talk to one of the kids. "Is Mom with Hayley?"

"Yeah, she's in rocking her to sleep." At least she knew where everyone was. "Joey is making big plans to paint Easter eggs," her dad continued. "We'll get you Thursday after school. You can paint lots of eggs and Zack will hide them, like last year, remember?"

"Yeah." Laughter was spilling out of the living room so loudly, she could hardly hear her dad. "I have to go."

Rachel hung up and ran to the living room. Her mother was on the coffee table, wearing her witch costume from Halloween, dancing to the loud music while holding a beer in her hand.

"This will liven this party up!" Jolene squealed. Everyone was laughing at her. She did look silly. Rachel laughed. And laughed and laughed, her wild and crazy laugh. It kept coming out of her and she couldn't stop it. This was fun. Her mom was funny. Everyone was having lots of fun. More fun than Maddie and Joey had just sleeping in bed, or Zack at Preston's house. She could eat all the chips and candy she wanted. She could drink all the soda she wanted. She could stay up as late as she wanted.

Her ribs hurt from laughing so hard. Rachel suddenly stopped and walked into her bedroom. Her shoulders drooped from fatigue. She closed the door to shut out the noise and the smoke, and stared at her bed. Her dad said she was big enough to sleep in it herself. Walking over to the edge of it, Rachel fell onto the soft comforter. She was so, so tired. Closing her eyes, she sang quietly, "It's mice, it's mice, it's mice that make the world go 'round..."

Her eyes had just closed when the door burst open. "Young lady, what are you doing in here? Will's here, and we're about to light the candles!" Her mother shook her arm. Rachel blinked at her, trying to remember if she had to get up for school already. She heard the music.

Nope, no school. The party.

"Come on, Rachel. I need you to help sing 'Happy Birthday' to Will." Rachel wanted to tell her mom to go away and let her sleep. Her eyes just would not stay open.

"Let's go, partner. Get up!" Her mother pulled her to her feet. Cola. She would have to drink another cola to stay awake. Her mom guided her out to the living room where everyone was waiting. While Jolene lit the candles, Rachel drank long gulps from her soda can.

Will was all smiles. He beamed while they sang to him then blew out all the candles.

"What was your wish, Will?" yelled Tina.

"That's my secret," he said and winked at Jolene. She smiled at him. Her mother had taken off the costume and was wearing the motorcycle jacket and jeans. Rachel didn't think she had a blouse on underneath it. She sure hoped her mother remembered that.

Penny announced one o'clock was late enough for her, and she and Camden left the party. Soon the others followed, and after Tina, the last one out the door left, Rachel heard the clock in the living room chime two times.

She couldn't find her mom, so Rachel dragged the mattress out from behind the sofa and threw sheets and blankets on it. She flopped down and closed her eyes on her pillow. She was thinking maybe she should try her bed again when Will and her mother came into the room and stood behind the sofa. They were kissing.

"Why don't you change your last name to Starks," Will said softly to Jolene, as he rubbed her back.

"Because of Rachel. I want us to have the same last name." They walked toward their bedroom, talking softly, as Rachel's eyes closed and she fell asleep. She was wakened by her mother's loud voice, yelling at Will to shut up.

"You're my wife. You're supposed to sleep with *me*." Will wasn't yelling back. He sounded hurt, not mad this time.

"I'll sleep where I please, mister." Then her mother called Will all kinds of bad things. On and on, she screamed at him. Rachel buried her head under the pillow and actually fell asleep.

But not for long. Her mother was making her sit up.

"Wake *up*, Rachel, for Pete's sake. We're getting out of here." Rachel rubbed her eyes and squinted at her mom. Will walked by, with his baseball cap on.

"Don't. I'll go. For God's sake, Jolene, she's just a kid, let her sleep." Will looked so sad. Rachel actually felt sorry for him.

"Go!" her mother screamed. He hurried out the front door.

"Good riddance," spit her mother. "He thinks just because he gave me this jacket I should do everything he wants."

"I could sleep in my bed, Mom. I think I'm big enough."

Jolene reached up and turned off the light on the end table. "Now what would happen if you had a bad dream, Baby? Who would be there to chase it away for you?"

Rachel opened her mouth to answer, but Jolene continued. "Close your angel eyes and go to sleep. You have sweet dreams. Mommy's so tired, so very, very tired..." Rachel heard her mother's light snores as she instantly fell asleep.

Sweet dreams? Those were kind of hard to have after all this fighting, all that yelling and screaming and ugly words. Not the things sweet dreams are made of.

Rachel squeezed her eyes shut and sang out into the darkness, "It's mice, it's mice, it's mice that make the world go 'round..."

SIX

Rachel was always feeling mixed up. She was happy her daddy was coming for her today. It would be a "long stretch," he said, because of Easter vacation. They would color and hide eggs, she and Joey would work on their fort, and the church would be filled with lilies on Sunday. Beautiful, graceful lilies that looked like white trumpets in flowerpots. They would bring one home to put on Mama Mae and Pa Luke's gravesite. Then they would feast on ham. Ham so yummy, it made her mouth water just thinking about it. Where was Daddy?

She looked out the window but didn't see his truck yet. Rachel hoped he could find the big, new house okay. She saw her mom outside, trying to start the lawn mower. Will told her if she wasn't going to keep the inside of their new home clean, then she was responsible for the yard. Rachel didn't know how her mother would ever budge that big mower.

She was also worried about leaving her mom alone. Four days was a long time to be without her. Her mom would be lonely. And if she and Will got into a bad fight...

He's here! Her dad's truck pulled slowly into the drive and Rachel heard the wail of the lawn mower stop as her mom walked over to the truck. She ran outside.

"Hi, Daddy, I'm ready!" He was standing beside his truck, arms outstretched, waiting for her. She flung herself into them. A moving van rumbled by.

"Slow down, you stupid truck!" yelled her mom. "This is a residential area!" She turned to them. "I don't know why they go so fast on this street. You'd think they'd know better, all these fancy homes and all." Her face was red, and her hair stuck to her neck.

Her daddy said nothing. "Did Mom boil the eggs?" she asked him.

"Yup. They're in the fridge, waiting for kids to color them. Ready?" A red sports car raced past them.

191

"Slow down, you stupid car!" hollered her mom. "Where are the cops when you need them?" She walked over to Rachel and kissed her. *Beer breath blah!* she thought. *Maybe it's from last night.* "I'll see you Monday night, Baby. Color an egg for me."

"I will, Mommy. I'll call you."

"Okay." Her mom's bottom lip pushed out as she pouted. "I'll miss my baby." She turned and started the mower. Rachel was mixed up again. She looked at her dad, all smiles as he buckled her in his truck. She watched her mom struggling with the mower, looking alone and sad.

"Bye, Mom," she yelled.

"She can't hear you, Sugar," said her dad. "The mower's too loud. But she heard you the first time. She'll be okay."

But Rachel wasn't so sure.

*****

Rachel had tried to call her mom last night, but without success. She was worried about her. "May I call my mom?" Rachel asked Laynie.

"Okay."

The phone rang and rang. The answering machine picked up. "Mommy, it's me, Rachel. Where are you?" She hung up and ran to her dad.

"She's not there! Where could she be?" Rachel searched her mind, trying to remember what her mom had said. Did she say she was going away? Who would be with her? Who would watch out for Will?

"Rachel, it's okay. Your mom goes away a lot when you're not there."

"No, she doesn't! She waits to do things with me." Her dad picked her up and carried her into the bedroom. He didn't seem worried at all. She could be hurt."

"She has friends. She's probably shopping or something."

"No, she isn't."

Laynie came in, frowning. "Isn't Tina her friend? And Nan?" She rubbed Rachel's arm as she spoke. It felt nice.

"Nan doesn't come over any more."

"But Tina does. I'll bet they're eating out somewhere," she soothed.

"You know your mom doesn't cook," said her dad. "I think Mom's right. She's probably eating with Tina, or maybe she and Will went out on a date."

It was true that her mom didn't cook. And Will had been nice to her mom lately. He said he was sure things would be different in the new house. But to be sure, Rachel called again. *No answer.*

"Where's Daddy?" she asked Laynie, who was changing Hayley's diaper.

"He's out getting eggs. Why don't you go help him?"

"My mom's not home yet. I called."

"Don't worry, Rachel. She's might be sleeping. Didn't you tell me you two like to sleep till lunch on Saturdays?"

"Can I call after lunch?"

"Sure. Now, go outside and find Joey or help Dad. You need to do something fun." The third try after lunch, Rachel finally got her mother on the phone.

"Where have you been?" she demanded. *Finally.*

"Right here, Rachel. You know I don't go anywhere without you."

"Why didn't you answer the phone last night?"

"I was mowing the yard, Silly."

"After dark?"

"I went to bed early. I miss you. Do you miss me?"

"The phone would have made you wake up. It always does."

"I was really tired, Baby. Did Laynie get your dress finished?"

"Yes."

"Do you like it? Bet it's not as nice as Aunt Tanya's." Rachel didn't know how to answer her. "I'll have a ton of Easter candy for you when you get home. And a stuffed Easter bunny. It's so cute. I got it last night."

"Where?"

"At the mall. Tina and I went."

"I thought you said you were home."

"I was. Except for getting you a present. Do you miss me, Rachel?"

Rachel was mad... and yet relieved. Her mom was okay.

"Say it. For your poor lonely mom."

"I miss you. I have to go."

"Is Laynie making you get off the phone?"

"I have to go help Dad get eggs."

"Poor baby. Try to have fun. I'll see you Monday night." Rachel was glad they were done talking. When she ran outside, Joey and Maddie were hollering for her to hurry up and help wash the dog in the big tub on the patio.

She forgot about the eggs and raced back inside to get some towels. She was going to have some *fun!* Then the phone rang again; Layne told her it was her mom.

"Mom! I forgot to tell you I'm going to do cool things today, like make pretty Easter eggs."

"I miss you, Baby."

"You already told me that last time."

"I haven't done anything because you're my best friend and you're not here to play with me. I haven't gone anywhere, done anything, because you're not with me." Rachel was speechless. She was starting to feel badly about all the fun she was going to have. "I miss you, Baby."

Laynie was looking at her, frowning. "Rachel, the kids are waiting for you outside," she said loudly. "If that's your mom, tell her you'll call later."

Rachel was never so glad to have Laynie tell her what to do. "I have to go, Mom. Call you later."

"Tell me you miss me."

"Miss you. Bye." She quickly put down the phone.

"Scoot!" laughed Laynie. "Go be a kid."

They washed the dog, colored eggs on the picnic table, and ate supper. It was a good day, a day off from being her mother's best friend, a day to just be a kid.

The next day Rachel and Maddie giggled as they looked at themselves in the mirror before going to church. Their look-alike dresses swirled about their legs as they turned and twirled. They arrived at church, barely on time. The sanctuary was beautiful and smelled how Rachel thought heaven would smell. The graceful lilies held their majestic blooms above white silk bows and white foil pots. They were a drastic contrast against the deep red carpet and cushioned pews. It was breath taking.

As Rachel sat on the pew next to her dad, she remembered what she had told her Sunday School teacher the last time she was here. They were talking about prayer, and Rachel asked if they could pray for her mom. She wanted her mom to stop drinking beer and stop smoking. She whispered that in Miss Granger's ear. She had smiled at Rachel and they went off together and prayed.

Suddenly, she wondered what her mother was doing. Where did she sleep last night? Who would help her remember where she put things today? She kept hearing her mother's voice on the phone, sounding sad and lonely. Rachel buried her face in her hands and burst into tears. Her dad swept her onto his lap and held her.

"What's wrong?" he whispered.

"I don't know." She had been so happy. Now this. All mixed up again. Rachel sobbed into her dad's shoulder. He rose and carried her outside the church. He sat on the bench under a tree and held her, patting her back, telling her it was all right. They stayed there until the rest of the family came out. Zack carried their lily and walked up to Rachel.

"Hey, Rach, you want to be the one to put this on Mama Mae and Pa Luke's grave?" He held the flower in front of her face, his brown eyes wide, waiting for her answer.

"Me 'n Maddie degreed. You can do it," added Joey.

"Oh, you degreed, did you?" laughed her dad. "I think that's a great idea."

It made Rachel smile. The whole family picked her to do something special. They would go to the cemetery first, then home to dinner, Laynie said. It was good not making all the decisions. It was good just being the little girl.

They hunted for the eggs Zack and Preston (who had come over) hid all over the yard. Laynie came out twice to announce that her mom had called. Rachel was glad she had told her she would call her back later. She was having too much fun to talk on the phone.

When she was hunting eggs for the contest to find the most, her mother called again so she asked Laynie to tell her mom to call after supper. Rachel, Maddie, and Joey raced around the yard, finding eggs until they were called in to eat.

A loud knock at the door interrupted their supper. Shawn opened it, and there was Will, telling him Jolene wanted to speak to him. All eyes around the table focused on the front door. He said she also wanted to see Rachel.

Her dad motioned for her to come along. "Hurry back for vassert," said Joey. "Mom made a pineapple upside over cake for you." Rachel nodded grimly at him and followed her dad.

"Preston and I will shoot some basketball while we wait," said Zack as they went out the back door. Rachel had that churning feeling in her stomach as she clutched her dad's hand and went out the front door. Her mother had never come before without phoning first.

A car door was open and her mother's legs were hanging out. When Rachel and her dad got close enough, Jolene grabbed her and clung to her. Rachel was startled by her mother's behavior, and struggled to get away. She reached toward her dad, but her mother held her firmly.

Rachel saw her dad open his mouth to speak, but her mom cut him off, screaming. "I couldn't even talk to my own daughter on the phone today. I called and called, but that conniving Laynie cut me off. She's dangerous, Shawn. You better watch her."

Rachel saw Zack and Preston stop playing basketball at the end of the driveway and stare at them. Zack dropped his head in shame. Poor Zack.

"Mommy, don't be so loud."

But her mother ignored her. Her dad told her to go inside, but her mom only held her tighter and yelled and yelled. Rachel shut her eyes, waiting for it to be over. But it was getting worse. Each time her dad tried to get Rachel from her mom, her mother's screams got louder and wilder. Rachel peeked at Zack and Preston, who stood watching the scene.

"All right, Jolene. You're not supposed to be drinking by the court's order, and it's obvious you have been doing a lot of that today," her dad said. Her mom looked at Will, who had his eyebrows way high up on his forehead. Rachel thought he looked surprised. But her mom looked madder than ever.

"I thought we were friends, Shawn, but now this!"

"What are you talking about?" asked her dad.

"Laynie. She's the cause of all this. You better watch her, mister. She's trying to take everything from me."

Her dad grabbed Rachel. "Go inside, I'll be in soon." Rachel looked at Will, who nodded. Avoiding her mother's eyes, she raced into the house and asked Laynie if she and Joey could go into their room alone.

"Sure, Sweetie. If you need me or anyone else, we're here." Rachel took Joey's hand and took him into the bedroom. As soon as the door shut, she burst into tears.

"This is just like at home, Joey. My mom yells and screams at Will. He gets so sad and mad. He doesn't know what to do, so he goes for a walk or gets really mean. Sometimes my mom takes me out of the house after I'm asleep and we stay at a friend's house."

Joey was crying, too. "What are you going to do, Rachel?"

"I don't know. It's awful."

"I think you should tell Mom or Dad."

"You think so?" *It would be nice to tell them.*

"I'll get Mom, okay?" He came back with Laynie, who sat on the floor with them and listened to what Rachel had told Joey.

"Oh, Rachel, I'm so sorry. That is not the way little girls are supposed to live. Look, Dad will be in soon, he's talking to Zack and Preston. Your mom and Will left. You know your mom, she'll calm down later." On and on Laynie talked, in a soft, soothing voice, until

Rachel felt better. After her dad came and talked some more, Rachel was exhausted. She cuddled her pillow and asked Laynie to sing to her. Joey handed her old stuffed puppy to her, sat with her on the floor, and listened to Rachel's song. The last thing Rachel saw was Joey's smile. The last thing she felt was her Dad's kiss on her cheek. The last thing she heard was Laynie's singing. Sleep, welcomed, needed sleep, brought her peace.

SEVEN

Rachel waited for her dad to take her back that Monday night. She stood outside their bedroom door, listening to Laynie and him talk. "I'll go along, Shawn. Zack can stay here with the others if we take Hayley."

"Did you call Jane?" her dad asked.

"Yeah, I told her what happened. She seemed indifferent to the whole thing."

Indifferent? That must be a good thing. Jane says she'll always look out for me.

"That whole family…let's go," her dad said. "I want to get this over with." Rachel ran outside.

Her mom was waiting for them when they arrived at Pueblo Avenue. "You're late, mister," she yelled at Shawn. "I'll have the judge look into this."

"Jolene, stop fighting in front of Rachel," her dad warned.

Her mom turned her back to him and yelled at Rachel, the whole way into the house. "You're late, young lady. You and your dad are late. I was waiting for you, wasting my time, and you're late."

"Sorry, Mommy. We didn't think we were late."

The following Wednesday Rachel watched for her dad's return. The last couple days had not been good. Several times she thought Will was going to explode because her mom would not quit yelling and yelling at him. She even yelled at Rachel, said she wasn't supposed to talk to Laynie any more. *She* was trying to take Rachel away from her, and Rachel didn't have to listen to *her*.

Rachel caught her mom dialing and hanging up on Laynie a few times. She'd peek around the corner and listen as her mom slammed down the phone and mutter, "Take that, Laynie!" and called Laynie a whole string of bad words.

Her dad's truck pulled into the drive. He came to the door and her mom told Rachel to sit on the sofa and be quiet. She opened the door. Rachel couldn't hear her dad, but she heard her mother.

"Get your butt off my property. Wait in your truck for her."

Her mom slammed the door and leaned against it. "Don't look at me like that, young lady. He won't leave without you. He used to want to be with *me*. We were a family. Then *she* came along and ruined everything. We'd be together again, if it wasn't for *her*."

"Daddy's waiting, Mommy. If you love him, why are you so mean to him?"

Her mother sobbed into her hands. "I don't know, Baby. I don't know. It's all Laynie's fault. I wish we were married, your daddy and me."

Rachel was mixed up again. She wanted to run from her mother, but she was afraid to leave her like this, crying. Rachel liked Laynie, but her mom said Laynie was the reason they weren't a family any more. She should hate Laynie, like her mom did.

"You're right, Rachel. Go. I shouldn't keep your daddy waiting. Lord knows he has enough on his mind taking care of all *her* kids." Rachel climbed off the sofa and kissed her mother goodbye. She ran out the door before she could change her mind.

When she first arrived at her dad's, Rachel was mean to Laynie. She knew it hurt her, she could see it on her face, but she had to do it for her mother. After all, Laynie was causing all this trouble between her dad and mom.

As if he could read her mind, her dad took her into his and Laynie's bedroom and sat on his desk chair. He motioned for Rachel to sit on his knee.

"I see you're giving Mom a hard time. Want to tell me why?" Rachel shrugged. "I bet I know," he continued, "you don't like it when she makes special food for you when you're here." Rachel cocked her head at her dad and laughed.

"No, Silly."

"You don't like her singing to you at night."

"No, Daddy, that's dumb."

"I'll tell you what's dumb. You like how Mom treats you, but you treat her mean. That's dumb, isn't it, Rachel?"

She dropped her head. "Yes,"

"Why do you do that to her?"

"I don't know." Her mom would be so mad if she told.

"I think your mom is saying unkind things about Mom. Things that aren't true. Don't believe them." That was hard to do when her mom told them to Rachel every day. And Laynie *was* with her dad. Shouldn't her mom be with him?

"I want to tell you something, Sugar. Some day, when you are older, I'll tell you everything you want to know about what happened between your mom and me. I think you need to know two things right now. Your mother was the one who didn't want to be married to me any longer. She left one day and took you from me. I wanted the both of you to come back home, but she didn't want to."

Her mother left him? No, that can't be right.

"You were very little. I missed you so much and tried to get you back, Rachel. I never wanted to live away from you."

She looked at her dad's blue eyes, and Rachel knew he was telling her the truth. But she had been so used to the other stories her mom had told her, she wasn't sure she could really believe this.

"One more thing. After your mom and I got a divorce, she changed her mind and said she wanted us to be together again. But I knew she would only change her mind again, and get tired of being with me. I couldn't go through that again. Your mom always changes her mind. She gets tired of things. It's the way she is, Rachel. She goes back and forth between being mad at me and then saying she wants to be with me. You know that, I know you do."

Rachel sighed.

"Two years later I fell in love with Laynie. I'll love her forever, Rachel. She's my wife and will always be. And even if I had never met Laynie or anyone else, I would never, ever go back with your mom. Do you understand that?"

Rachel slowly nodded. She thought she did. But it didn't fit in with all she'd been told by her mom. She needed time to think.

"So, I'd like to see you be nicer to Mom. She loves you a lot, and you know that."

Her dad was right. Even though Laynie had lots of rules they *had* to follow (and how she rebelled against them!) Rachel was sure of Laynie's love. Not a best friend's love, but a mother's. She would try to forget the things her mom had said, at least for now.

The rest of the evening went by so quickly, before she knew it, Laynie was taking her home. Dad said he had to get to the paper work that was piling up. Mom put Hayley in her car seat and buckled Rachel along side of her in the middle seat of the mini van. She never let her sit in the front seat. She said it was not safe for younger kids. Fussy! Rachel only grumbled about that a little. It was fun to play with her little sister, anyway. She was worried, though, how things would go between this mom and her mom.

When they arrived Will was out in the yard and came over while Laynie helped Rachel get out of the van. Rachel ran into the house while they talked, hoping to divert her mother's attention until Laynie left.

"Hi, Baby." Her mom was waiting for her in the living room. "I want you to do something for me. I want you to go tell Laynie I'm sorry I lost my temper at Daddy Sunday. Can you do that for me?"

Rachel was relieved. "Sure, Mom. Be right back."

Her feet flew over the grass to Laynie and Will. "Mom!" she burst out. "My mom said she's sorry she lost her temper at Daddy."

Laynie knelt down and placed her hand on Rachel's shoulders. "Your mother needs to tell Daddy that herself, not use you for her messenger, Rachel." Laynie stood and stared at Will. Somehow, she was sure Laynie meant Will to hear that. Anyway, she wasn't about to tell her mother that. Laynie left and the rest of the evening was one without yelling or fighting.

Almost every day when Rachel came home from school, her mother was on the phone, sometimes with someone she would not say, but usually with her dad. She got off right before Will came home. He'd ask her why he couldn't get through when he'd try to call her, and her mom said she was talking to Tina or Nan or Penny. She'd wink at Rachel, who winked back. *This is cool to trick Lieutenant Dan.*

Her mom had hidden some money in her car. She had told Rachel it was for clothing and toys, so she shouldn't tell Will because he said Rachel already had plenty of those. One Saturday, her mom came out of the bedroom, opening and slamming drawers, mumbling, "Where is it?" She looked in cupboards and under chair cushions.

"What are you looking for, Mom?" asked Rachel.

"My stash of money. I can't find it!" Her voice rose as she answered.

"Don't you remember? You hid it in the glove department. In the car."

Her mother laughed like she had just told the world's funniest joke. "That's so cute, Rachel! Glove department! What would I ever do without you? I sure need you to keep me straight."

Then the papers came again that always made her mom explode. They were watching TV in the living room when a man knocked at the door and handed them to her mom. She walked round and round the room, calling her dad and Laynie all the bad words Rachel had ever heard. Her mom sat next to her and showed Rachel the papers, as if she could read them.

"See? I told you we couldn't trust them. They're trying to take you away from me! Did you know about this?"

"No, Mommy. Honest."

"Of course you didn't. You would have told me. That's what girlfriends do. Oh, Rachel, what are we going to do?"

When Will came home, her mother shoved the papers in his face and demanded to know what *he* was going to do about this. He looked at Rachel. It was a weird look. A shiver went down her back.

"*I'm* going to take charge of things from now on, Jolene. I'll get a good lawyer, pay for anything you need to keep her, but you have to listen to me. *I'm* in charge."

Rachel couldn't believe her mother was agreeing. To *all* of it. Didn't she hear him? *He's in charge. Lieutenant Dan!*

Her extra time with her dad was taken away again. Rachel missed her family and was afraid Hayley would learn to do something while she was away. Laynie assured Rachel that the baby seemed to wait for Rachel to be there to do things for the first time.

The hearing was right before school let out. Her dad and Laynie didn't say much about it, only that they were trying to make her safe. But her mom, well, that was a different story. She went on and on about the big plan her dad and Laynie had to destroy her life. "They're out to get me," her mom said. "They know you're fine where you're at. They hate me, especially *her.* Your daddy would never do this to me on his own. This is *her* scheming, Rachel, to take away everything I have. First, she took your daddy. Now you. As if all those kids over there weren't enough, *she* has to have you. I'll do anything to win this. *Anything!"* Rachel's head hurt and her insides were on fire while her mother raged on and on. "That's why I have to let Will think he's running the show. I need him, Baby, to help me keep you."

"But the judge wouldn't take me from you, would he?"

"Oh, yes, Rachel. That's why you must never tell anyone about the belt. If it's brought up, you must say you made a mistake."

"But, Mom, that's lying."

Her mom squatted down and looked straight into her eyes. "Sometimes it's okay to lie. I only lie when I have to, Rachel, when it's important. We'll do anything to stay together, right? I don't know what I would do without you. How could I stand it if you weren't here? That judge might not let me ever see you again!"

Rachel panicked. Her mother was so infused in her young life, she couldn't imagine functioning without her. And who would look after her mom? Who would help her escape Will?

"Mom, why are we staying with Will?"

"Going to court is very expensive. We will be paying lots and lots of money to keep you. We'll get a good lawyer... lots and lots of money... but you don't have to worry about that." When her mom left her to get another beer, Rachel felt as though the only thing she could do was worry.

The next few days her mom didn't eat much. But she didn't drink beer quite so often and didn't smoke around Rachel. After a while, her mom wasn't drinking any beer. They even went to church a few times. Her mom said she was going to help teach Bible School, and she and Will went to a Bible study every week. She stopped calling her dad and didn't meet Stanley at the Corn Crib any more.

About the only thing she and Will fought about now was her sleeping with Rachel on the floor. Her mother yelled that she had given up everything else, and she would not that. She said Will should leave her alone, she was so nervous about the hearing. Then she would turn to Rachel and say, "I don't know how your father could do this to me."

The day of the hearing, Rachel came home from school to find her mother exuberant. "We won, Baby!" she proclaimed, hugging her. "That judge knows a child belongs to her mother." Rachel was glad her mother was happy. Now maybe she wouldn't be so nervous all the time.

"I'm going to call your dad tomorrow and tell him this has to stop, Rachel. It's too hard on me, all this court stuff. Then, after a while, I'll forgive him. He probably does it just to satisfy *her* anyway." She leaned down to Rachel and whispered, "But she'll never take you from me. You're *my* daughter. Don't forget that, Baby." She winked and walked into the kitchen.

"I feel like celebrating! Want a soda, Rachel?" Her mom handed her a cola. Rachel's stomach twisted when she saw her mom take a beer out for herself. She flipped back the tab and swallowed, swallowed, swallowed. Rachel wished she could make the beer stay in the can, because too much beer meant trouble.

"Will won't be home until late tonight. He's working overtime. Let's order pizza and eat it in the living room."

Rachel gasped. "Will doesn't let us to eat or drink in there! He said he wants to keep that room nice."

"Oh, Lieutenant Dan can cock-a-doodle-doo all he wants." Her mom picked up the phone and called in their order. Smiling, she said, "Want to have some real fun? Let's play telephone games."

Her mom got out another beer, and punched out numbers on the phone. "Hello?" she said in what her mom said was her sexy voice. "Is your refrigerator running? Well, you better catch it!" She slammed down the phone and laughed hysterically. Rachel joined her laughter, sipping her soda every time her mom drank her beer.

They made several more prank calls, then suddenly her mom grew bored with the game.

"Where is that pizza guy? Think he'll be cute?"

"Maybe." Rachel didn't know what to say. They sat in silence, her mother drinking until the doorbell rang. Her mom was disappointed when a young woman delivered the pizza. She pushed her lower lip out and pouted as she slid a video into the VCR.

"Want to watch <u>The Monster Monkey</u>?"

"It's kind of scary, Mommy. Laynie says it's not a good movie for kids."

"I'll bet she does. Miss Dr. Spock." Her mom laughed. "Well, we'll watch anything we want. Soon school will be out. We can watch something every night, and sleep till noon."

"Sounds cool, Mom." At that moment, somehow her mother knocked her beer to the floor. Rachel screamed.

"Oh, no, Mom! We better get it cleaned up! Will is going to be so mad!" They pushed towels into the puddle. Rachel got out a bucket and her mother filled it with soapy water. They scrubbed and blotted until it was barely visible where the beer had fallen.

"I think it will be fine after it dries," said her mom. "I never should have married him, Rachel."

"You mean Will?"

"Yeah. He's so different from the way he used to be. I'm going to call your Daddy. I miss him. You watch for Will." Rachel stood by the window as she listened to her mother talk to her dad, scared Will would somehow appear in the room and see what all was going on. *This is no good. Mom is talking so loud, Will could hear her if he's outside sneaking around, trying to catch us doing something wrong.*

"Shawn, I want us to get back to normal. I hope you have this court stuff all out of your system, I can't take any more of it. It makes me so nervous, so very, very nervous... Let me know when you want Rachel to come over... Rachel told me you opened up a sub and pizza shop. She said you decorated it like a train station. How cute. How's it doing? Good. Glad to hear it. Are you alone tonight? Poor baby. I could come to you … Bet you miss your nursery. Shame you had to close it. Guess it was because of all those kids. Hope the sub shop does better.

"I can't call you as often as before. Will thinks I just like to talk to you. You know, he's jealous… Maybe I'll bring Rachel for lunch sometime and try your pizza. She talks about your subs all the time. She misses you. So do I... I really screwed up, Shawn. I never should have left you. Guess you love Laynie...Wish you could love me just a little. Guess you love her a lot, don't you... that's good. You're Rachel's father and I love you. We'll always be together because of that. I'll always love you. Can you love me just a little-you have to go? Okay. I love you, Shawn. You take care. I love you."

Her mother thoughtfully put down the phone.

"I know he would have told me he loves me if he didn't have to go. He was about to say it. I could *feel* it." Her mom looked so sad. Rachel wished Laynie would go away. Just look at her mother, all alone and sad because she wanted to be with her dad. Her mom and dad together. It would be so nice...

Lights flashed through the mini blinds and raced across the living room wall.

"He's here! Mom, Will is home! Look at this mess in the living room!" Rachel's hands shook as she shoved napkins and paper plates under the sofa. Her mom gathered up empty cans and raced to the living room. They almost had everything cleaned up when the front door opened. Will's smile faded as he scanned the room. The pizza box was still on the coffee table, and a soda and beer can lay on the floor under it.

"What's going on here?" Rachel ran to her mother's side.

"We just had a little celebration, Will. You know, the hearing and all. I called you. Remember?"

"That's why I came home early. To celebrate! I brought something for the party!" He patted his pocket and winked at Jolene.

"You're not mad?" Rachel was shocked.

"No, little darlin'. Now, come here and kiss Daddy hello."

Daddy? No way. She only had one of those. Her mother said it often enough. "The only father you'll ever have." But she didn't want to make Will mad. She walked over and hugged him quickly. Her mother slid her arms around Will's neck and kissed him for a very long time.

"What'd you bring me, Baby?" Rachel could barely hear her mother talking to him.

Will patted his pocket again and grinned. "Rachel, watch the rest of your movie. Have a treat. We'll have ours in here." Her mom tilted her head back and laughed.

They walked down the hall, and Rachel heard their door close. From time to time she heard them laughing, but Rachel tried to concentrate on her movie. *What were they doing?*

She had fallen asleep and was dreaming her favorite dream about her house. It was a big house with a swimming pool with pink water. She could hear her favorite song being sung by her dad. They all lived there: her mom, her dad, Laynie, and all the kids. Sometimes Dara. Never Will. And they all got along.

Except this time someone was fighting. It was her mother. Rachel heard her voice. It was so real it woke her up.

It really was her mother, and she was screaming nasty words at Will. Rachel rubbed her eyes and tiptoed back the hall. They were in the bathroom.

"Leave me alone, Will!"

"I want to know who all you called today. Answer me!"

"If you were half the man you think you are, I wouldn't have to call anybody. You couldn't keep up with your other wife either."

"You whore!" he yelled. He pushed her mom against the wall. Her mom slid to the floor and looked at her elbow. It was bleeding. She shrieked, cursing at Will. He strode across the floor and grabbed her face. "You whore. You cheap whore. You're never happy with anything you have. I know you're seeing someone."

Her mother said a lot of ugly things back to Will. The look on his face scared Rachel. Suddenly, his hand was raised and he slapped her mother's mouth. She dropped her head and whimpered. Will turned and stomped out the door. Rachel hid behind the big plant in the hall, and watched him go into their bedroom and slam the door.

Rachel crawled over to her mother and touched her leg. "Mommy, are you all right?" she whispered, glancing over her shoulder to see if Will was coming back. Her heart thumped so loudly she couldn't hear her mom's answer.

"Can you get up, Mommy?" Her mother lifted her head and nodded. Rachel saw that her lower lip was puffy. "Are you hurt?"

Her mom smiled. "Nothing that a beer can't fix. Help me up, Baby. Help me to the kitchen." Rachel tugged on her arm until she was on her feet. Her mother's eyes looked like they were made of ice. Once she was on her feet, she paced around the bathroom, like the tiger Rachel had once seen at the zoo. Then it seemed as though she remembered something. She hurried through the door to the kitchen.

Rachel followed her and watched her put a beer can against her lip. Then she opened it and swallowed, swallowed, swallowed. Rachel had that funny feeling as if she had seen this all before.

Her mom lit a cigarette and blew out smoke. "Where is he?"

"In the bedroom."

"Let's go. Get in the car." She grabbed a second beer and her purse, and hurried Rachel out to the car.

"Where are we going, Mom?" They got in and headed toward the highway. "Mommy?"

"I don't know, I don't know where to go."

"Tina's?"

"She's out of town." They were swerving. Every time a car approached them, her mother drove so slowly Rachel felt she could walk faster than that.

"Nan?"

"I don't want her to know about this. Not Jane, not Penny, or Aunt Tanya."

"Maybe Daddy would let us stay."

"Think so? I mean, just for the night?" Rachel was ecstatic her mother was even considering it. Maybe they would all get together, just like in her dream.

"I think he would. He and Laynie wouldn't want us out on the road like this."

"That would be so nice, wouldn't it, Baby? We could be one big family. Zack and Maddie and Joey are so cute."

"So is Hayley, Mom. You should see her."

"I could stay in your room. We're used to sleeping together on the floor." They laughed. Rachel was starting to feel happy. "You really think they wouldn't mind, Rachel?"

209

"I'm sure. They wouldn't want us to be with Will when he's so mad. It's like the belt. Laynie says it's not normal. Kids shouldn't have to live like that."

Rachel's body jerked front as her mother's foot stomped on the brake. "What's wrong, Mommy? Why are we turning around?"

"We're going back."

"Home?" Rachel's heart raced.

"We have to. Don't worry, Will's probably asleep in our room. We'll be really, really quiet and sneak in." Her mother's eyelids drooped. She was getting harder and harder to understand.

"Why can't we go to Daddy's? Isn't that a good idea?" Rachel had to convince her. If they went back and Will was awake…

"We'll be okay! I know what I'm doing." But when they got back in their drive and her mother fell over nothing but her own feet, and Rachel knew she was not okay. She helped her mom up and steadied her while she made several tries to unlock the door. Rachel was deathly afraid Will would hear them.

Finally the door swung open, and her mother stumbled inside. The house was quiet.

"I'm going to be sick, Rachel. Help me get to the bathroom." They scampered to the toilet, where her mother leaned over and vomited. Rachel ran out to the mattress in the living room and buried her head into her pillow.

Why did she come back here? Will's going to hear her. What treat did they eat in their bedroom? I hope she doesn't die.

Rachel ran over to the bathroom door. "Are you all right, Mommy?" she called. She heard water running in the sink. Her mother came out, blotting her face with a towel. Her hair was stringy and matted against her head. Dark circles surrounded her eyes and her skin was gray. She was shaking.

"I'm okay now. Guess I ate too much pizza." Rachel was trying to remember if she had eaten any at all. That seemed like such a long time ago. "Did I wake up Will?"

Rachel shook her head. Now her stomach felt like it was eating itself. She wondered what her mom would do next

"Let's go to sleep. Come on, Rachel."

"I can't."

"Well, you better listen and not cause me any trouble. I can't take any more. You want to wake him up?" Rachel stared at her. "Be nice and quiet and come with me. Nothing's going to happen."

She followed her mom and lay down on the floor. After the lights were out, she thought about her bed at her dad's, and how quiet it was there after bedtime. No one ever wakes her up to run away because they're fighting. Staying there would have been a great idea.

She rolled over to tell her mom, but she was already asleep. Rachel heard a noise. She squeezed her eyes shut and prayed to God. Laynie said she asks God to protect Rachel. Maybe she had better do the same, especially if the noise was Will. The bathroom door closed and the light leaked under the door. It's rays stretched toward her, like they were trying to grab her. Rachel snuggled closer to her mom.

The bathroom door opened as the light blinked out. Rachel closed her eyes and pretended to sleep. *Don't cry, don't cry, don't cry!* She tried to slow down her breathing as she heard Will shuffle over to them.

"I know you're up to something, Jolene. Things have to improve around here. We'll talk tomorrow. Tomorrow things will be different. Big changes. I'll be keeping better tabs on you. And Rachel. You both need to know you can't cross the line any more."

He hunched down and turned her mother's face toward him. "Sleep it off, Jolene. You two aren't getting away with anything any more." He walked away. Rachel heard the bedroom door close. She peeked at her sleeping mother.

Rachel wondered how long it would take Will to fall asleep. She counted to one hundred, then sat up and looked toward the phone. She counted to seventy-five just to be sure. Rachel tiptoed over and picked up the phone. Her dad had explained about calling if things got too scary for her. He had told her to call them, or if she were in danger to call 911. This was danger.

Which number? Rachel remembered what her mother had said about the BELT. If the judge knew about this, he would definitely take her away from her mom. Forever.

She put the phone down and crept back to her mother's side. *Why did she ever come back here? She promised we would leave him.* But Rachel knew most her mother's promises weren't kept. She tried, but something always happened that prevented her mother from keeping them.

Rachel pulled the sheet up to her mother's chin, the way Laynie did hers when she tucked her in at night. Laynie wasn't so bad. She made Rachel feel safe. She just wished she didn't keep her mom from being with her dad.

She was so mixed up. Her tummy burned. Closing her eyes and pulling her own sheet up over her head, Rachel guessed her mom was right. Bad pizza.

EIGHT

School was out. Rachel and her mom had gotten in the routine of staying up late and sleeping until noon. Sometimes they didn't get dressed until supper.

They couldn't use the phone during the day. Will took a piece of the phone so her mom couldn't call anyone. Rachel noticed when her dad came to pick her up, Will would go out with her instead of her mom. Sometimes Will even locked the front door after them, like he was afraid to let her dad see her mom. How stupid.

Once they had a fight and Will said her mom let Rachel go to her dad's so much because she tried to "think of ways to see Shawn."

For now, Will was away and her dad was coming. Her mom had forgotten to give her lunch again, and Rachel was really hungry because they never ate breakfast any more. She found a piece of bread and some chips, and ate them with her soda. The clock in the living room chimed three times. They were still in their pajamas.

"Rachel, get me another beer, please, Baby." Her mother was watching her favorite soap. Rachel was glad her dad was coming early. The doorbell rang.

"He's here!" Rachel pulled her mother's arm. "Come on, Mom. I have to go."

"You go out yourself. Tell your dad I'll call him later from Tina's since you're staying an extra day."

"Will you be all right, Mommy?"

"I'll go to Tina's." The bell rang again. "Hurry!"

Rachel ran to the door and flew into her dad's arms. "Daddy!" He looked surprised as he carried her to the truck. While buckling her in he kissed her cheek and said, "Don't you think it's about time you got dressed?"

She had forgotten she was wearing her long green nightgown. Rachel giggled. "Should I go back and change?"

"No. Let's just get going." He seemed in a hurry. "I was going to stop at the grocery store on the way home, but I can't with you wearing that. For Pete's sake, Rachel, you're wearing a winter nightgown. Aren't you hot?"

"No. It's cold in our house. Mommy and I are always cold."

"Sugar, you're going to be six this summer. I know that's still young, but you're going to have to make sure about certain things, like being dressed when I pick you up. What if everyone was along and we were going to go to the museum or something?"

He sounded a little mad. He'd really be upset if he knew she didn't even have any underwear on. She had thrown out her sleep pants and forgotten to put on a pair of panties.

"I'm sorry."

"It's not your fault. Jolene should make sure you're ready. The day's half over and you're like this." He pressed his lips together like he was afraid more words would get out. "How are you? Is everything okay?"

"Fine." When they got to the house, she ran into her room and got dressed. Laynie let her nibble on grapes and cheese while she waited for supper. Joey and Maddie came in from the back pasture, surrounding her with smiles and chatter.

As always, Rachel had so much trouble falling asleep the first night or two at her dad's. They went to bed too early for her, so she would just lie in her bed and watch the clock hands go round and round until they would both point to the top. Laynie would make her get up before lunch, even if she was tired. She said it would be so Rachel would be ready for bed at a normal time. Laynie could be so bossy.

But when she and Laynie were alone, Rachel wanted to talk and tell her all about the bad stuff. Even though she was bossy and picky about so many things, Rachel felt safe with Laynie. She talked about the way things should be. Normal. Good for kids. Laynie talked about those things all the time.

Rachel told her about the fights, but only some of them. Laynie said it was no way for grownups to behave, especially around children. They talked again about what to do if she got scared. Laynie asked her about the neighbors: Did Rachel know them; could she run to them if the fights were really bad, things like that.

Her mother called twice. The first time she said she missed her best friend. The second time she told Rachel they would get a puppy when she came home. Will said it was okay.

But when it was time to go home, Rachel didn't want to go. She didn't want to face the screaming and bad words and waking up at night and driving around. She didn't want to leave Joey and the rest of her family here. She missed her dad when she was away from him. When she told Laynie she wished she didn't have to go, Laynie said she wished that, too. It seemed like she wanted to say more, but she just handed her Hayley so she could kiss her goodbye.

On the way home her dad told her he was worried about her. Was there anything she wanted to tell him? She looked at his anxious blue eyes and wished she could tell him all of it. But her mom would be mad. And that judge…

"I'm fine. Don't I come over soon to stay a long time?"

"Yeah, for a month. That will be great, won't it?"

Rachel nodded. Except for one thing. She would do a lot of worrying about her mother while she was away for so long.

Her dad grasped her hand as they pulled into the drive. "Here we are. I love you, Sugar. See you in a few days. Call me."

Rachel slammed the truck door shut and turned around to go inside. She almost ran into Will. He waved at her dad as he drove away. She strained her neck to watch the truck go out of sight. Will pulled on her arm. "Wait!" she yelled at Will. She could yell, too. Rachel waved frantically at her father, watching him drive away until he was just a small dot on the street.

"Where's my mom?" She yanked her arm out of Will's grip and marched inside.

"She's inside. Scrubbing the molding around the kitchen floor. Finally."

Rachel didn't know what molding was, but at least Will hadn't hurt her while she was away.

NINE

They were going to Big Plains Festival. Rachel begged to bring Dara, but for some reason they planned it for a weekend she was at her mom's. No kids were going, just her mom and Will. *Great. Just great.*

They were going to stay at a motel with a pool. But you had plenty of chances to get wet during the rides, so the pool was no big deal. Her mom seemed happy with the trip, but Rachel suspected she was faking it. She drank beer all the way there. By the time they checked into their motel, her mother was wobbly and talking slushy.

They finally got to the park and Rachel went on some of the rides with Will. She begged her mom to go with her, but she said they made her sick or she was too scared. Rachel wished Joey were along.

As the day wore on, they let her go on some of the rides alone. It was fun at first, but Rachel got bored after while. No one to scream with. No one to laugh with when she got wet from the rides. Just faces of people she didn't know.

Then she couldn't find her mom and Will. Rachel wandered around, getting a little scared. So many people. So many legs and feet. And the sun was hot. She went on another ride, just to cool off. Rachel scanned the crowd as she flew past them. No Mom. No Will.

Rachel climbed out of the ride and wondered what to do next. She rubbed her finger with her thumb. What if they were fighting somewhere? They'd forget all about her. What if it was a bad one and the police took them away?

Her heart thumped against her chest. She had to find them. Rachel was running toward a place that sold food when she saw them. Will was shooting his video camera at her mom while she walked around. Her mom turned and walked right up to the camera and said something that made Will laugh. Suddenly, her mom frowned and said loudly, "Where's Rachel?"

"I don't know," said Will. He kept on aiming his camera at her mom. Rachel ran up to her.

"Here I am, Mom!" She hugged her mom's waist and buried her head in her blouse. Her mother was all right.

Will put the camera down. "Let's go catch one of the shows." That was it. No one said things like don't you ever go off without us again, or, we were looking everywhere for you, or, you scared us out of our minds, young lady, like when she wandered away from her dad and Laynie. Although Rachel was glad she didn't have to bear another lecture, something inside her felt sad. She couldn't explain it. Just that mixed up feeling again.

She would be glad to go home tomorrow. She wished she could see her dad. Maybe her mom would let her. She would pester her after they were back. Her mom said Rachel drove her crazy sometimes, but it worked. You did what you had to do to get what you want.

*****

Rachel was happy her mom was letting her go to her dad's even though it wasn't his weekend. She didn't even have to pester much. Tomorrow night she would be dressed and ready for him, just like he wanted.

Her mom and Will were in a bad mood. It made Rachel nervous. She looked down and saw she was rubbing her finger again. The hard knot on it was about the size of a small marble now, and getting bigger. She should stop rubbing it, but she couldn't help it.

They were in the living room watching a boring show. Rachel went to her room and brought out some of her dolls and was playing with them on the floor. She counted six empty beer cans at her mother's feet. Will had a beer in his hand. "What should we do this weekend, Rachel?" he asked her.

"I'm going to my dad's." Will grabbed the arms of his chair and turned to her mom. She was staring at the TV.

"How come I didn't know about this?" he snapped.

Her mom faced Will. "It just happened today."

Will's neck was turning red and that meant trouble. "I let you have the phone for one day, and you call *him.*"

"No, he called me."

You're lying, Mom! You called Dad right after we got up and asked him if he wanted to come get me this weekend. Her mom was giving her that look, the one that said *be quiet.*

Her mom turned to Will again. "He wanted Rachel this weekend."

"Why didn't you say 'no'?"

Her mother set the beer can down on the coffee table and licked her lips. "You know how Shawn is. He wants everything his own way. He always bullies me. I tried to say 'no,' but he wouldn't hear of it."

Why are you getting Dad in trouble? Rachel screamed silently at her mother.

"Then he can deal with me!" Will jumped up and grabbed the phone, punching out numbers. "Laynie? I want to speak to Shawn. I'll wait until he can come to the phone. No, I said I'd wait. No, I don't want to talk to you, I want to talk to Shawn. I'll wait." Will turned to her mom. "She said he's out in the barn."

"She's probably lying," her mom said. "Or maybe she makes him sleep out there." She giggled.

"Shawn?" Will straightened up, like he was trying to be taller. "Will Starks here. I understand you want Rachel this weekend. It really isn't your weekend to have her. What?" Now Will's face was red. "He wants to talk to *you.*" He slapped the phone in her mom's palm.

"Hello?" Her mom sounded funny. "Will is looking out for my best interest, Shawn. Yes... I know... yes..." Will was glaring at her mom, so she turned her back to him. "Yes, Shawn. I guess I did. Sometimes I just forget. I did say that, you're right."

"Shut up!" Will ordered.

"Don't tell me to shut up, Will."

"You tell him she stays with us!"

"*I'll* decide where she goes, Will. She's *my* daughter."

"You whore! To hell with you." Her mom's eyes were huge. She covered the phone with her hand.

"You want them to hear that? You calm down, Will - what, Shawn? Everything's fine. Just forget the call." She threw the phone on the table and flopped into the sofa. Will grabbed her arm, jerking her to her feet.

"You think I can't figure out what's going on? " His hand clamped her chin. Will was shaking with anger. "Lie, lie, lie. I'm sick of it." He slapped her face. Her mother slapped him back. Rachel jumped up. "You stay where you are, Rachel, if you know what's good for you." Will's eyes were scary.

Her mom pushed Will against the wall, showering him with all the bad words she knew. Rachel's head ached as she furiously rubbed her finger, watching helplessly as Will shoved her mother down on the floor. With a sneer, Will leaned toward her, trying to grab her legs. Her mom kicked his shin. He yelped.

Rachel remembered the last time she had tried to stop their fight. She had tried to part them and had gotten hit by both of them. Her mom had ordered her to go to her room but they had kept on fighting. *This is going to be even worse. I wish Daddy were here.*

Will's face frightened her. They were threatening to kill each other. *I have to stop him.*

Rachel threw herself between them. "Stop! Stop fighting. Please, stop!" she screamed. All three of them tussled on the floor. Somebody tossed Rachel through the air, and she landed on the glass coffee table, her head banging into it. Will and her mother didn't notice. They kept fighting.

She carefully touched her forehead where it hurt. No blood. No crack in the glass. Rachel crawled to the kitchen as they yelled awful things about killing each other. When she stood up, her head throbbed. The room whirled around her like when she'd spin in circles. She put her fingers against her head again, and this time felt a bump. It hurt. "Mommy, I need you," she whimpered. Rachel started to cry. She cupped her hands at her throat and sobbed, "What can I do? What can I do?" Her own shrill voice sounded strange to her. Her mother's scream cut through the house. *They really are going to kill each other. With what? Knives. I have to hide the knives.*

Rachel ran into the kitchen and yanked open a drawer. The silverware rattled like bones. Her hands shook so violently, she could hardly pick up the butter knives. She got a garbage bag and frantically threw them into it. She pulled open the next drawer and saw more knives. Long, sharp ones. Rachel tossed them in the bag. After she had checked all the drawers, she hid the bag in the cupboard that had flour and sugar in it. No one would find it there.

She was considering hiding the forks when she noticed the silence. Too scared to open the door, Rachel counted to one hundred. A car's engine started up in the drive. She peeked out the window and saw Will drive away.

Rachel found her mother on the floor, staring at the wall. Her lip was bleeding and her blouse was torn. "Mommy? Are you all right?"

"That bastard. Is he gone?"

"Yes."

"When I told him I was going to call the police, he ran like a rat."

"Will they get him?"

"I really don't want to deal with the police, Baby. They ask too many questions." She wiped her lip with the edge of her blouse. "Bastard owes me a new blouse."

"Should we call Daddy?"

"And have him tell the judge? No way, José."

Rachel felt trapped. What could they do? What if Will came back, madder than ever?

"Some marriage, huh, Rachel?" Her mom struggled to get on her feet. Rachel hurried over to help her.

"What are you going to do, Mommy?"

Her mother shuffled over to the bookshelf and took down a picture album. "Never should have married him." She tore out the pictures, casting them to the floor after ripping them in half. Pictures of her and Will smiling on their wedding day. Cutting a cake. Opening presents. Kissing. Each one was yanked out of its place in the album and torn in two by her mother's trembling hands, then she kicked the pile of tattered pictures at her feet. Her mother walked to the phone, squinting as she picked out the numbers she wanted.

"Billy? Hi." Her mom was using her sexy voice again. "It's me. It was so good running into you yesterday. Are we still on? Good, I really need to talk. I can't wait." Her mother hugged the phone against her waist. *What was that all about?*

"Who were you talking to, Mom?"

"A friend. Someone nice. A person Mommy knew since kindergarten. Someone who Mommy hopes will help her."

"Help you what?"

"Never mind. Let's go to Jessica's tonight. Haven't talked to her for a while. We'll come back after Will goes to work tomorrow and get you ready to go to your Daddy's."

Like so many times before, Rachel and her mom were on the road late at night, fleeing to a place for safe sleeping. Rachel felt sick as she tried to shut out the images of her mom and Will fighting, of red faces and torn pictures. She tried to shut out the sounds of the shouting and screaming and bad words, of threats to kill and sharp knives in a bag. But they would not leave her alone.

The stars beckoned her through the car window. What was it like on a star? Laynie sang a song to her once about that. *Would you like to swing on a star?* It had to be nice. Peaceful. Everyone getting along. Kind words. Lots of singing. Soft voices... kids laughing... Rachel floated off to sleep, wishing she could live on a star.

TEN

They were talking at the table in the kitchen, sipping from coffee mugs. Her mom declined the donuts Jessica offered her, but Rachel put two on a paper plate.

"So you let Shawn take the rap for Rachel's visit. Bet that made Laynie mad."

Her mother lit a cigarette. "You don't even know her."

"I met her once. She came by work to tell me she thought I was doing a wonderful thing testifying in court for them."

"Boy, did she ever get a surprise!" Her mother laughed and blew smoke toward the ceiling. Rachel pretended to not be interested in their conversation. But they had been talking about her dad. She didn't want her mom getting him into any more trouble with anyone.

"I need more money, Jolene." Jessica licked her fingers like she was afraid one of those specks of glaze was going to get away.

Her mother's face darkened. "I paid you for your favor."

"I haven't found a job yet."

"Then get off your fat butt and get one."

"I don't see you gittin' a job. Just another man."

"I have to take care of Rachel somehow."

"I need more money, Jolene."

"I have to talk to Will."

"Well, talk soon. I'd hate to have to ask Shawn for money."

"He'd never pay you."

"You're right, but *you* will. You don't want me near him."

Why does Jessica think my mom should give her money?

"You'll have it this week. Let's go, Rachel."

"You said I could play with Bret when he comes back."

"Come on, Rachel. Don't give me a hard time."

"You promised. You always promise and then you lie."

"I don't lie. I just change my mind. Let's go home."

"Shut up. I'm staying."

"I'll stop and get you something. I'll let you pick out something for Joey and Maddie, too."

"And Hayley and Zack."

"Sure. Can we go now?"

They got in the car and sped away. "Why does Jessica want your money?" Rachel asked as she gripped the door handle.

"She's a fat pig with a fat butt, that's why. I don't want to talk about her." They drove in silence to the store. Rachel picked out candy and posters for the trip to her dad's. Her mom kept trying to tell her what to pick even though Rachel wanted to do it herself.

At home, Rachel noticed her mom wasn't paying much attention to her. She called her dad twice at the sub shop. Rachel was hoping her dad would tell her mom to bring her over there. She liked playing in the back and going out front to visit customers. Sometimes her dad let her clean off tables. Other times she would play with Hayley in the playpen if Laynie was working.

Her mom was drinking a lot and talking like she was half asleep. She was complaining to her dad about Jessica.

"She's on welfare. Imagine that, Shawn! What? I don't go over there. She comes by here. She always wants something... I don't know, I guess because I used to live near her and we were friends. She's a fat pig. She's always asking me for money... I don't know why, Shawn... I told her I'm not giving her any more money... I mean any money. 'Get a job', I said... What? ...Okay, she'll be ready."

Her mom took the phone into the kitchen to make her next call. Rachel put her ear to the door and heard her mother giggling, "Oh, Billy!" Rachel turned away. Her mother certainly liked talking to men. She was sure pulling one over on Will. He had no idea how much her mother liked men. She seemed to be calling this new guy, Billy, a lot lately. Which made Rachel wonder how her mother could always be wishing to be with her dad, yet always liking to be with other guys. She couldn't ask anyone this, because calling other men was a secret.

Secrets. They had a lot of secrets, her mother and Rachel. That was the way life had to be. Tell the truth when it won't get you in trouble. Don't talk about the things that will. And lie when the first two don't work. Rachel was learning fast.

ELEVEN

After coming back from her dad's one weekend, Rachel learned from her mother they no longer lived with Will. Just like that. While Rachel was relieved to be out of that house of terror, she wished her mom would let her in on all these changes. She still wasn't sure where they were living. Sometimes they would stay with Aunt Tanya, sometimes stay at Grandad's, but more and more they stayed at the new guy's place, Billy. Anyway, for tonight she knew where she was going to sleep. *Billy's.*

Billy's house was teeny compared to the one they lived in with Will, even smaller than the one they pretended to live in beside Paul's. But Billy was cool, and he didn't seem to mind Rachel sleeping in the same bed with her mom and him. He must really like her mom, for he had let them move in just like that, and given her mom a job of answering the phone for his construction company. Her mom stayed near the phone the first few days and did her job really well, but then Rachel noticed lately she let the answering machine do the talking because she was sleeping in or too busy to deal with it.

Rachel wasn't supposed to tell they kind of moved in with Billy. Another secret. Her mom said it was best not to let Will figure out where they were. That worried Rachel, for she still got scared when she thought of him.

She had her own room again, and she did most everything there but sleep. They had put a TV in for her, and she heard some talk about her own DVD player. They seemed to want to be sure Rachel liked it here. She met Billy's son, Sam, who was six years younger than her. Rachel only saw him every other weekend. Sam was okay, for a little boy, but Rachel got tired of playing baby games with him.

Her mother was calling her into the kitchen.

"What, Mom?" Rachel saw her toss a beer can into the trash and pointed to a blanket draped over a box.

"Look what Billy and Mommy got you." Rachel sprang over to the box and slid the blanket to the floor.

"A puppy! Oh, he's so cute!"

"Yes, he is. He is so precious! He's just an itty-bitty thing and needs his Rachel to take care of him. He's in a new home, too, just like you." Rachel frowned as an unwelcomed thought raced through her mind. *I wonder who will be leaving first.*

"I want to name him Frisky, Mom."

"Oh, I already named him, Baby. Besides, it's a girl. And what kind of name is Frisky for a girl?"

"I thought you said it was my puppy."

"She is. But she already had a name when we got her."

"You just said you named her."

"No, she came with a name. Her name is Megan."

"Megan? That's no name for a dog!"

Her mom picked up the puppy and handed it to her. The puppy licked Rachel's chin. "Just look at her, Baby. She loves you so much already. Don't you, Megan? You loves your wittle Rachel, don't you?" Her mom kissed the puppy's nose. Rachel clutched the warm, wriggling puppy, and sat on the floor to examine her.

"You are so sweet, girl. All right, I guess I have to call you Megan. We need to get you a bed and a dish."

"I got all that for you."

"But I wanted to pick them out," Rachel protested. "She's my dog."

"Don't be silly. You can pick out her collar and leash. And some chewy toys. She'll need lots of those so she doesn't chew up Billy's house. Two chomps and it would be gone." She and her mother giggled furiously at that.

"Can I take her into my room?"

"Sure can." Her mom got out another beer as Rachel hurried to her room. She sure was drinking a lot lately. Billy mostly pretended not to notice. He let her mom do anything she wanted. Talk on the phone, sleep late, call her dad, go shopping. And now this puppy. Billy was definitely cool.

Rachel put the puppy on her carpet and found the doggy bed her mom had bought. She unwrapped it and placed it at the foot of her bed. She put Megan in it, and laughed as the puppy chewed on a corner. She held the puppy close, snuggling her nose into the soft blond fur.

"Hey, Megan. You're so adorable. I love you, my puppy." Suddenly the puppy quieted and fell asleep, right there on Rachel's chest. Her small hand glided over the puppy's sleek back as she felt the warmth of her tummy on her belly. "I do love you, Megan. But what are we going to do when it's time for bed? I wonder if they'll let you in bed with us. Oh, I can't leave you all alone in here without me." Her mother was calling her again. She carefully laid the puppy on the dog bed.

"Hush, Mom, Megan's asleep," she scolded.

"Good. There's something I need you to do."

"Are we going away?" Rachel asked as her mother grabbed her keys.

"I have to get some more of our things out of Will's house before he gets back from work."

Rachel panicked. She didn't want to go back *there*. "But what if he comes home early?"

"That's why we have to hurry. I wanted to wait until it's dark, but we have to skeedattle before he comes home from work."

"But my puppy might wake up. She'll wonder where I am."

"She'll be fine. She has the whole house to explore if she wakes up."

"But it'll be dark and she'll be scared and all alone."

Her mom was pulling her arm. "That's why we have to hurry. We'll be real fast, you'll see."

"But I'm afraid of Will."

"*Rachel!*" They were getting in the car. "Don't you give me any trouble." They quickly pulled out of the drive.

"I thought we were done. You said Billy would buy us everything we needed. I had to leave my stuffed puppy and bunny pajamas, but you said we couldn't go back any more, it was too dangerous." They were driving fast, then slow, then fast, then slow as a snail.

"There's something... there's a few more things we have to get. It'll be okay, Baby. Mommy takes good care of her little girl."

We're here! Rachel's eyes searched the house for any signs of Will. Her stomach hurt, really, really hurt. She bent over in pain.

"Rachel, come on!" Her mom yanked her arm and fumbled with the keys.

"I have to go to the bathroom."

"When we get inside."

"Hurry, Mom. Here comes a car!" They froze like rabbits in car lights as a pick up truck drove by.

"We're okay, Rachel."

"I don't feel good. I want to go back."

Her mother stopped her struggle with the keys and put her face right in front of Rachel's. "All right. I'll take you back, and I'll come back here all by myself. No one will help me. I'll be alone, here in the dark, without my little best friend to watch for me."

Rachel swallowed. "Okay, I'll help you."

Her mom grinned and hugged her. "What would I ever do without you, Girlfriend?" She turned and cursed when she realized none of the keys worked. "Idiot! He's changed the locks! How will I ever get it? I have to get it."

"Get what, Mom?" Rachel eyed the road for lights.

"Never mind. I'll try again while you go visit your Grandma Stevens."

"Who will help you?" Rachel asked as they got in the car.

"I'll find someone. I have lots of friends." Rachel was all mixed up. *Lots of friends? How come you didn't ask them to come tonight?*

"Let's go home, Mom. I want to see Megan."

"Sure, Baby, after I stop for beer."

"But Megan will wonder where I am."

"I'll hurry. Want a soda and a candy bar?"

Rachel saw how wobbly her mom was and decided against having her do anything that would take up more time. "I'll wait here. Hurry up."

When they got home, she found Megan had soiled the kitchen floor. "Looks like a reason not to cook tonight," laughed her mom. Her mom found a reason every night not to cook.

The puppy was chewing on one of Billy's shoes. Rachel scooped her up and buried her face in puppy fur. "I don't like those ugly Velcro tennies either," she murmured as she took Megan to her room. She cuddled the dog and thought about the upcoming trip she was going to take to her Grandma and Grandpa Stevens'. It was Laynie's idea, one of her better ones. Rachel had been surprised her mother said she could go. "I wonder what she'll do without me while I'm with Grandma and Grandpa?" But that was weeks and weeks away. She'd figure out something.

"What am I going to do about you, Megan? Do you want me to sleep in here with you? Would you like that, girl?" Rachel laughed as the puppy's tongue tickled her cheek. "Oh, I love you, Megan. You're my very own puppy and I'll take good care of you." She carried her out to the living room where her mom was watching TV.

"Baby, get me another beer, would you? Can't live with without my beer!" Her mom laughed liked she had just told the craziest joke. Rachel laughed, too, although she didn't see the humor in it.

"I want to sleep in my room tonight with my puppy," she announced as she handed her mom a beer.

"Why?"

"So she won't be lonely."

"Oh. Well, you could have her sleep with us."

Rachel thought hard about her answer. She, for some reason, really wanted to just be with her puppy in her own room, in her own bed. "She might have to go to the bathroom. I'll take her at night. I'll just put her out the back door and she can run around till she goes. Then I'll take her back with me."

"I could put a mattress on the floor in the living room and you and I could sleep there. Just like old times."

It wasn't exactly what Rachel wanted. "What will Billy say?"

Her mom crinkled her brows. "Oh, don't worry about him. He's easy." So for the next few weeks, that was the sleeping arrangements. And Billy hadn't fussed. He never seemed to get mad at anything.

Then one evening as they were sitting around the coffee table eating a bucket of chicken while watching a video, the front door burst open. Rachel's stomach almost erupted when she saw Will, red-faced with fury, yelling for Jolene to come to the door. Billy jumped up and blocked his entrance.

"Get out of my way, Parker. I've come for my wife. She's still my wife and I want her back where she belongs. Jolene! I know you're in there, I can see Rachel. Get out here and I'll forget this whole mess you've made."

Rachel looked back in the corner where her mother cowered on the sofa. She just stared toward the doorway. Rachel was ready to throw herself in between them if she had to.

"Will, this is my house. Get out." The men stood nose to nose. Billy's hands were clenched in tight fists. His face was red as the tomato soup Rachel had for lunch.

"You can have your house, I'll have my wife. Jolene!"

Billy leaned front as Will stepped back. "You get out of here right now, or I'll mop up the floor with you." Will seemed to think about that, and took another step back.

"You'll be sorry, Jolene. I still have something you want." With that, he turned and disappeared into the darkness.

What do you know? Billy could get mad.

TWELVE

This Victor guy that kept coming around and Rachel didn't like it, not one little bit. The first time she met him, he gave her the creeps. She and her mom were in the front yard at Billy's (now officially where they lived since Will seemed to take to heart the floor-mopping threat) when he stopped by in his car to talk to her mother. His eyes were dark, his hair was dark, and he had a nose as big as a banana. Well, maybe a pickle. A very big pickle.

Anyway, he and her mom talked. And talked and talked and talked. She thought her mom had become glued to his car door. "Who was that?" Rachel demanded after he finally drove away.

"He's a poor soul. That poor, poor man." Her mom could be so... what was it Laynie said about Rachel sometimes? *Dramatic.* "It's sad. It's just so sad. Oh, Rachel. That poor man lost his wife."

"He better go find her."

Her mom snorted. "No, silly Milly. She *died.*" Her mom stroked Megan's back as Rachel held the puppy. "We must help him be happy again."

"How?" Megan was getting big already. She was pretty heavy to carry around. Rachel put the puppy down on the grass. "What can we do?"

"Oh, mostly just listen to him when he comes around. He needs someone to talk to. You know me, I'm a very good listener. I have that knack. People are always telling me their troubles."

Rachel frowned. *What is she talking about?* "So, when did she croak?"

"Rachel! Don't talk like that. It was so tragic. It just happened a little while ago. So, we'll help him. Billy would want us to."

Rachel watched Megan race around the yard. Her dog was so funny, she could watch her all day. "Billy knows him?"

"Of course. They're friends." Megan was digging beside the house. "Rachel, get after your puppy. She's not to do that. Hurry!"

But when Rachel went to stop Megan, she scooted away and headed for the goldfish pond. "Not the pond, Rachel! You know Billy doesn't want her messing it up."

Too late. Megan leaped and landed right smack in the middle, as water surged over the side and spilled out onto the lawn. One goldfish flopped on its side by the edge of the pond. Her mom was screaming and having an absolute fit.

"I'll get it, I'll get it, Mom. Geez, it's not like it never happened before." Rachel tossed the wriggling fish into the water.

"I knew we shouldn't have gotten you a retriever. We'll never be able to keep her out of that water." Rachel coaxed Megan out and laughed as the puppy rolled on her back on the grass. She was the coolest dog in the world.

Rachel later overheard her mom tell Billy she couldn't believe it was three years already since Betty, Victor's wife had died. She also said Victor wanted her to help him out every so often at his tee shirt shop. She would wait on customers and answer the phone. Billy said sure, no problem. Well, Rachel certainly didn't want to go along on those jobs. The more Victor stopped by, the less Rachel liked him. He was always, *always* saying bad words, even when he wasn't mad. Just regular talk and then, bingo, one bad word after another. Even worse than when her mom and Will had been fighting.

And when he visited, Rachel might as well have been air. Her mom forgot all about her. Oh well, at least she had Megan.

Once her mom even arrived at her dad's with Victor. Rachel was waiting and waiting for her to come and pick her up, and she was way late. Rachel had given up watching for her and played outside with Joey. Her dad was fixing fences near the barn and Laynie was hanging up wash. Rachel liked watching the clothes flapping in the wind, like they were little kites all in a row. Just when the sun started to disappear, her mom pulled in the drive in a car Rachel immediately recognized. Her mom jumped out and walked over to her dad, with Victor following. She was telling her dad this was Victor her boss, and she needed a ride, so he was just helping out.

Rachel was worried. Her mom always had this weird thing about introducing the men she liked to her dad. Now she was doing

231

that with Victor, and Rachel was not at all happy about that. She was just getting used to Billy. And she did not, no way, want to ride home with slick Vic. Too creepy.

Rachel ran over to Laynie. "Want me to hand the clothes to you, Mom?"

Laynie took her eyes off her mom and Victor and put her hand on Rachel's shoulder. It felt nice.

"Sure, Sweetie. But I only have a few left."

"That's okay. Looks like I have to go now." Her mom was yelling for her.

"Is that the man you told me about, Rachel? Victor?"

"Yes."

"Are you okay about him driving you home? If you feel uncomfortable, I'll take you home."

That would be so nice, but that would be big trouble. Rachel would never be able to choose Laynie over her mom. Never ever. Her mom believed her little candle flame was to burn only for her.

"It's okay."

"You sure?" Laynie looked worried.

"Yeah. I'm sure, Mom. I better go." She kissed Laynie and raced over to her dad. "Bye, Dad." He scooped her up as she threw her arms around him.

"Do I need to do something?" he whispered in her ear.

She quickly shook her head. Her mom was really nervous. She was biting her nails and wiggling her one leg. Rachel knew she had better get her home soon. Besides, Megan was waiting for her.

*****

Victor continued to stop by, and called her mom way too much on the phone. Rachel would disappear with Megan when he came over. In fact, her dog was her only close companion these days at home. For some weird reason, her mother had started to take long baths. She would order Rachel to busy herself with something so she could take a long, soaking bath. Her mom was now the cleanest person in the state, sometimes bathing three or four times a day, even if Billy was home.

One evening Rachel and Billy were in the kitchen eating supper (Chinese take out, yum) while her mother was bathing. Rachel was about to pop a shrimp in her mouth, when Victor walked into the room. Megan hadn't even heard him to bark a warning.

"Victor! What are you doing here?" asked Billy as he put down his soda. "Had supper? There's plenty here."

"Where's Jolene?" Victor looked like he was in a hurry.

"She's taking a bath."

"I want to talk to her." With that, he turned and headed for the bathroom. *How come he knows where the bathroom is?*

"I said she's taking a bath, Victor. Just wait a minute." Billy jumped up to block Victor's path.

"And I said I want to talk to her." He tried to continue his course, but Billy blocked him again. This was getting interesting.

Victor growled at Billy with an endless string of bad, dirty words. Billy glanced at Rachel and looked back at Victor. "Let's take this outside. You need to cool down." For some reason Victor thought that was okay and stalked out the door. Billy told her to keep eating (as if she could after all that) and followed Victor.

Rachel ran to her room and held Megan close. The men's angry voices filtered into her room from outside. She buried her face in Megan's fur. "Please, not again. No more fights. No more fights. No more fights." She could not stop saying her litany to Megan. The puppy licked her arm. Lick, lick, lick, it was so soothing. "What would I do without you, Megan? You make my insides get quiet. I love you so much."

Later that night, after Victor had gone home, her mom finally came out of the bathroom. They all sat in the living room and watched a video. Billy never mentioned Victor's visit.

THIRTEEN

Rachel had a wonderful time at Grandma and Grandpa Stevens' over spring break. She visited aunts and uncles and cousins she barely remembered seeing before. She didn't even get homesick, although she missed Megan. Her mom called every day and assured her she was feeding her dog and giving her clean water. She said Megan seemed sad Rachel was away for so long. That made her feel anxious.

That and the phone calls and letters from her mom and Jane. Every single day, like they were afraid she would forget to come home or something. No way. Megan needed her.

Rachel got out her slew of cards and letters and read some of them again. Jane's first.

Dear Sweet Rachel,　　　　　　　*Friday P.M.*
I haven't done much today, just a little sewing. We went to Captain Barney's to eat. Have you been there? We'll be sure to take you when you come home. Only 13 more days until your birthday! I have a surprise for you!
XXX OOO Jane

Dear Sweet Rachel,　　　　　　　*Saturday P.M.*
Only 12 more days until someone's birthday. I have several ideas what I might get that special someone. You've only been gone a few days but it seems forever!
Enjoy your time with your grandparents.
Love, Jane

Dear Sweet Rachel,　　　　　　　*Sunday A.M.*
11 more days until a very beautiful little girl's birthday. (This is getting a little sickening, thought Rachel). *I think she'll be 7 years old. Arnold and I went to church today. We are going on a little trip to LA. We will be back in 3 days.*

Then I will take you to the movies, OK?
Be sweet, Jane

Rachel put the postcards in her suitcase. She would be leaving tomorrow. Grandma had put her clothes, all nice and clean, in there, too. She would skim over a few of her mom's letters one more time.

Dear Rachel,
Hello Baby! I think you are really brave for taking this trip.
Billy and I are going to pump out the swimming pool to get it all ready for you when you come home. Rachel raced through the next part where her mom went on and on about Billy's brother who was getting surgery, and blah, blah, blah. Grown up stuff. Ah, here was the part she wanted.

Megan is being so naughty! I think it is because she misses you. She got in Billy's pond again and made a big mess. Billy was a little mad but he cleaned it up and it looks good as new.

I am taking good care of Megan. You do funny things to me... I never thought I would enjoy taking care of a puppy like this. But I enjoy her so!!! (What's up with that? thought Rachel. She doesn't talk like this. Bet she thinks I read my letters to Grandma.)

Well, I must get back to all the work I have to do. I love you bunches. Love, Mommie

"Mommie? I'm not a baby, Mom." Rachel picked up the next letter.

Dear Rachel,
It is hot here, and we need rain.
We finally got the pool drained and discovered another problem. Grass had grown up through the bottom of the liner! We bought another one, so that was another problem overcome!!!!

I also got you some school supplies. But I wish you could have been shopping with me. It felt funny without you along.

I've been doing some thinking and planning on your birthday party. Maybe we could put a bow on Megan. Hurry home so we can decide which theme you want.

I have enclosed some spending money for you. I love and miss you. So does Megan. She says, "Woof, woof, where is my Rachel?"

Love, Mommie

"Oh, my poor, poor Megan. I miss you so much. I'm coming home, girl. Tomorrow." Two more letters.

Dear Rachel,

*Hey, what's happening? I baked a cake today (*yeah, right, Mom) *to practice for your birthday. I wasn't quite satisfied, so I'll persevere and try again. Just like the pool.*

Grandad is coming over for coffee this morning. (I wonder why he's coming over. Mom said she never wanted to see him again). *Poor Billy is working hard out in this heat. He's been very busy. That's good. He bought you a birthday present yesterday. It's a funny gift. I know you'll get a kick out of it. He can be so silly!*

*I better stop here and get busy with housework. You know how I love to clean. (*Mom, is that you?) *I miss you. So does that puppy! She wishes you were here, right this minute! Hurry home to her! And the fixed-up pool!*

Love, Mommie

"I'm coming, Meagan," she whispered. One more letter, before going to bed. Then tomorrow it's back to her dad's and then home to her puppy. And the pool and her birthday and gifts and presents!

Dear Rachel,

It's 6:45 in the morning and I just woke up about 10 minutes ago. The phone rang and it was a wrong number. Oh, well, I'm an early riser and I have lots to do anyway!

The pool is coming along nice and is ready and waiting for you. Just like Megan.

*Well, Grandad is coming shortly for coffee. (*They sure are drinking a lot of coffee). *See you real soon. I'll kiss your puppy for you. I can't wait to see you.*
> *Love you,*
> *XXXX OOOO*
> *Mommie*

All those promises of the pool, gifts, movies. Some of it would come true, some not. But one thing for sure, she was going to hug and kiss Megan and beg her mom to let her take her dog to her dad's next weekend. She wanted to get a big red bow for her to wear at the birthday party. And she would tell her mom she was really ready to sleep in her own bed every night. With Megan, of course.

*****

Rachel thought they would never get home. She was really glad to see her dad and everybody, but she had to get home before Megan had forgotten her. No, she would never do that. Megan loved her and only her.

She kissed her dad and raced out of the truck into the house, thinking for sure her mom would be waiting for her on the porch, but it was only Billy. "Hey, Rachel," called Billy as she raced by.

"Where's Megan? Where's my puppy?" Billy followed her into the house.

"Don't you wonder where your mom is first?"

"No."

"She went to the store. She'll be-"

"Megan! Megan! Come here girl! I'm home. Your Rachel is home."

Billy caught up to her in the kitchen. "Your mom's just pulled in the drive, Rachel. She really missed you." The screen door slammed as her mom came through with two bags.

"My baby's home! Are you all right?" Her mom dropped the bags onto the table and opened her arms. Rachel went and hugged her.

"Of course I'm all right. I had fun."

Her mom tilted her head. "You're not at all sad?"

"She just got here, Jolene," said Billy. "All we got to do is say 'hello.'"

"Where are your bags?" her mom asked.

"I left everything with Dad. It was all my clothes and stuff from there anyway, remember? Mom, I want to go in my room and see Megan. And I want to tell you something else." Rachel swallowed. *Here goes.* "I want to sleep in my own room, in my own bed, so I can be with Megan. I'm old enough anyway."

"So you are. Getting older," agreed her mom as Billy left the room. Rachel heard the back door slam again. "Old enough to understand some things."

What are you talking about? I'm getting Megan. She pulled away from her mom and went into her room.

"Rachel! Rachel, come here!" Rachel ignored her mom; it wasn't the first time, and won't be the last. She pushed open her door, knowing Megan would be sitting there, waiting for her, ready to jump into her arms, with lots of licking and sniffing.

"Megan!" she squealed.

She couldn't find her. Well, it was no wonder, her room was a mess. Megan was probably hiding under her bed. No, there was too much stuff under there.

"Rachel, I said come here!" Her mom sounded mad. *Too bad, so sad.*

Rachel looked under the bed anyway. No puppy. She sat back on her haunches and scanned her room. "Where are you, my doggie? Are you trying to trick me?" She pawed through the piles of clothes on the floor around her bed. "Are you hiding in here?" Rachel said as she searched each one. *The closet.*

"Rachel!"

Her mom was just outside her door. Rachel started throwing everything out of her closet. *Where is Megan?* She was getting scared. What if a car hit her while she was gone? What if someone saw how cute she was in the yard and *stole* her?

"Baby, I have to tell you something." Rachel looked at her mom standing there with a beer in her hand, her mouth opened like she didn't know what it was she had to tell her.

But Rachel knew. She put her hands over her ears. If she could block out the words, then maybe it wouldn't come true.

"You know how Megan was always getting in Billy's pond?"
No!

"Rachel, she just wouldn't listen! She kept ruining everything." Rachel pressed her ears so hard they hurt. Her arms were shaking. But she had to keep the words out. Her mom tried to pry her hands off her head.

"We had to get rid of her," she yelled. "We found her a good home, Baby."

"Shut up!" Rachel pushed her mom back. Her mom looked surprised. Well, too bad. This was a day for surprises- bad ones. "You get her back! I want my puppy. I want my Megan, she's mine and you can't just give her away! You always give away my pets, Mom. I hate you! I really love Megan and she loves me! Is that why you got rid of her? Because you think it's like a pie and there's not a piece for you? You don't get it, do you? It's a candle, Mom, Oh, just shut up and get me my Megan. I have to have her back!"

Rachel felt as though her world was ripped apart. She had to find Megan. Her puppy would be wondering where Rachel was. She wouldn't understand why Rachel wasn't with her. Poor, poor, Megan would be lost and scared without her. Rachel's body shook as tears exploded from her. "I want my dog. I want my dog. I want Megan!" she sobbed.

"Oh, Rachel. You have to understand. We just couldn't keep her. She was too hard to train. Come on, you're old enough to understand that."

"You never gave me a chance to train her. She was *my* dog. Why did you do it while I was away? You always do it while I'm away."

"It just happened. Billy was working all the time, and I was here all alone and just couldn't handle her. I tried, Lord knows I tried, but it was so much work for me, it was so *hard* on me. Then we had to clean up her messes and fix the pond."

"I didn't even get to say goodbye." Tremendous sobs heaved from Rachel as she tried to speak. "I didn't get to hug and kiss her one more time." It was so hard to breathe. The thought of never seeing Megan again was crushing her chest.

"She's far away, but in a wonderful home. She's happy. That's what should be important to you. If you really love Megan, you'll get over this by knowing she's happy. Besides, we'll get you another puppy, Rachel. A calm one. Now, you have a good cry and then come out to the kitchen. We have a birthday party to plan!" Her mom quickly left the room and shut the door.

Rachel searched her room, whispering Megan's name, just to be sure. Maybe she was like those dogs in the stories where they miss their owners so much they come back home. Maybe she was hiding here in her room so her mom and Billy wouldn't find her.

But there was no Megan in her room. Rachel buried her face in her pillow, filling it with her agony as she sobbed. Her puppy was gone. Forever. She couldn't imagine never seeing her cute little face again, never feeling her loving, slurpy licks on her cheek. She would not feel her soft fur as she ran her hand over her back, nor feel her warm puppy tummy on hers when she held her close.

For months to come a heavy, suffocating feeling inside haunted her. She stayed in her room and slept there from that night on. And for the first time in weeks, Rachel wet the bed.

FOURTEEN

So much happened to Rachel she couldn't tell if it was a long or short time ago since they left Will. The calendar showed just a little over a month. And the month was July, and she was supposed to have, she was *promised,* a wonderful birthday party. Her dad had even made sure she would be home for her birthday because she was going to have a party. Well, somehow, her mom forgot all about it and tried to make it up by taking her and some of her girlfriends to the movies.

After Rachel was back in school, she had gotten a cat, but already it had been given away to Grandad. No surprise to her, he didn't keep it long. Grandad couldn't take care of himself, let alone a cat. Once they stopped in because they had gotten a call from Aunt Tanya that Grandad was in "bad shape." Grandad had answered the door, his face all stubby, his hair greasy, and Rachel would never forget, he had peed his pants. He had answered their knocking and stood there in the doorway, like peeing your pants was an everyday thing.

Grandad and her mom yelled at each other a lot these days. Her mom said they weren't going over there any more. Said he drank too much. It cracked Rachel up that she said that while she was wobbly and drinking a beer. At least her mom would never get *that* bad.

October arrived, and Rachel went to a carnival with one of her friends from school. She came back early and walked in the living room to surprise her mom. She and Billy were on the sofa, laughing and smoking something that really, really stank.

"Aren't you smoking your regular cigarettes any more, Mom?" she asked as they quickly stabbed their smokes in the ash try.

"Uh, yeah, Rachel. Just not this time."

"These are way fatter than yours. And they smell weird." Rachel wrinkled up her nose.

"They're a sample," said Billy. "Some guy gave it to me."

"I'm going to my room." Rachel felt dizzy and she wanted to get out of that stinky room. She wished Megan were waiting for her. She still missed her terribly.

Sometimes Rachel told Laynie about all the weird stuff going on at her mom's, but only when her stomach and head hurt. She liked the way Laynie listened, but was always afraid she would do something about it. If her mom found out, she would be madder than a wet hen she told someone, especially Laynie.

Rachel also told Zack and Joey some things, and sometimes Maddie. But most of it she had to keep a secret. She knew the judge didn't want her mom drinking beer. Her mom was pretty good at fooling everyone about that. And she wasn't supposed to smoke around Rachel. If she forgot or was too tired to go outside (which was most of the time) she would spray Rachel's hair with perfume before going to her dad's. Her mom was very smart.

School had started and she was surprised her mom came to school to help as a room mother. She was never wobbly when she came. That was good, because Rachel didn't want the judge to find out and take her far away from her mom. Her mother also brought her lunch every day and ate with her. She said it was to make sure she ate everything. No problem. Rachel liked fries and soda.

One evening they were at home in the living room. Rachel had just finished her homework while her mom and Billy were watching TV.

"Did I hear someone knock? asked her mom.

"I'll get it," said Rachel. She opened the door to see a tall man wearing a uniform.

"Hey, Mom," yelled Rachel. "The cops are here."

Part Three
LAYNIE

ONE

Laynie's life was chaos. Shawn and she had opened a sub/pizza shop and done well enough to hire a young woman named Amelia to help. But typical of the fickle clientele of Wesley, business was now dropping. Her relationship with Rachel was a tug of war. Maddie and Zack struggled to fit in at school.

Shawn would tell Laynie about Jolene's odd conversations. Laynie tried to be patient and keep silent, but Jolene's endless invitations to Shawn to come back to her were getting ridiculous.

Jolene called Laynie to say she'd been investigated by children's services, and did Laynie know who would have reported her. (Laynie wished she did. She would have pinned a medal on them.)

More calls: Could Shawn come over (*to play?*) and help with Rachel's science fair project; Rachel's bedwetting was so hard on *her;* Rachel was having a party for her "little friends," would Shawn provide the entertainment by singing and playing his guitar. Jolene was changing times to pick up Rachel so often, Laynie had to keep a calendar by the phone to keep track.

But the thing that she felt most helpless about was losing the hearing last summer. Even though Judge Jenkins had seemed disinterested (like they were intruding on his time) Laynie had hoped that, based on new evidence and Jolene's history, he would see Rachel needed to be removed from Jolene's care.

He had swiftly denied Shawn's request for custody. *The judge hadn't even remembered us.* There had to be a way to get him to think of their lives outside that courtroom.

Laynie recalled a Biblical parable where a woman went before a harsh judge, begging for him to listen to her, but was sent away. She came before him, again and again, pleading her case. Finally, the judge listened and granted her wish, just to be rid of her. *I will be that woman, Judge Jenkins.*

Thanks to Jolene, it wasn't long before Laynie started her pen pal relationship with the judge.

Dear Judge Jenkins,
    Just two weeks ago you denied my husband's request to have his daughter, Rachel, removed from her mother's care and given to us to raise. You have given her mother, Jolene, three reprimands to date, amid her promises to stop drinking and become a better mother. You never ordered her to AA or counseling, unrealistically supposing she would end years of uncontrolled drinking herself.
    She calls us constantly, drunk. She showed up here yesterday, demanding we cut short our time with Rachel. Jolene came unannounced, and if her current husband hadn't been in the driver's seat, we would have put up a fight not to let her take Rachel, for she was intoxicated. She slurred her words, she staggered on the front walk, and she smelled of alcohol. Rachel was obviously upset at the commotion, along with our other children. We couldn't stop her, for it was not our "regular" time with Rachel. Jolene had asked us to take Rachel so she and Will (her husband) could go away together. I guess they had another fight and canceled their plans.
    Rachel tells us about their fights, and I am frightened for her safety. She is witness to violence, and feels compelled to protect her mother, placing herself at times in the direct line of fire.
    Please help that little girl. We are helpless to do so.
    Sincerely,
    Laynie Stevens

Laynie was nervous about mailing it, but figured the way things were going, they had nothing to lose. Shawn had agreed with the letter, but muttered a fatalistic, "It won't change anything."

It had been hard for Laynie to focus on working at the sub shop with these thoughts of Rachel. Not to mention Hayley needed her shots, and Maddie heard about a birthday party all her friends had been invited to, but not her. Zack brought a rock home that had been thrown at him in agriculture class. Joey cried every time Rachel returned to her mother's.

With all this on her mind, Laynie had to call Jolene after closing the shop. They had been invited to Ron's (a long-time friend of Shawn's who often took the kids swimming and fishing) for barbecued ribs. He wanted Rachel to come along, but this wasn't their weekend to have her.

Laynie locked the door after Amelia left. She looked at the clock. Ten fifteen. *Shawn has all the kids in bed.* She opened the desk drawer and did the books for the day, glad to have an excuse not to call Jolene yet. She put the books back in the drawer and took out an envelope with pictures from Carol and Missy.

Laynie shuffled through the scenic Colorado pictures. The shot of their friends' house partially hidden by pines, built into the side of the mountain seemed like heaven. How wonderful it would be to wake up and see the Rockies every morning!

The phone was ringing. "Laynie? Is Shawn there?" Laynie's stomach twisted.

"No, Jolene, he's not. You're stuck with me."

"Don't be silly, I'm not shtuck with you."

Drunk again. "I was going to call you. Would you and Will check to see if it's okay for us to have Rachel Saturday night?"

"When it comes to Rachel, " Jolene said, "it's you, me, and Shawn. I think that's enough, don't you?"

Laynie didn't know how to answer her. "So, it's okay?"

"Sure, Laynie. You can have her the whole weekend if you want. In fact, I'll bring her out tomorrow afternoon."

"Good. You're sure the whole weekend is okay?"

"Laynie, Will and I are having a lot of problems right now. Some of it over Dara. She's so wild."

"She won't listen to you?" *Pffft.* Laynie heard a can pop open.

"I'm not much of a dishciplinarian," Jolene said slowly, "but I make her listen. Dara, that is. When she's here I take Rachel away, or have y'all have her. I don't want Will raising Rachel. You, Shawn, and me were doing that long before he came into the picture."

This is too weird. "Um, so you'll be able to bring her out to the sub shop tomorrow afternoon?"

"Yup."

"Does asking for extra time cause problems between you and Will?" Laynie pressed.

"Yes, and it's getting worse. There may be some major changes in the lineup here. Will gets upset when I give y'all extra time. I go to Daddy's a lot to get away."

As if that's a good place for Rachel. "I see."

"And when Will wants me to keep Dara, I don't, unless Rachel begs me to. But only for a little while. And now Dara's mother wants me to help her with her science project. I will not have Dara around Rachel."

"Jolene, I have to go. We'll look for Rachel tomorrow." Laynie hung up and looked at the pictures one more time. Somehow, she had to get her family there. Somehow.

Of course, the next day Jolene called Shawn and said she wasn't bringing Rachel out. Maybe Saturday.

*****

Saturday afternoon Jolene burst through the door at the sub shop with Rachel. Laynie was getting ready to go home with Hayley for her nap as Shawn sat down to see what he needed for that night.

"Bye, Baby," Jolene cooed as she pried Rachel from Shawn's knees. "Mommy will miss her wittle girl while she's gone. I'll be so sad without you." A frown of concern hovered over Rachel's eyes.

Stop, it, Jolene, Laynie screamed silently. "Thanks for bringing her, Jolene. Rachel, why don't you go to the bathroom since I'll be taking you home with Hayley and me in a few minutes." Laynie pressed Rachel's shoulder and guided her to the back.

On the way home Laynie tried to get her to talk, but Rachel gave only short answers and stared out the car window. Dark rings pooled under her eyes. The knot on the side of her knuckle looked like a smashed pea. "Rachel, is there something you need to talk about?"

"No."

"Maybe if there is, you could talk to Dad. Or Zack."

"Is Zack home?"

"Yes."

Rachel pressed her lips together and nodded once. She sought out Zack as soon as they were in the door. That night after the younger children were in bed, Zack called Laynie to come into his room. He had just finished hanging a new poster on his wall as she sat on the edge of his bed. He closed his door. "Is Rachel asleep?"

"Yes, why?"

Zack sat beside her; his dark eyes were full of worry. "Rachel told me some weird stuff this evening. Jolene told her the court is trying to take her away and she'll never see her again."

"I know. Jolene tells her that all the time."

"That's got to be so freaky for Rachel. You know what else? Jolene told her that the day she was born, Dad left her. Rach cried, Mom, when she told me that." Laynie's fingers dug into her palms.

"Dad tried to explain to Rachel what happened. But it's confusing for her, with her mother telling her all these lies," said Laynie.

"Rachel still is sleeping on the living room floor every night. She stays up late and tells me about shows that you won't even let *me* watch. She said something really scared her."

"What was it?"

Zack frowned. "She wouldn't tell me. Said she'd be in trouble if she told. What are you going to do?"

"I'll figure something out, Zack."

Zack paced the floor, frowning. "I'm worried about her, Mom. Can we get a new judge? Why would he keep letting Jolene win?"

"I guess he's stuck on tradition. You know, the mother gets the child, no matter what. Thanks for letting me know, Zack. You're a good brother."

Laynie went to the desk and typed out another letter to Judge Jenkins.

TWO

Only two people now remained in the shop after the short lunch rush. Laynie chatted with them a bit then went behind the counter to chop lettuce and onions for the supper crowd. She put the full containers in the refrigerator and counted the small mounds of pizza dough under the olive oil-soaked towels and decided the way business had been, there was enough. As she prepared the tomatoes for the slicer and adjusted the setting, her mind drifted to Rachel.

The violence between Will and Jolene seemed to be escalating. Rachel had tried to tell Shawn again about the belt incident, but Jolene had grabbed her arm, screaming that she was a liar and that nothing had happened.

Hot pain pierced her thumb. "Aaaa!" Laynie yelped as blood flooded out the gash. She switched off the slicer and hurried to the sink. The phone was ringing. *Of course.* She tore off a paper towel and squeezed it around her throbbing thumb. "Train Stop. May I help you?"

"So you took your little pink highlighter and sent me this article?"

"Excuse me?"

"I know you did it. You sent me this here newspaper article on the arrest of Jesse Bender. I'm *not* Jesse. My name is Jessica, you stupid woman."

"Jessica?" The two women eating subs were looking at her.

"You better watch yourself."

She turned her back to the women. Then Laynie heard Jolene's voice in the background, coaching Jessica. "You've been sending stuff in the mail to me and Jolene."

"I don't know what you're talking about." Laynie hung up. "Crazy drunks with nothing better to do," she muttered. The phone was ringing. Her thumb throbbed.

"Train Stop."

"You better be careful. I'm gonna get you."

"Jessica, why are you doing this?"

250

"You know why. You and your pink highlighter."

"What are you talking about? A highlighter?" Jolene was talking to Jessica again.

"And Shawn needs to pay more child support instead of wasting his money on stamps to mail this stuff."

Laynie slammed down the phone. She searched her mind, trying to figure out what Jessica could possibly be talking about. The phone rang again. She wanted to let it ring, but what if it was a customer? Her eyes met the two women's. "Want us to get that, Laynie?" one of them asked.

"I'll handle it." She picked up the phone. "Train Stop."

"You better watch your back, wherever you go, girl."

"Jessica, stop it." Laynie frantically searched for the record button on the answering machine. She pressed it. "What is it you think I did, Jessica?"

"You and your pink highlighter. You need to stop."

"Stop what?" But this time, Jessica hung up. Laynie had gotten little on the tape. She put the phone down and saw her hand was shaking.

"Laynie, are you all right?" asked the women. Laynie was going to shrug it off, but she was tired of pretending everything was fine. In her anger, she told the women about the conversation and a little about Jolene. They left only when Laynie promised them she would have the police walk her to her car after closing.

She kept her promise, although she felt a little silly and embarrassed. Officer Aiken listened intently as Laynie explained what happened. As he waited on her to lock up, he urged her to file a report. "The threats could be all talk, but you never know."

Great. Now there was a new nut in her life. Laynie went home and told Shawn what happened. "Funny," said Shawn, "Jolene called me today, ranting and raving about the same thing. From what I can understand, someone has been mailing articles about an arrest of a woman for writing hot checks, and a DWI."

"Do you have any idea who it might be?"

He shook his head. "I told her it wasn't us. She says it was you, and I said no way. She said her lawyer thought it was Grady."

"Our lawyer?"

Shawn laughed. "Yeah, Jolene was just babbling. Jessica showed her a newspaper article that was highlighted."

"Ah, in pink," mused Laynie.

"What?"

"Go on."

"Jolene thought Jessica was doing it because she wanted *more* money from her. Sounded like blackmail or something."

"I'm calling Jolene tomorrow, Shawn."

"All right."

Whoa, this is a surprise. Usually Shawn said things like it wouldn't do any good, or they would just lose time with Rachel.

Laynie waited until the next afternoon to call. "Jolene? What do you think you were doing by having Jessica call me last night?"

"I don't know what you're talking about." But Jolene's voice betrayed her.

"I had nothing to do with whatever mail the you and Jessica received."

"Maybe it was someone from your little blessed church."

"What?"

"If you didn't do it, you know who did."

"If you wanted to talk to me about this, why didn't you just call me yourself instead of have Jessica do your dirty work?"

"Laynie, I'm so tired of your bull-"

"And I'm tired of walking on eggshells around you. I know you had Jessica call me from your house. I know all about all your phone calls to Shawn. I know you're always after him. I know so much more than you think I do."

"And we'll just find out about *you.* " Jolene hung up. Laynie's whole body trembled. Living like this was crazy.

Monday morning Laynie filed a report against Jessica Bender at the police station. They convinced her to call the phone company and get a tracer put on the phone at the sub shop. She signed the agreement to file charges against Jessica if she was caught making threats over the phone

Tuesday evening, when Shawn was at the sub shop, Jolene called him. He played the recorded conversation for Laynie:

Jolene: Yeah, Jessica popped in on me this weekend again.
Shawn: Why are you letting her in?
Jolene: I don't know, I just don't know. She was all upset over those letters I told you about. You sure it's not you?
Shawn: Yes.
Jolene: She thinks it's you. Or Laynie.
Shawn: It's not her either.
Jolene: Not precious Laynie... Jessica is dangerous. She wants more money. She said she would go to Daddy for money. I told her to leave him alone.
Shawn: Why does she come to you and your family for money all the time?
Jolene: You know me, Shawn. I always feel sorry for people. That's just the way I am.

The rest of the week was quiet. No more calls came to the shop. Laynie stopped by the police station Wednesday and was told the report had been filed.

That evening Shawn called Laynie from the convenience store. Laynie told him of her progress. "You know the police might go to Jolene's and question her about this, Laynie."

"She's just as much a part of this as Jessica."

"Call and tell Jolene the police might come by to question her, that it couldn't be helped. You just want Jessica to stop."

Laynie was bewildered. "Why would I do that?"

"You know Jolene. She'll go ballistic. What if Rachel's there?" Laynie knew the next line. "And she'd punish us by taking time away with Rachel. Is that what you want?"

"No."

"So you'll call?"

"You ask me to do some awful things, Shawn."

"It's necessary."

"Jolene knows what buttons to push to get her own way. Oh, I'll call, don't worry."

Laynie was furious as she hung up the phone. *I wish I could send you to the moon, Jolene. Hey, I hear there's a man there. You'd love that.* Laynie smiled at her lame joke. She picked up the phone and put it down.

I just can't call her. She'll just hang up. I'll tell Shawn I couldn't get through or she wouldn't talk to me. But Laynie didn't want to start lying to her husband, so she forced herself to call. Four rings and she quickly put down the phone. *Good, I tried.* She checked on the kids. Zack was the only one still awake.

Laynie tried again at ten and was successful. "Will? This is Laynie. Is Jolene there?"

"Just a minute." Laynie heard him put the phone down and walk away. She faintly heard Jolene's voice answering him.

"She's asleep, Laynie."

"It's really important. Have her call me at home."

Laynie got a drink of water and tried to slow her breathing. The phone rang.

"Laynie? Will said you called and it's important. I don't appreciate being wakened up this late hour. I get up early."

Laynie took a deep breath. *Here goes...* "I just wanted to tell you I filed a report against Jessica, and the police may be there to question you about it."

"Fine." Jolene's voice seethed with anger. "See if I care."

"Jolene, I only wanted to let you know they have to talk to you since the calls were made from your house."

"No, they weren't. You're just trying to scare me."

"No, I'm not. Listen, Jolene, you're not being charged." *But you should be.* "I didn't even want to call you, but Shawn said I should. You told him Jessica was dangerous, and if you really feel that way, you need to tell that to the police."

"The police are going to be talking to *you!*" Jolene yelled. Laynie was listening to a dial tone.

She called Shawn to tell him what happened. He cut her off because he had a line of customers in front of him. She was holding the phone against her chest when Zack came out and kissed her goodnight. "What's wrong, Mom?" he asked, patting her shoulder.

"Oh, just Jolene stuff."

"I hate what she does to our family. I wonder if she ever thinks about that."

"Enough of her. Is Preston picking you up in the morning?"

He grinned. "Yeah, we're going to the lake. His dad said he'd teach me how to ski."

"You be careful."

"I know, I know. Wear a life jacket. I will, Mom, just for you. And Mr. Matthews. He's a stickler, too."

"Good for him. Now get to bed." She kissed his forehead. "Night, Pumpkin."

"You haven't called me that in a long time."

"I'll try to do it more. Especially in front of your friends."

"Gee, thanks, Mom." He waved one more time, and then shut his door. The band of light underneath his door disappeared.

Laynie had just sat down to write in her journal when the phone rang. Maybe it was Shawn.

"Laynie? Will Stark here."

Will Stark here. This guy cracks me up. "Hello, Will Stark."

"Why did you call Jolene?"

Laynie related what had happened at the sub shop and that she had been to the police station. "Jessica is mostly hot air, Laynie. If the letters stop, she'll chill out."

"I have no control over the letters."

"You must tell these people it's causing problems."

"Listen, Will Stark, I don't know who it is, and I want Jessica out of my life."

"Well, we all agree on that, don't we, Laynie?"

"The calls were made from your house."

"No. Only the initial call was."

"No, Will, all three calls were made from there." Laynie heard him put the phone down to talk to Jolene.

"No, *Laynie*, only the initial call came from here."

255

"I hate to tell you, *Will,* all of them came from your house. I heard Jolene telling Jessica what to say. She brought up child support, and you and I know that came from Jolene." Laynie heard Jolene screaming in the background. *Finally got caught in one of your lies.* "Jolene knew of the calls," Laynie pushed on deliberately, "she called my husband and told him Jessica made those calls from your house, and that Jessica is dangerous."

"This is a complete mess and it needs to stop, Laynie."

"Now that's something you and I agree on, isn't it, Will Stark?" Jolene's hysterics almost drowned out Will's voice.

"Laynie, I have to go. There are things I need to tend to so I can get to bed."

"Just a minute, Will. If Jolene says she wants Jessica out of her life, why did she let her in your house and use the phone? You don't know what all goes on while you're away."

She heard Jolene shrieking at Will. "I have to go," Will snapped and hung up.

Laynie called Shawn, hoping he was able to talk. She needed to hear his deep, soothing voice assuring her they would get through this. Of course, just as he answered, people flocked into the store. She could hear their commotion as he told her he'd try to call later. Laynie told him not to bother, that she was going to bed.

She went to bed, but not to sleep. Jolene's shrieks and Will's condescending voice filled her mind with worry for Rachel. *How does she live with that, day after day? Why doesn't Tanya or Jane ever check up on her? They don't want any waves in their smooth little pond.*

Laynie stared out the window. The bright, full moon bathed the cows grazing in the front pasture. The peaceful scene did not calm her tonight. School would start soon. It would be a tremendous adjustment for Rachel after this crazy summer. Where was Rachel right now? Was she safe? Was she scared?

Laynie stared at the ceiling and watched reflections from the windowpane dance across it. A hot breeze puffed in the window. She wished she could turn on the air conditioner, but they had to scrape money together to pay bills, court costs, and child support, leaving no money for the luxury of a cool house. Colorado would not be possible this summer. She drifted from Oklahoma and imagined they lived on the side of a mountain, among the pines, in a two-story house with a porch that wrapped all the way around it. The breeze was cool and whistled gently through the pines. She was watching the moonrise over their pond, sitting on one of the wooden rockers with her feet curled up under her, waiting for Shawn. She would tell Shawn how great the kids were doing in school, and how friendly everyone was every time she went to town.

"Hi, Babe." Shawn's voice startled her. Colorado flew away from her as she blinked back to reality.

"You're home! How'd you manage that?"

He sat on the edge of the bed. "I closed for Sandy last night, remember? Tonight she's closing for me."

Laynie sat up. "I'm so glad you're home. I had a round with both Jolene and Will."

"I know. Jolene called me at work."

"You had time to talk to *her*?" Laynie heard the anger in her own voice.

"I didn't have much of a choice. She said we couldn't get Rachel tomorrow." Laynie sighed. It was all so predictable. "I told you she would do this, Laynie."

"Look, Shawn, she didn't do *this* until I called tonight to warn her of the police. And if you recall, *you* told me to do that."

"Then it would have happened after the police visited her."

"So either way it's my fault."

"That's not what I mean. But this whole deal with the police has only brought more trouble."

"I was supposed to do nothing?"

"It doesn't do any good."

"We should let Jolene threaten me?"

"That's not what I said."

"Our lives revolve around Rachel. Jolene controls Rachel, so she controls us."

"What are we to do, Laynie?"

Laynie faced him. "Make Jolene responsible for what she does."

"And how do we do that?" She heard the anger in his voice.

"I *did* do something this week and it's got you upset with me. You're more upset with me than with her."

"Trying to correct her won't do any good. It's just the way it is and you have to accept that." Shawn shrugged. "You'll never change her."

"I know that, but I'm tired of letting her change us."

"It's not worth getting all worked up over, Laynie." He turned to leave the room. She grabbed his arm.

"You know, just once I'd like you to be on my side."

"What do you mean?" He sat back down on the bed.

"Every time we have this discussion, you're always on the other side of the fence. Just once, I'd like you to say, 'Yes, Laynie, I know how you feel,' or 'It gets to me, too.' But you always lecture me how things will never change and we should just accept it. I can't just push all this out of my mind."

"Then it will drive you crazy, Laynie."

"It drives me crazy not to talk about it."

"But you never stop."

Laynie let go of his arm. "Maybe that's because you never really listen to me." He stared at her for a minute, then left the room. Laynie slid under the sheet and hugged her pillow whispering her troubled prayer. "The fight is going out of me, God. It's a bad thing, this Jolene business. My whole family suffers. Give Judge Jenkins wisdom. Open his eyes, please, open his heart..." Laynie drifted into a troubled sleep.

THREE

The next few weeks Laynie had to weather Jolene's revenge. When she'd answer the phone, Jolene would hang up. When she picked up Rachel, Jolene would never talk directly to Laynie, but rather talked to Rachel, who relayed her mother's messages. It was almost funny.

Shawn came home one day and took her into the living room. "I got a call from Jolene today."

"Wow, there's a surprise. Too bad you were too busy to talk to her."

"She's still on the warpath. She said you ruined some of Rachel's clothes and she doesn't want you to wash them any more."

Laynie laughed. "Good one. And you, of course, stuck up for me. You told her she's being ridiculous and I certainly know how to do the wash by now. You told her you're much too busy to be listening to her ridiculous antics, and she has to stop bothering you at work."

"I just let her talk."

"Wow, another surprise, Shawn." He shook his head and left the room. Laynie continued to do Rachel's wash.

When the calls to Shawn increased to three times a day, Laynie felt as though she was strangling on her anger.

After a particularly long phone conversation at home with Jolene, Laynie confronted Shawn. "Maybe, since you seem to spend so much of your time on the phone with your ex-wife, you should get together and say all the things you need to say to each other. Maybe you need to just leave and be with *her*."

Shawn's mouth dropped. "What are you saying?"

Laynie wasn't sure, but the words tumbled out of her. "Just go and be with her. It seems to be what you want. If I got you to spend just half the time talking to me you do her, I'd be ecstatic."

Shawn took her hands and pulled her to him. "It's *you* I love, Laynie. You know that."

She looked into his blue eyes, searching for a sign of understanding. "It's awfully hard to know that, when you spend all that time with Jolene on the phone and never have time to talk with me. You don't let me talk to you about how she makes me feel. You make excuses for her. And don't tell me it's because of Rachel. I don't want to hear it." She dropped her head, drained of all hope. She knew what he would say. Shawn left the room for a moment and came back with a plaque from the living room. He held it in front of her and pointed to it.

"See this? You hung this up, Laynie. The Serenity Prayer. What's this say?" He pointed to the words "to accept the things I cannot change." Laynie was furious. Her heart raced as she grabbed the plaque from him. She had to get outside.

"Where are you going?" Shawn asked her.

"Do you really care, Shawn? You used to be my best friend. You *wanted* me to talk to you about everything. Now it's so limited what I can say and when I can say it, I feel like a stranger." She felt like slamming the back door, she really deserved to be able to do it, but she didn't want to wake the kids.

Anger boiled through every cell in Laynie's body. Rage at Jolene and her lousy parenting, her meddling in their marriage and family. She was angry with Shawn and his tolerance of Jolene, angry with Judge Jenkins and his ridiculous rulings, Will and his uncontrolled temper. *And where are you, God? I could use a little help here.* She turned and hurled the plaque into the night.

Laynie sat on the glider and wept. She put her fist to her mouth to muffle her cries. Shawn must not hear. Her tears used to fill him with compassion for her; now they only seemed to annoy him.

The back door swung open and in the bright moonlight she saw him coming. Laynie quickly wiped away her tears. "Want some company?" he said softly.

"It's up to you." He sat beside her and looked at the sky.

"Sure is a pretty night. Remember the night we went to the lake and the moon was like this?"

"That was a million years ago," Laynie murmured.

"We've had a lot happen in our short marriage, haven't we, Laynie? More than our share of turmoil."

"Yes."

"We're going to get through this, Sugar. I know it's hard, for all of us, especially for you."

Shawn took her hands in his. "You and I look at things differently, Laynie. I try to take one day at a time and deal with it. You are a very reflective person. You look at the past and wish it was different."

"I look at the past to do everything I can to make our future better."

"You have dreams. I'm too tired to have them."

"Dreams keep me going, Shawn. They dim my troubles."

"But sometimes they make you impatient."

Laynie sighed. "Perhaps that's not always bad. We waste too much time while life speeds by."

"Like me on the phone with Jolene."

"I didn't say that... this time." They laughed.

"You're right, Laynie. It's been too much too long. I'll stop it somehow. Not all of it, though. I need to know what she's up to with Rachel."

"You'll really put a stop to it?"

"Yeah, and it's about time. I'm getting calluses on my ear." They laughed again and Laynie felt some of her anger ebb. "You are the love of my life, Laynie. You got that?"

She looked at him. "It's hard to feel that with all this stuff going on. I miss the way we used to be."

He hung his head. "I know, I do, too." Shawn took her hand and pulled her up. "We have to make sure none of this hurts our love for each other. I'll never love anyone else."

"I love you, too." Under the night's canopy, they kissed and held each other close. Laynie felt her anger die. Her love for Shawn pushed it away into the hot, Oklahoma wind.

FOUR

It was hot as blazes. The dogs were digging holes all over the yard and in Laynie's flowerbeds, trying to find a cooler spot. The chickens fluffed dust over themselves continuously. Even the cats were panting, which made the kids laugh. Laynie brought towels out for the children swimming. The yard had deep cracks and was hard as cement. Laynie splashed water on her herb garden.

Maddie and Rachel were screaming, more than the "stop splashing me" squeals to the boys. Laynie dropped her watering can and ran to the pool.

"Quiet!" Zack was ordering. "I can't even talk to Mom."

"Be quiet!" added Joey. "My ears will go *death.*"

They were staring and pointing several yards away. "Mom, there behind the bush. Cookie found a rattlesnake!" It slid under the leaves as their gray and white cat sat intently watching it. Laynie herded the children onto the patio, a trail of water marking their passage. "Stay here. I have to get the snake gun."

Rachel squealed.

"Stop it, Rachel. You'll scare him away before Mom can shoot it. Then we'll wonder where he is," said Joey.

"Snakes can't hear," said Maddie.

"Can, too," retorted Joey.

"Cannot." Maddie folded her arms.

"Then how come it heard what Eve was saying in the Garden of Eden? Huh, Maddie?"

"Zack, make sure no one leaves this spot," ordered Laynie. She hurried inside and pulled out the stool, reaching for the small shotgun on the top shelf over the washing machine. Her hands were shaking as she loaded the gun.

"Oh, Lord, I have a gun in my hands and I have to shoot a snake." Her heart raced. "I have to get close to a snake and shoot a gun. Oh, Lord, oh Lordy me." Keeping the gun cocked open until she was outside, Laynie muttered her mantra of dread. She snapped it closed. Maddie screamed.

"Mamma! Cookie's going to get bit!" Laynie followed Maddie's pointing finger and saw that the cat was sneaking up on the snake.

"I'll get her," declared Zack.

"You stay where you are!" commanded Laynie. She was trembling. "Cookie, here, kitty, kitty," she coaxed. But Cookie was focused. Crouching low to the ground, she inched toward the rattlesnake, never taking her eyes off it.

"Cookie, please, kitty, don't." Laynie was crying. The snake sensed the cat and coiled. Its tail sprung up and vibrated with warning, but Cookie paused at the rattling alarm only a moment. *I have to hurry before she's too close. I don't even know if I can hit it.* Laynie hurried towards the snake. Cookie moved in quickly, determined not to lose her prey. Laynie clicked the safety off, and pointed the gun at the snake's head. Her finger pressed against the trigger as she held her breath.

Cookie lunged for the rattler. The snake struck her head as the cat shrieked in pain, racing off to the front of the house. The children were screaming and crying.

"Mom, shoot it!" yelled Zack. The snake was quickly retreating to the honeysuckle bush. She would never find it under there. Laynie pointed and squeezed. The gun lightly bumped her chest as it exploded. She realized she had closed her eyes and missed. Laynie forced herself to watch as she discharged the second shell. Even though it tore open the middle of the rattler, it still wriggled slowly toward the bush. Laynie ran to the barn and grabbed the hoe. She returned to the snake and hacked at its head.

"Get him, Mom! Kill him!" the children were yelling. Again and again, she struck the snake with the hoe. It struggled to get away as she chopped its head off.

"Where's Cookie?" she asked, sweat racing down her back. "Kids, go find her. If she's still alive we have to get her to the vet." The children immediately scattered and searched for their cat.

It was after supper when they finally found her, crouching under a bush, her head the size and shape of a small football. Shawn helped Laynie load up the cat to see Dr. Cooper, who gave Cookie shots and medication. "She has a fifty-fifty chance, Laynie," he said. "But she's lucky that she got it in the head. That's actually the best place for an animal to get bitten." Laynie put Cookie on her lap and cried the whole way home. She looked so pitiful.

"Thank you, Cookie. You protected the children. You're a hero and don't even know it," Laynie whispered as she gently stroked the cat.

Laynie kept Cookie in the house. She would hold the cat after giving her the medication, talking to her and tenderly stroking her back, coaxing her to eat and drink. Finally, on the third day, Cookie started eating. Although it would take over a month for her head to go back to its normal size, Cookie recovered from the snakebite.

*****

Shawn had asked Laynie to take Rachel back that Sunday so he could fix fences in the back pasture. After an early supper Laynie announced there was ice cream or chocolate cake for dessert. The ice cream was the unanimous winner.

"You know what's so sad?" asked Rachel as she chopped up her ice cream with her spoon. "Poor Dara didn't have a birthday cake."

"How come?" asked Joey, vigorously stirring his ice scream until it made soft peaks.

"I wanted my mom to bake a cake, but she wouldn't. I asked her to buy one but she said 'no.'"

"We could give her our cake!" declared Joey.

"Yeah," added Maddie, "Mom can turn it into a birthday cake!"

"Could you, Mom?" asked Rachel, her eyes full of pleading.

"Sure. I've got some decorator's icing and M&M's. How's that sound?"

"Sounds like a plan," said Zack. "But do you know where Dara lives, Rachel?"

She nodded. "She and her mom live with her great aunt near the water tower. My mom and I used to go along with Will to get her and take her back."

"How come you don't any more?" asked Joey.

"Because she says bad words and doesn't listen to my mom. But I still think she should have a birthday cake."

So on the trip to return Rachel, Laynie hunted for Dara's home. They had to drive up and down several streets until Rachel recognized the house. Laynie helped her get out and watched her carry the cake and knock on the door. A woman with her gray hair pulled back in a bun said something to Rachel and smiled.

"Dara's not there," said Rachel as she got back in the mini van. "But her aunt said she'll give it to her. Won't she be surprised!"

Laynie drove toward Rachel's house. Rachel was staring at her feet. "You're awfully quiet, Sweetie."

"Mom, don't tell my mom about the cake, okay?"

"Okay."

"It might make her mad."

"I won't say anything, Rachel."

As they pulled in the drive, Jolene drove in behind them and parked on the other side of the drive.

"She must have found her keys," said Rachel, watching her mother. "If Will sees them, he takes them so she can't go anywhere. So my mom hides her keys from him."

"Oh, my," said Laynie. "Rachel, are you going to be okay?" The little girl nodded as she unbuckled to get out. She kissed Laynie and threw her arms around her neck for an extra squeeze. "You call me if you need me, Rachel. If you're scared or-"

The car door was jerked open. Jolene reached over and plucked Rachel off Laynie's lap. "Let's go inside, Baby. I got you something." Laynie watched them go into the house, Rachel giving her one last wave before the door closed.

FIVE

Fall brought cooler weather as the children settled into school. Zack, Maddie, and Joey settled into their routine quickly, but Rachel was struggling to survive; Laynie could see it in her eyes. The callous on her finger had grown, her stomach hurt her every time she came out, and she lost weight. She was wetting the bed again, and there were times Rachel would burst into tears and not know why.

Right before Thanksgiving, Laynie and Rachel were walking the back pasture together, checking up on a newborn calf. "I played hooky from school again," volunteered Rachel. Laynie tried not to look shocked.

"Really? How many times?"

"Two times this week. One time last week."

"What did you do?"

Rachel grabbed a weed and yanked it out of the hard ground. "I had lots to do. I cleaned my room and stuff. We were just too busy for school."

"Who?"

"Me and my mom. We made snowflakes."

"Snowflakes?"

"For the Christmas play next month. Lots and lots of them. Wait until you see them."

"But you weren't sick, Rachel?"

She threw the weed down. "No ... but we had to tell them I was or, you know..."

"You mean your mother didn't tell the truth when the school called."

"We couldn't, Mom! We *had* to lie."

Laynie stopped walking and stooped down to Rachel. "Listen, Rachel, lying is not good. Lying so you won't get into trouble doesn't make it okay. School is much too important to be missing so you can stay home and make snowflakes or clean your room."

"But we had fun." Laynie sighed. How was she ever going to teach Rachel what was right? What was normal?

"Look, Rachel, over there!" The calf turned to inspect them as they inched forward. It stepped closer to its mother, its brown ears flicking above its white face. "See, she's going to nurse."

"It's a girl?"

"Yes. Don't go any closer. She looks like she's doing fine."

When they returned to the house, Maddie said Jolene was on the phone. Laynie reluctantly put the phone to her ear.

"Laynie, did Shawn try to call me?"

"I don't think so. He's working and usually doesn't have time."

"Well my phone's not working and I thought maybe he tried to get a hold of me."

You mean Will took a piece of the phone again. "Don't think so, Jolene."

"How's Rachel?"

"She's fine."

"Well, I wanted to be sure she didn't change her mind about staying an extra day since they don't have school tomorrow. She changes her mind all the time, in the blink of an eye, like her mother."

"So it's still okay to keep her until tomorrow, like you told Shawn?"

"Yes, ma'am."

After they hung up, Laynie glanced at the clock. Almost two. Shawn would be home soon. After she'd waken Hayley, they were going to the aquarium.

The children were excited about the trip. They stayed until the aquarium was closed and stopped in the sub shop to treat the kids. Amelia pulled them to the side, her face crinkled with worry.

"That crazy Jolene and Will called here seven times- seven times-asking if I knew where you were!"

"Did they say why?" asked Shawn.

"No, just asked me over and over where you were. Said they were going to get me in trouble if I didn't tell. Called seven times, and all in one hour! I'm fixin' to file charges against them."

Shawn looked at Laynie. "I guess we better head home as soon as they're finished eating and see what this is all about."

"So much for our nice day," Laynie said to Amelia.

"How do you do it, Laynie? I would have knocked their blocks off by now." Amelia wagged her finger at her.

"Don't think I haven't felt that way. I'm really sorry you had to be involved in this."

Amelia wiped off the counter. "I hope they stop or I might have to quit. I can't take this."

"Please don't do that, Amelia. We'll do everything we can to stop this."

"It better stop soon. They're nuts."

As they ushered the children to the mini van, Laynie had to agree with Amelia. *Nuts. Bananas. The whole enchilada.*

As they approached home, they saw Will's truck waiting for them at the gate. Shawn pulled along side of the truck and rolled down his window.

Laynie could see Jolene beside him, her stringy hair pulled back in a red handkerchief. *Death warmed over would be a compliment for her tonight*, thought Laynie.

"Hey, Jolene, what's up?" asked Shawn.

"Why haven't you brought Rachel back tonight at six oh-oh like you're supposed to?" She was slurring and talking slowly. She didn't look at Shawn, but stared straight ahead.

Will leaned out the window. "What's going on, Shawn? Rachel was to be back tonight."

"No, Jolene said it would be fine to bring her back tomorrow. Remember, Jolene?" Shawn strained to see Jolene but she only looked straight into the windshield.

"No," said Will, "I quizzed Jolene quite extensively and Rachel was to be back tonight at six."

Laynie's heart was pounding. *I can't let this get out of hand. Not in front of the kids.* She leaned toward the truck. "No, Will, Shawn came home very happy Friday because we could keep Rachel until Monday."

"No, that's not the way it is."

"And now Amelia's upset," said Jolene. "We've called the county cops on you." The kids in the seats behind them gasped.

"Yeah, we called the sheriff's office about this," Will added.

"Shawn didn't do anything wrong," Laynie yelled at them. She glanced back at the children. Their eyes were wide with fear.

"Jolene, Jolene!" pleaded Shawn. "Look at me, Jolene. We talked about this. You know it." But Jolene would not turn her head.

Will leaned back in his seat. "You want to pass her over here?" He had his arms through the window.

Laynie held her breath. That would be devastating for Rachel. "No," said Shawn, "We'll bring her back in the morning." Jolene was babbling as Will stuck his head out the window.

"You better watch out, hot shot," he warned and sped away in his truck. Laynie heard crying in the back seat. Rachel, Joey, and Maddie were sobbing while Zack tried to console them. Hayley gawked at her brothers and sisters, and then broke into sorrowful wails.

It took hours to calm them down enough and get them to bed. Laynie felt like she would explode from the anger she harbored for Will and Jolene. Their beautiful day had been ruined.

All the children except Rachel were finally asleep when Laynie checked them later. She knelt beside her bed and brushed back her hair.

"This is just like home, Mom. All the yelling and fighting. Now it's here, too."

"It caught us by surprise, Rachel. I won't let that awful fighting be done here any more. I promise."

"Did you know Will shoved my mom once and she had him arrested?"

"I heard that."

"But my mom changed her mind. I wished she wouldn't have. She always changes her mind. She should have put him in jail."

"Yes, she should have. Men should not hurt women, Rachel. Some do, but they're cowards. I want you to know that. Real men do not hurt women."

Rachel nodded. "And my mom says when she and Dad aren't fighting, she wishes they could be together again."

"I wish she wouldn't say that to you. It must mix you up and make you feel funny about me."

Rachel's eyes were closed and Laynie thought she was asleep. "Sing to me, Mommy," she whispered. Laynie struggled to hold back her tears.

"Your favorite?"

"Not tonight. Sing the one about the star."

Laynie caressed Rachel's hair and sang, "Would you like to swing on a star..."

After Rachel finally fell asleep, Laynie told Shawn she was calling Jane. "Won't do much good," he predicted.

Shawn was right. Jane was unresponsive as usual. She brushed Laynie off with, "Well, I don't know... I wasn't there..."

"There's someone else who is going to know about this," said Laynie as she turned on the computer. "Dear Judge Jenkins" she began. She would be persistent and chip away at his wall of indifference. Before it was too late.

*****

Jolene called Shawn at the sub shop later that week and apologized for Sunday night. He told Laynie she was so drunk during the phone conversation he could hardly understand her. She wanted them to take Rachel again this weekend.

Joey showed Rachel the new kittens. Laynie was at the open kitchen window, watching and listening with amusement as they looked into the box of newborns on the patio.

"I saw her lay them," said Joey as they peered into the cardboard box. "They were slimy, and Cookie licked it off. It was gross."

"Gross," agreed Rachel. "But they're so cute now. I want one of them."

"Aren't you afraid Will might hurt it?" asked Joey. Their heads hovered over the box.

"If he would, I'd kill him." Laynie held her breath. "Sometimes, Joey, Will locks us out of the house. He always thinks my mom is with a man."

"Is she?"

"Sometimes. But they're just friends. Stanley or this new guy, Billy. I only saw him once. My mom usually drops me off somewhere. Aunt Tanya's, Tina's."

"You get to go a lot of places."

Rachel sat down beside the kittens. "I don't like it, Joey. I never know where I'm staying over night. I guess it's better than at my house."

"Why?" Joey sat beside her.

"Well, one time Will hit my mom and she cried. Me and my mom went into my room and lay down on my bed. Will came in and just stared at us. My mom said, 'Leave me alone.' He wouldn't leave, so my mom gathered up the sheets and we went to the mattress in the living room. I was so scared I couldn't sleep."

"Why does your mom stay with him?"

"I don't know. Maybe because we have nowhere else to go. I wish we could all live here. My mom says that, too. But this mom wouldn't like that."

Laynie back away from the window. Shawn came into the kitchen. "Jolene's out front and wants Rachel."

"What this time? Another scene?"

"No, she's with Tanya. Edna died. I want to talk to Rachel before she goes out. I want to be the one to tell her that Granny died. Who knows how Jolene will handle this." Shawn squeezed Laynie's hand and went out the back door.

After Shawn talked to Rachel and delivered a tearful little girl to Jolene, he came inside and found Laynie in the living room. He stared at her silently. "What is it, Shawn?" Laynie frowned as she tried to guess what the next episode might be.

"They want me to be a pall bearer."

This gave new meaning to the rug being pulled out from under your feet. "*You*? It's been years since you've seen Edna. You said she was always telling Jolene she let you have Rachel too much."

"But when we were married, she liked me a lot. Said I was the best thing that ever happened to Jolene."

"But your relationship changed with the divorce."

"Edna was... good to me."

"But she didn't do what was best for Rachel. She knew what her daughter was like."

"So I should hold that against her."

Laynie didn't know what to say. How could he even be considering this? "You've told Rachel we can't be one big family. But there you'll be..."

"What? Going to the other side? This is a funeral, Laynie, not a battle." He stared into her eyes.

"Everything's a battle with Jolene, a chance to get to you. You'll see, Shawn. She'll be there, all weepy, wanting your sympathy."

"You're being silly." He was leaving the room. "I want to be there for Rachel. And the other family members."

The other family members? Laynie followed him into the dining room. "Oh, you mean the ones who have helped Rachel so much? The ones who all pretend everything's going to turn out wonderful if they bury their heads in the sand and cross their fingers? This... *stupid* family with brains the size of peas! Well, yee haw, Shawn, circle the wagons and make camp, they sound like our kind of people. No wonder you want to be with them!"

Shawn blinked at her in a way she knew he didn't understand her. How could he be so blind! How could he consider being in a room full of them? Had her husband lived so long wallowing in their quicksand of bazaar rationale it had sucked him in until he had forgotten what normal was? *Well, I know, I know what's normal and this is insane.* Her fury did not change his mind. Shawn went to the services. Laynie refused to ask anything about them or acknowledge Shawn's participation.

To add salt to her wound, one week later, Laynie saw a card lying by Shawn's wallet. She read the outside:

The honor that you conferred upon our loved one

by acting as a casket bearer
is gratefully acknowledged
and deeply appreciated

Laynie opened it and read:

Dear Shawn,
Thanks for acting as a casket bearer for Aunt Edna. She
loved you!
Thank you for giving her a beautiful granddaughter. Rachel
was the joy of her life.
I would also appreciate the values you and Laynie are
teaching Rachel. I love you both for this.
Jane

Laynie held the card in her hands, thinking of the many
things she'd like to do with it. *What a weird family. Weird, weird,*
weird. She blew out a long sigh and laid the card down, listening to
see if Hayley was awake. She needed to hold someone innocent and
gentle, to help make sense of the crazy world.

"Mommy," she heard when she peeked in Hayley's door.
Laynie hurried over to the toddler's outstretched arms and picked her
up.

"I will always try to do the right thing, Hayley. I promise to
be the kind of mother mine was. You and the children deserve that."
She held her baby against her and closed her eyes, shutting out Jolene
and Will and fights and funerals and her own growing loneliness.

SIX

Maddie came into their bedroom where Laynie was making the bed. Laynie looked up and saw her deep frown, her green eyes squinting as she folded her arms in exasperation. "Mom, I just answered the phone and was talking to Rachel, then someone else got on. She said she was Snow White. I said that can't be and she laughed wild like Rachel does sometimes, and said she was the real Snow White. I think it was Jolene."

Laynie heard the phone ringing. "I'll get that, Maddie."

"She's weird, Mom. She should grow up."

Sorry, Maddie, I think we've run out of hope there. Laynie answered the phone.

"Mom! It's me, Rachel. Guess what? Will is so cool."

"Will?" *Will Stark?*

"Yeah. He bought me a color TV and remote. It's mine and it's in my room."

"My, that's quite a gift for a second grader. So, Rachel, why did your mom tell Maddie she was Snow White?"

"She didn't do that."

"Are you alone right now? Where's your mom?"

"She had to go to the bathroom."

"Okay, now you can tell me the truth. It was your mom who did that, right?"

Silence. "Yeah."

"Rachel, people need to do better things than play games on the phone. Especially adults, doing it to children."

"Okay."

"What are you doing?"

"Having a snack. Me 'n my mom. Graham crackers."

"What are you two drinking?"

"Milk and beer." *Geez, Jolene, it's not even noon.* "Hey, Mom, there were no fights this week."

"Good. That's the way it should be, Rachel."

"My mom's coming."

274

The next thing Laynie knew, she was listening to Jolene. "Is Shawn there?"

"No, he's at the sub shop, Jolene."

"Good. I'll call him there."

I'll bet you will. Laynie wondered what the excuse was this time. She hung up, envious of the time she knew Jolene would spend talking to her husband. *Snow White is on the hunt, Prince Charming. And you thought the wicked witch was the one to watch out for...*

*****

Shawn came home late from closing the shop that night.

"Another lousy day," he said as he settled on the sofa beside her. "Guess we need to think about shutting it down. I don't get it. Everyone raves about our food and service. The prices are right and the place is clean as a whistle." He took off the engineer's cap and rubbed his head in puzzlement.

"It's this town, Babe." Laynie took his hand. "Look how many businesses have come and gone."

"Jolene called." He shook his head and took off his glasses, rubbing his eyes. "She said, 'there's going to be a change in the line-up.' That it has to do with Will. She wanted to meet me at the Longhorn and talk."

"Uh, oh, watch out. She's up to her old tricks."

"This was different. I called her to see if she still wanted to meet, and she said she's leaving Will. Said he's a good person but Rachel doesn't like him. I told her Rachel needed to be out of that dangerous environment but she acted like I said nothing. She wants me to come early Friday, because she has stuff packed in her trunk for the weekend and wants to go before Will comes home."

"This surprises me, Shawn. Rachel called here and said things were going better. Guess Jolene's putting on a good show so Will might let his guard down. Sounds like he better check his charge cards."

"Boy, howdy! I remember that trick," said Shawn. "I'll be able to get Rachel at school. At least we'll have her so she can miss the big dramatic exodus."

The weekend went quickly. Sunday they went to Ron's for ribs and brisket. As the sun traveled closer to the western horizon, Rachel announced that she didn't want to go back home that evening. Just as they were getting her things together to leave, Jolene called and told Shawn to bring Rachel to Tanya's house. When Shawn told Rachel what happened, she hooted an ecstatic "yippee" and was suddenly ready to go.

When Shawn returned home he told Laynie Jolene was very nice and promised them consecutive weekends with Rachel while she was getting the rest of her things out of the house. The next week she called him every day, telling him about moving and leaving Will.

Rachel wasn't sure where Jolene was most evenings. She was worried about her mother because Jolene said she had to figure a way to get her things out of Will's house since he changed the locks. "My mom needs me to come along when she goes to get our clothes out of the house. It makes me scared to go there."

"Tell her you don't want to go," said Laynie. "She needs to get a grown up to do that, not a kid."

Rachel shook her head. "My mom doesn't have any friends but me. Once Will walked in while we were at his house and he asked her to come back home. I thought she might say 'okay' but she didn't. Will got mad so we got out of there in a hurry."

Jolene had told Laynie to meet her in the parking lot of a bank near Tanya's when she brought Rachel back. It was odd she asked her to meet there, when she was so close to Tanya's house. Laynie suspected Jolene and Rachel were not really living there. Rachel was back to not knowing where she was sleeping at night.

Jolene climbed out of her car and stumbled over to the mini van. Rachel got out and stood by her mother. Hayley waved from her car seat.

"She is so cute!" declared Jolene as she leaned in the passenger window. Laynie was shocked at her brazenness of not hiding the fact she was very drunk. The van was filled with the smell of alcohol. "Hayley is so beautiful, she's so pretty," Jolene gushed. "Her hair has such pretty curls and her eyes are so big and brown and cute and pretty and she's just so ... precious!" She looked at Laynie and smiled. "Thank y'all for watching Rachel while I move. That's so nice. You look nice today, too, Laynie."

"Come on, Mom, let's go!" demanded Rachel, pulling on her mother's dress. "I want to go now!"

Laynie didn't want to let Jolene drive off with Rachel, even if it was for a short distance. Did she have a right to stop her? Would she be arrested for contempt?

This was silly. Rachel's safety was threatened, arrest or no arrest. But she had Hayley along. They were pulling away. Laynie put the van in gear and followed. Jolene drove very slowly to the grocery store. Laynie parked and waited. Hayley was getting fussy. *Come on, Jolene, hurry up.* They finally came out and Laynie followed them onto the street. Jolene made a right hand turn at a red light, but Laynie was unable to follow because of traffic. She lost her and frantically scanned the street, driving around trying to find Jolene's car. It was gone. Hayley was still crying.

Laynie pulled into a parking lot and got Hayley out of her seat to nurse her. "How could I have let her go with her!" she whispered as she held her child. Hayley stopped nursing to look at Laynie, troubled. "I'm okay, Hayley, Mommy's okay." Laynie stared out at the traffic. "God, send your angels to surround Rachel and protect her," she murmured. "Don't let her be hurt because of my mistake."

As she strapped Hayley back in her car seat, Laynie vowed she would never let Jolene leave again with Rachel when she was drunk.

SEVEN

Their lawyer, Grady, had told Shawn that the judge mentioned he was getting letters from Laynie. Then one morning, Laynie was shocked to get a phone call from Judge Jenkins.

"Miz Stevens, I've been getting your letters, and that's okay, but there's nothing I can do about this situation unless you bring this matter to the court."

"I realize that, Judge Jenkins, but we've come before you three times and each time Rachel is returned to her dangerous environment. If we go before we have something that is good enough evidence, we will lose and have to wait another year. By then, Rachel will be dead."

"All I can say is you must bring this before me in court before I can do anything about it."

"I understand." Laynie couldn't wait to tell Shawn. She caught him on the way out the door and told him of the conversation. "I felt he wanted to say more but couldn't."

Laynie insisted Shawn keep entering events in their diary. He declared it wouldn't do any good, but she was adamant about it. She opened to read his latest entry:

October 11
When I picked up Rachel this weekend Jolene came out and demanded to know why I was drilling Rachel about having a boyfriend. I told her I needed to know what was going on in my daughter's life. When I took Rachel back Sunday night to Jolene's dad's house, as instructed, no one was home. I sat in the truck with Rachel and after a while a red pick up truck pulled up and Jolene and some guy got out. She was stone drunk. Jolene introduced him as Billy Parker and then said to me, "I guess you two have a lot to talk about," and took Rachel inside.

Billy said Will had forced Jolene out. Jolene came back outside with Rachel, and said Billy was creating a job for her at his construction company. Rachel clung to my legs. Then out of the blue

278

Jolene asked Rachel where she wanted to live, that she wanted Rachel to "be happy." Rachel was flabbergasted and remained silent. (She's too young to make a decision like that.) Jolene started in on Rachel saying she has to stop her lying, that first Rachel said Will hit her with a belt, now she's saying Laynie hit her with a belt. Rachel said, "Will hit me with a belt. He did! It was Will."

Wednesday: Jolene said I was to pick up Rachel at her lawyer's (she's divorcing Will). I told her I was going to the bank, first. She showed up at the bank with Rachel and a bird in a cage (!!!) that I was to now take care of for Rachel. She told me she and Rachel stay either at her dad's or Tanya's.

On the way home, Rachel told me she was not supposed to tell us certain things, like they stayed at Billy's house all week, and they all sleep in one bed. Rachel said her stomach hurt her. I pressed her to tell me what was bothering her. She said a while ago she and Jolene were at Billy's when Will tried to break into the house. Rachel started to cry as she told me this story. It really scared her. Will was yelling he wanted Jolene to come back and Billy yelled at Will.

Rachel said her mother gets mad when she's out of beer and says, "I have to have my beer," and keeps some in the "ice box" at Billy's. Jolene hides her car behind the gate so Will won't see it. All this deceit and calamity in front of my daughter.

When I took Rachel back, I walked over to Jolene's car. She had a beer between her legs and tried to hide it under her dress. When Jolene told me they were living at Billy's house, but he's not there (yeah, right) Rachel just hung her head. She sees and hears her mother lie over and over again. (Is this not child abuse- teaching your child to lie?)

I asked Rachel to go back to my truck so I could talk to her mom. I asked Jolene about what she had said, about whom Rachel should live with. She said Rachel would live with her, it will be "just Rachel and me, but I want joint custody because I'm tired of making all the decisions myself."

Laynie felt a wave of nausea wash over her. She put the diary away and went to the kitchen for a cracker. She would go to the clinic tomorrow, but she already knew. She was over three months late.

Another child amid all this turmoil. They really couldn't afford any more expenses. Hayley was still so young, in diapers and toddling, the constant vigil stage. And Laynie was no spring chicken any more. The doctors had made such a production over her being thirty-five with Hayley, they'd have a real drama on their hands now.

A baby. A new life. *It'll be okay.*

The next day after her exam, Laynie sat across from a tired looking nurse at the clinic, holding her folder on her lap, declaring, "Well, you're pregnant."

Laynie sat back in her chair. "I am! I guess I knew, but to hear you say it..."

"What do you want to do about it?" Laynie was stunned. She stared at the woman's crucifix and couldn't believe she had asked her that question like she wanted to know what she would do with an extra pair of socks.

"What do you mean, what do I want to do about it?"

"Well, you already have so many children, and your age, your financial circumstance..."

"Listen to me," fumed Laynie, "Just because I come to this free clinic does not mean I am the type of person who should not have a baby."

"I'm sorry. I had to ask you."

"I might not be able to pay for expensive doctor's visits at this time in my life, but that doesn't mean you should judge me as less desirable to have a baby."

Laynie took the file out of the woman's hands. "You can't take that," she snapped. "It belongs to the clinic."

"I wouldn't want my file to take up any unnecessary space in your righteous clinic. It might contaminate the others." Laynie drove home, gripping the steering wheel. She had to calm down. All this stress was not good for the baby. Her hand rested on her abdomen. "A baby," she whispered. "A brand new person." The smile that broke out pushed away her anger and all the reasons why it was not the best time to have a child.

"You're here, now, and we'll be ready when you come." Her mind was already rearranging the house, trying to figure out who would sleep where. She wondered how the children would react. Shawn would be excited.

Later that night, after the children were in bed, Laynie broke the news to Shawn. His elation kept them both awake, then he finally went to sleep with his hand on Laynie's tummy.

They decided to wait until the weekend to tell the children, when Rachel would be with them. It was Thursday night and they were going to the church for a special service. Laynie finished the dishes when the phone rang.

"Laynie? This is Jolene. Tell Shawn he can forget getting Rachel this weekend. I heard he was talking to her teacher again and I don't appreciate all the slander. I'm going to sue. Tell him that." Laynie was listening to a dial tone.

So much for telling the kids this weekend about the baby. Her energy drained out of her. Laynie was tired, so tired she felt as though she could barely make it to the sofa. "Shawn," she called into their bedroom, "can you finish getting Hayley ready?"

"Sure, Babe," he answered.

"What's wrong, Mom? You look all pale," said Zack as he sat next to her.

"I'm not feeling too great. I'll let you in on a secret. I'm pregnant, Zack."

His eyes widened. "Really? Wow! When will it be here?"

"I'm four months along. It won't be long." Laynie leaned front as her abdomen tightened. "Oh, my!"

"Mom, what is it?" Zack put his arm around her shoulder.

"I don't know." Laynie was alarmed as it swept over her again. She feared she was in trouble.

"Do you want me to get dad? He's in Joey's room with Hayley."

"Yes. I'm going to our bed." *I don't want to lose this baby, dear God. Please.* When Shawn found her she was in the bathroom.

"Do you want me to come in, Laynie?" he called through the door.

"Oh, Shawn, I think I'm losing the baby." Her voice shook with anxiety.

"What do you want me to do? Tell me what to do, Laynie."

"We can't do anything. I can't stop it," she sobbed. It happened so quickly. When she came out of the bathroom numbness shrouded her as she looked at Shawn's puzzled face. "Our baby..." she whispered.

"Oh, Darlin', is there something we should do?" Shawn's voice was filled with helplessness.

Laynie ran her hand through her hair and stood there for a moment, searching the floor like it held the answer. She lifted her head slowly and turned to her husband. "We should go to church."

"Don't you need to see a doctor? Shouldn't you rest?" Shawn put his arm around her waist and guided her to the sofa.

"Just let me rest a minute. Make sure the kids are ready, we don't want to be late." Laynie felt like a robot, like she was on autopilot. Un-human. Disconnected from her feelings.

"Mom, are you all right?" Zack was back beside her.

"I lost the baby, Zack, " she whispered. "There was nothing I could do. It happened so fast." She stared straight ahead, then as if someone had whispered in her ear, she tilted her head and said, "But now we have to get to church. Help Dad load up the children." Detached from herself, Laynie heard herself dictating directions, like she was directing the scene of a play from the audience. Zack patted her shoulder, not sure he should talk her out of this or listen to her.

"Why don't you stay home, Mom? We could all stay home."

"No, no. We need to go. There have been enough of bad things ... I'm so tired of the bad things, Zack. We have to go."

Laynie needed to do something normal. She made herself go through the motions of the church service, her mind numb from the shock of her loss. They returned home and put the children to bed. Zack reluctantly left her side to go to his room. Laynie felt guilty at the bewildered look as he left her, yet she was helpless to do anything about it.

Shawn held her in bed that night. She turned to him, searching for the right words. "At first, when I wasn't sure I was pregnant, I prayed not to be. Gave God all the reasons why it was not a good time to have a baby. Then I came to terms with it, Shawn, I really did. I wanted this child."

"I know you did, Laynie."

"I should never have said I didn't want to be pregnant," she sobbed.

"That's not why you lost this baby. You know that, Laynie. God's not that cruel. God knew you really did want this baby. Something must have been very wrong."

In her head Laynie knew Shawn was right, but the next few days she wrestled with her grief and guilt. She didn't know why, but she instructed Shawn and Zack not to tell anyone about the miscarriage. Shawn thought it best to act like nothing happened. Laynie wished they would talk about how it felt to lose the baby. The small person she had carried under her heart was dead.

In her sorrow, Laynie called an old high school friend, Taylor Bridges, who was still living in her hometown. She and Laynie didn't see much of each other, but they remained best friends.

Laynie dialed her number. "Taylor?"

"Laynie! I was just going to call you. What's wrong?"

Somehow, Taylor always knew when she needed her. Laynie cried as she told her what happened. Her friend listened and comforted. "I'll light a candle for your baby, Laynie. I'll pray for you and the baby." Even though she was not Catholic, the thought of a candle being lit for her baby was a comfort to Laynie. An acknowledgment of a passing life, no matter how small it was.

That evening Shawn came home and put his arms around her as she was washing the dishes. "How are you handling all this? I know it must be a terrible load for you. Taking care of the kids, worrying about Rachel, dealing with Jolene, and now this."

"This? What, Shawn. Say it." She turned and faced him.

Shawn took her hands and pulled her closer to him. "Losing our baby."

Hearing the man she loved more than her own life say it strangely released Laynie from the grip of isolation that had held her since losing the baby. "It fills me with such grief, Shawn, such deep, deep, grief. We lost a child. I never even got to hold it." She wept against his chest. "I never got to look into its eyes, to hear it cry or coo. I never got to touch her soft skin."

"Her?" whispered Shawn into Laynie's hair.

"What?"

"You said her."

"I just have a feeling. I named her Taylor. But if it was a boy, Taylor would be all right."

"Taylor," murmured Shawn. "We won't forget about Taylor, Laynie. I didn't know it bothered you this much."

"You never asked."

"But you wanted to keep it all quiet."

Laynie looked up at Shawn, recognizing the sorrow in his eyes. This *had* been difficult for him. "I can't explain that, but I want to share this with *you*. We had a child, Shawn, and now... she's gone." They stood there holding each other, their sorrow divided by embracing each other.

The child they would never know. A life so brief, so fragile, so fleeting.

EIGHT

Jolene called Shawn daily with incessant questions about Rachel. She also phoned Laynie asking how to cook something or how were the kids or what could she buy Shawn for his birthday. To that one Laynie told her she would get Shawn a gift from Rachel and the children, all together.

Laynie wasted her breath. Jolene bought Shawn underwear, along with a shirt and *The Farmer's Almanac.* Laynie fumed. *Underwear! Is he supposed to wear it and think of her? Oooh, baby.* Like she was supposed to be stupid enough to believe Rachel would pick that out for her dad. Laynie picked up the not so subtle message loud and clear.

But not so Shawn, at least he wouldn't admit it. He simply shook his head, amazed at Laynie's anger. "You know she does this every year. I don't see why you let this upset you." She wondered how he'd handle it if the tables were turned.

Laynie gave the birthday clothing to Goodwill, but the almanac disappeared before she could rid her home of the intruder. She hunted high and low for it, wondering what was its fate. She found out one night when they went to bed early, and looked over from her book to see Shawn lying on his pillow with the almanac propped on his chest. She opened her mouth to ask him how he could bring that book, Jolene's gift to him, to their bed, but she knew he would tell her she was being silly. *How can he lie there with it and not know it bothers me?* Closing her book, she rolled on her side away from him.

"Tired?" asked Shawn as he patted her shoulder. She turned her head and saw his eyes never left the almanac.

"Yeah," she sighed, laying her head back on her pillow. "Real tired." *Of Jolene.* Laynie fell asleep, praying what she'd been praying for four years. *I feel as though I can't take any more. Every day, every single day, it's something about Jolene. I want to scream and scream until I lose my voice.*

Instead, Laynie pulled her pillow close and shut out the light by which Shawn was reading the almanac.

*****

The clock showed 8:45 on a Wednesday morning when Shawn came into the kitchen. "Laynie," was all he said. She couldn't read his face. He looked like he might cry, but yet a smile tugged at his mouth.

"What is it, Shawn? Who was that on the phone?"

"It was Will."

"Will?"

"He said Jolene was in trouble last night. Wouldn't say much else, just that Rachel was okay, and I am to 'call where I need to call' to find out. I called Wagontown police. Laynie, Jolene was arrested for public intoxication. I'm going to meet with the arresting officer to get more information. I called the school to see if Rachel is there and she is."

The phone was ringing again. As Laynie digested this new information she heard Shawn consoling someone on the phone. Several minutes later Shawn returned. "That was Jane. She heard, too. She realizes Jolene will never change. She confessed she knew Jolene's sober at school when she does volunteer work, but drinks when she's at home with Rachel. Jane's tired of people coming up and telling her things about Jolene. She said she would help us in whatever way possible."

"What are you going to do?"

"I'm meeting with the arresting officer right before I pick up Rachel. I'll just hang around Wagontown with her."

"Do you know where to get Rachel?"

"Yeah, Jolene finally admitted they're living with Billy." Shawn leaned toward her "I wonder what Jolene did last night."

That was what Laynie wanted to know. She watched the clock all evening, anxiously waiting for Shawn's return. The dogs outside barked as headlights came up the drive.

"How is Rachel?" she asked Shawn as he came through the door.

"Quiet. I hated dropping her off."

"What did the arresting officer say?" Laynie pulled Shawn over to the sofa where they sat down. He gripped her hand, holding on as he explained the latest escapade.

"Jolene had broken into Will's house to get some things. Someone saw her and called the cops. They stopped her out on the street and the officer was suspicious she was drunk. He gave her a test and arrested her for Public Intoxication." Shawn's eyes widened as he continued his story. "When I took Rachel back this evening, Jolene acted like nothing happened."

"What do we do now?" asked Laynie.

"I called Grady and he's working on it. We might be able to have an emergency hearing. I want Jane to go to Grady's tomorrow to give her statement on what she's been witnessing. I want her to get Tanya there, too."

Shawn came back and told Laynie about the last phone call he would make that night. Tanya opened up and told him all she knew about Jolene and her drinking, ending by saying "Jolene's so messed up she'd be happy to live in a prairie dog hole." She agreed to help them. It seemed too good to be true.

The next afternoon Laynie went by Grady's office and brought home copies of their statements. She read them:

STATE OF OKLAHOMA
Supporting Affidavit for Extraordinary Relief

On this day Jane Morgan appeared before me. After being sworn and while under oath she told me the following:

"My name is Jane Morgan. Jolene Cheyenne Stevens is my cousin. Rachel Stevens is her daughter. I am not party to the lawsuit concerning custody of Rachel Sue Stevens. I live in Wagontown, Oklahoma. Jolene has a severe problem abusing alcohol, which also is done in the presence of her daughter. Last Saturday I went to her house and she was intoxicated while she was alone with Rachel.

In June of this year, Rachel was with me at Pinto Park when Jolene came to pick up Rachel. Jolene was obviously drunk, and left with Rachel in her car. Rachel was in the front seat, and did not buckle up her seat belt.

Jolene's continuous abuse of alcohol puts Rachel's health and welfare in serious jeopardy. Rachel needs a change in her surroundings and care until Jolene can overcome her problems."

Signed this ____ day of October, _____

_____
Jane Morgan

SUBSCRIBED AND SWORN TO before me this ____ day of October, _____

_____Notary Public
My commission expires _____

STATE OF OKLAHOMA
Supporting Affidavit for Extraordinary Relief

On this day Tanya Savannah Longer appeared before me. After being sworn and while under oath she told me the following:

"My name is Tanya Savannah Longer. Jolene Cheyenne Stevens is my older sister. Rachel Sue Stevens is my niece. I am not party to the lawsuit concerning custody of Rachel Sue Stevens.

Jolene drinks alcohol excessively. I have been witness to her inebriation and obvious bouts of being drunk. Rachel is totally aware of Jolene's lifestyle. Rachel suffers from emotional trauma, weight loss, outbursts of crying, and bedwetting. This is because she lives with her mother who abuses alcohol.

Rachel needs a change in her surroundings until Jolene can control her alcohol abuse."

_____

Tanya Savannah Longer

SUBSCRIBED AND SWORN TO before me this _____ day of October, _____

_____

Notary Public
My commission expires _____

Something about the statements bothered Laynie. She read the copies again and it hit her. When Shawn came home she showed him the end of each woman's statement.

"Look, Shawn. They both say Rachel needs to be taken from Jolene until she recovers. What do they think Rachel is, the brass ring on the carousel?"

"I think it's the only way they could bring themselves to sign a statement like that against Jolene."

"It's not against Jolene. It's *for* Rachel. Why is that so difficult for people to see?" Laynie handed him the papers.

Shawn shook his head. "I know one person that better get it this time. I don't know what I'll do if Judge Jenkins gives Jolene another chance."

"What happens now?"

Shawn took off his glasses and rubbed his eyes. "Grady says we go before the judge tomorrow morning. Then if we get Rachel, an officer of the court will go get her. I told Grady I don't want that to happen at school, in front of all those kids. I asked him if I could go along, but I'll have to wait for them just outside Wagontown. At least she won't have to ride the whole way home with a stranger." Laynie could see he was troubled by the effect this would have on his little girl.

"Ask him if he would take one of her stuffed animals along and give her. Something she can hold onto until she's with you," she suggested.

After a sleepless night they waited for Delilah to come and be with Hayley while they went to the hearing. They hadn't seen much of her and Henry since the hay-burning incident, but now their friends were making themselves available to help get Rachel any way they could. Driving in silence, Laynie was trying desperately to suppress her hopefulness at today's outcome. The bleak, beige courthouse loomed ahead. She clasped Shawn's hand as they climbed the cement stairs. Everything about the building was cold, hard, stark. Laynie watched her feet cross the mud brown tiles.

"I hate this place," she whispered as they searched for Grady in the hallway. "It ties my stomach in a knot just coming in here."

Shawn took her hand. "This time it will be different. It *has* to be." Laynie spied their lawyer approaching them with a smile. The roller coaster ride was about to begin.

"Hey, Laynie, hey, Shawn. You got everything?" Grady asked Shawn as they rose to meet him.

"Yeah, we're ready." Shawn clutched the folder containing the arrest report. They followed Grady up the winding steps. Laynie gripped the metal railing because her knees threatened to collapse. They sat in the front row of the courtroom, and waited while Grady stood off to the side. Prisoners in bright orange jumpsuits shuffled in, wearing handcuffs. Lawyers hurried in and out, toting briefcases and files, looking important. There was constant movement in the courtroom.

They all rose when Judge Jenkins entered and sat on the bench. Laynie wondered how long it would take for all that rising-as-you-enter-and- leave-a-room to affect a judge's ego.

290

They didn't wait long until Grady came to them and told Shawn to follow him up front to the judge. Laynie remained in her seat, straining to listen. Grady did most of the talking, reviewing their attempts to get Rachel out of a dangerous environment, showing Judge Jenkins the affidavits from Tanya and Jane, and explaining the Public Intoxication arrest. Shawn handed over the police report. He only spoke once, pleading with the judge to grant him custody of Rachel.

Remember us, Judge Jenkins! Laynie stared at him. He glanced up and met her eyes for just a second, but quickly looked away. An icy fear raced through her body. *You DO remember us, don't you?*

His Honor brushed back the sleeves of his robe like he was ready to get to work. "I warned this woman," the ruddy-complected man declared loud enough for the whole room to hear. "I warned her about this drinking. I hereby order that the child should be delivered safely to Shawn Stevens immediately. Jolene Stevens is ordered to appear before this court on October 22 for a temporary custody hearing."

Laynie was stunned. Even though it was what they had been anticipating, a part of her mind refused to believe what she had just heard. Shawn turned to her, beaming. He listened and nodded as Grady shuffled through papers, explaining the procedure for getting Rachel.

Shawn put his arm around her and guided her out of the room. "We did it, Babe. I can't believe it!"

"What do we do now?" Laynie's heart pounded.

"We go down the street and get the papers filed and give a set to the constable. He's going to get Rachel. I know him, he's a nice guy. He'll make it as easy as possible for her. Then I'll leave with him and wait for him to get her after school at Billy's house. She'll be home with us tonight, Laynie. At last." He kissed her and held her against him. Shawn was trembling.

How long he's waited to rescue his little girl! Even before I knew him, he began this battle all alone.

They went to the sub shop to tell Amelia the news. As soon as they walked in, the young woman wiped her hands on her apron and motioned them to the back. "Jolene called and said something about you stopping payment on your last two support checks. She thinks Will may have gotten them. She went on and on about how she's had to change her life because of Will. Like I care." Amelia giggled. "So why are you two here now, anyway?"

Elated at their news she squealed with delight as she grabbed the ringing phone. "Train Stop Sub Shop," she sang. Her eyes expanded as she handed the phone to Laynie. "Its Jolene! She wants *you*!"

Laynie panicked. The last person she wanted to talk to was Jolene. "Hello?"

"Laynie? This is Jolene. I'm in charge of a parent volunteer luncheon tomorrow at school, and I want to make those ham subs like y'all make there. Do y'all put mayonnaise on them?"

Laynie shook her head. She felt horrible, talking to Jolene like nothing was going to happen. Even after all Jolene had done, a part of Laynie felt sorry for her.

"Laynie? You there?"

"You can use mayonnaise. But not everyone wants that."

Jolene giggled. Laynie realized she was drunk. "I have to go, Jolene."

"Thank you, Laynie. I'm too stupid to do this myself." Laynie hung up and stared at Shawn.

He waved his hand. "I don't even want to know. I have to get you home so I can drive over to Wagontown and wait for Rachel." Amelia hugged them both and they hurried home. After Shawn left, Laynie waited for the other children to arrive from school. They bustled in, tossing backpacks on the bench, searching the kitchen for a snack. Laynie explained what happened while they waited impatiently for Shawn to return with Rachel.

"This doesn't mean she's definitely going to stay here. It's just the first step," she explained to their beaming faces. "This was an emergency hearing. The next step is a hearing for temporary custody. Then we have to have a hearing for permanent custody."

"That's dumb, " said Maddie. "Why don't they just decide everything at one hearing?"

"So the lawyers can make more money," stated Zack.

"Will Rachel go to school with us on Monday?" asked Joey. Laynie nodded.

"They wouldn't have her start a new school and change it in a little while, would they Mom?" asked Joey. "Aren't they sure she's going to stay with us?"

"I certainly hope so. I guess they feel it's necessary to go through all these steps."

"So they get more money out of you. See, I'm right." Zack's dark eyes were full of teenage wisdom.

"The judge finally got it right," declared Maddie. "Maybe he just can't say 'no' to Jolene when she's there." Laynie silently wondered if Maddie was right.

"Mom," said Joey, "make Rachel's favorite supper tonight."

"You must have read my mind," answered Laynie. "I have a big pot of ham, beans, and potatoes on the stove."

"They're here!" yelled Zack. Maddie squealed and Hayley rose from her toys on the floor to toddle toward the door. Laynie was shocked as Rachel strolled through the door as if nothing had happened.

"Hi, y'all," she called as she sat on the sofa, holding the stuffed bear. "I'll be going to your school with you Monday. Dad says we can have a tour of it tomorrow. I'll be riding the bus with you guys and everything."

Laynie raised her eyebrows at Shawn as he came through the door carrying dresses on hangers and a suitcase. He took them in and laid them on Rachel's bed and returned to the living room. "Why don't you go out and play before supper," said Laynie. Shawn watched them playing through the kitchen window.

"I can't believe how well she's taking this. Do we wait for a delayed reaction?" Laynie asked as she put her arms around Shawn's waist and kissed him.

"When the constable first brought her to me, she was crying. Rachel hugged me and held on tight for a long time, while I tried to explain to her what was going on. After a while she grew still and I pulled her away to look at her. She wanted to know if her mother would be all right, and I told her Billy would take care of her, and that her mom needed to get help to get better. Rachel nodded and accepted that. The rest of the way home the conversation was normal."

"Did the constable tell you much?"

"He said Rachel was doing all right until Jolene got hysterical. He asked Jolene if she wanted to send along anything, that's what I brought home."

Laynie thought for a moment how it would feel to have your child taken from you like that. But her common sense pushed away a pang of pity as she recalled all the reasons why things had come to this.

Rachel seemed almost relieved at the supper table as she chatted about what they would do after supper and whose turn it was to be "it" for "Kick the Tin Can." She ate two platefuls of supper and a dish of pineapples. Laynie cut up the brownies she had made and placed them in small dishes, and put a scoop of vanilla ice cream on top. Then she squeezed chocolate syrup over it and added, to the delighted squeals of the children, sprinkles.

"Wow, Mom, ice cream and sprinkles!" said Joey. "You should come and live with us more often, Rachel!" They all laughed.

"No, Joey once is enough. I don't want us to ever have to go through this again," said Shawn. "Let's hope after all these hearings, Rachel will be with us forever."

"Yeah, now we're a real family," said Maddie.

"The hole's filled up," added Joey.

He's little but he's got it right. There was one more thing Laynie felt she had to do. Oh, she didn't want to, but she knew she must. While they were all outside she walked over to the phone and stared at it. She quickly picked it up and punched out the numbers before losing her nerve. She was relieved to hear Billy's voice.

"Crosstown Construction."

"Billy? This is Laynie. I... I was wondering if Jolene is okay."

"She's doing as well as can be expected."

"You're able to stay home with her tonight?"

"Yes."

"Tell her Rachel is fine. She wasn't crying once she got to be with her dad. I mean, if she's worried how all this-"

"She wasn't drunk, you know."

"What?"

"Jolene. She wasn't really drunk outside Will's house."

"Oh, Billy."

"No, she really should not have been arrested. She wasn't drunk, Laynie."

"But the police-"

"They were wrong."

"Jolene told you this, right, Billy?" Laynie wanted to tell him to open his eyes. He should read the Breathalyzer test report and talk to the officer. But she knew, like all the other men Jolene somehow captured under her spell, Billy would cling to what Jolene told him. "You really should talk to the police, Billy. But I didn't call to get into that. I just wanted to see if Jolene was all right."

"I'll take care of her."

"Good." She quickly hung up the phone and walked over to the back door. Daylight was dimming as the children played their game. Shawn was pushing Hayley in her swing. No judges, no courts, no fighting, no accusations, no lies. Just her family, all together, all safe. Laynie wanted it to stay this way forever. Rachel ran past the door and waved at her, making a funny face.

She was safe at last.

NINE

For the next two weeks they heard nothing from Jolene. No calls, no notes in the mail, no visits. They received notice of postponement of the temporary hearing because Jolene was "receiving professional care." In the mean time Shawn and Laynie thought it would be good to get Rachel involved with things like scouts and piano lessons. Now she would be able to attend church with them every Sunday and participate in children's choir.

Rachel's frantic finger rubbing stopped. Each night she fell asleep more quickly after assurances that her mother was all right. The sudden outburst of tears ceased. She gained weight. Rachel loved her second grade teacher and made lots of friends at school.

Jolene called and asked to come out for a couple of hours. She and Billy came one Sunday afternoon and took Rachel out for supper. Shawn met them outside, where Jolene gave him an expected chilling reception.

But she was warm to Shawn on the phone the next day. He told Laynie she called him at work to explain her disappearance was because she was in rehab for a week. She said she had no choice, which Laynie guessed to mean her lawyer advised her to do so. Jolene explained to Shawn she was in an outpatient program and attending AA.

At the temporary hearing, Shawn was appointed "Sole Managing Conservator," but Jolene was given more visitation rights than Shawn ever had over the years. She did not have to pay child support at this point.

Rachel handled the visitations well, except for the night Jolene took her along to search through Will's mail at his house. Rachel had been terrified. Laynie called Jolene and told her it was not a good idea to take Rachel along on these trips to Will's. Jolene told her that Rachel was her daughter and Laynie should mind her own business.

The permanent trial loomed ahead of them. Even though it wasn't to occur until September of next year, Laynie and Shawn continuously poured over their diaries, notes, and tapes. Their lawyer said Laynie could no longer write to the judge while the case was pending. She focused her energy on keeping records of everything that happened until the trial.

After the holidays they received an "anonymous" phone call that they should check their mailbox. (Shawn was sure it was Will Stark.) They found a video and watched as it showed Will's last attempt of a family vacation. His voice narrated their trip where Jolene stumbled around the amusement park, her speech slurred and her face sagging from intoxication. Rachel seemed unaware- or used to- her mother's condition. Laynie held her breath as they came to the part where neither Will nor Jolene knew where Rachel was. After two minutes of Jolene searching and tripping while Will kept on filming, they found her.

Jolene turned her slackened face to the camera and walked up to the lens. "Laynie," she stated, "I said, Laynie and Shawn. I'm going back to my room, smoke me a cigarette, and chug me a six pack, so get off my back!" She cursed, and then grinned into the camera.

A chill shivered through Laynie. Here was Jolene, miles away on a vacation with her husband and daughter, yet obsessed with her and Shawn.

"I bet this is why Jolene broke into Will's house. Boy, howdy! She sure as heck wanted to get this!" said Shawn. They watched the tape again, Laynie shocked at how drunken Jolene allowed herself to be while Rachel was in her care.

"This ought to prove to the judge she's outright defiant about his orders to stop drinking and smoking around Rachel," Shawn said as he rose and ejected the tape. "We need to put this up where kids won't see it."

As she lay in bed that night, Laynie wondered how much trouble Jolene was going to give her family in the future. *Please change her,* prayed Laynie. *Help her fight her demons. Or at least leave us alone.* Laynie fell into a troubled sleep.

*****

At Rachel's teacher's conference that spring, Mrs. Green sat across from Laynie at Rachel's desk. "Let me take a guess at something," she said as she took papers from a folder. "Rachel sees her mother Wednesday evenings, doesn't she?"

"Yes, how did you know?"

The smiling woman leaned over and laid papers before her. "Look, see these papers?" Rachel's written work was neat and clear. "These are papers from most of the week. Now look at these."

If Rachel's name hadn't been at the top of the papers, Laynie would have thought Mrs. Green had another child's work before her. The writing was difficult to read. "Are these Rachel's?"

Mrs. Green was nodding. "Those are Wednesday afternoon and Thursday's work. It's the same every week."

"The visits affect her that much? What should we do?"

"What you're doing now. Give her consistency. I've met Jolene; she comes in often to eat lunch with Rachel. Rachel instantly turns into this wild, unruly child and Jolene hasn't a clue what to do. She's such a nervous person and... odd."

"I know." Laynie knew she shouldn't feel embarrassed, but she did.

"Just keep loving and guiding and disciplining Rachel like you have been. She's a survivor. I think you got her just in time. Now I hope to God you keep her."

Mrs. Green's words rang in Laynie's ears. "You got her just in time."

Laynie thought of her own parents. All their lives they had helped other people, from relatives to acquaintances. One day Randy, a foster child they had taken care of for only two weeks, showed up on their front porch, all grown, with wife and baby in tow. After introductions and catching up on each other's lives, Randy rose to leave, and put his arms around Laynie's parents.

"I was only here two weeks," he told them, "but I never forgot it. They were the best weeks of my life. I've always remembered the things you did, the things that you taught me. You treated me with respect. You loved me enough to discipline me. I'm here today to thank you for that." He hugged them again. "I want us to be the kind of parents you two were to me. You didn't just drop me off at church, but we went as a family. Now I go to church. I don't know how I could handle things if I didn't go. It makes me a better person. It makes us a stronger family."

If her parents had influenced Randy's life after just two weeks, Laynie had to believe she and Shawn could give Rachel some of the upbringing she so desperately needed, enough to sustain her as she made decisions and matured. The longer they would be allowed to keep her, the better the chances were for Rachel.

TEN

Rachel was in the third grade for a month when the trial for permanent custody took place. Laynie and Shawn had answered pages of "Interrogatories" and read the answers to Jolene's. They scoured all their records, making lists of questions for Grady, reviewing the tapes, diaries, and the video. Their lawyer gave the assurance that the longer they had Rachel, the better it was for them. Since it had been almost a year, they had nothing to worry about.

The night before the hearing, Laynie heard Joey in his bedroom. She could see by the night-light he was on his knees beside his bed. She put her ear to the door.

"Dear God," he murmured, "please make the judge be as wise as King Solomon. It's me, Joey in Oklahoma, asking. The judge's name is Jenkins. Do you know him? I guess so, you're really smart. Dad says you're the smartest of all, so maybe you could give some of your smart to that judge so he sees Rachel is supposed to be with us, God. Dad needs to stop worrying about her. And Mom needs to stop crying. Don't forget. Tomorrow morning. My sister, Rachel, at the courthouse in Oklahoma. Amen." He scooted back under his sheet and squeezed his eyes shut. Laynie couldn't resist the urge to tip toe in and put her arms around him.

"Hey, Jelly Bean," she whispered. "Do you know how special you are?" He grinned up at her. "Now, you get to sleep. You have school tomorrow."

"I wish I could go with you and Dad."

"It's not for kids, Joey."

He frowned. "Mom, it's too hard to fall asleep. My brain is spinning. Would you sing to me?"

"All right. 'Yellow Bird,' right?"

The little boy's frown deepened. "No. Sing Rachel's song." Laynie swallowed, afraid she was going to cry in front of Joey. This small person had the love of a giant inside him for his sister. She sang quietly, caressing his hair until he fell asleep.

300

"I love you, Joey." She kissed him and rose to the top bunk to check on Rachel. She never stirred as Laynie pulled the sheet to her chin and kissed her forehead.

Laynie looked at her and thought about the progress they had made that year. Rachel was finally dry all night. She sat at the table without continuously jumping up and down and she no longer complained about tummy aches.

Don't let Judge Jenkins undo all this tomorrow, dear God. Give him the courage to go against tradition. Give him the wisdom Joey prayed for tonight, the wisdom to give a child to her better parent. Please.

That night Laynie stared at the ceiling, praying again, or watching the clock blink another minute away. Strands of sunlight snaked under the blinds and slithered to the carpet. She slid out of bed and went to the kitchen to make Shawn's coffee.

After getting the children off to school and Hayley ready for the day, Shawn and Laynie said goodbye to their toddler and Delilah. They carted folders and envelopes and boxes to the van. "I sure wouldn't want to be the one getting all my dirty laundry aired this morning," said Shawn.

"I just can't imagine what it would be like to sit there and listen to all the crazy things you've done," agreed Laynie.

They drove to town and toted their things inside the courthouse, depositing all of it on a wooden bench in the hallway. Henry, Mrs. Green, (Rachel's teacher), Amelia, two men from church, and their other witnesses sat near them. Laynie saw Jolene come in. The only person with her was Jane, who sheepishly smiled at her. She had called the day before, telling Laynie she would be with Jolene, just to ask for continued visitation. She said she wanted to help Jolene because she was really trying to change. Jane had said she wanted to be "up front" with Laynie, since Laynie was always that way with her. But it made Laynie nervous to see her with Jolene.

Grady bustled in, smiling and scanning the row of witnesses. He told them it would take a few minutes, that he and Jolene's lawyer were conferring

"You know," said Shawn as he leaned toward Laynie, "I'm almost looking forward to getting all this stuff about Jolene out in the open. It's about time."

"Do you think the world's ready for that?"

Shawn chuckled and patted her knee. "Boy howdy, I'm ready! I wish we could get this started." As if he heard him, Grady motioned for Shawn to come to the end of the hall. Jolene and her attorney swept passed them.

The four of them hunched over a small table, talking. A head would nod, papers would shuffle, a voice would rise. Grady and Hagley disappeared through a door and Jolene stared straight ahead as she marched past Laynie. Shawn strolled over, grinning.

"Y'all can go home," he told their witnesses. "It's over. Jolene signed the papers. Rachel stays with us."

A small cheer rose from their crowd of friends as hand shakes and hugs were exchanged. Shawn turned and swept Laynie into his arms. "At last," he said, "after all these years we won."

"What happened?" asked Laynie.

"I guess the evidence was so overwhelming her lawyer advised her to settle before the trial. Let's get out of here."

They carried all their things back to the van and hurried home to tell Delilah. "I can't believe it's over so quickly. I'm glad we won," said Shawn, "but I wish we would have had our day in court. Know what I mean?"

Laynie nodded. She really did understand. After all the years of frustration, of the lies and deception, of the crazy antics of Jolene, they felt as though it would at last be revealed.

"But what really matters is we have Rachel," added Shawn.

"Yes," agreed Laynie. "At last. Now let's get home and call the schools. I have a feeling Zack, Maddie, and Joey are suddenly going to have a great day."

ELEVEN

Jane showered all the children with presents at Christmas accepted an invitation for dinner. Laynie wanted her to get the chance to really know the family Rachel was with now. She appreciated Jane's statement when she left, saying, "*This* is where I want Rachel to stay."

As summer neared, Laynie convinced Shawn they could squeeze enough money out of their budget to visit Carol and Missy in Colorado. About a week before they were leaving for their trip, Jolene called them. Laynie thought it was to say goodbye to Rachel, but she spent the entire conversation talking about herself. She told Laynie she and Billy had gotten married, that he was "such a good man," and that he would never put up with her drinking, since he doesn't drink alcohol himself. *Funny*, thought Laynie, *he took you in when you were three sheets to the wind.*

Jolene prattled on about her AA meetings, how terrible her father was because he asked her to get liquor for him when he knew she was still in rehab. Then she said, "I thank God you and Shawn were there for Rachel. I don't know what I... I just, well, it was good y'all were there for her."

Laynie wasn't sure what that was all about, so she called their new pastor, who had shared his story in church about his past life as an uncontrolled alcoholic. "She's doing what's called 'crying in your beer,'" he told her. "We do it all the time. We feel sorry for ourselves and want others to feel the same. It happens a lot in the early stages of recovery. She's not stable yet. Not by a long shot."

Jolene was now calling daily, reporting the condition of her father's failing health. After his death Shawn chose to go to the memorial service for him. *Here we go again...* But Laynie chose to be silent.

*****

Laynie got out the maps for their trip and spread them on the kitchen table while Hayley was napping and the other children were outside in the pool. She examined the highlighted highways that snaked across the map, then opened the travel books and looked at the pictures of the Rockies, knowing she was smiling.

The phone rang.

"Hello, Laynie. It's Jolene. I need to ask you something."

"Okay."

"The cutest thing happened the other day. Sam was here- that's Billy's little boy- and I was taking a bath and he walked in on me. 'Why, Miss Jolene!' he said, 'you have a chest just like mine!' Isn't that cute? He's right, you know. I'm so thin. Nothing up top, flat as a pancake, that's me. I *am* trying to gain weight. I've taken a course at the high school on nutri-shun. And I'm going to quit smoking. After watching what cigarettes did to my mom and dad, I'm going to the doctor and get help. What do you think?"

I think you've been drinking.

"Laynie, you there?"

"That would mean so much to Rachel if you would quit, Jolene." Laynie longingly stared at the maps on the table. "I have to go now."

"Oh, so do I. I have to make an appointment for my pap smear."

That was more than Laynie cared to know. "Bye," she said and quickly hung up. She sat down at the table and rubbed her temples, closing her eyes, shutting out the conversation. Laynie got up and rummaged through her old albums, putting the John Denver one on the turntable. Carefully placing the needle on her selection, she sang along with his soothing, mellow voice and sorted through the brochures. "Rocky Mountain high... Colorado."

One more week, and they would be there.

TWELVE

When they crossed the border to Colorado and stopped to take their first pictures in the Rocky Mountains, Laynie looked at the splendor of the scene before her. She couldn't believe they were really there. *God must have modeled this like heaven, it's so beautiful.* The children crossed over and under the guardrail and ran across a meadow. Zack toted Hayley on his hip while Maddie, Rachel, and Joey jumped up and down in glee. Shawn came over and put his arm around Laynie. "Can you believe we're really here?" he grinned at her.

"No. And don't pinch me. I don't want to wake up if it's a dream." Laynie's eyes captured the panorama she hoped would stay in her memory forever. They reluctantly piled back into the van and traveled the last leg of the trip. After they arrived at Carol and Missy's they found themselves puffing as they took in suitcases and put them upstairs in their rooms.

"I feel like I ran the mile," said Shawn as he plopped into a chair. Carol grinned and handed him an iced tea.

"It's the altitude. You'll get used to it after three or four days." Their friends were wonderful hosts, sharing their home with them, taking them to "The Garden of the Gods" where the children climbed boulders and rocks; Echo Lake where they picnicked and touched snow on the mountain top; and of course, Pike's Peak.

Laynie fell in love with the area, but Shawn was troubled by the up springing developments. "Looks like they took a bunch of houses and shoved them together with a bulldozer," he said. Laynie had to admit he was right.

"The new governor is putting a stop to that," said Missy. "It's time to control our growth in this area. We're already having water problems."

But Laynie was in love. There was something about the Rockies that brought her peace. It was easy to see and feel God everywhere. Carol recognized her enchantment. "I get up every morning and look out that window and say, "Ho, hum. Another day in the Rocky Mountains," she teased Laynie.

Laynie convinced Shawn to look at some homes for sale with acreage in the area. Even though the property was quite a bit higher priced than in Wesley, Laynie still dreamed. "Carol and Missy said a sub shop would do great there," she told Shawn on their drive back to Oklahoma.

"But you know Jolene would take us to court to get Rachel back," he answered.

Jolene.

"That's why we should do it now. The judge remembers us and there's no way Jolene can prove she's rehabilitated in this short time. We should move *now*."

"I can't go home and just put a 'For Sale' sign in the yard."

"Why not?"

"I have too much to take care of. The cattle. And what about the greenhouse we just built and our plans for wholesaling plants? Just throw that all away?" Laynie was surprised at Shawn's anger. "I just bought all that equipment to cut hay, and now you want to move, like that?" He snapped his fingers.

"Why did you go along with looking at property, Shawn?"

"You wanted to so badly."

"I thought you wanted to consider moving there. I watched your face as you looked at the mountains. I saw you get caught up in their beauty."

"I *did* like it there. A lot. But it'll take time to move anywhere. Probably years."

Years. Laynie's heart sank. The thought of remaining in Wesley indefinitely depressed her. Nearing home, a familiar heavy dread settled in her stomach. As they bounced down the drive to their house, Laynie tried to see things through Shawn's eyes: their home on land that was filled with pecan, live oak, and olive trees; his growing herd; his hay equipment he bartered and paid for; his greenhouse for another plan to make money. *His.* Through no fault of Shawn's, Laynie never felt these things or plans were hers. They were not her dreams.

Laynie did love their yard, but she had to constantly watch out for rattlesnakes, scorpions, and fire ants. The summer heat could be oppressive. The plants in the shade house required constant watering and fertilizing, and they had to cart all of them into the greenhouse for the winter. Cattle were always going through fences, especially when they were ready to go somewhere, or when Shawn was working. The cutter needed welding, and the round baler broke down again. The tractor always needed a new part or repair. Laynie swore Shawn spent more time under the equipment fixing it rather than actually using it.

Another school year was coming up and Laynie felt guilty about sending their children back to the Wesley schools. She had constantly battled the administration for changes for safety of the children. Zack was sitting on the floor because there weren't enough desks while they were building a new gymnasium. He had to share textbooks because there was no money to buy more while the school put lights on the football field.

Laynie had never felt comfortable at school events or ball games. *People don't look you in the eye here.* At the grocery store, she would smile and say hello, mostly to be met with downcast eyes and silence. Laynie recalled watching two women fight right in the aisle, pulling hair and striking each other with their fists. She had hurried away with Hayley while her little girl asked, "Mommy, are they fighting over the macaroni and cheese?" And when Shawn would say, "You hate it here, don't you?" Laynie wanted to scream "Yes!"

But she didn't.

So they stayed. Rachel thrived with them during fourth grade. Laynie sent a card to Judge Jenkins, telling him how well Rachel was doing, and thanking him for saving her life. It was also the year Laynie found out she was going to have another baby.

THIRTEEN

One sizzling afternoon Laynie was coming out of the library and discovered her tire was flat. Even though she was very pregnant, she was sure she could change the tire herself. Before jacking up the car, she struggled to loosen the lugs on the wheel. They would not budge.

Remembering Shawn had them put on at the tire shop, she murmured, "I'll never be able to get these off." Returning to the library, she called the Wesley police and asked for help. Fifteen minutes later, a cruiser pulled in the lot beside her minivan. A very large officer wriggled out of the car and immediately began to sweat after leaving the air-conditioned cruiser.

"What's the problem, Ma'am?" he barked. He was not a happy camper.

"I'm so sorry to bother you, but I can't get the lugs off. I really shouldn't strain too much." He looked at her blankly. "I'm pregnant."

"You got all the tools you need?"

"Yes, you can see I tried to do it, but I just couldn't. I'm sorry." Laynie was angry he made her feel as though she needed to apologize. Kneeling on one knee, the man grunted as he pulled the wrench. Beads of sweat popped out and streamed down his cheeks, dripping off his brows and chin. *It's a downpour,* mused Laynie. As he loosened the lugs his face turned redder and redder, like the burner on Laynie's stove.

"There," he announced. "They're loose. I got to go now, I'm needed somewhere else." The lug wrench clanged on the macadam. He mopped his face with a handkerchief and plopped into his car. Laynie held the jack in her hand as she watched him drive off.

"Wesley hospitality," Laynie muttered as she finished the job, her own back trickling with sweat. "I hate this town."

On her way home, she saw the officer coming out of a coffee shop.

FOURTEEN

In February, Laynie gave birth to Dottie Marie. Henry had found Shawn a good job with a great salary as office supervisor at an air conditioning service center. They made the decision to home school the children next fall, since they were getting nowhere with the Wesley schools. Zack was preparing to go to college after receiving a grant and a scholarship. Things were looking up.

When Shawn made his dreaded call to tell Jolene of their decision to home school Rachel, Jolene's response was, "I would be too stupid to do that." That was it. Not one question about the curriculum, not one word of protest.

Laynie enjoyed actually having some cash in her wallet. It was nice to catch up on all the bills and not fall asleep nights wondering where the money would come from for next month's expenses. They even had money to occasionally do things with the children, like go to the movies and eat out. It was a good feeling to be able to buy shoes the first week it was reported they were too small or had "a blow-out," as Joey called a hole in his sneakers.

The third week in March, Shawn came home and took Laynie into their bedroom. They sat on the bed as he gripped her hand. She recognized the look in his eyes, the one that accompanies another crisis to come. "What is it, Shawn? What's wrong?"

The exasperated man shook his head and stared at the wall. "I can't believe this, Laynie. I'm out of a job as of next week."

Laynie's throat tightened. "What happened?"

"Seems as though the owner of the company made lots of loans without his wife's knowledge. He up and leaves her with all the debts. Now the banks are calling and she's going belly up with the company." A tremor in his voice betrayed his struggle to be calm.

Laynie gently caressed his arm. "She had no idea this was coming when she hired you?"

"She won't admit to it, but, boy howdy, she knew," Shawn answered bitterly. "I'll start looking for a job right away. It never seems to be good for us very long, does it, Laynie?"

Laynie took a deep breath. "Maybe this would be a good time to look out of state. I looked at online job banks and there's plenty of jobs out there for you."

Shawn nodded slowly. "Maybe you're right. Let's start looking for a good place to raise our family. The timing seems right, with the kids being home schooled and all. The move would be easier for them now. And we'd find a good school system so you can concentrate on chasing Dottie."

Out of despair sprang hope for Laynie, and the possibility of a better life for her family.

*****

Summer passed quickly and the day came for Zack's departure to college. Laynie kidded with him as they loaded the little red pick up truck Shawn had managed to pay off in trade for work from a neighbor. The back was weighted down, ropes and twine holding in Zack's college cargo. Everyone came out to shower him with hugs and kisses, as Laynie followed her oldest son to the driver's seat. She slammed the door and leaned inside to kiss his cheek one more time. "You be the best you can be, Pumpkin." She smiled as she blinked back her tears. "Be safe, be happy, work hard."

"I will, Mommy," teased Zack as he buckled his seat belt. "I'll be able to come home Thanksgiving. That's not far away."

Shawn leaned in and tousled his hair. "Almost all grown up, Zackie. Almost. Still got a lot to learn about the world."

"I know, I know, Dad."

Suddenly Laynie wanted to put the brakes on this whole scene. Once Zack drove off, he would literally be driving into a different world, an unfamiliar place, where he would be without his family. *Without me.* This, her first child went and grew up too fast. Would he be able to keep up with the pressure? How will he handle all the temptation waiting for him? Would he eat right...

"Did you pack your vitamins?"

"Yes, Mom, for the third time." He shook his head and chuckled.

Zack was right. She was being silly. This is what Shawn and she had been preparing him for. *But I'll miss him so much.* Laynie and the family watched and waved wildly, hands flapping frantically, voices shouting goodbye until the truck disappeared. *There you go. Be careful, Pumpkin.*

Laynie was surprised how she wrestled with her anxiety. Praying for her son in his new venture of life, she felt Shawn's arm around her, drawing her to his side.

"He's gonna be okay, Babe." His nearness comforted her.

"I know, I know. This is harder than I thought."

As everyone went off to do whatever they had to do, Laynie drifted into Zack's room. She looked around at his posters on the walls, his skateboard under his desk, his baby picture on his bookshelf. She picked up the photo of the grinning, chubby baby, running her hand across the cold glass. "I miss you already," she whispered.

In the days ahead, she would catch herself listening for Zack's voice in the house somewhere. She would strain to hear his laughter in the living room as the children watched TV. Once she caught herself watching for him to pop out of the school bus before the others. His empty chair at the dinner table, his quiet bedroom, even noticing less dirty laundry all weighed heavily on Laynie as she struggled to adjust to Zack's absence. *It's not that big a deal. Really. This is the way it is to be. It's just that, well, there's a hole in my family. One of mine no longer lives here. I can't check on him every day to see how he's doing. I can't peek at him at night to watch him sleep. My son has left the nest. And that, dear God, is a hard pill to swallow. Help me accept this change... Fly, little bird, fly.*

FIFTEEN

Taking care of Dottie and Hayley, and home schooling overwhelmed Laynie, but she was determined to make it work after noticing positive changes in Maddie, Joey, and Rachel. Fortunately Dottie took long morning naps and Hayley learned to entertain herself or quietly listen to the classes that interested her. Shawn noticed the children were more relaxed when he came home.

But Maddie missed playing her flute with the band. And now, for some reason, Rachel had started to complain about home schooling.

"You were the one who wanted to do it more than anyone, remember?" Laynie told her one morning as she balked at doing her math. "You didn't even want to finish last year at Wesley."

"I changed my mind. And this math is too hard. And it's boring. And you're not a real teacher, anyway."

Laynie leaned on Rachel's desk. "Ah ha, I see. And where's all this coming from, Rachel?"

Rachel rolled her eyes. "What do you mean?"

"You never said these things before. Has someone been saying these things to you?"

Rachel dropped her eyes to the floor. "No."

"Sounds like it to me. If your mom or anyone wants to know about home schooling, tell them to call me. I'd be more than happy to talk to them about it."

Laynie noticed Rachel was pulling away from her, ever since Shawn told the children he was looking for a job and they might need to move. They were all elated at first, but now Rachel didn't join the other children in their excitement. Laynie thought it was the idea of moving away from her mother. But Rachel now returned from Jolene's with an attitude that frustrated them all. She would isolate herself at first, snubbing Joey in particular. She argued with Laynie more and more, and no longer confided in her.

One morning, Maddie came into the kitchen, her green eyes wide against her pale face. "Sweetie, what's wrong?" asked Laynie as her hand felt Maddie's forehead. "Are you sick?"

"I just heard the most awful thing, Mom. Rachel said her mom's going to court to get her back. Jolene can't do that, can she?"

An old, familiar steely chill gripped Laynie's body. "I guess she can try."

"We won't lose Rachel, will we, Mom?"

"The judge certainly has more sense than that."

"Jolene had her chance being Rachel's mom. A whole lot of chances! I don't want Rachel to leave us. I hate Jolene."

Laynie put her arms around her daughter. Maddie had learned at an early age that life was not fair.

"Don't hate Jolene, Maddie. Your hatred will hurt you the most. It won't change Jolene at all, but it will change you. You let Dad and I worry about this court stuff."

"But Rachel's my sister. I worry about her, too."

"I know you do." Laynie hugged her, not knowing what else to say, knowing nothing could be said to sweep away the fear of losing Rachel.

It was back.

*****

Rachel returned from Jolene's with a BB gun, announcing, "My mom bought it for me."

Laynie heard the tone of defiance in her voice. *Thanks, Jolene.* "I wish you would leave it at your mom's, Rachel. Has anyone bothered going over rules about this with you?"

"No, but I guess you will," sighed Rachel. So Laynie stressed the usual rules of safety, especially the part about putting it out of Hayley's reach when she was not using it. "But you are only allowed to use it if you follow the rules. If not, it will be put away, Rachel. Do you understand?" Rachel looked at her solemnly and nodded.

It was that same afternoon Laynie heard Hayley in the bedroom she and Rachel shared. When she looked in, the little girl was awkwardly holding the BB gun at her waist. Laynie raced in and grabbed it. "Where did you find this, Hayley?"

"On Rachel's bed, Mommy."

"You must never touch a gun, any gun, Hayley. Run away from them, and tell Daddy or me about it. Understand?"

Hayley's brown eyes filled with tears. "You didn't do anything wrong, Hayley. You didn't know. But never, ever touch a gun, or you will be in trouble. Okay?" Laynie took the BB gun out of Hayley's small hands and put it on the top shelf of a cupboard. She told Shawn of the incident when he came home from his job at the convenience store. Rachel protested when she was told she would not be able to shoot the BB gun.

"I'll just take it with me when I go to my mom's," she shot back at Laynie.

"No, you won't, young lady. You've lost your privilege to use it. I'd feel horrible if I let you take it and you hurt Billy's son, Sam, with it," Laynie scolded.

"I won't do it again."

"Sorry, Rachel, but we don't go by what you say you *will* do, but by what you've already done. You know that."

"You'll be in big trouble with my mom. You'll see."

Laynie put her hands on Rachel's shoulders. "The rules about this weren't just made up as a test to see if you would follow them or not, Rachel. They are very important rules of safety, and I certainly hope your mother will agree with them."

But the next afternoon when Rachel went out to go to Jolene's car, she immediately returned and marched up to Laynie, her chin held high. "My mom said if y'all don't hand over the BB gun right now, she's going to bring Billy back with us and Dad will have to deal with him!"

Laynie didn't know whether to be angry or laugh at the threat. She heard Shawn coming in from the barn, and she called him into the room and told Rachel to tell him what she had said. He laughed.

"Okay. Take it." Rachel grinned at her. Shawn shook his head and left the room. Surprised at his response, Laynie had Rachel wait in her room while she took the gun down.

"Come here, Rachel," she called. The victorious girl still had a grin on her face as she held out her arms for the gun. Laynie handed it to her but didn't let go of it. Rachel pressed her lips together as her icy blue eyes glared at Laynie. "Rachel, don't you *ever* bring this back home. I will not have you jeopardize the safety of this family. Understand?"

"What if I do bring it back?" Rachel pulled on the gun but Laynie held firm.

"Then I will take it and smash it into a thousand pieces."

"My mom will be really mad at you!"

"I'm not afraid of your mother or her threats. I will *not* let her dictate how I run my home. Do you understand what I'm saying?" Rachel nodded. Laynie let go of the gun and Rachel raced out the door. They never saw the BB gun again.

*****

Rachel returned that evening with another message from Jolene. Laynie watched her sit on Shawn's lap as he sank into the rocker. "How was your evening, Sugar?" He brushed her long auburn hair away from her face.

"Okay. We went to the bank. My mom made a deposit of $600. She said she would give it to you if you wanted it."

"What?" Shawn stopped rocking.

"She knows how hard it is for you to take care of this big family. All these kids! She said you could have it if you wanted."

Air streamed out of Laynie's nose. *All right, Shawn. You better not act like this is nothing.* Shawn turned Rachel toward him.

"Rachel, I will *not* take money from your mom. She's not part of this family. She, Billy, and Sam, are one of your families. Over here, we're another. A different one. A *separate* one. Do you understand that?" Rachel nodded as she looked into Shawn's eyes. "Now give me a hug and get ready for bed."

"Jolene never stops, Shawn," said Laynie after Rachel left the living room.

Shawn shrugged. "She's just remorseful because of the threat she had Rachel deliver about the BB gun. It's the same old pattern."

"It's nice to know you understand her logic. Logic, that's a joke. I wish she wouldn't use Rachel for her messenger. Can't you speak to Jolene about that?"

"It wouldn't do any good. She'd look me right in the eye and agree and go right on doing it, or she'd go ballistic. It's no use." Shawn put up the newspaper like a wall to block out any further conversation. But Laynie wasn't finished.

"Can't you even try? Last week Rachel said Jolene was sad because she wished you two were back together. Think how that must mix up Rachel. Can't you even try to make Jolene see that?"

"She'd only see it as a personal attack, not something we're trying to do to protect Rachel," came his voice from behind the paper.

"But that's the point, Shawn. By not talking to Jolene, we're not even trying to protect Rachel. It's all chalked up to 'that's the way Jolene is and will always be so let's not even try.'"

Shawn lowered the newspaper. "I'd be wasting my breath. All I can do is try to teach Rachel the way things should be."

SIXTEEN

Shawn had to work Labor Day weekend, so they didn't make plans to go anywhere. They wouldn't have had the money, anyway. Laynie waited that Friday night for him to come home from work, to tell him of her plans for a picnic at the lake. With wild eyes he came into the room, his hand clutching papers.

"Shawn, what's wrong?" He plopped down of the sofa beside her.

"She sure planned this right. I can't call a lawyer until Tuesday. Made sure our holiday weekend was miserable."

"What did Jolene do now?"

"Served me with papers- at work, in front of a whole line of customers. I get this kind of news in front of all those people. I couldn't think. I didn't think even Jolene would do this to me!"

Laynie put her arms around Shawn. "How bad is it?"

"Oh, it's bad. She's trying to get her back. And she's put an order on us so we can't move."

"Can she do that? I mean, this is America! We haven't committed any crime, we're not wanted for anything. Can we be ordered not to move?"

"Seems so." Shawn tossed the papers on the coffee table. "I'm going to change lawyers. Remember Jennie, who came into the sub shop? She's set up her own practice and specializes in custody cases. When she comes by the store to get gas, I tell her about what's been going on. I'll talk to Grady, I'm sure he'll understand about the change. We need to meet with Jennie right away, but we can't till next week. We need to find out what they think they have to go on."

Shawn was rattled. He went on and on about what they should do. Laynie saw the desperation in his eyes and heard it in his voice as he struggled to get a handle on this latest catastrophe. Jolene was once again assaulting this man she loved so much.

Shawn got out paper and pencil, and started making some kind of list. Laynie hoped once he met with Jennie, he would feel better after finding out exactly what Jolene thought she had for court.

Shawn did find out, and it wasn't much. When he returned from his meeting with Jennie on Tuesday, all he had to tell Laynie was that Jolene was against home schooling and didn't like the way Laynie disciplined Rachel. "The home schooling should be a dead issue. We were going to get the kids back in public school in the fall anyway," said Shawn. They had, in fact, applied at a small school in the next district and were waiting to see if the children would be accepted.

"And there's nothing wrong with the way you're raising the kids, Laynie. We know that, and so does Jolene. She's grasping at straws."

"Anything else?"

"They're saying Rachel wants to move back with her mother."

Laynie considered this. "Rachel doesn't know what she wants, Shawn, she's so mixed up, thanks to Jolene. She loves us and deep down she knows this is where it's better for her. The court will see a child can't make such an important decision at this age."

"I don't trust the court," Shawn snapped. "You've seen what happened before."

"But we've had her almost four years! Surely that means something," Laynie declared.

Shawn nodded. "It's the longest she's lived anywhere. No judge in his right mind would tear her from this family on the slim, and I mean slim chance Jolene isn't drinking."

"Even if she isn't, Shawn, that's no reason to jerk Rachel around."

"I'll talk to Jane. See where she stands on all this."

Shawn stopped by Jane's the next day. Laynie could tell the meeting did not go well when she saw his face. "I think she's going to testify for Jolene. Seems she's more worried about Jolene than Rachel."

Laynie's heart sank. She thought she would be able to count on Jane to stand up for what was best for Rachel. "Jane once said she wanted Rachel to stay with us. Remember?"

Shawn laughed. "'That whole family is screwy. A bunch of warped, self-serving... I'm done with them. The whole lot."

A few days later they received confirmation the children were accepted at Twin Oaks School. The hearing was set for the end of September, so Rachel would be back in public school a couple of weeks.

Rachel and Laynie's relationship suffered. They argued constantly. Laynie felt all she was doing was disciplining her. Rachel seemed happiest when she upset Joey or got Maddie angry. "I think she's doing this to keep from being close to them," Laynie told Shawn. "I'm afraid in her mind she's already said 'goodbye.' It's easier to do if you don't get close to your family. Jolene is poison to our family. Look what she's done." And it had only begun.

One afternoon that summer, Laynie heard the children talking in Maddie's room. "My mom's getting all ready for court," stated Rachel.

"Don't you want to stay with us?" asked Joey.

"It's really cool at my mom's. She got me so much stuff this summer. I have a TV, VCR, and a new CD player in my room."

"Wow," exclaimed Maddie.

"And I just got a go-cart."

"Really?" said Joey.

"Uh, huh. And I can stay up as late as I want and watch any TV show I want. Not like here, where *Mom* won't let us."

"They're Dad's rules, too," said Joey.

"But Mom's the one who always makes us follow them."

"That's 'cause Dad's working all the time, Rachel. And he works all the time because he can't find a good job here." Maddie's voice was firm.

"You guys would like it at my mom's. We eat out a lot. You know what she said? She thinks y'all are really cute, and if you want, she'll go to court to get you, too."

"We would never do that," said Maddie.

"No way," added Joey.

"Well, my mom's my best friend. She says that all the time to me. She lets *me* decide everything about myself. She tells me everything."

"So what." Laynie smiled at Joey's response.

Laynie heard enough and walked away. She wondered if Jolene would completely destroy her relationship with Rachel. Her heart was heavy as she considered the possibility of losing her.

They increased her counseling with Dr. Janson, hoping it would help Rachel cope with the impending hearing. Shawn came home angry after a meeting with the counselor. Laynie was changing Dottie's diaper when he found her in the bathroom. "You'll never guess what stunt Jolene's pulled now. I went into Dr. Janson's and the receptionist looked surprised to see me. She said Jolene had been in, demanding to see Rachel's records. Dr. Janson told her it would not be a good idea to break Rachel's trust in her. Jolene threatened to talk to her lawyer. She made an appointment for herself and left. Then she called yesterday and canceled her appointment *and Rachel's*! Boy, howdy, of all the stupid…Dr. Janson said she'd do all she can to keep Rachel's files confidential. Heck, we don't even see them."

"The doctor doesn't have to show them to Jolene, does she?"

"Maybe, since Rachel's a minor." Shawn paced the room, shaking his head. "Can you believe Jolene canceling something that's good for her own daughter?"

"She's desperate, Shawn. Jolene will do anything because she's afraid if we win we'll move away."

"It would be better for Rachel not to have to deal with this going back and forth every week. It's tough on her. It would be better if we would move."

Laynie handed Dottie to Shawn. "I'm seeing Jennie tomorrow. She wants me to bring all the evidence we have so far."

Shawn lifted Dottie over his head while she squealed with delight. "Bet you think Daddy's ignoring you through all this. You're getting so big so fast." Rachel ran into the room and reached for Dottie.

"May I hold her, please, Dad?" He handed her over to Rachel. "Oh, Dottie you are so sweet," she cooed. "I could never live without you."

Shawn raised his brows and looked at Laynie "You know, Rachel, if you moved with your mother, you wouldn't see Dottie as much."

"I know. And look at how she likes me. She is so cute. I could never leave her."

After she walked out of the room, Laynie whispered, "She's so mixed up."

They watched Rachel's head hover over her little sister. Would she be here for Dottie's next birthday? Would they continue to be able to fall asleep nights knowing she was home safe, or lie awake again, wondering where she was?

With so little to even consider from Jolene, Laynie hoped Judge Jenkins would remember Jolene's history and the decision would be easy. Surely.

SEVENTEEN

Laynie put the box of "evidence" on Jennie's kitchen table. She was relieved Jennie wanted to meet in her home in Wesley rather than an office. "Let me see what all you have there," said the petite lawyer as she looked into the box. Jennie picked up a stack of cards and notes and began reading them. "Are these the ones Jolene and her cousin wrote when Rachel was visiting Shawn's parents?"

"Strange, isn't it?"

"It's weird. They bombarded her. Two letters every day. I wonder what they thought they were doing?"

"Trying to make her homesick, I guess."

"Seems so," Jennie's eyes raced over the remaining cards. She peered at Laynie over her glasses. "If I have to read one more time about how the pool is almost ready for her, I'll puke. What else you got?"

"Here's the original court transcript that says Jolene's not to drink or smoke around Rachel. Here are the pictures you wanted of our family, the house." Laynie opened a calendar. "This keeps track of things like how often Rachel returned late, which was most times, usually just twenty minutes or so, when she returned smelling of smoke, which was almost every time, and when Rachel told us they went to church."

"Which was twice."

"Yes. Is religious training important to Judge Jenkins?"

"I believe Judge J. is quite religious. But you have to realize these judges bring their own issues to court. He's from the old school where the mother should have the child."

"Do you think we should be worried?"

"You've had her almost four years. That's a long time, Laynie. Jolene has to prove circumstances have changed enough that Rachel needs to be taken from Shawn. You're great parents. You've got a really nice family. Rachel's not some brass ring."

"The judge *will* place her where it's best for her, right?" Laynie needed Jennie's assurance.

"That's what he's supposed to do. Now, let's see what else you got. What's this?" She held up a long, rectangular plastic box and rattled it. "A pill box?"

"Jolene sent it home filled with antihistamines for Rachel. I found it lying on her bed, where Hayley or Dottie could get it."

"Jolene just sent them home with Rachel, not letting you know she had them?"

"Yes."

Jennie shook her head. "What else?"

"Here are books and magazines I took from Rachel that came from her mother's. The magazines are for older teenagers. Look at the stuff in here." Laynie turned the pages. "I want to keep her informed, but this..."

Jennie flipped through them. "Wow, there's stuff in here *I* didn't know. Lots of talk about sex, how to get a boy interested in you, hardly stuff for an eleven-year-old kid like Rachel."

"Here's the curriculum list for home schooling, and the results of the home study ordered by the judge."

"That looks good." Jennie placed the report on the pile of evidence. "Okay. Now I have to show you something that I think is crappy." Laynie took a paper from Jennie and plowed through all the legal mumbo jumbo, noticing a child's printed signature at the bottom.

"They had Rachel sign a paper saying she wants to live with her mother?"

"It's the low of lows. This isn't usually done unless the child is over twelve."

"There's no way she realized what she was doing, Jennie." Laynie was angry. Angry at the low-life lawyer who dreamed this up and angry with the manipulative mother that would use her child like this. "I could barely understand what this means, how could Rachel?"

"I told Hagley, her lawyer, this was a crappy move."

"Will it mean much to the judge?"

"I don't think Judge J. will like it. Did you see the report from Jolene's psychologist?" Jennie smiled. "The part about the doctor going to Jolene's house and finding stuffed animals on Rachel's bed in a loving home almost made me gag."

"Now, Jennie, you don't mean these things were staged, do you?" It felt good to laugh with their lawyer. Laynie felt some of the tension leave her. "Wouldn't a judge be pretty dumb to not see through the report? It's not like it's been her ongoing therapist."

"You would think. We're in good shape, Laynie. I can't believe Hagley didn't talk Jolene out of this. He hates to lose."

"I'm so glad to hear you say that." They shook hands and Laynie hurried home to her children. Dottie was standing in her playpen when she walked in the door, and Hayley came out to hug her. Laynie was surprised to see tears in the little girl's eyes.

"What's wrong, Hayley?" Laynie stroked her hair.

"Rachel is crying and crying. Maddie can't get her to stop."

Laynie heard sobbing coming from Maddie's room. "I'll be right back, Sweetie. You stay here and keep Dottie happy. It'll be okay." Hayley nodded and walked over to the playpen. When Laynie opened the door, Maddie and Rachel were sitting on the bed, arms wrapped around each other.

"Maddie, what's the matter?"

"When I told Rachel you were at the lawyer's she started crying and crying. She doesn't want to talk to the judge and she doesn't want to tell him where she wants to live. She doesn't want to go to court."

Laynie sat next to Rachel and put her arms around the trembling child. Immediately, her arms wrapped around Laynie. "I don't want to see the judge," the child wailed.

"Did someone say you had to?"

"My, my Mom."

"But you don't want to?"

"No." Rachel's chest heaved as she wept. She buried her head against Laynie.

"Maddie, please go check on the little girls while I talk to Rachel."

"Sure, Mom." Maddie closed the door behind her.

"Rachel, I think you would feel better if you told me what's been going on."

"What, what do you mean, Mom?"

"About this court stuff. It's too much for a kid to handle." But Laynie could see it had been drilled in her to remain silent. "Okay. How about I ask you a few questions? You can answer what you want, and I'll tell you what I think is going on." Laynie tugged a tissue out of the box on Maddie's nightstand and wiped Rachel's face.

"Rachel, I saw the paper you signed."

"What paper?"

"The one that says that you want to go live with your mom."

"My mom took me to this office and I sat down at a table and she told me to sign a paper... Is that what it was?"

"Yes, Rachel."

"I didn't know, Mom! My mom said it would help her in court. I never should have signed it."

Laynie took Rachel's face and cupped it in her hands. "Listen to me, Rachel. Dad and I aren't mad at you. You're just a kid and you're all mixed up. The judge should figure that out. That's his job." Rachel started crying again. "I still love you, no matter what. Maddie told me about the list you and your mom are making up about me, things to tell the judge. I know your mom said it doesn't matter if they aren't true. That isn't something you really wanted to do, is it?"

Rachel shook her head. "No. I love you, Mom."

"Okay, Sweetie, I understand. I love you anyway, no matter what has happened. I'll never stop loving you. And I'm not mad at you."

Rachel's streaked face looked up at her. "I don't want to talk to the judge, Mom."

"*We* won't make you, but your mom might. But guess what I found out about him."

"What?" Her blue eyes were round with anticipation.

"He's a grandfather. He's got grandkids your age."

"Really?" Relief flooded her face.

"Yeah, so how scary can that be?"

Rachel smiled though her tears and hugged Laynie again. "He's somebody's grandpa? That's cool, Mom." Maddie came in and took Rachel's hand.

"Come on, Rach, let's do something outside. Want to draw chalk pictures?" Laynie watched them leave, holding hands, heads huddled in earnest conversation.

Another stunt by Jolene. Another storm to weather. Another prayer for help. It was a normal part of Laynie's life by now.

*****

The next few weeks, Laynie tried to run her home as normal as possible. But the new dreaded court date loomed ahead of them like an ominous dark thunderhead billowing up from the flat horizon. Although both Jane and Tanya were going to testify for Jolene, it was the cousin's reversal that smacked of betrayal. "I should have seen it coming," fumed Shawn. "What did I expect from anyone in that family?" Laynie bit her tongue.

She sat down and typed out a list of events and information to take along as notes for the trial. She would be ready for the battle ahead:

1. June-Jolene sent Rachel home with a week's supply of antihistamines in plastic box. In her backpack. No note, etc.

2. June- Rachel told me her mom is "sad," wishes she were back with Shawn. Rachel very mixed up.

3. Home school- Jolene's response- didn't care.

4. Jolene's many men friends- Victor scares Rachel.

5. Jolene told me she thanks God for us being there.

6. They smoke around Rachel indifferent to judge's orders. Rachel wrote notes asking Jolene to stop smoking around her.

7. Jolene took Rachel to church only twice.

8. Support- behind, unpaid medical bills.

9. Pets- gives and takes away from Rachel. 4 dogs, 3 or 4 cats. Rachel hurt and angry.

10. Rachel has bonded to this family- pictures, notes, etc.

11. Jolene treats Rachel as girlfriend. Shares inappropriate information.

12. Extravagant-with clothing and things. Magazines too old for her age, watches inappropriate TV shows and movies.

13. Rachel expresses need to protect her mother.

14. Rachel told Maddie she and Jolene had a list of "mean things about this mom, and it's OK to lie about it because that's how much my mom (Jolene) loves me and wants me back." Also- Jolene said if Maddie & Joey wanted to live w/ her she would try to get them, too.

15. Cards & letters Jolene & Jane swamped Rachel w/ on visits to grandparents.

EVIDENCE
Notes & cards from Rachel to us
Photos
Transcript not to smoke
Letters sent to Jolene & Billy for back support, one returned unopened
Plastic pillbox
Books and magazines
Home school texts and curriculum

Laynie carefully packed all the things they would take to the courthouse in a box. She put her hands on the top and prayed, begging God to let Rachel stay with them.

EIGHTEEN

Laynie was too nervous to put in her earrings. Her hands shook. Her insides felt like they had been put in a blender and someone hit the puree button. She wasn't handling this day well at all.

The older children had pleaded to stay home from school, but Laynie insisted they go. With great reluctance they said goodbye, then hurried out the door to catch their ride. Delilah arrived to stay with Rachel, Hayley, and Dottie.

As Shawn and Laynie walked up the steps to the courtroom, she was afraid she was going to get very sick, right there in front of everyone. They scanned the papers posted outside the judge's office and went down the steps to the ground floor. Shawn gripped Laynie's hand as they made the long journey to the courtroom in silence. When they rounded the corner, there was Jolene, huddled with Billy, Tanya, and Jane. *Get your stories straight,* thought Laynie as she stared at them. Jane quickly turned her back to them. "Wow, they're dressed to kill," whispered Laynie. She looked at her own very worn outfit.

Jennie popped out of the courtroom. "Hey, you guys! We got a small problem." Laynie sat on the bench in the hall. She didn't think she could handle any more problems, even small ones. Shawn slowly sat down bedside her, frowning with worry. "Judge J. is sick," their lawyer announced, "so you can have a substitute judge or wait until tomorrow. It's up to you."

"What do you think, Jennie?" asked Shawn. Laynie saw the hollow look in his eyes, realizing the huge toll this was taking on her husband. He had been struggling to keep it all together- juggling bills, getting ready for the hearing, all while being husband and father. Laynie wanted to chase everyone away and hold him, to make all of this disappear for the man she loved so deeply.

Jennie rearranged papers in her folder as she considered Shawn's question. "Well, this substitute guy is a real good ol' boy red-neck. He's the kind that thinks Mamma gets the baby, no matter what. Even if Mamma has a lot of problems."

"Let's wait, right, Babe?" Shawn turned to Laynie.

"Sure, Shawn, we'll wait."

"Good." With that, Jennie left them and disappeared into the courtroom. Laynie looked down at the enemy camp. Jolene was quite animated, exaggerating her gestures and laughing wildly. Jennie returned with the news that the hearing was rescheduled for tomorrow, nine o'clock.

*****

The postponement gave Laynie another night to shower God with her prayers for help. It gave her another morning to do normal things before this surreal event. Somehow, it seemed a little easier to get ready and go to the courthouse the next day. A steady determination replaced most of the fear; Shawn and Laynie paused outside the double doors of the courthouse, arm in arm. "I feel pretty good about this," he said. His blue eyes didn't have his sparkle. The darkness under his eyes betrayed his worry. "I mean, how can Jolene possibly persuade the judge to jerk Rachel around? Even if he buys what she says today, how could he uproot her from her home?"

Laynie rested her head against Shawn's chest and held him close, listening to his steady heartbeat, feeling safe in his arms. She wanted to stay like that and put the world on hold, but the clacking of a lawyer's hurried shoes across the cement pulled her away from the haven of her husband's embrace. Laynie stepped back and looked into Shawn's worried face. "That's what everyone's been telling us, Shawn. I think that's why Rachel doesn't want to talk to the judge. She doesn't want to have to come right out and say anything against her mother; afraid it would get back to Jolene, somehow. So she's banking on the fact that Judge Jenkins will see she needs to remain with us. I've read that a good judge knows how to ask questions so a child doesn't realize he's really asking where she wants to live."

Shawn nodded. "Yeah... that way she can look her mother in the eye and say this wasn't her fault. I wish she didn't have to be on call like this. This waiting to talk to him has to be killing her."

Shawn slid his arm around Laynie as they found their way down into the gloomy hall outside the courtroom. *Jolene's here with her troops again.* Jennie came out, smiling.

"All ready? Laynie this is different from before. You can't sit beside Shawn."

"Why not?" Laynie wanted to hear the lies Jolene would be telling so she could straighten out the judge. Even more, she wanted desperately to be near Shawn.

"Actually, you were lucky to have been in there before."

Lucky. Laynie sighed, resolved to being, once again, on the outside. "I'll watch for Henry and our pastor."

"Good." Jennie tugged on Shawn's sleeve. "You ready?"

"Yeah. Let's go." He leaned over and kissed Laynie. "I love you." Laynie watched him pass through the door to the courtroom. It closed, shutting her out, the one who took care of Rachel every day, who prayed for her every night. The Stepmother. Step. What a funny word to use to describe a relationship. A step what? Back? To the side? On?

Later Henry and Pastor Lowell came and kept her company as the morning dragged on. Henry was called in, then the minister, both returning to encourage Laynie that all was going well. They prayed yet another fervent prayer, then the men left for work. Henry would later stay with Hayley and Dottie when Delilah brought Rachel to talk to the judge.

Laynie studied her notes. She had to remember all the important things- Rachel's life depended on it. Jane and Tanya sat with Billy on a bench down the hall. The women had gone in earlier, and decided to leave now, evidently tired of waiting. Billy got up and paced back and forth. "I hate these things," he said. Laynie knew she was supposed to hear him, and what, feel sorry for him? She turned back to her notes. *What about what it does to Rachel? You're putting up the bucks for this, Billy. You had a choice. You could have refused...*

The door opened as Shawn walked out and took her hand to help her to her feet. "It's going really great, Babe." Ah, the sparkle was back. Laynie smiled at him as he added, "Jennie's a terrific

330

lawyer. Look, everyone's going to lunch. Let's go get a bite to eat, and then we have to call Delilah and tell her to bring in Rachel. The judge is going to speak to her in his chambers after you're finished."

All through lunch Shawn was excited about how the hearing was progressing. "I can't talk to you about the details. It's not allowed. But things are looking real good for us."

"I'll be glad when this is over."

"Boy, howdy." Shawn leaned forward and took Laynie's hand. "Thank you for hanging in there with me. I never could have done all this without you. Everyone in there knows you're the one who's been with Rachel the most. You are the one who's taken care of her, watched out for her, got her to talk about things that upset her. I love you so much for that." Her husband smiled, something Laynie realized he hadn't done for weeks.

"*You* are a wonderful father. To Rachel and all the children, even through all this and everything else you've had to deal with. As for me, how could I have done anything else? She's our daughter. I only did what any mother would have done."

"Any normal mother," he corrected. Shawn was so encouraging, Laynie was actually able to send some food peacefully down to her stomach. But as they walked out to the car, she wished she hadn't eaten. Her day in court was yet to come, and someone had turned on the blender in her stomach again.

Laynie sat alone on the bench as she waited to be called. She started to read her notes, then put them away. There was only so much of Jolene's history she could take, and she was way past that point. Thinking about what was at stake, pain stabbed at her middle, and she wondered if she had time to go to the bathroom.

The door swung open and Jennie grinned at her. "Your turn, Laynie. Just be your usual warm, assured, perky self, and you'll do fine."

Perky? Not one of the buttons on the blender today. Laynie took a deep breath and followed Jennie. Shawn smiled at her as he sat at the table where Jennie was sliding into a chair. Jolene stared straight ahead at the judge like an ice sculpture. Laynie was sworn in and she sat next to the judge. It was then she realized she had left her notes out in the hall. Laynie swallowed her panic, trying to think about something other than this tremendous error she had just committed. She looked at His Honor.

Wow, he's lost more hair. Gained a little more weight, too. He'll have to get a size "tent" robe soon. She cleared her throat. *He looks like a bowling ball. A bowling ball with a head on top... stop it, Laynie. Get serious.* She was afraid she was going to laugh, and never be able to stop. The wacky witness. The mad mamma. Loony Laynie. As Jennie approached her, Laynie glanced at the judge again. *He looks grumpy today. Has his usual reading material with him. Geez, there's this morning's paper. Sorry to interrupt your daily input, Robert, but would you mind paying attention to a little thing called a hearing? Reading the funnies or looking for a job in the want ads? Got something going in the personals?* Laynie pressed her lips together and closed her eyes. *God, please help me. I'm losing it.*

She opened her eyes and Jennie was directly in front of her. The help she had prayed for came and quieted her. Laynie focused on the questions Jennie asked her, pausing to think, trying not to talk too much, making sure what she said was exactly how it happened. There was so much to tell. But it seemed only moments later that their lawyer was finished with her. Laynie couldn't believe she didn't ask for more. Jennie announced she was done with this witness, and went to sit next to Shawn.

Wait! I have to tell how she tortures Rachel with dreaming of her being with Shawn again. I have to tell how she lies, how Jolene never gets Rachel to church, and lets Rachel stay up too late watching shows she shouldn't see and she doesn't give Rachel her vitamins or make her drink milk and Jolene still drinks! She's way too familiar with this Victor guy, and she's poisoning Rachel's health with her cigarette smoke. The woman is odd, weird, wacko and hasn't a clue what normal is. The pills, the BB gun, the missing pets, Jennie, there's so much more!

Oh, boy - Jolene's fancy lawyer (*Hagley?*) with his cocky smile was actually adjusting his tie as he came near. *Watched one too many lawyer shows, Mr. Larry Lawyer.* She looked at Shawn. He nodded and smiled.

Laynie volleyed his questions better than she thought she would. Hagley seemed intent on tripping her, humiliating her. Once, Judge Jenkins even woke from his coma to scold him. *He lives!* She focused back on her testimony.

"You seem very icy toward my client, Ms. Stevens. What has she ever done to make you react this way?"

Laynie couldn't believe she was asked the million-dollar question. The trouble was, so many answers bombarded her, she didn't know where to begin. "Mr. Hagley, you want to know what she's done to make me feel this way?"

"Yes, Ms. Stevens. That's what I said. Do you understand my question?" He said it like she was deficient in brain matter. Laynie was angry.

"For starters, she's always calling my husband, telling him she loves him." Hagley was clearly startled. "She tells Rachel she wants them to get back together, but I'm in the way." *Too bad Billy's out in the hall. You're always so lucky, Jolene. Always.* Laynie raced on, afraid she was going to be stopped.

"Jolene told Rachel she would get the judge to give her the rest of my kids if they wanted to come live with her because she thinks they're so cute."

Jolene's eyes bugged. "I did not!" she blurted, sounding absolutely indignant. Judge Jenkins blinked as though he missed something. Hagley turned to Jolene and shook his head in disapproval at her outburst. Laynie plowed ahead.

"Jolene has her friends call me and harass me at work. She calls and hangs up on me. She tries to turn Rachel against me."

"So Rachel and you don't get along?" Hagley raised his eyebrows and smiled.

Laynie stopped cold. "Our relationship is good, despite Jolene's attempts at sabotaging it."

"That sounds a little paranoid, Ms. Stevens."

"He's not asking a question, your Honor," Jennie called from her table.

"All right. I'll ask a question. You've spoken of children's diets, sleeping times, what's appropriate and what's inappropriate for children to your attorney, as though you're some kind of expert. What gives you the authority to make these judgments?" Hagley's Cheshire cat smile was back.

Laynie sighed. "I have six children. That tends to teach you something. Shawn and I have taken a parenting class. I've read many parenting magazines and books. I had excellent parents to model after."

"This makes you an expert?" The metamorphic smile was now a sneer.

"No, it makes me a mother who wants to be the best she can be. I'm not perfect, but I learn from my mistakes."

"You've made mistakes?"

"Of course. I'm sure you're not a perfect lawyer."

Hagley looked at Laynie like she was a naughty child. "So, you're like everyone else?"

Laynie frowned. What was he up to now? She thought of something. "Well, I have had some special training."

"Special?" The man was jeering at her. "And what was that? A Red Cross baby-sitting course?"

Laynie smiled. "No, I used to attend monthly training on child care, on special needs children, and on distressed children while I was a foster mother when I lived in Wyoming."

Hagley looked like a gaping goldfish. Shawn was smiling. Jennie looked at His Honor, grinning. Judge Jenkins yawned.

"Nothing else." Laynie watched the attorney strut back to his seat beside Jolene. Jennie was nodding at her as she motioned for her to cross the floor and sit beside Shawn. Halfway across the room, Laynie feared her legs were going to buckle.

"You did great, Babe," said Shawn as he took her hand. She sank into the wooden chair and realized she had been holding her breath.

"Good job, Laynie," praised Jennie.

"You through?" asked the judge to the lawyers. "If so, then I am going to talk to the child in chambers. We'll meet back here at 5:00."

"I can't take this," whined Jolene as she pulled her sweater around her shoulders. "This is so hard on me."

"Let's get out of here," said Shawn as he guided Laynie through the door. They walked down the hall toward the stairs. At the door at the top, Rachel peeked through, waving at them. "This is killing her," Shawn mumbled as they smiled and waved back, "and I can't even go to her. I'm her father and I can't comfort her."

"That's right," admonished Jennie behind them. "You can't speak to her until this is over. We're almost through, Shawn, hang in there. See you at five." Jennie ducked into a doorway. Delilah came and waved, then took Rachel's hand and disappeared. Laynie and Shawn pushed open the door and watched Rachel go into the courthouse.

"There she goes," said Shawn. "I hope she finds the courage to tell the truth."

"I don't know if Rachel has an inkling what the truth is," sighed Laynie. "She must feel like she's in a pressure cooker."

"She's just a kid, going through all this. But I feel real good about today, Laynie. You did great. I did well. Jolene's psychologist was so fake. Anyone could see her testimony was staged. She's a doctor with her professional advice for sale. It's evident Jolene no longer goes to AA or church or anything that would help her with her drinking."

"So what is her defense?"

Shawn squinted. "All she says is Rachel wants to come back to her, and that everyone's supposed to believe Jolene's sober just because she says so. She said she went to a rehab center and continued to be an outpatient for a while. For a while. Boy Howdy. Knowing her, that's about two hours."

"Did she show any papers to prove this?"

Shawn shook his head. "I don't get it. We always had to prove everything when we were trying to get Rachel. All Jolene has to do is sit there and say so. Oh, yeah, she also said she could give Rachel more individual attention than we could because of our large family and the attention demanded by the other kids. Boy, was she coached!"

Laynie took Shawn's hand. "You really think she'll stay with us, don't you?"

Shawn's arms encircled her. "Yes. I got to hear all of it. I can't think of one reason why that judge would put her back in Jolene's care."

Laynie nodded. "But why does the judge seem so... irritated? Like this hearing is such an annoyance to him."

"Yeah, like he's mad he's involved in this whole thing. Well, Laynie, that's what he's sitting up there and getting paid for. If he can't stand doing this, he needs to change his day job."

They decided to go for a short walk around the block to pass time. Walking felt good, and Laynie entertained the thought, only for a moment, to keep walking, to never return to that courthouse. When they came back, Jennie was waiting for them. "That was good timing," she said as she pulled the door open. "The judge is ready to give his decision." Shawn looked at Laynie and smiled. "Let's get this settled once and for all." He took her hand and they walked down the steps.

"Where's Rachel?" asked Shawn as they were seated at Jennie's table in the courtroom. Jolene and her lawyer took their seats at the other table.

"She's outside with Delilah waiting for you two." Jennie smiled.

The announcement to rise came as Judge Jenkins walked in, scowling. Everyone was seated. The room was engulfed in a suffocating silence. His Honor briefly scanned the room, and then started his litany of long-suffering.

"Cases like these are extremely difficult. Matters with children... difficult. I spoke with the child, and not much was accomplished... this is a hard thing to... it is difficult for me..." He sat back, shaking his head. "This has been a most difficult case." Laynie gawked at Shawn, who was frowning.

What in the world is he saying? Are we to come back again?

The judge cleared his throat. All eyes in the room were on him, each face staring at him in puzzlement.

"The court is going to modify conservatorship in the interest of the minor child, Rachel Stevens, to the respondent. The request of the petition by the respondent to be possessory conservator is granted and will be Managing Conservator of the child. All parties must consult with their attorneys to sign the appropriate papers and documentation. All papers shall be signed and put into effect ten days from today. This hearing is over. You are dismissed." He slammed his gavel and hurried out of the room. Everyone sat blinking, trying to decipher what Jenkins said.

"We won, right?" Laynie whispered to Shawn. He turned to Jennie. Laynie saw Jolene staring straight ahead where the judge had been seated with a look of confusion.

Shawn grabbed Jennie's arm. "What in the world did he say?" Jennie drooped her head. "We lost."

Shawn's eyes wildly scoured the room, as if he were searching for something. Jolene leaned toward her attorney and listened, then started laughing. She jumped out of her seat and rushed out of the room.

"We lost her?" whispered Laynie. "We lost her? How could he do that?" She closed her eyes to try and stop the tears. She wept, her face buried in her hands, sobbing, "How can he do this?"

Shawn helped Laynie get out of her chair. "Let's go find Rachel. We have to tell her." His voice was tight, his face pale. Laynie let him guide her through the door as Jennie trailed behind them. Their attorney looked as though she had lost all her senses. Walking out into the dimming sunlight, Laynie frantically wiped her face as she saw Rachel and Delilah sitting on a bench.

"I'm so sorry," muttered Jennie. "I'm so very, very sorry. I can't believe this. I don't understand how this could happen."

Rachel jumped up and raced to them. She flung her arms around Shawn and looked into his face. "Is it finally over, Dad? Can we please go home now? This is so boring and I want to play with Joey." Laynie saw Delilah's questioning look, and only trusted herself to shake her head. Her friend's mouth gaped.

"Rachel," Shawn said softly.

"What, Daddy, what's wrong?" The little girl stared at her
dad. "Tell me. Did you win me?"

Shawn looked helplessly at Laynie, then took a deep breath.
"No, we didn't. The judge said your mom won." Rachel slid down her
dad's legs and collapsed on the lawn.

"I don't want to go. I don't want to go," she sobbed. "I want to
stay with my family. I don't want to go. Go back and tell the judge he
made a mistake. Please, Daddy, make that judge change his mind."

Jennie squatted down beside Rachel. "Rachel, I have to know
what you told the judge." Shawn picked her up and wiped off her
tears.

"Tell Jennie, Sugar. What went on in there?"

Rachel's blue eyes were swimming in tears. "First he asked
me where I wanted to live. I told him fifty- fifty. Both dad and my
mom. Then he said that his grandchildren go to school where my
mom lives, that it's a good school and why wouldn't I want to go
there. I didn't know what I was supposed to say. Then he asked me
again where I wanted to live. I couldn't say it to him. I just couldn't
say it. My head hurt too much. He was scaring me because of what
else he said."

"What else did he say?" asked Shawn.

"He, he said he might just have to get a gun and shoot
someone, and is that what I want. He said I was making it hell for him
to decide. I was too scared to talk. Then he got madder."

"This is crazy!" declared Shawn. "Jennie, I want you to go
back in there and demand to see him. He can't talk to a kid like this."

"I'll try." Jennie disappeared into the courthouse. Laynie
looked around the grounds to see if Jolene was in sight. She wished
the woman could see what she had done to Rachel. *Probably off
having a celebration drink somewhere.* Rachel was stretching her
arms toward her. Laynie walked over and took her from Shawn.

"I don't want to leave our home," whispered Rachel. Laynie
couldn't stop her own tears.

"I don't want you to leave, Rachel. But we don't know how to
stop this."

"It's not over," said Shawn. "People just can't do this to a child. To a *family*. That judge sits up there and makes an arbitrary ruling on what's just another case to him. He leaves this place to do all the things he normally does when he goes home. What do *we* go home to? A family torn apart by his insane decision." Shawn looked at Rachel and stopped himself.

Jennie was back with them. "He wouldn't see me. I told the clerk about Rachel's collapse and that she wants to tell him she wants to stay where she is. The clerk returned with a message that it's too late now, that the only thing Rachel can do is convince her mother to change her mind." It was then Laynie knew they were going to lose Rachel.

Our little girl. Just a bone for the dog.

"Don't give up yet," whispered Shawn to her as he took Rachel back into his arms. "Rachel just might convince Jolene." Laynie saw the despair in her husband's sad eyes.

"Let's go home," she said. Her heart was heavy with the task ahead.

Telling the rest of the children.

NINETEEN

When Rachel pleaded with Jolene to let her stay, her mother simply responded with, "Oh, so now you want to change your mind." So Laynie made preparations for Rachel to exit her school while their stunned family and friends learned of the judge's shocking decision. Zack was angry when they called and told him. Maddie and Joey cried every night. Laynie listened to their desperate prayers asking God to make Jolene change her mind. She struggled to answer their questions about why God let the judge do this, questions she was asking herself. Hayley struggled to understand how her sister, whom in her memory had always been there, was now getting ready to leave them. Rachel would hold Dottie and rock her in her room, telling her over and over not to forget her.

The day Rachel was to leave them Maddie and Joey said their tearful goodbyes before they left for school. Shawn and Laynie sat on the sofa with Rachel in between them, Shawn holding Hayley as Rachel cuddled Dottie. The clock on the mantle kept hurling time toward the hour Rachel was to leave.

"Don't you forget me," whispered Rachel as she tickled Dottie's cheek. "Rachel won't be here as much as before. Don't think Rachel doesn't want to be with you, my baby, baby sister." She handed Dottie to Laynie.

"Do you really have to go?" asked Hayley. Her brown eyes misted. "I don't want you to go, Rachel. I want you to live in our house. Like always before."

"I have to, Hayley. That judge said so. But I'll still be your sister. I'll still come over."

"But you won't be here like before." Hayley flung her arms around Rachel's neck and the girls cried. Laynie watched them cling to each. This fateful proclamation had rippled out to injure and scar even the young children. Especially the children.

"Rachel, do you have your vitamins?" asked Laynie as she searched her backpack. "Be sure to take them every day. And drink milk, not soda. And go out of the room if someone is smoking."

340

"Okay, Mom."

Mom. How can I let her go? How will she survive? What kind of man is Billy? Will they say prayers with her and get her to bed early enough? Will they check her homework?

"Do all your school work. And don't worry about making friends at your new school. You'll have plenty. Be sure to always buckle up. Every time, Rachel, whether anyone tells you to or not. Okay, Sweetie?" *What else have I forgotten?*

The dogs were barking outside. Hayley slid off Shawn's lap and looked out the picture window. "Oh, no! Rachel, your mom's here. Make her go away. Tell her you won't go. We can hide in my room." Hayley burst into tears.

"Rachel can't do that, Hayley," said Shawn. "We have to say goodbye and let her go. We'll see her next week, Baby Doll. Come, kiss your sister." Hayley ran to Rachel and held her, sobbing.

"Doesn't *anybody* care about sisters? " she cried. Rachel kissed her cheek. "I have to go to my room, Rach. I can't see you go away. I have to go pretend you're in your room." Hayley fled to her room and shut the door, her sobs muffled by her pillow. Someone was blowing a car horn in the driveway.

"Bye, baby, baby sister," whispered Rachel to Dottie. Her trembling lips kissed the toddler's forehead and cheeks. "Don't forget Rachel, okay? I'll be back soon, Dottie." Rachel's tears splattered Dottie's head. Laynie put her arm around Rachel and drew her close.

"I love you so, Rachel. I want you to know you'll be just as important to us as when you lived here. You're still part of this family. I don't want to let you go, but I can't stop this. You know where we are, and we'll come any time you need us. Oh, I'm going to miss you!" Laynie was strangling on her grief.

"I'll miss you, too, Mom." Rachel buried her head against Laynie and they both sobbed. The front doorbell was ringing.

"Come on, Rachel," said Shawn as he scooped her up in his arms. He held her and finally gave way to the dammed up sorrow inside him, heaving great sobs. Rachel's hands caressed his hair as she cried into his shoulder, whispering, "Daddy, Daddy, oh my Daddy!" Someone was knocking on the door.

"I love you, Sugar. I tried to make this different." Shawn's voice cracked. "I wanted you here with us. I want you to know that I tried, I tried. Remember that I love you, more than you'll ever know. Come to us for anything. You're going to be all right. I will miss you every minute you're not here. This part is very hard, Rachel, but you're going to do okay. Understand?"

Rachel looked at him and nodded. "You can't fix this, can you, Daddy?"

Shawn sobbed. "I wish I could, but I can't." Rachel clung to him, her knuckles white from gripping her father's neck. The knocking on the door was louder. Rachel looked at him.

Shawn kissed her. "We have to. Now." Laynie watched them go to the door. It felt as though she was watching something die. Shawn opened the door as Jolene stood there, arms folded, foot tapping. He pried Rachel's arms from him and kissed her one more time. "I love you."

"I love you, too, Daddy," she cried desperately as Jolene pulled her from him and quickly shut the door. Shawn sat at Laynie's feet and buried his head in her lap, crying as a perplexed Dottie looked on. Laynie laid her head on top of his, their sorrow overcoming them as they cried. They stayed like that for a while, entwined, too exhausted to move, too numb to talk. The doorbell was ringing.

"Guess Jolene came back to rag me about making her wait," said Shawn as he rose and opened the door. It was Rachel.

Jolene changed her mind!

"Dad, I left my backpack here." Rachel ran into the living room and picked it up. "I...I-" Shawn picked her up again as she dampened his shirt with new tears. Through her own tears, Laynie smiled. Rachel had managed to delay her departure, if only a few minutes. She had found a way to gain a little of that power back.

"I better go before my mom amps out," said Rachel. "Don't come out, Dad. She thinks you kept my backpack on purpose."

"I don't care what she thinks. Do you want me to come out with you?"

"Nah. Uh, oh, there's the horn again. How rude." Rachel laughed, then burst into tears again as she gave them another round of hugs and kisses.

"I love you, Mom. I love you, Daddy, oh, my one and only daddy."

Rachel closed the door.

Epilogue

Guess it's time to start keeping a diary again, even though I think Rachel's soon old enough she can decide where she wants to live. Jolene must know that, she has pulled out all the stops to buy Rachel things to make her want to stay with her. For what it's worth, here goes:

1. Rachel says she is embarrassed the way her backpack "stinks" (cigarette smoke) when she opens it at school - kids comment on "that awful smell." Rachel was apologetic to us because all her Christmas gifts (stuffed animals) for the kids smelled. I pitied her.
2. Rachel wears make up- pretty heavy most times.
3. Jolene drives Rachel and her "boyfriend" on dates. (She's only 11).
4. Rachel is falling asleep in class.
5. Jolene had promised to keep taking Rachel to scouts and dance lessons. She has not.
6. Rachel is having episodes of dizziness in school; the last one resulted in her having to leave school. She's back on junk food and soda, I suspect malnutrition. Jolene is supposed to get her in for a check-up.
7 Rachel has become very argumentative, doesn't follow our family rules, and is careless with her possessions.
8. Rachel said there isn't even a table for them to eat their meals on. She often eats in her room alone, watching TV. Saddens me. I miss her at our table.
9. Jolene gave Rachel $140.00 to buy herself an outfit for the band concert. She came over here with a $50 bill in her pocket.
10. Rachel misses school sometimes because she's tired. She blames herself because her mother can't wake her up.

Laynie dropped the pen and closed the notebook. She shut her eyes, feeling herself being pulled into the vacuum once again. *A black hole.* It sucks in everything around it with no concern of its effect. Laynie knew well the definition of a black hole. *Jolene.*

As Laynie stood and put the notebook in the hutch drawer, a folded paper fluttered down to her feet. She picked it up, smiling. It was a homemade card Rachel had made her when she was so terribly homesick at scout camp last year. A heart was drawn on the outside over "MOM." Inside Laynie read:

> *Dear Mom,*
> *I hope you like the present I picked out for you at the camp store. I love you and missed you a lot while I was at camp. I don't think I will ever go AGAIN!*
> *I love YOU!*
> *Love,*
> *Rachel*
> *PS I LOVE YOU*

Laynie closed the card and remembered how when they had arrived to take her home, Rachel asked if she could stay another week.

Rachel could adapt. She was a survivor.

A bottomless sigh escaped her as she listened to the children in the living room. Dottie was squealing with laughter as Maddie played with her. Joey was telling Hayley about his field trip to the bird sanctuary while she asked him endless questions about it. Laynie caught herself listening for another child's voice, and then remembered.

It was like that, all the time. She knew Rachel was not there, yet she listened for her, looked for her, waited for her to be the last one in the door. The hardest of all was seeing her empty chair at the supper table next to Zack's. Every night it was a silent proclamation of their missing child. Sometimes Maddie would forget and set Rachel's place at the table. Sometimes Shawn would come home with donuts for the kids, nobody having the heart to point out the extra one.

The fifth donut. The extra place at the table. The silent chair at supper. Some things you just never get used to. Boy howdy.

Printed in the United States
124148LV00001B/34/A

9 781591 134978